Shattered revelations

Jo McCall

Jo McCall

Shattered Revelations: Shattered World Series Finale

Copyright Jo McCall 2022
All Rights Reserved
First Published 2022

No part of this book may be reproduced, stores in a retrieval system or transmitted in any form by any means, without prior authorization in writing of the publisher *Wicked Romance Publication*, nor can it be otherwise circulated in any form of binding or cover other than that which it is published and without a similar condition, including this condition, being imposed on the subsequent purchaser. All characters and places in this publication other than those clearly in the public domain are fictitious, and any resemblance of actual persons, living or dead, is purely coincidental.

Cover design: Kate Farlow @ Ya'll That Graphic
Editing: Beth @VBProofreads
Formatted by: WickedGypsyDesigns

DEDICATION

TO THOSE WHO SAID I WOULD NEVER MAKE IT.
THE NAYSAYERS, THE HALF-HAZARDS, THE
BOOERS IN THE CROWD.

FUCK OFF.

LOOK AT ME NOW, BITCHES.

"You never know what's around the corner. It could be everything. Or it could be nothing. You keep putting one foot in front of the other, and then one day you look back and you've climbed a mountain."
-Tom Hiddleston

WARNING

The content within this book is DARK and may be triggering to some.
For a full list of triggers for this particular book go to jomccallauthor.com

TKACHENKO family

- Malik Tkachenko
  - ◇ Yelena Morisov
  - Unknown
- Kirill Tkachenko
- Andrei Tkachenko
  - Amalia Sidorova
    - Antony Tkachenko
    - Ivan Tkachenko
    - Matthias Tkachenko/Dashkov

WARD *family*

- **Benedito Romano** ◇—◇ **Lucia Rosstyena** → See Romano Family
- **Benedito Romano** — **Melissa Ward** (Mistress)
  - **Jerry Ward** — **Mariah Keller**
    - **Giano Ward**
    - **Rico Ward**
    - **Davis Ward**
    - **Elias Ward** — **Kendra Mareno** — **Dante Romano**
      - **Christian Ward**
      - **Libby Ward**
      - **Kenzi Ward**

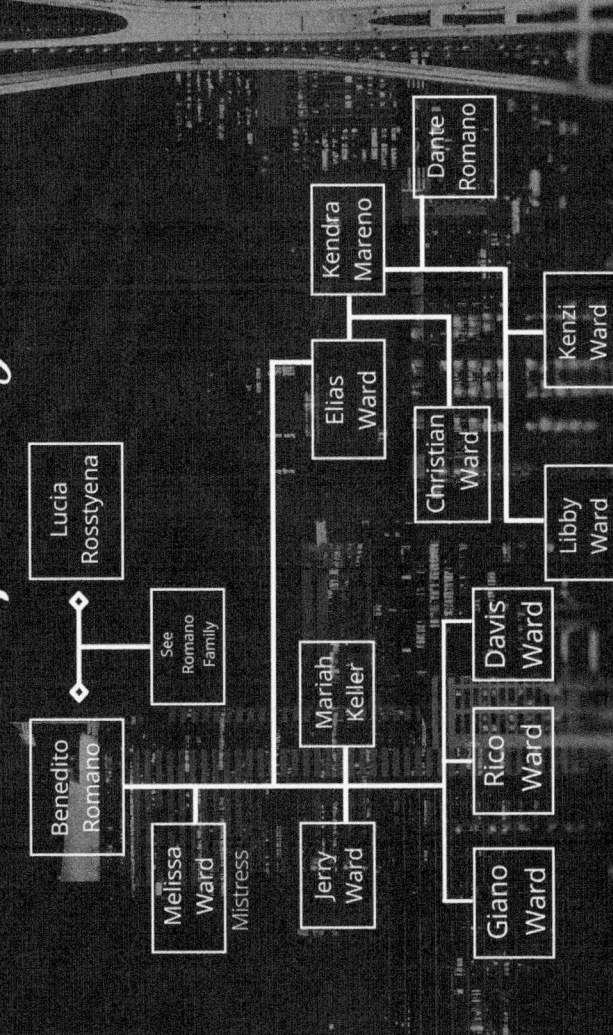

ROMANO *family*

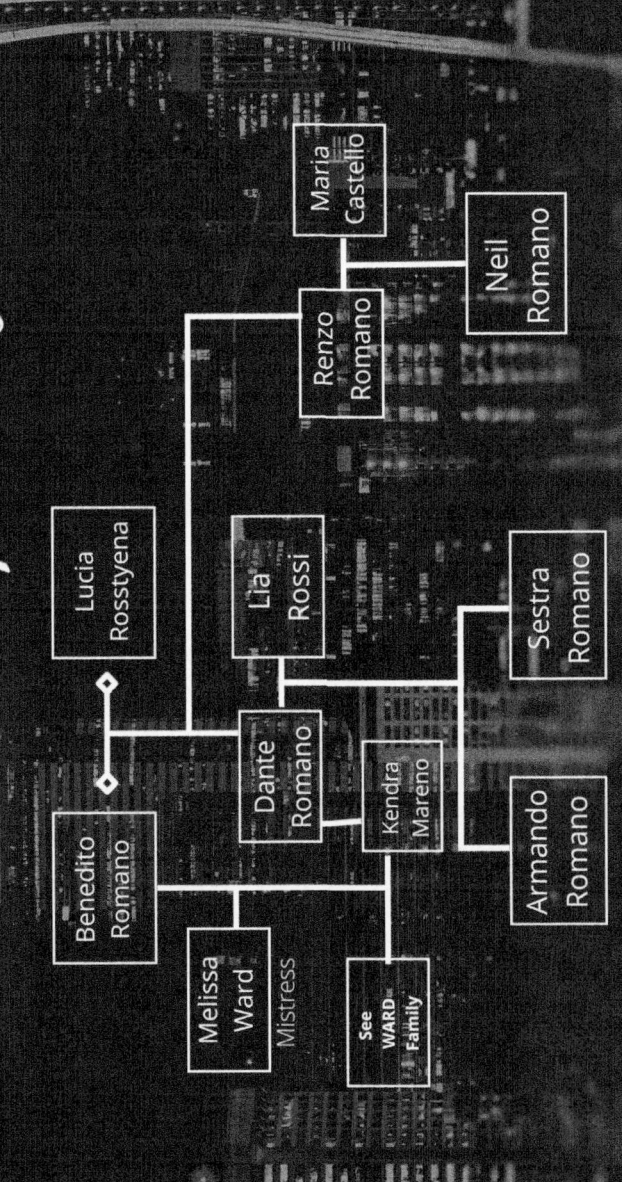

- Lucia Rosstyena ◇—◇ Benedito Romano
  - Benedito Romano & Melissa Ward (Mistress) → See WARD Family
  - Dante Romano — Kendra Mareno
  - Lia Rossi
    - Sestra Romano
    - Armando Romano
- Renzo Romano — Maria Castello
  - Neil Romano

Kavanaugh family

- Finn Kavanaugh — Ava Connors
  - Lachlan Kavanaugh — Maeve O'Connor
    - Cara Kavanaugh
    - Ioan Kavanaugh
  - Liam Kavanaugh — Marianne Murphy
    - (Liam Kavanaugh) — Katherine McDonough
      - Seamus Kavanaugh
      - Kiernan Kavanaugh
      - Connor Kavanaugh
      - Soairsi Kavanaugh
    - Matthias Dashköy — Avaleigh McDonough

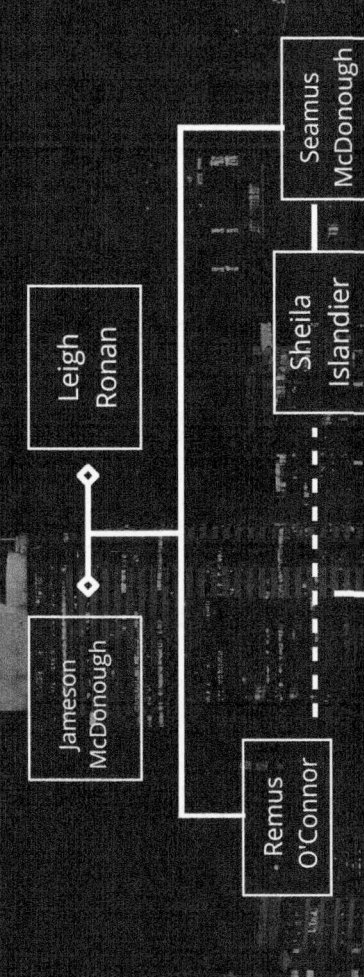

McDonough *family*

- Jameson McDonough ◇—◇ Leigh Ronan
  - Remus O'Connor ┄┄ Seamus McDonough — Sheila Islandier
    - Katherine McDonough — Avaleigh McDonough
    - Marianne Murphy / See Kavanaugh

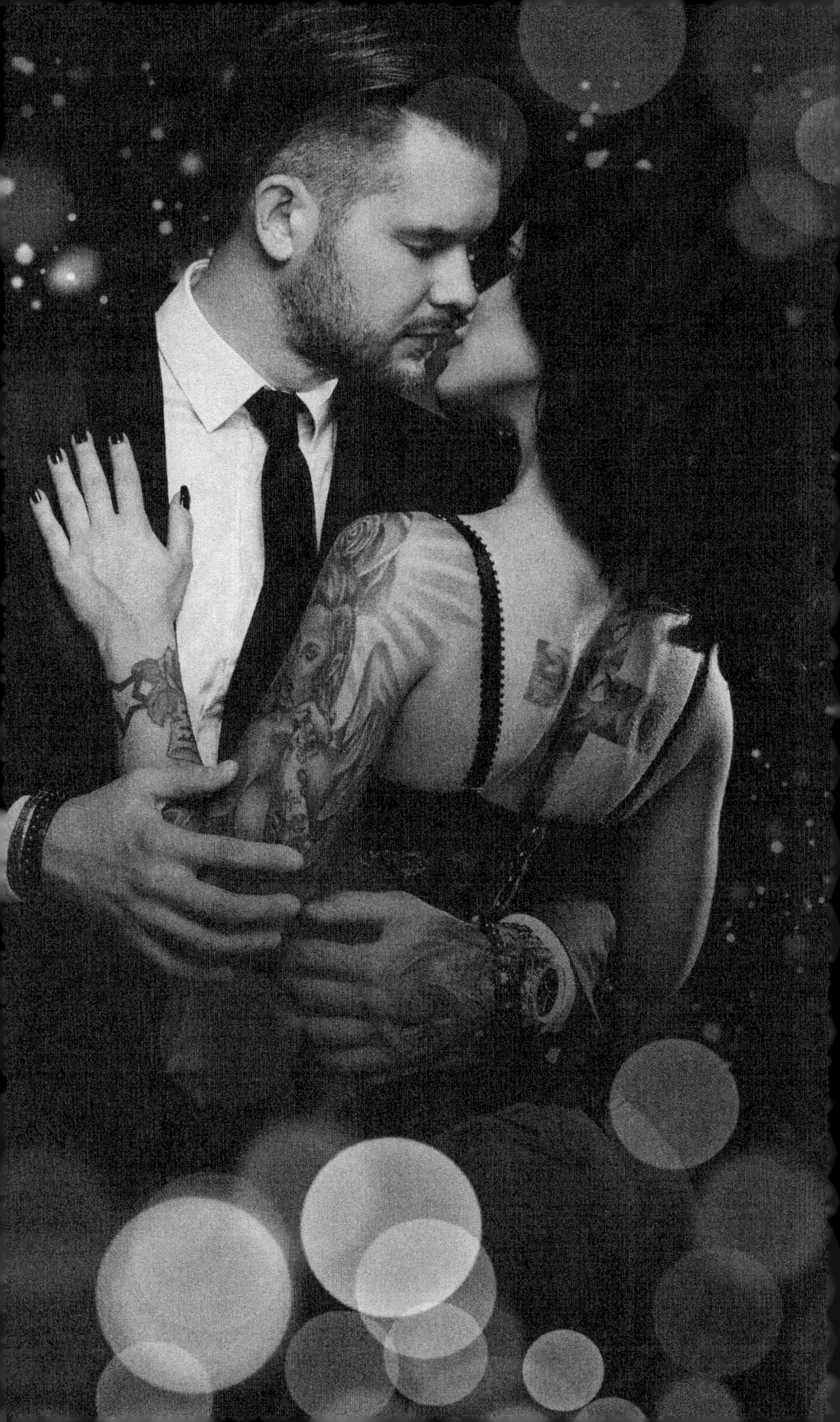

ONE

Ava

Well, this was boring.

Drumming my fingers on my knee, I tapped out the rhythm to "Dead or Alive" by Bon Jovi on my dirt-marred skin. Hunger was gnawing at my bones, my stomach growling in protest at the lack of nutrients. I'd refused to eat the plates of food they sent in through the slot at the bottom of my prison door.

They were drugged.

It had only been a few days since the Dashkov building collapsed, and I hadn't heard anything. Not a peep. If they were truly dead, I would have expected my distasteful, backstabbing grandmother to be down here gloating.

They're alive.

The mantra ran through my head on repeat. A welcome broken record of reassurance. If they were in the vault, they would have survived. It was a genius system. The vault worked on a separate system from the rest of the building. If for any reason the surface building was breached, the underground would remain untouched. Matthias even had the foresight to make sure the vault had its own life support system. Oxygen, electricity, air. Everything in the vault was self-contained.

They had to be alive.

Which begged the question of why the fuck I was still sitting in this god-forsaken cell. I couldn't be all that hard to find, especially since I was still wearing the tracking necklace Vas had given me a few days after I became *Pakhan*.

It was small and unassuming. Perfect to hide in plain sight. No one was the wiser that the gold anchor on my neck would spell their doom.

The shuffling of feet sounded outside my cell door. Dinnertime. Right on cue. My stomach growled in protest, but there was no way in hell I was falling for that trick again. The door to the cell swung open, the hinges creaking noisily. I winced at the obtrusive sound in the otherwise silent room.

Huh, usually they didn't come in when it was chow time.

"You're still alive, I see." A smooth voice interrupted the silence. "Surprising."

I scoffed. "Did you want me to die? You don't sound too disappointed that I'm still breathing."

"Why would I be disappointed, dear?" the woman asked, her head tilted slightly. "If I wanted you dead, I wouldn't have brought you here."

Fair point.

"What do you want, then?" My patience was wearing thin with this woman. "Family bonding time?"

The woman's Cheshire grin beamed at me through the

dark. "For you to have supper with me." Her painted smile and dark eyes made her look unhinged, and for a moment, I wondered what she would do if I told her to shove the food straight up her tight asshole.

Thoughts loading...

Nah, not gonna risk it.

"I'm not exactly dressed for dinner." My gaze shifted pointedly down to my dust-covered and torn clothing that also lacked foot apparel.

"Narana will take you to bathe and change," my grandmother assured me before turning to leave. She stopped at the door, and turning her head, she warned, "And in case you get any bright ideas about attempting to run—know that every inch of this house is guarded, and you will be put down like a dog if you try."

"And here I thought you didn't want me dead."

Her smile turned vicious. "Let me spell it out for you then," she elaborated. "You try and run, and I will make sure each of my guards has a turn fucking you like the bitch you are. How's that?"

I swallowed hard, my face paling at her words. "Much better. Crystal clear." Keeping the tremor from my voice was near impossible. "Five stars."

"Good."

And then she was gone. Like Dracula through the mist. If I found a stake and drove it through her withering heart, I wondered if she'd turn to dust.

"Let's go." Narana, a brawny older woman with a square face and peg-shaped nose, stepped toward me, grabbing my upper arm in a bruising grip. "Follow me. No trouble."

Hulk. Smash.

Well, with that accent, she wasn't Irish.

I let her lead me from the cell and down the corridor toward the stairs that led up to the main house. Or what I hoped was the main house. I hadn't been conscious when they brought me in. Cement stairs ended at a large wooden door, and when Narana opened it, the smell of spice engulfed me.

Definitely a step up from the mold and piss smell downstairs.

A few more sharp turns and a flight of stairs later, we landed in front of another wooden door that Narana told me was my temporary suite.

How nice of grandmother to give me such luxuries.

"Shower," Narana demanded, shoving me toward the en suite bathroom. "You have ten minutes. No more. I come back to do hair."

"Sure," I muttered as she stalked from the room, her tree-trunk legs moving much faster than I would have thought. The slam of the door and the click of the lock sealed me inside. Alone.

Great. I was locked in.

I made my way into the lavish, overly tiled bathroom and turned on the shower to warm before sliding out of my dirt-encrusted clothes. Did I want to have dinner with my psychotic grandmother? No. But I did want a shower, and that was enough to get me to cooperate.

For now.

They're alive.

Stepping under the warm spray, I tilted my head back and let the water drown away the only tears I would allow myself in this house. No matter what happened after I stepped outside the bubble of this space, I wouldn't let it break me.

But I did need a plan.

Escape wasn't going to be easy, and my grandmother's threat wasn't an idle one, so I needed to be careful.

Very careful.

Matthias would come for me.

He was just running late.

Super late.

Fucker.

Grabbing the body wash and the brand-new grotesquely pink loofa that was strung up, I vigorously washed at the dust and dirt that had accumulated in that cell. The clear water ran muddy as I stripped away every vulnerability until there was nothing left but a clean canvas.

One I would paint with their blood.

"Time is up, girl," crooked-nose Narana commanded. "Out now."

Reluctantly, I turned off the flow of heavenly water with a heavy sigh and stepped from the shower. Narana waited expectantly with a towel in her hand. When I grabbed for it, she shook her head and instructed me to lift my arms.

Great, Porky the pig nose was going to dry me.

She toweled me roughly, getting every uncomfortable crevice, before wrapping me in a black silk robe and instructing me to sit on one of the vanity stools.

"Good girl," she praised me when I did as she instructed. My skin crawled at her approval, like ants scurrying through an anthill. That was the last thing she said as she lotioned, polished, sugared, and primped my body and hair for the next two hours. By the time she was done, my ginger hair was curled, my face painted, and my skin shining like a brand-new car at the dealership.

I had a sinking feeling there was more to tonight than a simple dinner request. That feeling grew the moment I saw the dress laid out for me on the bed. It was a simple yet luxurious maroon velvet strapless cocktail dress with a sweetheart neckline that dipped just low enough to hint at inappropriate. The bosom was slightly ruched, and the hem barely fell to mid-thigh when I stretched the fabric over my curvy frame.

Wonderful.

"Come," Narana commanded. She took me roughly by the elbow and led me, stumbling in my stripper heels, from the room. After another few twists and turns, and a few stairs I nearly broke my neck on, we arrived.

"Jesus," I muttered distastefully. There had to be a worse word than gaudy. Horrendously opulent, maybe? The walls were painted a deep red, and the wood beneath my feet was blacker than charcoal. The dark cherry dining room table spanned the room seating for over a dozen guests, yet only five seats had place settings.

Also in black.

Maybe my Dracula theory had merit.

Or the bitch just liked the color that represented her soul.

One thing was for sure, this room was where they sacrificed the virgins on the full moon.

At least I could breathe easy on that front.

"Finally." My grandmother's voice filled the large expanse, echoing mildly off the low ceiling. She inclined her head at my pug-nosed handler. "Thank you, Narana. That will be all." Narana bowed and let go of my elbow before she retreated from the room.

What a good little pet for master.

Sheila turned her attention to me. "Much better." She raised an appraising, well-manicured eyebrow. "A good cleansing can do so much for a person."

Resisting the urge to roll my eyes, I said, "Yes. I've always wanted to be washed and primped like a prize cow before auction. I may not be a virgin, but from the way your maid was scrubbing at my vagina, it's probably shining like gold right now."

A snarl painted my grandmother's red lips. "Your attitude could use some work," she groused primly, her head high, nose in the air. "So could your crass words. Picked up from those Russian barbarians, no doubt. Not to worry, dear. Those are things easily beaten from a woman."

"Touch me, and you'll find out in surprising detail what happens to people who don't respect my boundaries." I shrugged a shoulder nonchalantly. "Shall I grab one of the candlesticks and give it a go? Miss Scarlett in the dining room with the candlestick sounds like a good narrative for me."

Ah, there was the reaction I wanted. The ice beneath the prim façade. Sheila's brown eyes narrowed, her face darkening like thunderclouds. I could see the faint lines of her Botoxed forehead twitching, yearning to get free and wrinkle the smooth expanse.

"I'd watch your tongue if I were you," she hissed. "You have no idea what I am capable of."

I smirked. "Maybe it's you who should watch yourself, *grandmother*." Her eye twitched. She didn't like that name. Not one bit. "You have no idea what *I* am capable of. Remember that."

Silence.

Then she chuckled darkly and, with a grand gesture, took her seat at the end of the table. "I have no doubt," she admitted. "Now sit. I was told you haven't been taking advantage of my hospitality and eating the food supplied to you."

This woman was bipolar.

Or psycho.

Maybe both.

Yep. She was both. There was no way a normal person could easily switch their mood like that. Certifiable, this one. Looney as a tune.

"I'm not in the habit of eating food that's been drugged," I bit out, recalling the first few meals that had me feeling woozy and sick for several hours. Drugs and my body never melded well.

The bitch smirked.

"And I'm not in the habit of abiding by anything other than docility in my property." The smile she gave me was all stepford and plastic. Or it was all Botox. Couldn't be sure. No matter. If her intention was to warn me, it didn't work. It did, however, creep me out.

"It's cute you think I'm your property," I sneered. "I didn't realize a bag of bones could own property."

Sheila's smile fell flat.

"You're a pathetic little bitch." Her hands tightened on the arms of her chair hard enough to turn her knuckles white. "Just like your mother."

I took a threatening step toward her, eyes hard and teeth bared. "Don't talk about my mother, you fucking—"

"I see we're all getting along then," a deep rumbling voice interrupted. It was tinged with an Irish accent that melted seamlessly with his Boston drawl. "Sit down, Avaleigh. Stop being dramatic."

The ease of familiarity with which he commanded me left me uneasy. We'd never met, but here he was, acting as if he had known me my entire life.

Scoffing, I did as he said, but only so I wouldn't hit a bitch like a Whack-a-Mole at the county fair. Sheila smirked triumphantly, as if she'd won something. The only thing she won was me not shoving a fork into her carotid and watching her bleed out on her ridiculously priced rug.

"And you are?" My gaze followed the man as he made his way to his seat across the table from me on my grandmother's right side.

He gave me a disarming smile. "I'm your grandfather, of course."

"Yeah," I snorted. How stupid did this man think I was? "If you're Seamus McDonough, then I'm Hilary Clinton. You're either a twin or a really close doppelgänger."

His eyes shifted to Sheila. "I told you she is perceptive."

Sheila huffed a mirthless laugh. "But easily conned."

What the fuck were these two nutcases on about?

"I admit, though," my evil grandmother kept on. "I was truly touched when word reached me that you were concerned about my safety. Those small fear responses are always so helpful in gaining access to one's emotions and using it against them."

Well, suck a duck.

Karma really was a bitch.

"You played me." I scoffed in disbelief. "You knew I was going to be at the gala, didn't you?"

"And you played your part so spectacularly well, little Ava."

"What part?" I asked. "You didn't gain anything that night."

"Didn't I?" She cocked her head to the side and smiled. "You did the one thing I needed the most, and that was to reveal the mole in my operation. Two, actually. And you did it so well."

Seamus's look-alike nodded and smiled at her words.

"Not only that, Avaleigh," he told me, "but you helped us to eliminate some of our loose ends along the way."

"Dr. Martin." My grandmother rolled her eyes. "That horrible offspring of Cartwright's."

"He was particularly foul, wasn't he?" the man agreed. "Nasty for business."

"And of course, your carelessness and urge for vengeance allowed us to easily access the Dashkov building."

"God rest their souls." Seamus's doppelgänger shook his head in mock solemnities before calling for the waitstaff to bring out food and drinks. My stomach growled as the room filled with fragrant spices and sizzling hot plates as the waitstaff rushed in from the kitchens holding trays of decadent goodness. My body had been starved of nutrients for the last three days, and it took every ounce of control I had not to grab up the spiced apple roast and dig in like the Grinch at a Christmas feast.

"Do eat, dear," my grandmother urged me. "I promise I didn't drug any of it this time. We are sharing from the same dishes, after all."

The old crone was right. There was no reason not to eat. If she wanted to drug me, she would have had them deliver an individual plate instead of allowing me to serve myself from the same dishes as them.

"As long as you cooperate, there will be no reason to drug you." It was a warning, and it wasn't subtle. Behave or back to woozy land I would go.

I loaded up my plate with the roast, potatoes, green beans, and a few other vegetables I could reach before sitting back in my chair and slowly beginning to make a dent in my food. Several quiet minutes passed, and I hated to say that it wasn't an uncomfortable silence.

It wasn't cozy either, but at least they weren't hurling death threats at me. They probably had that saved for dessert.

"So." Yep, I wasn't going to let the silence go on forever. It was beginning to grate on me. "What's your actual name? You know, the one you were born with."

The man sitting across from me, the enigma I hadn't been able to place on the chessboard, beamed at me.

"I'll tell you if you tell me how you figured out I wasn't Seamus," he compromised.

I could do that.

"The Seattle police took photos of my mother's dorm room after she disappeared," I told him. "One of the photos easily seen is of her, Seamus, and Cruella here on the day of her graduation, which was also the day you were seen meeting with Dante Romano's father here in Washington."

"Clever girl," he praised me. "A keen eye for detail."

Sheila snorted. "Stop pandering to her, Remus. It's below you."

Remus.

It wasn't a name I recognized.

"Whether you like it or not, she is our granddaughter, dear," he chided her gently. Sheila harrumphed indelicately.

"And soon she won't be our problem any longer."

That certainly had my attention.

"There you go again." Remus sighed. "Giving away the plot."

Before I had a chance to ask what the hell either one of them was talking about, the doorbell rang.

"It would appear our guests have finally arrived." My grandmother let out a pleased smile. I looked over at her.

"Who did you invite?" I hissed. "Voldemort?"

All right, so I was deflecting. Using humor to counteract the raging heartbeat that thrummed beneath my ribcage. There was only one man I could think of that they would have walking through those pocket doors. I'd escaped him—twice—and I would be damned if I let him take me again. Because if he did, there wouldn't be any escaping.

While the two of them were focused on awaiting their guest, I slowly slid the heavy silver knife off the table and gripped it tightly in my hand. Christian or not, I wouldn't let anyone take me. Not without a fight.

"Ah, here is the pair of the hour," Remus exclaimed brightly as he stood and walked around the table to greet his guest. "Welcome."

I turned in my seat and nearly dropped the knife in my hand at the sight of their guests standing before me.

Damn, it felt good to be right.

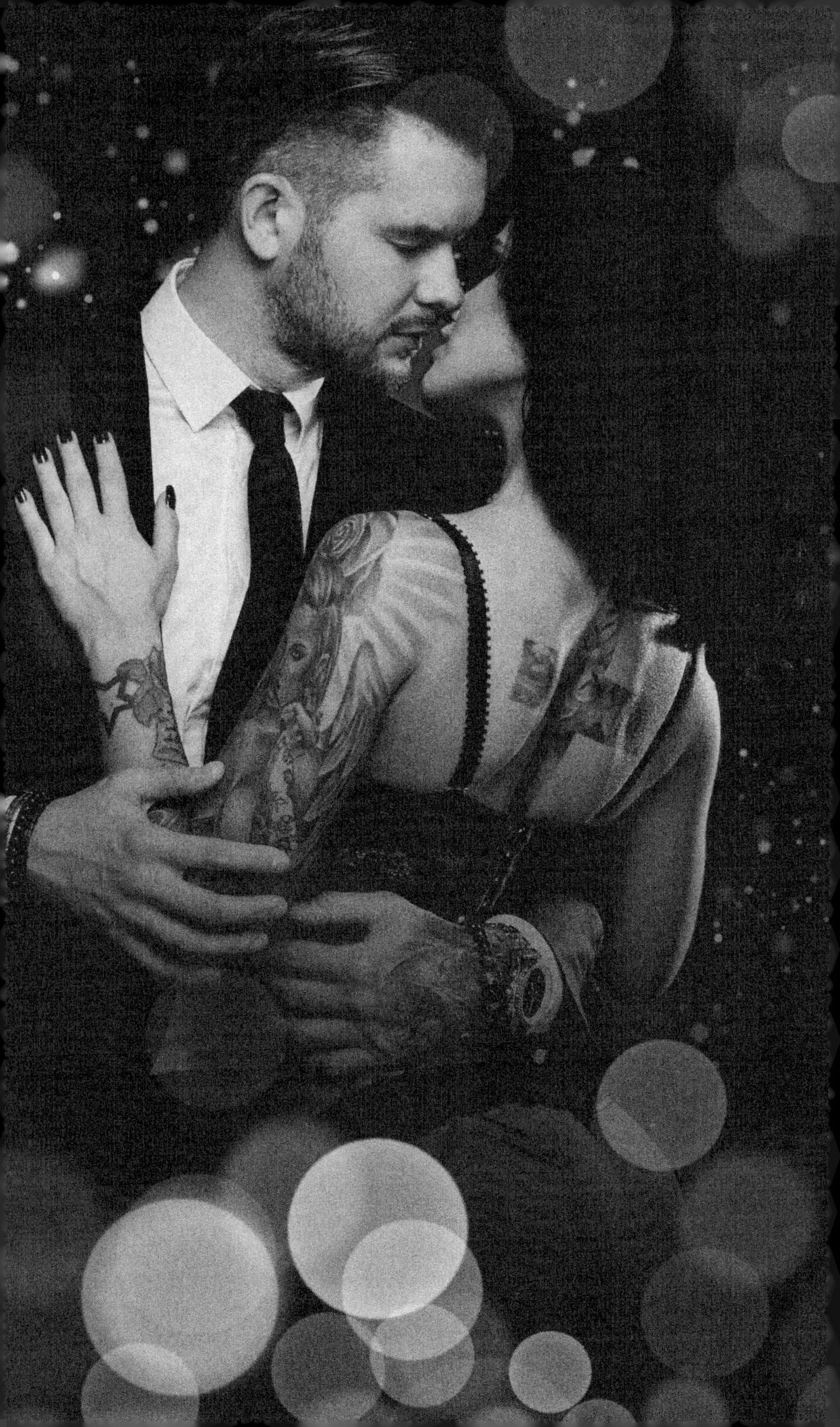

TWO

Ava

Honestly, there wasn't much in this world that surprised me any longer, and the sight of Marianne entering the dining room wasn't shocking in the least. I'd known the manipulative snake had been involved in the conspiracy the entire time, but I hadn't known why.

Or what she had to gain.

"Mother." Marianne stepped forward to embrace Sheila, a smile on her face.

Wait...What?

Flashes of the small box in the cell at the barn came back to me. A baby's tooth, a lock of hair, a photo of a baby with a woman I hadn't been able to identify. All right, I could now say I was surprised.

This was something I hadn't seen coming, but now that they were both standing before me, side by side, I could see it. The same dirt-colored eyes and fair complexion. The pair were alike in almost every way. From the color of their hair to the shape of their faces. They even shared the same slender nose and cut jaw.

How had no one seen those similarities before now?

When all this was over, I was going to get my eyes checked.

"Hello, dear." Sheila smiled at Marianne before turning her attention to the man who'd accompanied her. I recognized him from the gala. "Kellan, welcome. Please, have a seat." She motioned to the empty place settings, one of which was next to mine, while the other had been placed beside Remus.

"Thank you for having me," Kellan told her graciously, his eyes roaming over my body as he took his seat. It wasn't a lecherous stare. That was something I would have been able to handle. No, this stare was calculated. I had seen Elias and Christian make a similar expression dozens of times throughout my childhood when examining the women in the *stables*. He was appraising me like livestock. "I can see it was certainly worth the drive."

Whoever this man was, he was Irish. His voice with thick and broguish compared to my father's, which barely existed beyond the few typical Irish slangs he never rid himself of.

"We are so fortunate you could come down on such short notice." Sheila waited for her guests to be seated before taking her own. "Please," she motioned to the trays of food set out, "help yourself."

This was all very Norman Rockwell.

The table descended into silence as Marianne and her guests loaded up their plates and dug in. I just stared, however, not reaching to touch my food again. My mind had shifted into overdrive as it tried to push the pieces of the puzzle together.

Who was Marianne's father?

Remus? Or someone else Sheila had sought company with?

And how did no one notice how similar the pair looked when standing next to one another?

"Did you know, Ava," Sheila's voice broke through my reverie. She'd cleared her plate and had another glass of her expensive merlot poured for her as she gazed at me, "that twins run in the McDonough family?"

That explained Seamus and Kiernan.

She waved her hand dismissively before answering her own question. "Of course not," she chuckled mirthlessly. "Your mother never told you anything about your family, did she?"

"I'm starting to see why," I muttered.

"Your grandfather..." She paused for a moment, her eyes flitting up to the ceilings as she rethought what she was about to say. "The man you believe to be your grandfather, Seamus, was a twin as well. In fact, you were the first child born to the McDonough clan in over a hundred years who wasn't a twin."

My eyes darted up to Remus.

I hadn't missed the truth bomb Sheila had dropped. It was nuclear. Seamus McDonough hadn't been my grandfather. He hadn't been mother's father.

Not her biological one, at least.

One thing didn't fit, however.

"There was no record of Seamus McDonough ever having a twin," I reminded them. No hospital records. No pictures. Nothing. It wasn't that I doubted the sincerity of Sheila's words. It was clear as day that the man who sat before me was Seamus's twin. A doppelgänger, even the best one, wouldn't have been able to fool my father. Plus, doppelgängers were similar but rarely, if ever, exact carbon copies.

Remus sneered at my words and pushed his unfinished plate away. "Of course not." He wiped his mouth with the linen napkin. "They fixed everything so we didn't exist. If we did, it meant a power struggle between two heirs, and they couldn't have that. Not again."

Huh?

The confusion must have shown on my face. "The McDonoughs have a dark, dirty secret," Sheila sneered. "For a little over a hundred years, they killed the second-born twin of every McDonough leader."

Even Oppenheimer couldn't have constructed a bigger bomb than the one Sheila just unleashed on me.

"As time grew, however, they realized that those forgotten twins could be utilized in different manners. Just like my poor Marianne." Sympathy played gracefully across Sheila's face. It was fake, though. The words didn't match the expression appropriately. It didn't reflect in her eyes or in her posture. Unfortunately, Marianne was eating it up like a starving child.

"My mother wasn't a twin."

Someone would have known this fact. Someone would have told me if my mother had a twin running around in the world.

"Not in the traditional sense, no," Sheila explained. "Marianne and your mother were fraternal twins. Up until they were born, there had only ever been identical twins born."

"If they weren't identical," I asked. "Why give Marianne up? Just because she was second-born?"

This family was growing more messed up by the second.

"I never gave my child away!" Sheila screamed, her face contorting in anger, hand clenched tightly around her wineglass. Remus leaned in and patted her on her arm, calming her with a few whispered words. Once she was settled, she continued. "Your great-grandmother came to me that day with Seamus and took her from my arms. I begged. Pleaded. But they said it had to be this way. That twins, identical or not, would never be allowed to grow together. They. Stole. Her. From. Me."

"You see, the McDonoughs have a rule about succession," Remus interjected, allowing Sheila to pull herself together. "There can't be any contestation for the throne."

"That makes no sense." I shook my head. "One twin would always be older, even if only by a few minutes. That makes them the firstborn and secure in their right to inherit."

Remus smiled sadly, and for a moment, he was almost human to me. His green eyes were burdened with sorrow and rejection. I could only imagine how it must have felt to be the forgotten brother. The unloved brother. The brother who was cast out and tossed aside.

"I can see you haven't done much research into your heritage." He shook his head in disappointment. "The McDonough roots can be traced back as far as the fifth century. They were one of the most powerful clans in Ireland and shaped a lot of how the country developed over time. The first set of twins to be recorded was in 1458, and for a hundred years, there never appeared to be a problem."

"Until you looked beneath the surface," Marianne spat bitterly from her seat.

"Yes," Remus nodded in agreement. "Viability of both fetuses back then was slim. Usually only one survived childbirth. In the rare cases, when both twins survived, there never seemed to be any issues in succession of clan power, until you discover that at least one twin died under mysterious circumstances 90 percent of the time."

"Most circumstances appeared to be accidental," Marianne chimed in. "Other times, they were murdered by a rival clan or in a dark alley somewhere."

"Always the second-born?" I was curious and unable to stop myself from wanting to learn more.

Remus smirked. "No one can be sure," he admitted. "There was never a set pattern. Sometimes it was the first-born. Other times it was the second. But who's to say the second-born didn't become the first?"

How very Man in the Iron Mask.

"That's not uncommon in history," I pointed out. "Brothers killed brothers for power all the time. History is littered with power struggles among siblings. That is nothing new."

"No, it isn't," Remus agreed. "But in 1569, two brothers waged the bloodiest war against one another, splitting the clan straight down the middle. And later, the country."

"It nearly cost the McDonough clan everything," Sheila murmured. "More than half the clan was killed in the brothers' feud, and the aftermath nearly ended the clan altogether."

"Who won the war?"

"Both brothers declared a cease-fire." Kellan, who'd been silently listening up to this point, spoke up. "When they realized how much the war was costing them and how the destruction of their clan was imminent, they agreed to terms brought to the table."

"Terms about killing babies." Yeah, that was a bitter taste in my mouth.

Remus nodded grimly. "That was part of it, yes," he confirmed. "No second-born would be allowed to live past their birth."

"And the other terms?"

"One brother would get the north and another would claim the south," Kellan stated. "They split the country down the middle."

"I thought that had to do with the partition of Ireland in the early 1900s."

"The partition was its own event." Kellan leaned back in his chair and took a sip of wine. His green eyes bored into me, assessing me. "But it did solidify a few things."

"When did it change?" My gaze shifted away from the haunting emerald stare of the man next to me and back to Remus. "When did the second-born babies stop being murdered?"

"We believe it was sometime in the early eighteen hundreds." Remus's fingers tapped the table. "But no one can be sure."

"Why? What changed?"

"People were dying." My eyes shifted back to Kellan. "Politics and religion were heating up the country. Who better to train and send into battle than those who were never wanted?"

"They were used as cannon fodder," I sneered.

"Yes." Kellan smirked. "Sacrifices for the greater good."

"Don't sound so happy about it," I bit at him. "It's disgusting."

"But a necessity."

I turned to Sheila. "Is that what you think? Is that why you've done all this? Because I think you want it all to end." I shifted in my seat to face Marianne. "You certainly didn't follow McDonough procedure, did you? Both Seamus and Kiernan are alive and well."

Marianne snarled. "Leave my sons out of this."

"Like you left my mother out of it?" I hissed. "Like you, she was innocent."

"No firstborn is innocent in this." She scoffed.

"Why?" I questioned her. "Because she got everything you never did? How was that her fault?"

Crickets.

"It wasn't," I argued further. "What are you trying to do? Seamus is dead. The woman who took you is dead. There is no one left to uphold those sick, twisted rules. You got what you wanted."

"But there is always more to claim." Sheila smiled behind her glass of wine. "Always more to be had that was never given to us."

And there it was.

The real reason behind what they were doing.

This wasn't about righting the wrongs against them or getting justice.

No. This was about power and money. Their collective pasts gave them a reason to justify it all. The people they hurt. The blood on their hands. None of that mattered to them.

"You really had me feeling just a twinge of sympathy for you." I barked a laugh and let out a long, languid sigh. "Jesus. You are all pieces of shit."

"Watch your tone, young lady." Remus growled. "Show some respect."

Another laugh. "For you?" I scoffed and shook my head. "You know, the funny thing about history is it always forgets to mention the catalyst behind each takeover. Each decision. The one who whispers in the ear of the monarchy.

The snake in the tree tempting Eve. Anne Boleyn. Cleopatra. Helen of Troy. Jezebel. The list goes on and on."

I turned to Sheila. "So which one are you?" My gaze shifted to Marianne. "If you believe for one second that she did any of this for you—then you are a fool. Sheila doesn't care about you. She is using you as a tool to do her bidding."

Sheila remained calm in her seat. The Botox was really doing something for her. Marianne was redder than a ripe tomato. Her grip on the fork in her hand was tight. Enough that I could see her knuckles whiten as her anger took over. I had a feeling I was confirming something she had already been struggling with.

She didn't like my confirmation.

"Maybe now's a good time to teach that lesson, Kellan." Sheila's eyes turned to the man beside me.

Kellan's lips turned up in a feral smile.

"I couldn't agree more."

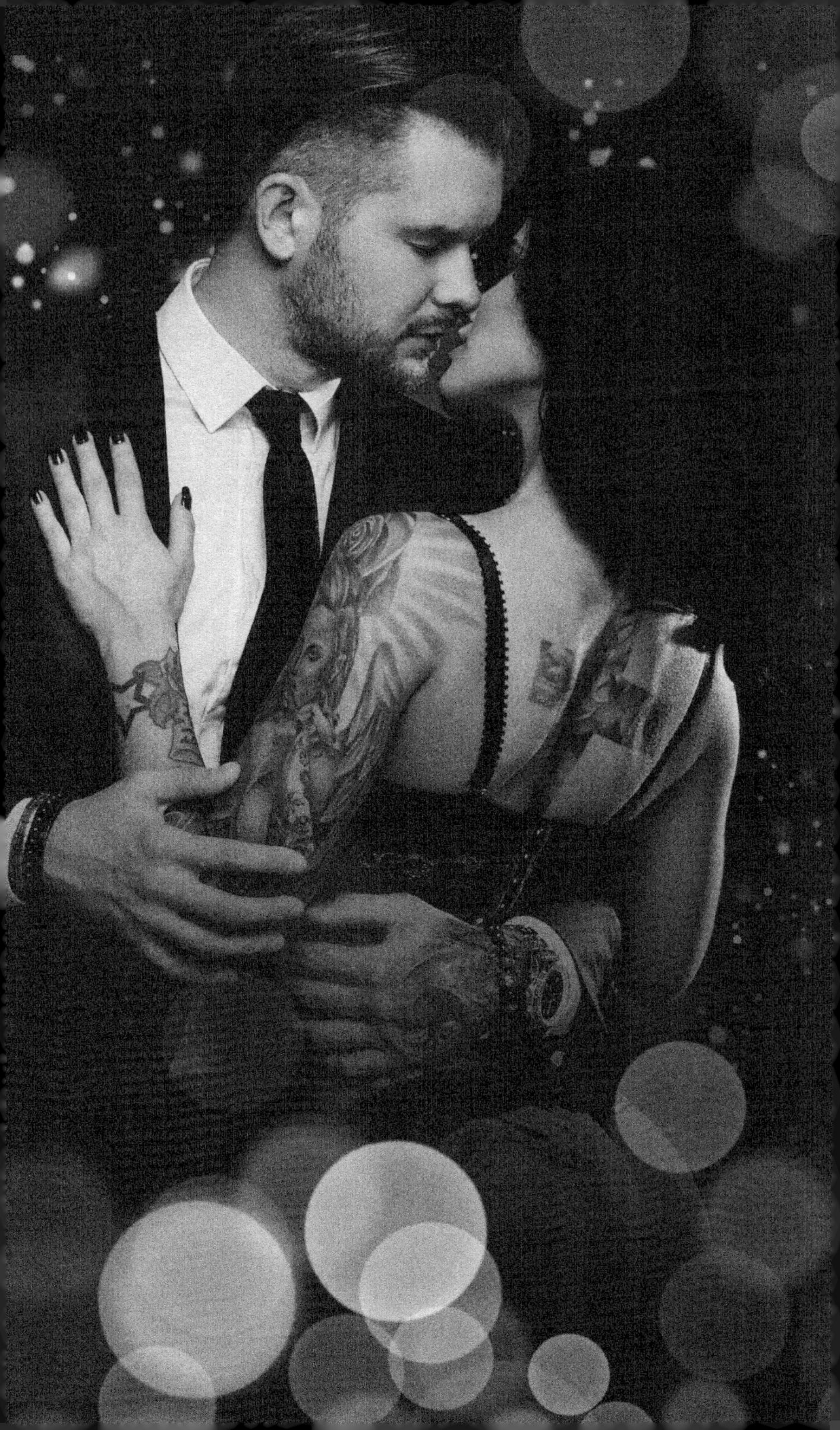

THREE

Ava

The moment Kellan reached for me, I struck. Kellan cursed as the steak knife slashed across his right forearm. My chair toppled to the floor as I bolted from the dining room and into the open foyer. Sheila's threat rang heavy in my mind as I madly dashed for the front door.

My bare feet slid to a stop on the polished wooden floor. I'd kicked off my hooker heels beneath the table before making my mad dash. Two of my grandmother's guards blocked my exit, their arms crossed against their chests, wearing matching smirks. They were at least twice my size, with a good hundred or so pounds on me. I wasn't going to let that stop me from cutting through them.

Theoretically.

I stared at the pair, doe-eyed and innocent, as my lips fell open slightly in fear as I took them in. The grins that spread across their smooshed potato faces told me they were buying what I was selling. "Please..." The small word fell from my trembling lips in a desperate plea.

One of the men took a step forward and tilted his head toward the dining room. "Get back in there before things get worse," he advised me. "Go on."

My parted lips twisted into a snarl, and the man's eyes widened in surprise when I lunged forward, knife ready to strike. I couldn't let them get on the offensive. The sudden, bold move was unexpected, and I managed to bury the knife in the thigh of the man closest to me before the second attacked.

"Little bitch," the second man screamed. He reached out to snag me, but I was quicker. Striking out with my palm, I thrust the heel upward, giving a satisfied smile when I felt the bones of his nose crack beneath my stroke. "Fuck," he cursed, his hand going to his nose.

With both men occupied with their wounds, I reached for the golden door handle, a triumphant smile on my face.

One step closer to freedom.

That was what I needed.

Just one step closer.

The handle was in my grasp, the cold metal turning beneath my hand as the hinges creaked beneath the weight.

One more step.

I could smell the fresh air burst through the crack in the door when it began to open. Pine and fresh rain washed over me, then—

A scream rent the air. Lightning surged through me, my breath rushing from my lungs. My muscles seized, my body pulling tight as I struggled to take in air. The floor rushed up to greet me, and I grunted painfully as I landed on the cold wood. The muscles in my neck strained painfully under my clenched jaw as my body writhed without my consent.

Some fucker had tased me.

Footsteps echoed beside me, but my body wouldn't move. The lids of my eyes were heavy as they fought the overwhelming need to close. A pair of black blood-stained Gucci men's shoes came into view.

"That was a very good attempt, little one." Kellan applauded me as he crouched down in front of me. A broad smile stained his face, and his blood stained the kitchen towel wrapped around the cut I'd given him. "Very well done. It won't save you from your lesson, though." He tsked. "Although I am certainly more pleased to administer it than I was before."

"Fuck"—I struggled to get the words out. My throat was tight, tongue heavy, and it felt like I was breathing through a straw—"you."

"I'm sure we'll get to that eventually." He winked at me before pulling me into his arms and rising to his feet. "But not today. Bad girls don't get rewards."

"As if fucking your micro-dick would be a reward," I spat at him, the power of the words lost with how weak and exhausted they came out.

Kellan simply hummed at my outburst. He didn't put me down. Instead, he carried me through the long corridors and back down the stairs to the cellar I'd spent the last few days in. He cradled me to his chest like a lover, his movements barely hindered by my weight or the gash in his arm.

He will come for me.

Matthias had to. He wouldn't leave me here; I was sure of it.

Once inside my prison cell, Kellan set me down on the dingy mattress that rested on the floor.

"Just in case." He winked at me, and my sluggish, taser-fried brain caught on a second too late.

"No." My free hand clawed at the manacle he'd fastened around my wrist. The chain clanked loudly in the small space. "Take it off," I snarled.

Kellan's smirk deepened. "You aren't the one who makes demands here, little one," he reminded me. I yelped when he squeezed one of my breasts roughly to prove a point. "I am."

"Fuck you, you bastard." Kicking as hard as I could, I aimed for the side of Kellan's head. He was too busy playing with my breast to note the sudden movement.

The kick wasn't hard enough to do any real damage. It was just hard enough to knock him off balance, but not having his slimy hand on me was worth it. I had one moment to bask in the smug satisfaction at the sight of his bleeding lip and the surprise on his face before bitter outrage engulfed him. He lurched toward me, his hand grabbing at the collar of my dress as he dragged me to my feet, his left hand striking my cheek in a slap that had me seeing stars.

And not the fun kind.

My ears rang, and the muscles in my neck strained against the force of his slap.

"You want to play rough?" he snarled, his hand gripping my jaw painfully as he shoved his thumb between my lips. "Go on. Suck on my thumb, you fucking whore, because soon you're going to be down on your knees sucking a whole lot more."

Oh hell no.

I bit down on Kellan's thumb, my teeth sinking into his flesh until I tasted the sweet copper of his blood. His sharp cry of pain was music to my ears, and I bit down harder, wanting to hear it again.

"Bitch." That was the only thing I heard before he landed a punch to my side, the air whooshing from my lungs. My jaw dropped open, releasing his injured finger, and pain twisted violently through my stomach. "You're going to regret that." He shouted for someone, and a few seconds later, another set of footsteps entered the room.

Looking up, I saw smushed potato face number two with his broken nose and angry eyes. The guard whose nose I butchered upstairs licked his lips as his lecherous gaze wandered over me. "I'm going to have a whole lot of fun with you."

Fuck me like a duck.

I was really in for it now.

I let loose a tidal scream when Kellan's hand wrapped itself in my hair, pulling my head backward into his lap, forcing me to stare up at him while smushed nose landed one blow after another on various parts of my body.

Kellan's grip on my hair tightened when I tried to move my head, his eyes staring down at me, a dark grin splashed across his face. Sick fuck was enjoying seeing my pain. I fought back as much as I could, refusing to lie there docilely and take the beating. It wasn't long before I could feel my body growing limp, the pain swallowing me whole, like Jonah and the whale.

Darkness seeped into my vision as another blow landed on the side of my face. My vision blurred, Kellan's gloating mug growing more and more out of focus. The sound of the guard's blows was becoming distant as well, and all I could hear were Kellan's soft, reassuring shushes, telling me that everything was going to be all right.

He better hope this killed me.

If it didn't, I'd be back for his blood.

With that last thought, I let the familiar tide of darkness wash over me once again.

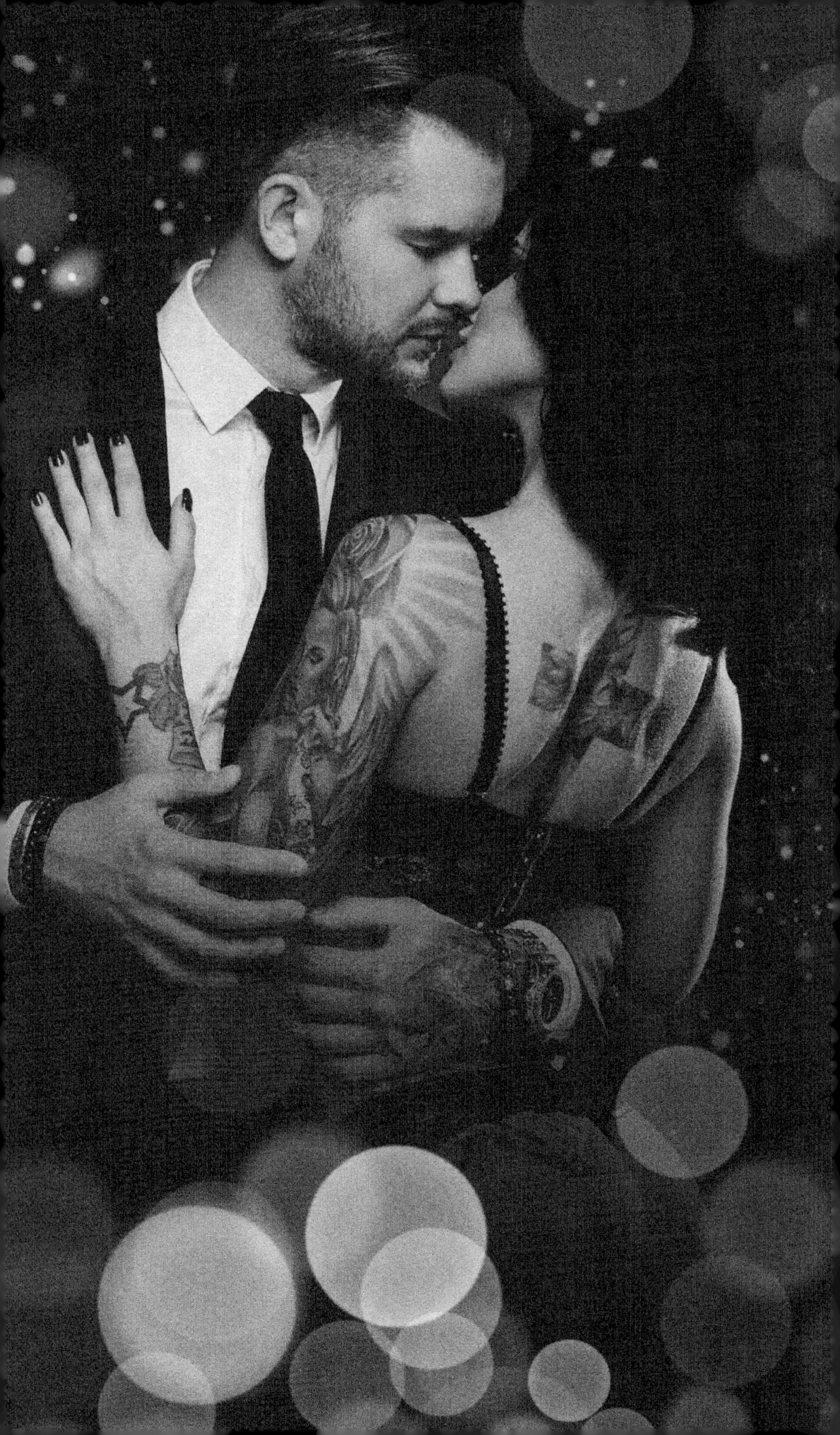

FOUR

BEFORE THE EXPLOSION

Matthias

"I told you something didn't feel right." Leon inclined his head to me respectfully as I exited the lobby, a large smile on his face despite the circumstances. Returning his smile, I embraced the young Italian before taking a step back and checking the feed that was displayed on the monitors in the security corridor.

He was right. Something was off.

"You cleared the building?"

Leon nodded. "The minute the breach was flagged, we called a code black," he confirmed. "We're the only ones here besides the men guarding the vault."

"Good." I took a deep, calming breath as Leon led us to the stairs that descended into the parking garage. The entrance to the vault sat on the other side of the parking garage, concealed beneath one of the many grates that dotted the underground structure. Whoever had breached our security system last night was careless.

They had wanted to be seen.

But why?

My gut twisted, telling me that nothing was adding up. The obvious play would be to go for the money we'd secured from the cargo container. But we'd already shuffled most of that cash through our businesses. It wasn't in the vault any longer. There was a possibility that whoever breached our system didn't know that, but I didn't believe that was the case.

There was something we hadn't seen yet.

A missing piece of the puzzle we hadn't found.

Protocol during a breach meant clearing the entire building. We didn't know what the hacker had managed to mess with. Security. Employee IDs. Mark was still working on finding any corrupt data. He'd come up short.

It would be difficult to sneak a physical person past me or my men, but most of us had been absent since my supposed death. I couldn't discount the distinct possibility that this wasn't the first security breach.

"Found anything?" I asked Mark over the comm line.

"No," Mark huffed angrily. I could hear the sounds of his fingers pounding against his keyboard. "Nothing. They didn't touch any of the systems. It's like they showed up, waited, and left."

"That doesn't make any sense," Andrei muttered. I had to agree with my father. Why bother infiltrating one of the most secure buildings in the city if you weren't there to obtain information? Was it to clear the building? No one outside of the organization knew of our protocols.

Unless we had a mole.

Rage simmered in my chest at the mere thought of one of my soldiers betraying me.

"Help me here," Vas muttered to Leon when we'd reached the far end of the parking garage. The pair grabbed hold of the wrought-iron grate, and with a short grunt, they lifted. We descended the stairs one at a time before making our way down the singular hallway that ended at the vault door.

I let my gaze wander the area, searching for discrepancies once we reached the door. Nothing was out of place. The two guards posted outside were the same pair that had been assigned the post for the last year. Their eyes widened in shock when they saw me.

"*Pakhan*," they whispered in awe-tinged voices.

"Marius." I nodded at the first guard before turning my gaze to the second. "George. How are you?"

"G-good," Marius stuttered slightly. "We're good. It's damn good to see you alive, sir."

"Thank you," I told him sincerely. "Anything to report?" The two men straightened up and shook their heads.

"No, sir," George reported. "No sign of movement. Nothing out of the ordinary."

"That's good to hear." My head turned toward Leon. "Let's get this over with."

Leon nodded and stepped toward the vault. It was lined with concrete and steel thick enough to keep out most radioactivity and withstand a nuclear bomb. The vault was more like a bunker. The door was made of carbon steel and completely independent from the rest of the building. From the Wi-Fi to the life support system.

Completely impenetrable.

A keypad sat on either side of the door, along with a

retina scanner. The only ones with access were the men in my upper circle. And Ava. But I didn't think anyone had told her that yet.

Each person was assigned their own code. For security reasons, a new code was generated at the start of every week to help prevent breaches. One code needed to be used in conjunction with another code, or the door wouldn't open, and the retinal scans had to be done at the same time.

Stepping up to my keypad, I gave Leon the signal to start entering his code. The system beeped, accepting the individual entries before the retinal scanner dinged. We leaned forward, our right eyes focused on the scanner.

"Wait—" Mark shouted over the comm line. It was too late. The scanner had already imprinted our retinas. The building rumbled beneath our feet, concrete shifting as an explosion rang out above our heads.

"Your retinal scan triggered the building's self-destruct mechanism," Mark cried. "Every one of the devices has been activated. You have less than sixty seconds to get the hell out of there."

"Motherfucker," I cursed. The door to the vault had already opened. It was our only chance. "Everyone inside the vault. Now."

The sound of falling rubble was deafening. "Mark, tell Kristian to get Ava away from the building or they'll be caught in the collapse."

Static.

"Mark."

Shit.

"*Mark!*"

"Son," my father urged from the doorway. "Your wife is strong. She will be fine. Get inside before you go down with the ship."

Cursing, I strode quickly through the door, helping my father pull it closed. The electronic click of the lock was music to my ears.

"We should be safe in here," Vas assured everyone.

"Should be?" Andrei frowned.

"Well," Vas smirked grimly, "we haven't exactly tested it out before."

Andrei chuckled.

Then the last few bombs detonated.

Hindsight was a bitch. In the early days of construction, we'd implanted explosive devices into the major fault lines of the building so that if worse came to worse, the building could be reduced to a pile of ash and rubble. Along with any evidence.

Not that I was careless.

No one outside my organization knew about those devices. There were only a handful of men who were aware of them. One of them had to be the mole.

Fuck.

The vault rumbled and shook as steel and concrete rained down on top of us. For the first time in years, I prayed. I prayed that the vault would hold under the weight of the upper building's collapse, and I prayed that my wife managed to get free of the collapse zone.

I wasn't a religious man, but in that moment, as the lights flickered and stalled, leaving us in an embankment of darkness, I'd pray to whoever would listen.

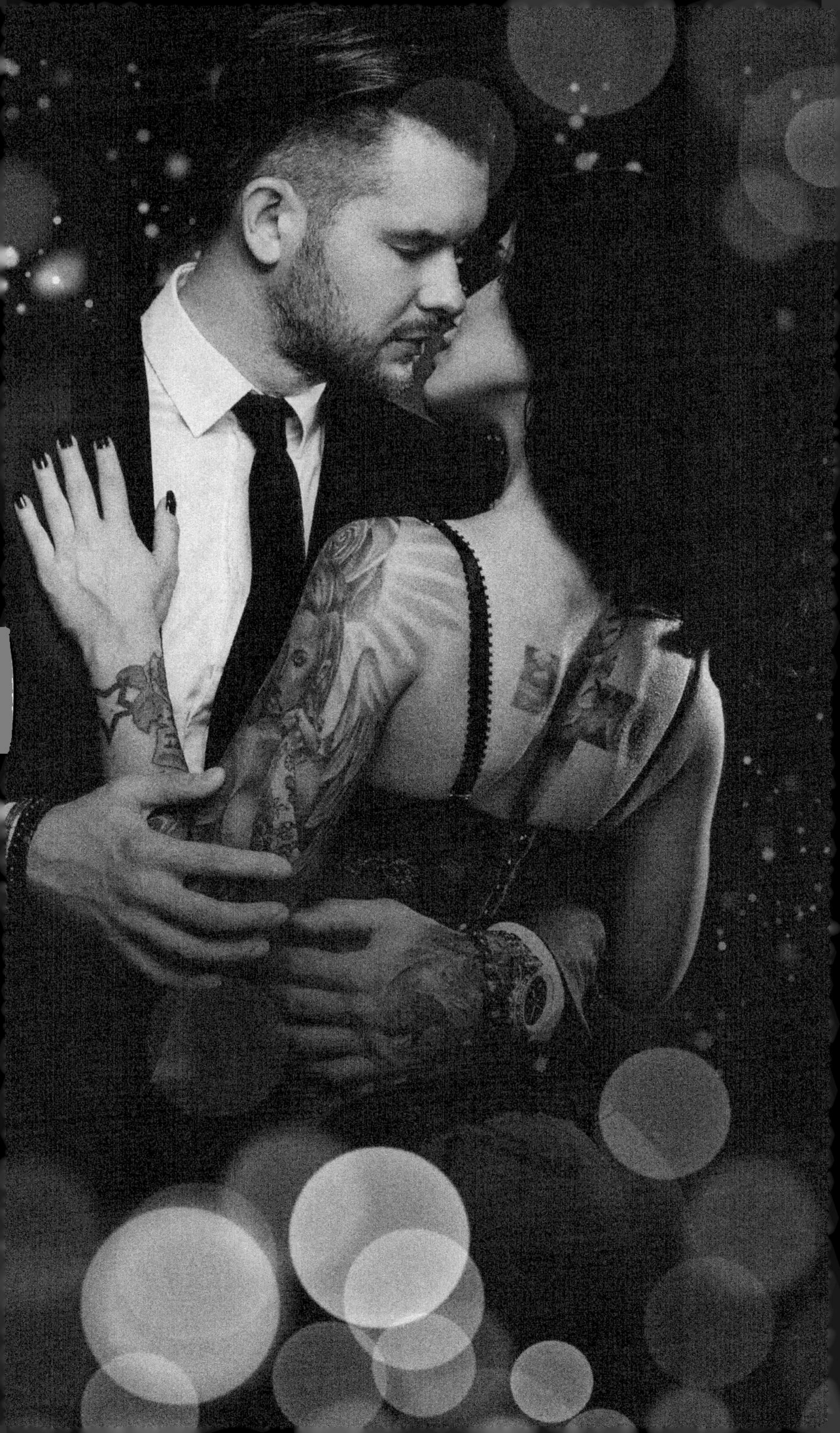

FIVE

Matthias

Agony was tearing at my chest like a wild animal.

Three days.

Ava had already been missing for three days without any trace of where she had gone. The tracker Vas had installed in her necklace was silent. Not even a blip. Footage from our security satellite showed her abduction just minutes after the building collapse, but there was no way to gain facial images. They were too distorted.

"Fuck," I roared, sweeping my hand across the desk. Glass shattered, screens cracked, and papers scattered under the weight of my frustration. The monster inside me wanted blood. When I got my hands on whoever had betrayed us, on whoever had taken my wife, I would rip them apart piece by piece and bathe in their blood.

"You know—" I looked up to see Vas leaning against the doorframe of my office. "There was some good whiskey in that glass. Expensive too." He shook his head in mock disappointment. "What a waste."

My lips curled in a sneer, and I shot him an icy glare. "Stuff it," I grumbled.

Vas shrugged. "I'm just saying," he advised with a smartass smile. "Kavanaugh won't be too happy that you're destroying his things."

I groaned. Running a hand down my face, I stood from my chair and slowly began to clean up the mess I had made. "Fucking stuck here," I mumbled. "No idea where my wife is. There's a mole somewhere in our operation. Whole place reeks of piss poor beer."

"That's Corona you're thinking of." Liam's voice drifted in behind Vas. "We serve Guinness. Big difference. Not that I expect you to understand such finer tastes when all you drink is that swill you call vodka."

"It is not swill."

"Tastes like water," Liam countered. "Stale water, in fact."

"Says the man whose beer curdles when you drink it," I sneered. "And who always stinks like cabbage."

"And you smell so much better?"

"Anything is better than cabbage."

"You reek of desperation." The leprechaun sniffed. "That's definitely worse than cabbage."

"That's the pot calling the pan, don't you think?"

"Kettle." The Irish asshat smirked. "It's the pot calling the kettle."

I shot him a confused look. "What? That makes no sense. Pots and pans go together. Why a kettle?"

Liam thought about that for a moment before he shrugged. "Have no idea," he admitted nonchalantly. "Now, if we're done, my hacker and yours have something for us."

He looked down at the mess I'd created in his spare office. "Unless you'd like to continue with your Neanderthal temper tantrum, that is."

I growled when he turned his back and strode from the room. "Neanderthal," I hissed. "I'll show you a fucking Neanderthal, you fucking leprechaun. Choke you on your goddamn Lucky Charms."

Vas barked a laugh as we exited the room, following my wife's father. Since the collapse of the Dashkov building, he'd graciously allowed us to take over one of the empty floors in the building above his bar. Most of my men had been assigned to the compound to continue training and preparing our people for war, but it was too far away from the city for me to set up shop at.

Kavanaugh had his own similar setup in the basement that rivaled ours back at the bunker. It was more rustic than what I was used to, but it did the job, and that was what mattered.

Mark sat at one of the operation stations next to a blond girl whose hair was tied up in space buns. She was wearing bright red flare pants and an orange tank top. Her face was covered in a layer of heavy makeup of bright rainbow colors. Bridget, I believed, was her name. She was the Kavanaugh family's hacker, with a resume that left most speechless. Ivy league graduate. Valedictorian. Bridget Jones was a mechanical and technological prodigy, and yet she was down here in the basement of a bar, working for a crime syndicate.

"Where are we at with finding my daughter?" Liam questioned the pair as he stalked through the door. Neither hacker turned to look at him, their hands busy flying across their keyboards, eyes scanning the brightly lit monitors in front of them.

"Her tracker just became active," Mark announced.

"Why weren't we able to get a reading until now?" I asked. "Or at least track where she's been?" The tracker should have had the capability to store Ava's route inside of the mainframe, giving us her GPS footprint.

"The tracker wasn't activated," Bridget explained. "Your wife probably never had a chance to activate it before she was taken from the scene. She probably tried to activate it sometime later, after we had already tried, but there was something blocking it. A jammer of some sort, most likely."

"Why can we see it now?" I wondered.

"We think that wherever she's being held has a similar setup to the Ward *stables*," Mark commented. "The jammer only worked *below* the surface of the barn. Just in case someone came snooping around. Cops would be more suspicious if they suddenly couldn't make a radio or cell phone call."

"Where is she now?" Liam stepped forward, peering at the screens.

Mark pointed at a large piece of green land near a small town called Kangley. Houses out there were few and far between. "Here."

"We believe she's still there," Bridget sniffed, "but her tracker cut out again about five minutes ago.

"Is that land registered to anyone?" Kavanaugh asked tersely. His eyes were narrowed at the screen, jaw tight. Did he recognize that area?

"Um..." Mark input the address into the federal database. "Yeah. It is registered to a Dearbhla O'Malley, but according to record, she died several years ago in a car crash."

"Who inherited it?" I asked. Mark scrolled through the documents, trying to source a name.

"Seamus McDonough," Liam hissed. "Seamus McDonough inherited that land."

I frowned. "Ava's grandfather?" He'd been at the gala. I remember the way Ava looked at him. Not with the newfound awe of meeting her biological grandfather, but with suspicion and fear.

"Whoever is holding her isn't her grandfather," Liam sneered. "He's just wearing his face."

Bridget snorted. "That's not creepy."

Liam rolled his eyes. "You know what I mean." He gave her a pointed look. "The man may look like Seamus McDonough, but he isn't."

"Then what happened to the real Seamus McDonough?" Mark's brow furrowed. "If this man has been parading around as him, he would have had to get rid of him, right?"

Liam nodded. "Ava suspected that whoever this guy is, he's been playing at being Seamus for a while now."

"How long?" I wondered. "Someone would have had to notice at some point that he wasn't really Seamus. Mannerisms. Vocal pitch. The way he drank his coffee. Unless he'd been studying Seamus for years and practicing each and every little thing, someone would have picked up on the fact that he wasn't who he appeared to be."

"Someone like Katherine McDonough." Vas spoke up from behind me. He was leaning against the wooden table situated in the middle of the room.

Liam turned to my *Sovietnik*. "Why do you say that?" he demanded roughly.

Vas smirked, his eyes lighting up with a challenge. He knew something that Liam didn't or something Liam already knew but refused to acknowledge.

"You should really listen when your daughter tries to talk to you about her," he reprimanded.

"Katherine ran away," Liam snarled. "There was nothing to talk about."

"We all know that isn't true," Vas barked. "The proof was in Portland. You're just refusing to accept it because you know what it means."

"It doesn't mean anything!" Liam roared. The Irish leader took a heavy step in Vas's direction. I was tempted to intercede, but something told me a few fists might need to fly in order for Liam to see some sense. "Katherine McDonough ran because she was scared. She didn't want to commit. She didn't want the pressure. She caved, and she told me as much."

Vas snorted. "A letter told you as much," he pointed out.

"A letter in her handwriting." His words dripped venom.

"And someone's handwriting can't be replicated?" I asked, tilting my head at him. "Like two people can't be in one place or share the same face?"

"That's not the point..." He trailed off.

"Think, Kavanaugh," Vas hissed at him. "Think about everything Ava has told you. About how her mother first disappeared. It was the day after Seamus sent you to Portland, right?"

Liam paused for a moment, his eyes raising up and to the left.

"She went missing the day after you left," Vas told him. "Katherine didn't show up for class that day. Another student went to check on her because they were supposed to meet for lunch. That student found her apartment door open and the room trashed."

"That wasn't in the report."

"Of course it wasn't," Vas sniffed. "Whoever took her wanted it to seem like she disappeared. You know this. Neil Romano told you this. His parents died saving her the first time."

"Just because he said it—"

"Why would he lie?" I questioned Liam. "Stop blinding yourself to the truth, Kavanaugh, when it's written in blood right before your eyes."

"There is something big going on here," Vas continued. "It's been going on longer than any of us could imagine, and if we don't get to the bottom of this, none of us will survive this war."

Liam hung his head. His shoulders were stiff, fists clenched at his sides as he warred with himself. Everything he had known was being obliterated, piece by piece. Katherine being abducted meant he had failed to protect her. To believe her. The man he looked up to wasn't who he appeared to be, and if I was right, reality was about to get even harder for him and his family.

But that wasn't my story to tell.

"What do you want to do?" He raised his head and stared at me. "My men will follow your lead."

I nodded at him graciously and turned to the hackers. "Get me a layout of the house and the surrounding terrain. See if we can get our security satellite in place. I want infrared alerts."

"Got it," the two acknowledged in unison.

Closing my eyes, I breathed in, taking a long, calming breath before letting it back out.

My eyes flew open, and I stared at my father-in-law.

"Let's go get my wife."

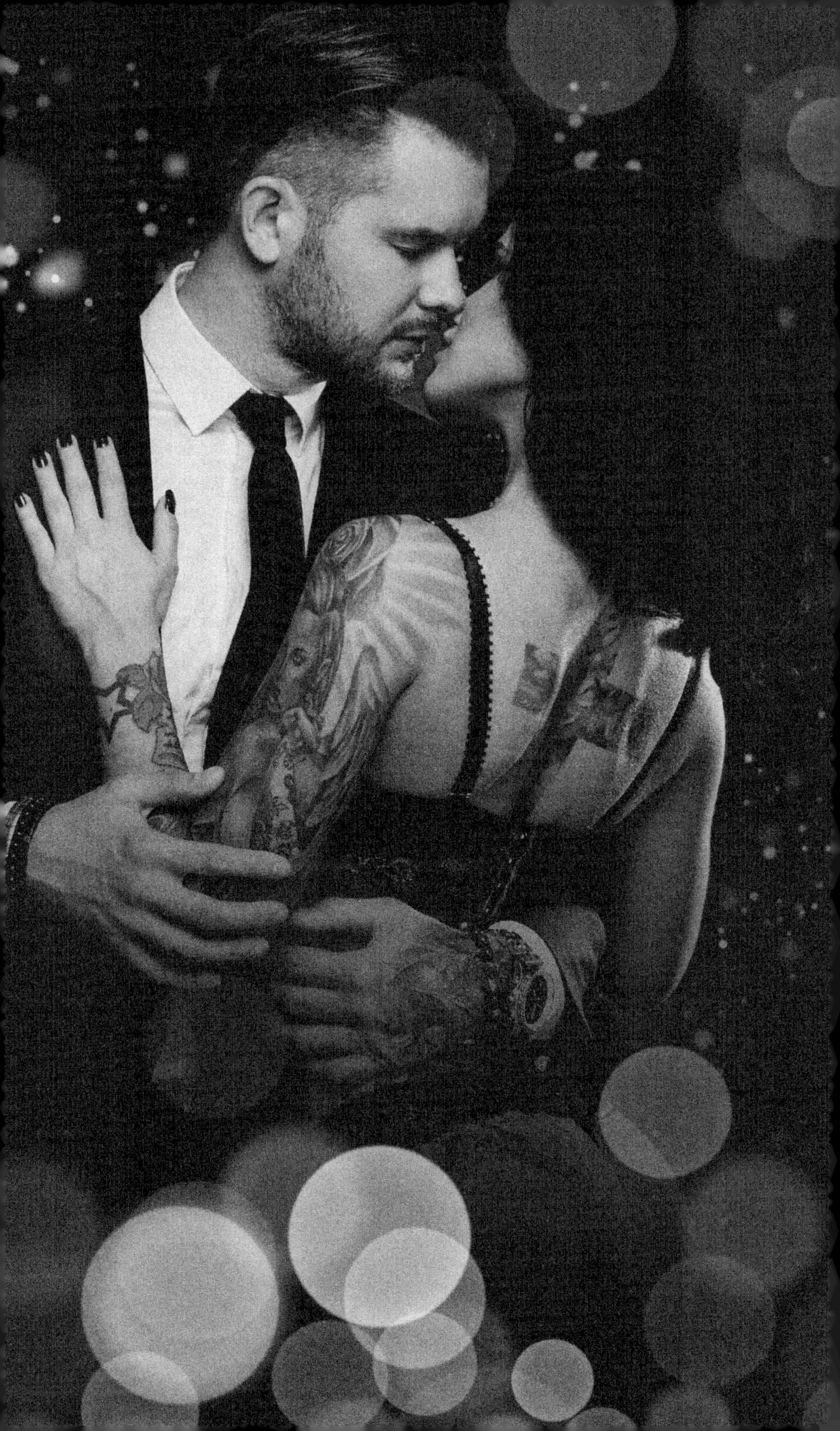

SIX

Ava

I startled awake, gasping for air. My fingers clawed at my neck, struggling to tear away the invisible noose wrapped around it.

It was dark outside. Slivers of the moon's rays danced along the floor as clouds shift along its surface. I could barely pry my eyes open—my eyelashes were stuck together, a thin layer of crust running along the edge. My face was swollen, and the metallic taste of blood lingered inside my mouth. I felt lethargic, and my body ached something fierce.

It took me a second to orient myself. I was still locked inside my prison cell. The manacles gripped my wrists tightly, chafing the sensitive skin. My dress was torn. The velvet was dirty and ripped in several places. It was held together by only a few seams along the top and one long seam at the skirt.

I had to get out of here, but the thought of escape sent a

horrified shiver up my spine, causing my heart to race. The manacles were hammered into the concrete wall behind me and barely allowed for any range of motion.

The last time I was chained up like this, Neil was holding my head, forcing me to watch Christian rape my best friend. The faded imagery caused my gut to protest as bile surged toward the surface. I barely managed to hold it back.

Matthias, where are you?

Why haven't you come for me?

I leaned my head back against the wall, silent tears tracking down my dirt-marred cheeks as I sent a silent prayer out to the universe. Was I still pissed off at him for pretending to be dead all those months? Fuck yeah. Was I planning on making him work to earn back my trust? Hell fucking yeah.

But did I really need him to burst through the door right now like the monster he was and take me in his arms?

With all of my heart, yes.

Was he out there looking for me? Wondering where I was? Worried about me?

I scoffed.

Who knew if he was even alive?

He is alive.

I repeated the mantra in my head like a broken record.

It was such a ridiculous thing to do that I started to laugh, and immediately stopped as my chest twisted painfully. I was going to kill them all.

Every motherfucking one of them.

Teach her a lesson.

What lesson? Was my cold-hearted grandmother planning on selling me to Kellan? Or was Kellan the proxy? I could briefly recall seeing him at the gala. His eyes had been trained on Bailey as she'd danced with my brother on the floor. After that, I couldn't remember seeing him again.

Would he take me away? Sell me? Use me? The icy, cruel smile he'd worn when he'd held me down for the guard to beat on spoke volumes about him. I had no doubt that he would do everything in his power to break me.

I let out a soft cry when I tried to move my feet out from under me. The pain in my ribs was intense. Fire licked up my body, and I let a few more tears leak down my face.

For the first time in years, I wanted my mother. She wasn't coming, but he would. The man who'd rescued me from the clutches of Christian. Who showed me immediate, unconditional love. He would come for me like he had before.

Matthias was my monster. The demon lurking in the darkest corners of my soul. The man who forged me from fire.

But my father was my knight in shining armor.

The man on the white steed.

He was the hero I never knew I needed.

And when a monster and knight joined forces, they were unstoppable.

They would come for me.

They would always come for me.

Daddy, please.

I let the silent prayer be carried by the darkness as I closed my eyes and surrendered myself to sleep, my soul battered but not broken.

"*Hó bha ín, Hó bha ín.*
Hó bha ín, mo ghrá.

*Hó bha ín, mo leana,
Agus codail, go lá.*

*Hó bha ín, mo leana,
'Is hó bha ín mo roghain.
Hó bha ín, mo leana,
Is gabh amach a bhadhbh badhbh.*

*Hó bha ín, Hó bha ín.
Hó bha ín, mo ghrá.
Hó bha ín, mo leana,
Agus codail, go lá."*

She was singing again. The hauntingly beautiful melody she sang to me each night before bed echoed through the dark kitchen in the middle of the night. I'd gone to bed hours ago, readying for another day of school, but she was still awake.

And crying.

This wasn't the first time I had come downstairs to find her weeping at the kitchen island, her golden locket clenched tight between her hands as she sobbed.

Alone.

She never spoke of my father. I didn't even know his name, but I'd peeked at the man inside the locket. His hair was red like mine, eyes the same shining green. It definitely seemed like it would be him.

Where was he?

Had he left us by choice?

"Mama," I whispered sadly as I walked into the kitchen, rubbing at my tired eyes.

"Avaleigh." Turning away, she quickly wiped at her wet eyes and cleared her throat before she turned back to face me. "What are you doing up, mo réalta?"

I stepped into her side and wrapped my arms around her waist. "It's okay to be sad, Mommy," I told her. "You don't have to hide it from me."

My mother smiled down at me gently. Tears still clung to her thin, fragile lashes, and pain danced across her face so starkly it almost looked physical.

"Some tears need to be shed alone, my star," she whispered, her words dripping sorrowfully. I crawled onto the stool next to her and leaned in, surveying the picture she had tucked away. The one she always cried over.

"Who is he, Mama?" I asked, running my finger along the outside of the picture.

Her mouth twitched on one side and her throat bobbed. "My knight in shining armor."

"Then why isn't he here?" I wondered. "Aren't knights supposed to be with their princesses?"

"Not all princesses get their happily ever after." Clearing her throat, she snapped the locket shut. "And some princesses have a bedtime. Go get your water."

Giggling, I hopped down from the chair to grab a glass of water. Once I was done, I placed it in the sink and held out my arms. Smiling, my mother lifted me into her arms, cradling me to her chest like I was the most precious thing she owned.

"One day," I yawned. "I'm going to have a knight of my own."

"Not all knights have shining armor, little one," she warned me, her voice low and thoughtful.

"Mine will," I told her stubbornly as my eyes began to close. "And he will never leave me."

The door to the cell creaked open, letting in a stream of dim yellow light from the hall. I didn't open my eyes, but I could hear his voice. It was low and garbled, as if he was trying to talk to me while I was underwater. Smooshed nose had no doubt done some form of damage to my ears. Upside, I didn't have to listen to their shit.

Kellan's footsteps echoed loudly in the quiet room. I kept my breathing even, eyes shut, hoping he would think I was still asleep and leave me in peace.

I was never that lucky.

"I know you're awake, little one," he sneered. His hand clenched around my jaw, gripping it tight enough to bruise. "No need to pretend."

His cold eyes greeted me when I opened mine. He was only inches from my face. My heart thumped in my chest wildly when I saw the long, curved blade in his hand. My jaw clenched, the pain grounding me. I refused to show this fucker any ounce of fear.

"Stay still," he whispered to me seductively. He pressed the tip of the blade between my breasts and slid the knife slowly through the fabric. "You won't need this much longer." He smiled down at me, like I was his lover and he wasn't forcibly undressing me. The velvet fabric gave way easily beneath the sharpness of his blade. He mumbled an insincere apology each time the tip of the knife nicked at my skin, causing blood to swell to the surface.

I gritted my teeth, refusing to make a sound.

"Your grandmother informed me that you were such a docile little lamb," Kellan murmured. He kept stripping at my dress, piece by piece, until it lay in ribbons surrounding me. I lay before him, shackled in nothing but my underwear. My breasts were on full display, and the lascivious way he licked his lips told me he wasn't hiding his attraction to my body.

"I'm not," I snarled at him. "You should ask for a refund."

Kellan chuckled darkly and pressed the blade against my right nipple. I hissed at the pain that bloomed when he sliced a shallow cut across my areola.

"There are so many ways to break someone, you know," he kept on murmuring. At this point, I was sure he was simply talking to hear his own voice. He didn't care what I had to say on the subject. He just wanted me to listen to his endless droning. If I wasn't tied down, I'd slam that knife through his vocal cords. Then no one would have to hear him speak again. "Pain is the most common, of course. Cutting. Sawing. Beating." He let out a wistful sigh, like he was recalling a happy memory. "But from what I've learned about you, that won't really work."

He grinned down at me when he felt my body stiffen in response to his words.

"That's what I thought." He chuckled like it was the best news he'd ever received. "You know pain all too well because of that wretched Christian Ward. The man doesn't know the art of torture and making someone fear it instead of leading the subject to adapt to it. A waste, really."

"No," he continued, the knife in his hand skating along my pebbled skin. "But I've watched how you respond to looks...touches..." He trailed off, his free hand running up my inner thigh. I kicked my leg out, which wasn't shackled, and nailed him in the stomach.

My reward was a slice of the knife down the middle of my upper thigh. I screamed, unable to contain the sudden pain that swept through me.

"Keep it up, little one," he growled. "I don't need all your body parts. Just the useful ones."

"Yeah?" I sneered. "I doubt any of your body parts are useful, so feel free to swap places with me. I'll gladly remove some of your appendages."

The fucker laughed. Not one of those half-assed ones either. He let out a full belly laugh that, if under different circumstances, was attractive as fuck. Too bad he was the creepy-ass villain in this story. He'd sure as hell make an amazing mafia bad boy in one of those smutty romance novels I loved so much.

"Did you get anything from her yet?" Marianne's cool voice seeped into the room. Kellan smirked.

"We were just about to get started."

They wanted information. Wonderful.

My stepmother's heels clicked annoyingly against the concrete floor as she stepped toward us. She quirked a well-manicured eyebrow when she stepped into view.

"And she had to be naked for this?"

Kellan, the psychopath, shrugged. "More of a canvas to work with. Plus, a pleasure to look at." Marianne grunted her disagreement and waved her hand dismissively.

"Well, get to it, then."

I couldn't help but give a low laugh. My throat was still fucked up from smooshed nose choking me. "My father is going to kill you so, so slowly," I taunted her. "He hates traitors."

She chuckled mirthlessly, her lips tipping up scornfully. "Who do you think your father will believe?" She cocked her head to the side. "You, the daughter he just met? Or me, his loving wife? Even if you managed to get out of here alive, he'll never believe you over me. Just like he didn't believe Katherine."

"You forged that note, didn't you?" I shook my head in disgust. "You're the one who turned her in to Elias after she escaped."

Marianne dragged in a short, contempt-filled laugh, her tongue dancing along her upper teeth. "Your dear mother wrote that note all on her own," Marianne admitted gleefully. "All I had to do was threaten to slit his throat in their bed. Easy peasy. She would have done anything for Liam."

"You convinced her not to tell him what happened in the first place." I knew the answers to these questions already. Most of them. But I needed to hear them out loud. I needed to hear it from the mouth of the monster who had taken away everything my mother cared about.

"That was a little harder, I must admit," she shrugged. "But victims' shame is such a powerful thing."

My heart broke for my mother. Shattering into tiny pieces like it had done so many times before when I dug through her past. The more I learned, the more I hated the world she had been forced into. This was someone she'd trusted. She'd treated Marianne like a sister without even knowing their connection.

"Why did you—"

"Enough with the questions," Kellan spouted. "We're the ones who will be asking them from now on. And how you answer will dictate how much suffering you go through."

Marianne tightened her jaw and stepped back, watching from the shadows. Was she relishing in what was about to happen? In my pain? Had she done the same to my mother?

"Good girl." He praised my silence as he dragged the tip of the knife over my uninjured breast before circling my nipple. "I want to know where the compound is, Mrs. Dashkova."

Kellan used the feminine version of my last name. Adding the extra syllable. It was a common practice in Russian culture, but I'd found that very few of Matthias's people adhered to that rule. Especially once I became *Pakhan*.

"I don't know what you're talking about," I told him calmly. "I've never heard about a compound."

Kellan smiled cruelly. "I think you're lying." He licked his lips. "Remember, little one, I can make you suffer in ways that Christian could never dream of. If you think your time with him was painful, just wait until I'm done with you."

Try me.

"I don't know anything about a compound," I repeated firmly. "I was leader in name only. Vas ran the business in my stead."

The blunt edge of the knife tapped against my nipple, causing my body to jerk unexpectedly. "Now," Kellan frowned, "I think you're lying, and I hate liars."

And he showed me just how much that statement was true. With every lie came a punch, a slap, a nick of the knife. My stomach was covered in a mix of shallow and deep cuts, my blood smeared across my body like a Picasso painting.

When the knife didn't work, he turned to needles. Digging them into the most excruciating places he could find. A few on my feet, so that if I flexed them, I'd cry out as they dug further into my body. A line of them up my belly. The inside of my elbows.

By the time he was out of needles, I was a ball of excruciating pain, and I wanted it to end. After a few hours, I was unable to answer him at all. Not that he seemed to care. It didn't stop him from removing one needle to move it somewhere different. At least he hadn't removed my fingernails or tried to shove the needles beneath them. I'd read about that in some yakuza mafia book somewhere, and it sounded worse than death.

My stomach felt like an empty pit by the time Kellan was finished with me. Marianne had left the room once he'd started cutting into my skin. Her face had been pale, eyes glassy. Guess she couldn't stomach it.

Weak-ass bitch.

The psychopath lifted the needles from my skin one by one, placing a soft kiss against the skin he'd abused, murmuring about how he didn't want to hurt me and I should just give in.

Yeah, sure, buddy. I'll give in when you're hanging out the window by your entrails.

Jesus, I needed so much therapy.

"Don't worry, little one," he cooed at me once he'd removed the last needle. "I'll make you feel better."

I was so out of it that my mind barely registered the feeling of his fingertips brushing along the seam of my cunt. He wouldn't find anything down there. It was as dry as sandpaper. The only pain I craved was the pain Matthias gave me. Erotic. Steamy. Consensual.

This fucker didn't know the meaning of the word.

I winced when he dug his fingers inside me. He'd spit on them first. Racked with pain, my body hardly acknowledged the intrusion.

But my mind did.

And it didn't like what he was doing.

"Stop," I whimpered, tears leaking from my eyes. Who knew I had any of those left? "Stop."

He shushed me, his eyes roaming over my bruised and

battered body. I was once again struck by how loving his gaze was. Did he honestly believe I was his? Was he that delusional, or was this part of a game to trick me into falling for his scheme?

"It's all right, Ava," he soothed. "Soon—"

An explosion from above rocked the room. Kellan pulled his fingers from inside me and jumped to his feet.

"We've got a problem, boss." The guard outside the door was frantic. "They're calling for you upstairs. We need to go."

"Dammit," he cursed. "Stay outside this door. Kill anyone you don't recognize and make sure she doesn't leave." The guard nodded and took up his post. Kellan turned to me and smirked. "Don't think this is over, little one. I'm going to enjoy fucking you like a bitch in heat while your husband watches. Then I'll slit his fucking throat, and you can watch him bleed out while I make you orgasm."

I snickered, suddenly feeling oddly renewed. "As if you could make me orgasm."

Kellan growled but said nothing, choosing instead to stride from the room, slamming the door harshly behind him.

Matthias had come for me, and god help anyone who got in his way.

They were going to need it.

was all the confirmation we needed. The plan was meticulously drawn to prevent unnecessary casualties on our end.

I could give two fucks about anyone else, but there were a few people I was looking at keeping alive.

Whoever held Seamus McDonough's face and whoever the woman was who had taken my wife.

I'd add more as necessary.

"You've got four bogies just inside the back door," Mark informed us over the comm line. "Two inside the front. Huh..." He paused dramatically.

"What is wrong?" I asked. "Why the pause?"

"There should be more people," he said. "The heat signatures inside the house are all roaming. They're obviously guards, but no one is just sitting still or doing normal activities. No staff. Nothing."

"Are you saying Ava might not be here?" I snarled.

"No." Bridget spoke up, her husky voice calm and weirdly soothing. "It just means that whoever took Ava might not be there. But she still could be."

"Do you think they were expecting us?" Seamus whispered next to me. I shook my head.

"I doubt it," I assured him. "Otherwise, this place would be abandoned, or we'd be looking at an ambush."

"Still could be," Liam admitted. "If the basement blocks RFID and GPS, it might block infrared."

I shrugged. "I'll risk it."

And that was when hellfire rained down.

Maksim and Leon had planted C4 along the outer banks of the house. Nothing structural. It was just enough to shake the mansion and maybe knock a few bricks loose. The walls shook, glass shattering, and shouts from inside of the house grew louder.

I surged forward, taking out the first guard who came toward the shattered sliding glass door with ease.

Then another explosion. This one was closer to the front of the house. We didn't slow our pace as we cleared a path through the back of the house toward the basement door that was just off the servants' quarters. We didn't have a lot of time before the enemy's reinforcements arrived or the building collapsed beneath the strain of the explosions.

I took out my Beretta. Subtly wasn't necessary any longer. They knew we were here to take back what was ours. A bullet whizzed past my head, missing me by mere centimeters, burying itself in the pillar behind me. A flash of ginger hair caught my eye.

He'd come out of the basement.

"What a way to meet," the man yelled. His Irish accent was rough, more pronounced than any of the Kavanaughs. He'd grown up on the island. "I'm a huge fan of your wife, Mr. Dashkov."

I growled, my chest rumbling with the depth of the vibration. "You're about to be a dead fan, stranger."

The man had the gall to laugh.

"That isn't how my story ends, I'm afraid." Another bullet left his chamber. I didn't bother to fire back. He was too well hidden, and it was a waste of ammo. "But I was so glad to get a taste of that sweet Irish homeland while I was here. I can see why you married her."

"Come out here and face us, you *sap*," Liam roared from my side. "I'll give you a taste of the homeland myself."

"Is that the famous Liam Kavanaugh?" the man crowed. "Oh, wait until I tell the boys back home all about this. They'll be singing my name down at the pub."

"Can't sing if you're dead, mate," he hollered.

The man laughed again. "One day, Kavanaugh," he hollered back. "Until then, though, I'll tell you this: Noah Kelly sends his regards."

Liam tensed next to me. Whoever this Kelly man was, he wasn't a friend of his. Another explosion rocked the mansion. This one wasn't ours.

I could hear the man's retreating footsteps on the wooden floor.

He was gone.

But that didn't matter.

The only thing that mattered was getting to my wife.

"Let's go." I inclined my head at the open door the man had entered from.

Slowly, we descended the steps into the basement and into the dimly lit corridor. We followed the dark hallway deeper into the house, our eyes alert. Most of the doors were open. Some hung off their hinges. Damage that hadn't been caused by the explosions. The air was damp and smelled of mildew. The rough, concrete walls closed in the space surrounding us, swallowing the dim lights that swung from above.

The sound of shuffling feet stopped me cold.

I held up my fist to stop the others. Pointing at my ear to convey that I'd heard a sound, I peeked around the corner where the hallway diverged into a sharp turn that led into a larger room. Another sound. This time, it was the sound of a rifle bolt.

More shuffling of feet, but it was just one pair.

Turning back to the others, I signaled my findings.

One man.

Large room.

On my mark.

Bang.

I fired a shot from my gun, a feminine scream sounding from behind the large wooden door that stood to one side as the guard dropped to the floor.

Ava.

I found her.

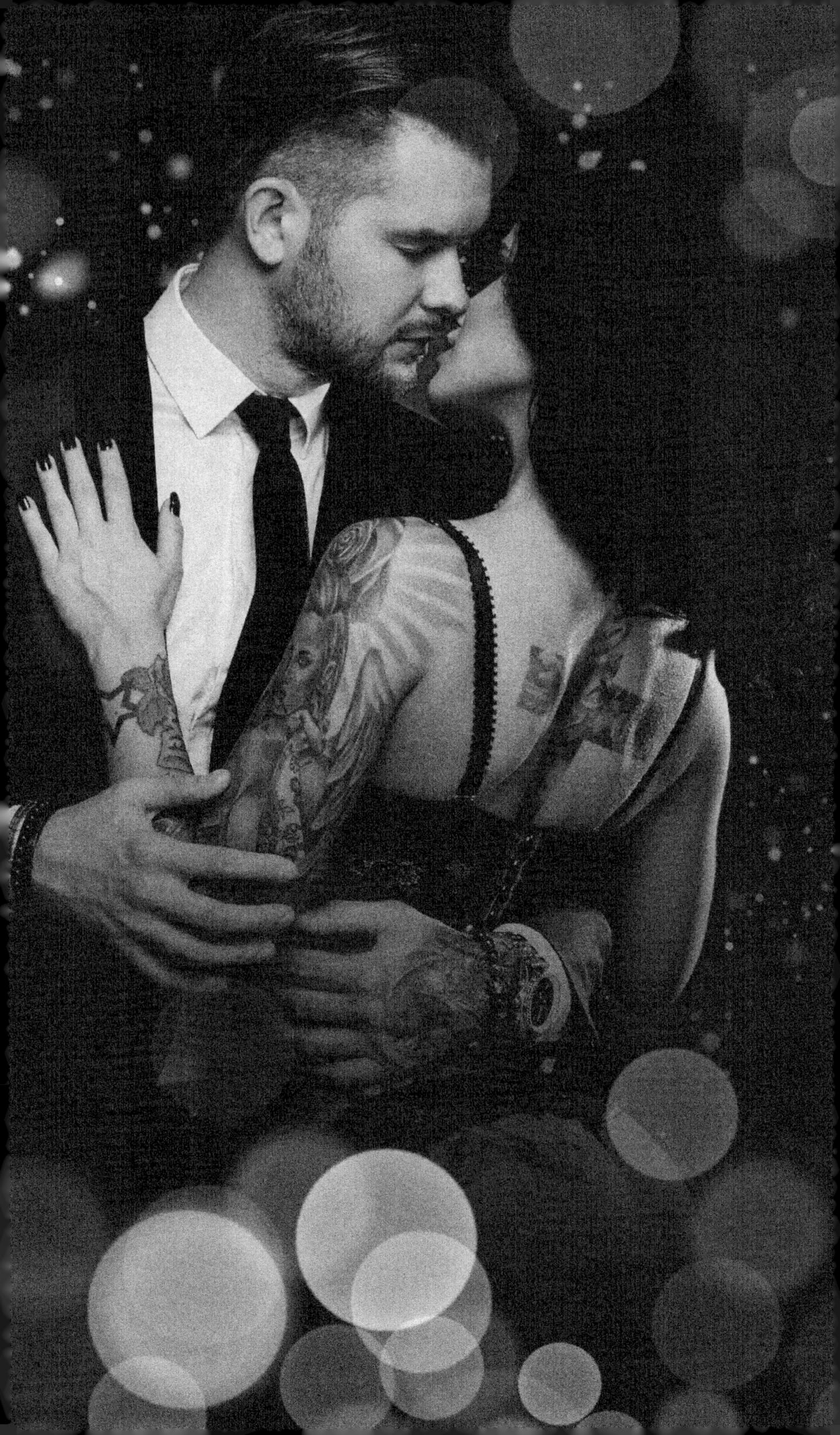

EIGHT

Ava

The walls rattled, shaking with the force of an unknown explosion.

My body trembled, the adrenaline fading as I lay half-sitting on the blood-covered mattress beneath me. The manacles were just long enough to allow me to grab the blanket that had been shoved near my head earlier. Even with the blanket, however, shock was keeping me cold.

The room was beginning to dim, and lights danced across my vision. Blood loss was starting to settle in, and it wouldn't be long before the hallucinations began to claim me. He came for me.

My devil.

My monster.

I could hear men shouting through the small window. Gunfire erupted in the distance. But I was safe because the devil and I had made a bargain. He would never let me die.

I leaned my head back against the wall, closing my eyes. They were too heavy anyway. Like cinderblocks.

A shot erupted outside my door, and I screamed, my eyes flying open as I groped for the blanket. That was close. Too close.

My breath stalled in my lungs; my gaze locked on the door. Was it him? The monster who invaded my dreams? Or was it the demon who'd tortured me? Would Kellan come back to finish what he started, just to spite my husband? Kill me before he could rescue me?

Was this all staged?

My thoughts stalled as the hinges on the warped wooden door creaked ominously, filling the dark silence that had been stifling me. My breath caught in my throat, heart hammering away in my chest as the soft light from the other room bathed his lean frame in an almost angelic glow, while his face remained entrenched in the lurking shadows.

I could almost sense his stormy gray eyes roaming my nearly naked body with such intensity it made my skin crawl. His hands rested lazily in his trouser pockets, his head tilted slightly, as if I was a mystery he needed to unravel.

This was not my avenging angel. Nor was he my white knight. The man standing before me was nothing more than a demon with a devilish smile wrapped in an expensive suit. A snake in the garden, ready to strike.

Instinctively, I brought my arms up to shield myself as he stepped froward, ignoring the chafing of the manacles against my already raw wrists. The soles of his shoes echoed loudly against the concrete floor, signaling his approach. The sound echoed like thunder in my ears.

There was nowhere to run. I was trapped, like a caged animal. Even if I could escape, if these manacles didn't chain me to the wall, there was nowhere for me to go. The approaching demon had taken everything from me. As he always promised he would do. Now there was only him.

Just like he wanted all along.

And I wouldn't have it any other way.

"It took you long enough." My body was tense, but having my monster so near set me at ease. The pain that racked through me seemed to lessen as his angry gaze assessed me from head to toe. "You were always horrible at asking for directions."

The pain in his eyes made me want to reach out and take him in my arms.

They say monsters don't feel pain, but that was far from the truth.

Monsters felt more than anyone. Pain. Love. Sorrow. That was why they became monsters. To leave behind the overwhelming emotion that clung to them like frost clinging to the last vestiges of winter before spring bloomed.

"*Moya lyubov'*," he whispered brokenly.

I smiled at the endearment, replaying it in my head before the darkness suffocated me once again.

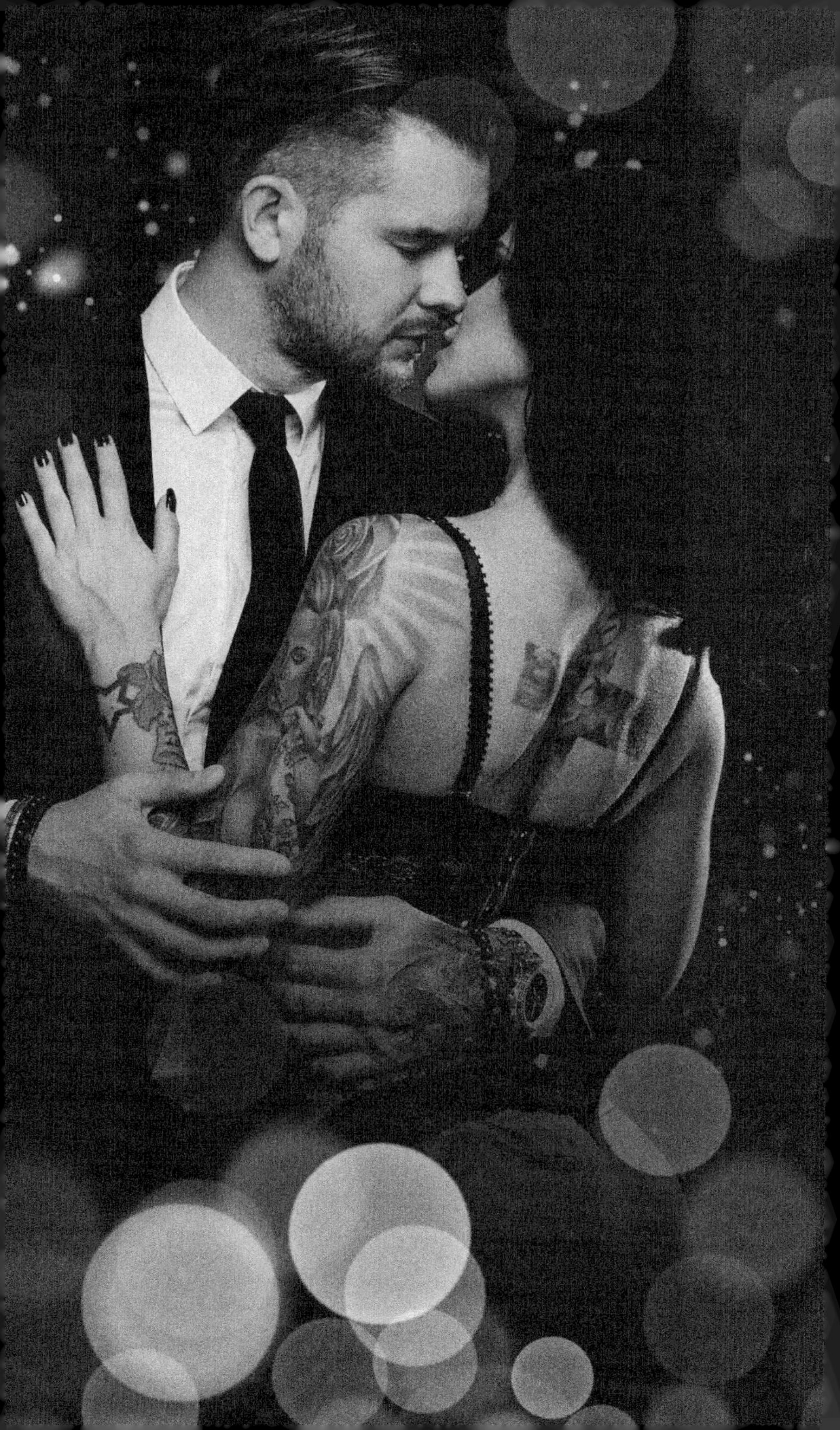

NINE

Matthias

"*Moya lyubov'*," I whispered as I approached her, my steps slow and calculated. She smiled up at me, but something about it didn't sit right. Her eyes were lazy and unfocused, skin pale. She repeated the words I'd said drunkenly, and then she was out. Ava's eyes rolled back in her head, and she slumped against the wall behind her.

My heart stuttered.

Don't let her be dead.

I rushed forward, two fingers going for her carotid. Her pulse was weak, but it was there, and I breathed a sigh of relief.

"Motherfuckers," Liam hissed at the sight of his daughter. Dirt and blood marred her skin and hair. The usual bright ginger locks were wet and clung to her fevered brow. She was chained to the wall by her wrists. The skin beneath the manacles was shredded and raw. Pride swelled in my chest despite the pain of seeing her injured. Those wounds told me she'd fought to get free.

My little psycho.

"Seamus," Liam shouted to his son. "Search the guard for keys."

The youngest of the twins stood rooted to his spot in the doorway, eyes round as saucers, mouth gaping in horror as he stared at his sister. He hadn't moved, not until Kiernan approached him from behind and whispered something in his ear.

The kid looked wrecked at the scene before him. Meanwhile, Kiernan shoved it all down, his eyes empty and cold. The pair were perfect copies of one another in every way except personality. Seamus wore his emotions like a shield, carrying it all on his sleeve, while Kiernan repressed until it exploded.

A blanket lay over her chest, barely covering her. It was soaked in blood. I shucked it aside, hissing angrily at the sight of her. Pain reverberated through me deeper than the slices through her skin.

I'm so sorry, my love.

I'd prayed to find my wife, and it had been answered. I only wished it was sooner.

Every inch of her was covered in cuts. Some shallow, others so deep they would need stitches. Her face was bloodied, but I could make out the bruising beneath the caked blood. Her ribs were marred black and blue.

If I ever got my hands on the person who did this to her, they would beg for death by the time I was through with them, and I still wouldn't let them die. I'd make them suffer as they had made her suffer. Cut them up piece by piece until there was nothing left.

Seamus rushed back into the room, fumbling with a set of keys. Liam made quick work of the manacles. Ava didn't move as he removed them. The right first, then the left.

She was too fucking still.

"Please, Red." I gently took her in my arms, cradling her to my chest. "Please don't leave me."

Fuck, she was cold. Too cold.

"Let's get this on her." Liam pulled a small container of Quick Clot from his bag. Opening the top, he slowly poured the powder over her wounds, his gaze traveling to her face every few seconds, making sure he wasn't causing her any pain. Once he was done coating her in the powder, he removed his jacket, his sons following suit, and covered her naked body in them. It wasn't much, but it would help conserve any heat she had left.

"Let's get her the fuck out of here," Liam growled, his eyes lit up like a raging inferno as he stared down at his daughter. "We don't have much time before the shock becomes irreversible."

Nodding in agreement, I hoisted her further into my arms, careful not to jostle her too much. Her body was listless against mine, and my heart fucking shattered into a million pieces as regret just as palpable as the rage coursed through me.

What if I never saw her open those beautiful emerald eyes again? I still hadn't apologized or made my amends. All I wanted to do was tell her I loved her. That I needed her, and that the months we spent apart were agony.

This was my fault. I'd been blind and selfish. I was the one who pushed her away time after time because I was too afraid to face my fears. To face the truth.

That she was mine and I was hers.

Ava owned me.

Heart and soul.

I'd known that from the moment she cast her fearful eyes on me in Elias's office over a year ago. I had just been too blind and stupid to see it.

And now it might be too late.

"Don't leave me, *Krasnyy*," I whispered desperately into her hair as we made our way back into the main house. The minute we stepped out of the doorway, the comm signal registered our movement.

"We've got a helicopter standing by on the front lawn," Mark informed me. He must have been monitoring our signals.

"Inform Dr. Radick that he needs to have a team meet me at the Kavanaughs' within the hour," I instructed him as I strode through the front door of the mansion. "Tell him I'll pay him double his usual rate."

Mark cursed. "Will do."

"We're ready to go, Matt." Vas motioned for me to follow him to where our transportation waited, ready to takeoff. It was a hot load. We kept our heads low, avoiding the blades. Liam nodded at his two sons as he trailed behind me. Once we reached the helicopter, he loaded himself inside, motioning for me to hand Ava to him.

I hesitated to let her go, even to him, but it was foolish to think I could get us both inside with her in my arms.

"It's okay," Liam yelled over the whir of the blades. "You'll get her right back, I promise."

Swallowing back the lump of anxiety in my throat, I nodded, carefully placing my wife in his arms before climbing up myself. Liam gently kissed her forehead before he arranged her on my lap. When we were all settled, Vas signaled the pilot, and we were off, the ground fading fast below us.

Vas positioned a pair of headphones over my ears that held a mic so we could communicate. Helicopters weren't quiet by any means.

"No sign of any Seamus look-alike," he informed me, a scowl covering his face as he took in my wife's battered state. "But we did take some of the guards alive."

"You can use my place if you need to," Liam offered, but Vas shook his head.

"Thanks, but we have a special place just for this." He smirked cruelly. "And trust me when I say we're all gonna take pleasure in what comes next."

I agreed.

"Have Mark check to see if he can get any footage from the cameras inside the house and basement. There were several set up."

Vas nodded and took out his phone.

Leaning my head back against the seat, I closed my eyes and let the comfort of having my wife in my arms wash over me.

"She'll have a long road ahead of her." Liam sighed. "Ava might try to push you away, but she'll need you."

I was well aware of my wife's stubbornness, and I had no intention of letting her block my help at every turn. I'd be there for her every step of the way, whether she liked it or not.

"Who is Noah Kelly?" I asked my father-in-law. Liam tensed in his seat, just like he had at the mansion.

"A ghost," he snarled. "A dead one."

"How dead?"

"Shot him point blank through the head with a forty-five."

"That's pretty dead," I agreed. Liam nodded.

"Who was he to you?"

Liam Kavanaugh was not known for being easily rattled, but the mention of one man's name shook him off balance.

"A long time ago, the McDonough clan was split in two." He let out a frustrated sigh, running a hand down his face, looking defeated. "There had been a long bloody war between two brothers. Twins, funnily enough."

"What does that have to do with anything?"

Liam blew out his cheeks. "Ava belongs to the McDonoughs of the north. What many in Ireland consider the 'true blood' clan. Noah Kelly is the descendant of the second clan. A clan so far removed from McDonough blood that they are barely recognized anymore."

I kept silent, letting him continue. "We grew up together in Boston. Noah and me. We were best mates until his father and Katherine's arranged for them to be married."

"Because you loved her." It didn't take a psychic to know that.

Liam nodded. "We'd been seeing each other for some time behind our families' backs," he admitted. "They were friends, but my family didn't come from wealth and prestige like Ava's. My grandfather was her grandfather's second. A soldier. And my father followed suit."

"I assume you told them."

"Yeah." Liam chuckled. "Seamus..." He paused for a moment, pain lancing through his grief-stricken eyes. "The man I believed was Seamus was furious. He told us to end it. That he wouldn't put the treaty at risk for a silly infatuation." He took a breath before continuing. "Katherine was a firecracker, though. Stubborn as a mule too."

I chuckled at that. Ava was just like her then.

"She threatened to disown him." He snorted in amusement. "Strolled right into his office during a meeting and told him that if he didn't call off the arranged marriage, she would leave, and he'd be left with no heir."

"He could have just appointed someone," I pointed out, but Liam shook his head.

"It may work that way in the *Bratva*, but clans are blood-only successions," Liam divulged. "No one but a blood relative can inherit. That means not even a wife."

"And Katherine was an only child."

"She was." He hesitated again, thinking over what he was about to divulge to me. "Part of me thinks she wasn't, though."

"Why do you say that?" Nothing in Katherine McDonough's history gave way to the theory that she wasn't an only child. I'd searched through Sheila McDonough's hospital report the night she gave birth, and there didn't appear to be any discrepancies.

"Right before we moved to Seattle for college, Katherine started acting...off." Liam tapped his fingers on his jean-clad knee. "She was spitting out nonsense about her father not being her father."

"Which we now know is the truth," I reminded him.

"That we were being watched," he kept going. "She began to distance herself from Marianne. Katherine had been planning to move in with me after I got back from my Portland trip. The two of them had been falling out for a while, but I never knew why."

"You."

Liam shot me a puzzled look.

"Me?" he questioned. "That makes no sense. Marianne never had any interest in me. She'd always been head over heels for Noah. Another reason why I shot him."

"I'm going to throw you a bone here, because I think

you deserve it." I cleared my throat. "But Ava needs to be the one to tell you the whole story and what she found."

"If this is about her theory that Marianne was somehow involved in Katherine's disappearance," he grumbled, "she already told me."

"Did you listen?" I wondered. "Or did you brush her off like you did when she tried to warn you about the Seamus doppelgänger?"

Shame was etched into every pore, his shoulders sagging with the weight of his guilt.

"I can understand that her poking at the people you've known your entire life can be painful," I assured him. "But if you ever make my wife feel like she is worthless or crazy, or you make her cry because you dismiss her thoughts again," my voice turned cold, venomous, "I'll kill you."

Silence followed my declaration. The only sound in the copter came from the blades slicing through the chilly air and the hum of the motor that shook our feet. Liam's gaze held mine, unblinking for several moments, before he gradually shook his head, acknowledging my words with a deep smirk.

"Break my daughter's heart again, and I'll give her yours."

I chuckled. "Deal."

"You two are fucked up," Vas grunted from his seat, rolling his eyes. "Seek therapy."

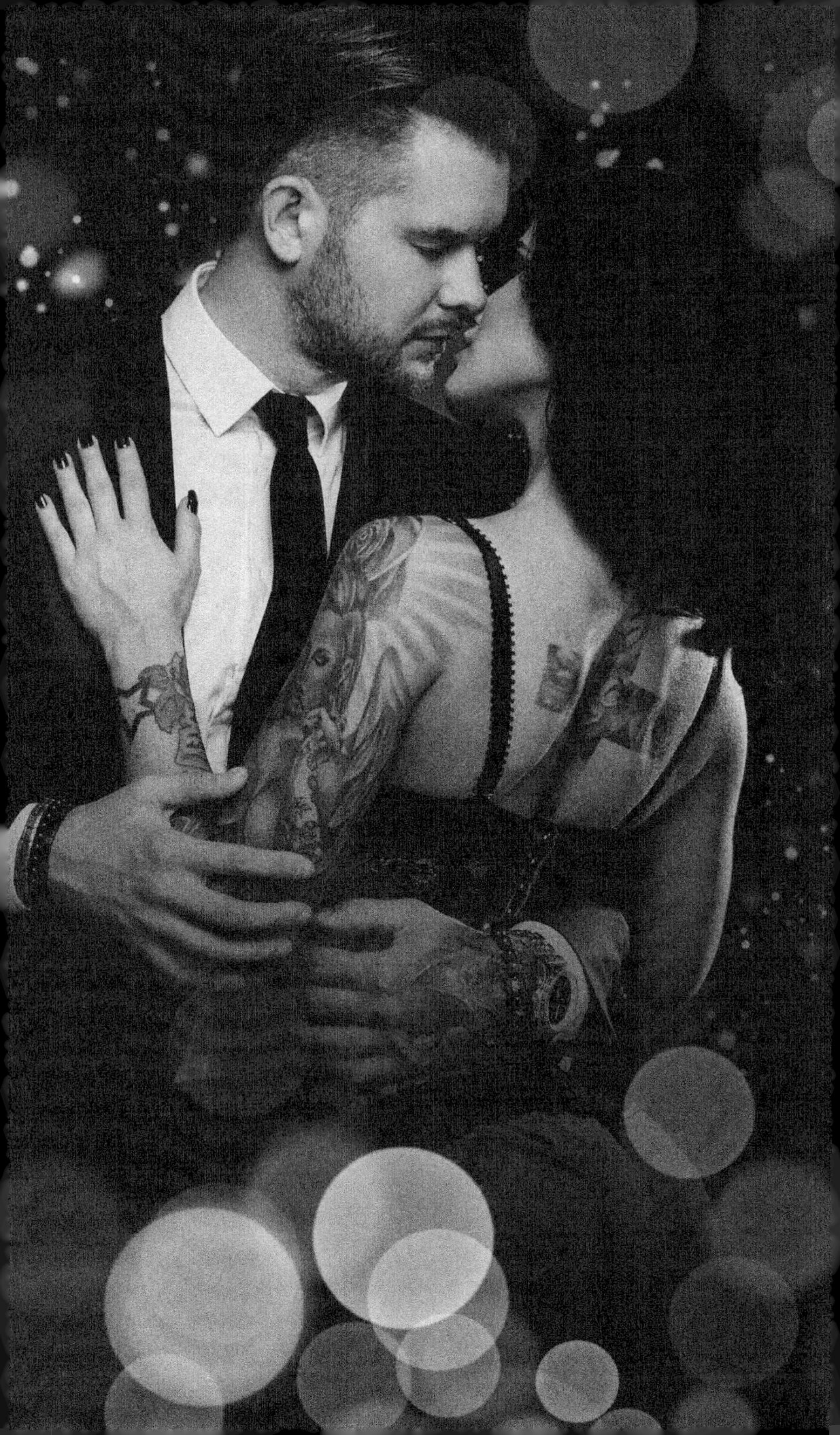

TEN

Ava

W*here am I?*
The scent of pine and spices filled the air outside my closed lids. I didn't need to open them to know that I was no longer in my cell at my grandmother's mansion. Something heavy was draped over my body, but it was soft and silky. Not the scratchy wool that had been covering me before. My eyes felt swollen and as heavy as lead bricks. My lashes were glued shut, and it took considerable force on my part to pry them apart. When I did, my vision was foggy and blurred.

There was a soft voice filling the space. Rough and sensual. His words were honey on his tongue as he read out loud from a small book in his hands. I could just make out the shape of him through my bleary eyes. He was sitting right in front of me, at the side of the bed normally designated for a night table. My ears were still ringing from the beating I'd taken, but his soft murmur was soothing to my wounds.

He wore a pair of light gray joggers and a fitted white shirt that stretched across his broad muscles, melding to him like a second skin.

Shit, was that drool?

Too late to be worried about that now since he'd stopped reading and was looking down at me with a knowing smirk.

My cheeks heated. My husband had caught me ogling him, and I doubted it looked sexy.

A choked sob broke free, and tears managed to escape from my swollen eyes. I didn't think I had any left in me to shed.

"It's all right, *Krasnyy*," Matthias cooed at me. He rose from his chair and tucked himself into the small space beside me, drawing me gently into his chest. I winced at the pain the movement provoked, but I didn't push him away. The warmth of his chest and the steady beat of his heart soothed the ache that seared through my belabored body. "I'm here, my love."

My love.

That wasn't the first time he'd said those words to me.

My love.

Those two little words made me cry harder, clinging to the man I loved with all my heart. Who had cracked it too many times to count. Who had nearly broken it when he'd come back to life after making me believe he was dead.

"It hurts," I cried, clinging to him. The long, measured breath he took told me he knew I wasn't talking about my physical pain.

"I know," he whispered into my hair as he gently rocked

his body back and forth to soothe me. "I'm so sorry, Red. So sorry."

He held me as I wept for the pain and suffering I'd endured. Not just in that cell at the hands of a sadist, but also during the months he'd been gone. I wept for the life I could have had with my mother and father if the world hadn't been so fucked up.

I wept until my eyes were heavy with sleep and hiccups turned to yawns.

"Sleep," Matthias's deep voice susurrated in my ear as he ran his hand through my hair. "The doctor will be here soon to check in on you. I won't leave your side. I promise."

I wanted to argue. To tell him that he'd already left me, but I didn't. Instead, I gave over to my body's demand and closed my eyes, praying that my monster would keep the nightmares at bay.

An entire week.

I drifted through feverish dreams for an entire week. Images of monsters and knights danced through my mind, the darkness refusing to let me go. I could hear my mother's shattering screams. Kellan's twisted laugh as he plunged yet another needle through my skin, his hands wandering, caressing, pinching. Marianne's cold eyes watched me like a hawk, her face morphing into my mother's, and then back again.

Over and over again, this played, and each time, I could hear his soothing voice drifting through the fog. He whispered words of comfort and love. His gentle hand wiping at my brow, lips caressing my forehead so lightly I was unsure if it was happening at all.

Hushed tones filled the space around me as my nightmares shifted and faded into oblivion. Gone, yet not completely forgotten. They'd always linger.

Just like the pain.

Pine and leather mixed with the familiar scent of orange and cloves.

Safety. I was safe.

The early tendrils of the morning sun highlighted the man sitting next to me, his hand buried in my hair, thumb rubbing soothing circles along my scalp. My monster.

"We need to tell her." That was Matthias. His voice was tense, fraught with frustration, but the hand on me was nothing but gentle.

"She's been through enough already," my father hissed in a low tone. "Telling her without having all the facts could damage her further."

"She isn't a piece of china," Matthias snarled. "And I made a promise that there would be no more secrets. Ava deserves the truth, even if it only brings more questions than answers."

My father sighed heavily and paced in front of the bed. He ran a hand roughly through his unkempt hair. He looked as if he hadn't slept in days.

"I don't understand how this is possible," my father choked. "Her body should be there."

"It could have been dug up before they got there," Matthias pointed out. Who were they talking about?

Father shook his head. "Sully said the ground was undisturbed, and Mark circled through the footage. No one has disturbed Katherine's grave."

My gasp gave me away. The two men turned, their faces etched with concern as they stared down at me. I took in the two most important men in my life. My monster and my knight. Two people who had both cracked me and built me back up. Who had come for me in my darkest moments, when everything seemed lost.

Matthias was right.

No more secrets. Between any of us. We couldn't let our allies live in the shadows. Or ourselves.

"Avaleigh." My father gave a tired sigh of relief at seeing me awake. "We were so worried, *mo réalta*." My heart. He'd never called me that before. It made me smile.

"I'm fine," I whispered, my voice hoarse. Matthias sensed my need and grabbed a glass of water from the nightstand next to his chair. He held the glass out to me, the straw perching on my bottom lip.

"Slowly," he instructed sternly when I tried to gulp down half the glass. Damn, getting the shit beat out of me sure as hell made me thirsty. The blood loss probably didn't help. Once I was finished, he set the glass back down on the table and helped me sit up against the headboard.

"How are you feeling?" my husband asked.

I grimaced. "Sore," I answered honestly. "But nothing I won't recover from. I think I prefer Christian's cattle prod."

Both of them growled, and the sound caused my eyes to widen. They didn't feel swollen anymore, just a bit heavy and thick.

"Don't joke about that." Father shook his head.

I waved it off. "If you can't joke about your trauma, then you're already half defeated." Or something like that.

"*Krasnyy*," Matthias warned, but I just smiled at him.

Okay, that action hurt a little too much, but I was happy.

"Tell me what I've missed."

They shook their heads in disbelief.

"You need time to heal, Ava." Matthias's gentle tone

was unnerving. Who knew I'd miss his alpha assholeness. Now I was hoping it came back soon. Maybe if I annoyed him enough, it would make a sudden reappearance. Gentle Matthias was just plain creepy. "Dr. Radick is on his way over now."

In a good way, to be honest, but I didn't want gentle right now.

I wanted answers.

And revenge.

Again.

Damn, my life had become a mafia soap opera.

"I need you to not treat me as if I am fragile," I scolded them. "I understand where this is coming from, but I have information you need, and apparently you have your own information to share."

The pair exchanged a look.

I liked it better when they couldn't stand each other.

"All right, Avaleigh." My father gave in with a sigh. "But you need to let Dr. Radick check you over without a fuss. Understood?"

I held up three fingers and smiled at him. "Scout's honor."

He rolled his eyes at me, mumbling under his breath about me never being a girl scout. Eh, that was true, but still, the sentiment was the same.

"Tell us what happened after the building collapsed," Matthias prompted after a beat of silence. Closing my eyes, I took a deep breath, centering myself before opening them again.

"Well, my mother's family is batshit crazy," I admitted. "Apparently psycho runs in the family as far back as anyone can measure."

Matthias snorted, but my father did not look amused.

"Kristian knocked me out of the way of the building's debris." I swallowed back the rising emotion. "I knocked my head on something, and when I came to, the building was destroyed, and she was waiting for me."

"Who?" my father asked. My gaze flitted to him, holding it steady.

"Sheila."

My father's forehead puckered. "Your grandmother?" he questioned. "She should be back in Boston."

"She's not," I told him. "Her plan was to not go back to Boston until she had Seattle under her control. All this time, it was her." I paused and blew out my cheeks. "Well, her and Seamus McDonough's twin."

"What?" The two men stared at me in disbelief.

"Okay, so there is a lot to tell you so—buckle up or something."

My father sat at the edge of the bed, his soft emerald eyes on mine. He was listening. Not arguing about how it wasn't possible or doubting what I was saying.

He was focused on me, his expression open and not closed off like it usually was when I brought up one of my theories.

"Okay, *mo réalta*," he whispered. "Tell us what you found, little spy."

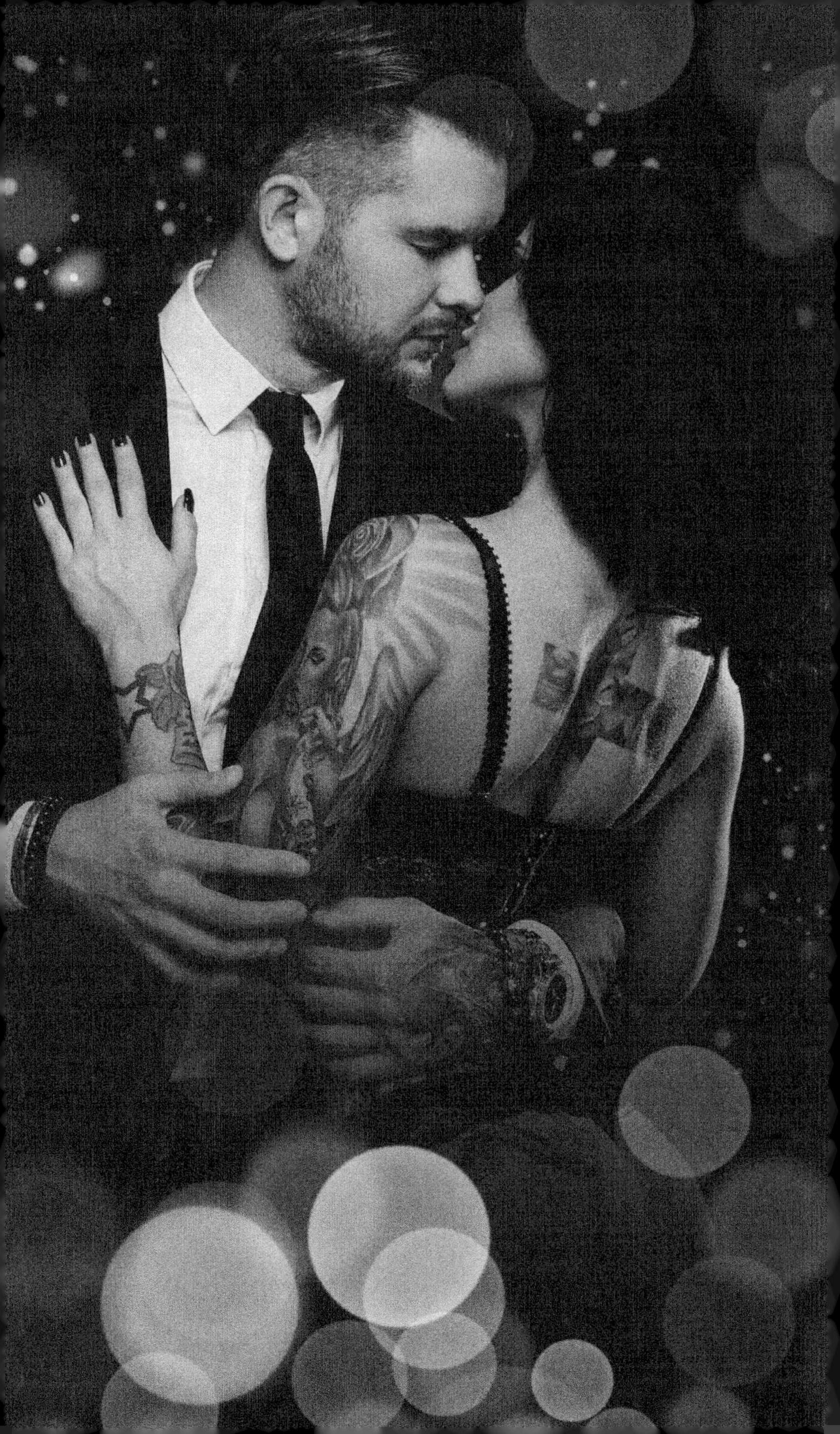

ELEVEN

Liam

There was violence coursing through my veins as my daughter told us her story.

Everything I knew had been a lie. One after another. By the very people who had practically raised me alongside Katherine. I always knew there was something off with Sheila when it came to her relationship with her daughter, but Kat never said anything. Never made mention of the kind of loneliness and abuse she suffered at the hands of her own kin.

Even Seamus was a disappointment. Knowing that he wasn't the one responsible for Kat's suffering eased only a fraction of the fury at what he and his mother had done. What every McDonough had done for too many years.

It made me wonder how long everything with Sheila had been in motion. Ava said that she had told her rather directly that Seamus wasn't Katherine and Marianne's father.

Marianne.

I'd tried to reach out to my wife several times over the last week while Ava fought for her life against fever and blood loss. She never once answered. Even the twins had tried to reach her.

Nothing.

What part had she played in Katherine's death?

Ava was holding something back. I could feel it and see it in her face as she talked about what had gone down just hours before we rescued her. Her face flooded with doubt and apprehension when it came time to tell us about what the man named Kellan had done.

While Marianne watched.

Except I already knew.

Not that it made a difference. I would listen to what she had to say about Marianne either way. Ava pushed forward in her story, her breaths accelerating the closer she got to describing her torture.

Torture that my wife watched and did nothing about.

"All I had to do was threaten to slit his throat in their bed. Easy peasy. She would have done anything for Liam."

There had been no small amount of glee in her voice when she'd told my daughter that. It was the very note that had caused me to doubt my daughter's words. I used it as a barrier to keep the truth at bay. The truth I had always known but refused to reconcile.

The more Ava unraveled Marianne's treachery, the more the picture revealed itself to me. Missing pieces from so many years ago slid into place without resistance.

I'd never questioned it before, but now I marveled at how easily Marianne had suddenly fit into our lives. We were kids at the time. Thirteen or fourteen, and she'd moved in down the street. She had been in all our classes and in Katherine's after-school activities.

Her parents had been friends with Seamus. He'd had them over for dinner a few times. Those were the nights Sheila was away doing work for her charity out here. Now that I thought back on it, I never once saw Marianne and Sheila in the same room together. Not once.

Marianne was everywhere in our lives, and we just accepted that. When Katherine's father had promised her to Noah Kelly, it was Marianne who had volunteered to take her place, and it was Marianne who ran to me crying with a broken face. She'd had proof that Noah had raped and beaten her because she wasn't Katherine. Wasn't what he wanted.

Another part of the puzzle that never quite fit correctly.

Noah had been adamant about his innocence. Said he couldn't remember anything about that night. I'd chalked it up to him beating her while he was drunk. What if it had been more than that?

What if she had drugged him?

My stomach churned, twisting itself in knots. I barely remembered the night I got Marianne pregnant. Katherine's note had broken something in me, but I'd had a plan to run after her. Drag her back kicking and screaming because our love was forever. It always would be. Even after all these years. It was her and me. There would be no one else.

A sick sense of dread spread over me. Marianne had tried to stop me. Telling me to give her space. She'd handed me a beer. Just one beer, and that was all I remembered about that night. About most of the nights we had sex.

Shit.

I rushed from Ava's room and into the hallway, my

breaths heavy as I beelined for the guest bathroom. Ava didn't need to see me like this. Slamming the door behind me, I heaved the contents of my meager breakfast into the porcelain toilet, tears streaking down my face as I struggled to come to terms with everything.

She'd fucking drugged me.

The bitch. Marianne had taken away my choice. I loved my children. They were all more like me than like that ragged whore, but it didn't take away the stabbing pain in my heart. Katherine had loved me so much that she sacrificed her freedom for my life, and all I'd ever done was sulk and curse her name.

"Da," Seamus called with a slight knock on the door. "Are you all right in there?"

Swallowing back the bitter pain, I closed the lid and flushed the toilet before turning to the sink.

"Yeah," I hollered at him through the door. "Must have been something I ate."

Seamus chuckled. "Don't let Nan hear you say that," he teased and then paused. "Are you sure you're okay?"

I rinsed my face and patted it dry. Checking myself in the mirror, I nodded at my reflection and turned to exit the bathroom. Seamus stood on the other side, worry etched into the lines of his face.

"What's with the concern, son?" I asked him. "Just a stomach problem is all."

He didn't look convinced. The boy had always been perceptive. He wore his heart on his sleeve and his emotions like a shield. It didn't surprise me that he could pick up on them just as easily. I had a thought or two about having Matthias train him in looking for micro-expressions. Even if I did think it was nothing more than voodoo witchcraft.

"I just—" He hesitated, rubbing a hand on the back of

his neck. "I know there was never any love lost between you and"—he couldn't say her name. Jesus, she had fucked us all up—"but I also know it can't be easy. You still trusted her. She was your wife."

I stared at him for a moment, taking him in. There were traces of Marianne in his face, but those emerald eyes and red hair were all me. And funnily enough, he looked more like Katherine. The McDonough gene had certainly favored him and his brother.

"Is it hard?" I asked. "Yes. But it is harder knowing I fell into her web of lies. But I don't regret it, my son." I clasped a hand on the back of his neck, bringing our foreheads together. I stared him straight in the eye. "Because even though the pain is throbbing and heartache is piercing, she gave me the most wonderful gifts I could ever ask for."

"A sky-high credit card bill," he joked. I smiled at his antics.

"You and your siblings," I told him seriously. "The five of you are the most important things in my life, and I wouldn't change that for the world. Understand?"

Seamus nodded, his Adam's apple bobbing in his throat as he swallowed back the emotion.

"Nothing could ever make me not love you or turn my back on you."

"I love you too, Da," he assured me. "I just don't like to see you hurting."

I kissed his forehead like I used to when he was a child. "Pain reminds us that we are human." I released my hold. "It reminds us to be humble."

Seamus smiled at me. The fucker had gotten so tall over the years that he was now eye level with me. Katherine had been the love of my life, and although it hurt to have lost her and it hurt to know that the one we'd called our friend had betrayed us all along, I wouldn't change anything for the world.

I may have lost Katherine, but I gained something in her absence. Children that I loved with all my heart. The family I'd always dreamed of having. I wouldn't let anyone take that away from me.

Fola roimh gach ní eile.

Blood before all else.

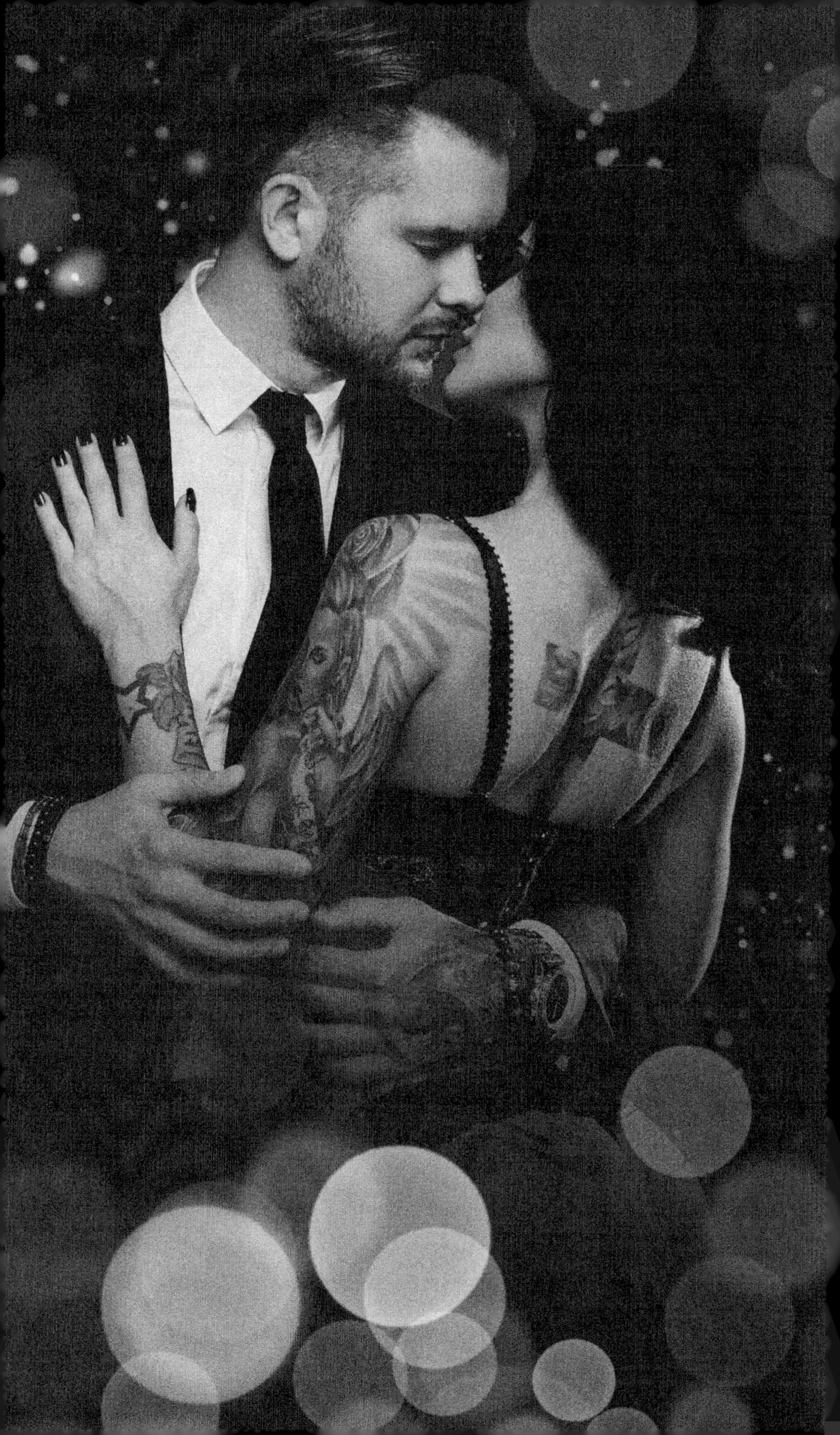

TWELVE

Ava

My father rushed from the room. His face had paled dramatically as I told my story, eyes wide with horror. It hurt to have to tell him that his wife had betrayed him. She meant nothing to me, but she was the mother of his children, the one he'd given his last name to. Everything that should have been my mother's.

I couldn't think that way, though. Without her, the twins wouldn't exist, nor the other siblings I had yet to meet. They were in Ireland, as tradition called for. Training for their respective roles inside the family. Seamus had brought it up a few times, but no one had gone into the specifics.

From what I gathered, it wasn't much different from the Dashkov compound, where we trained the next generation of men and women to be soldiers and leaders within the *Bratva* and its civilian companies. I'd learned that even those who worked at our civilian offices were part of the mafia. From the janitors to the receptionists. Even the lawyers were on the mafia payroll.

Most, if not all, were trained at the compound.

The Kavanaugh school didn't sound much different.

The silence inside the room grew stifling after my father left. Everything was finally out on the table. Well, almost everything. As much as I turned to Matthias for support, there was a heavy wall between us that felt immovable.

"Don't shut me out," he breathed, his voice low and regretful. "I can see the wheels turning in your head. Talk to me."

I snorted a laugh. "Where do you want me to begin?" I rasped. "The divorce papers? Or how about the gala? Should we discuss that? How you broke my heart and shut me out after making me believe we'd finally come to some sort of peace? You ignored me. Treated me like I was nothing but your whore in front of the people who should have known me as your wife."

"Ava—" he pleaded, his eyes brimming with regret and sadness.

"No," I cut him off sharply. "I'm tired of excuses, Matthias. I heard what you told Leon. That once the gala was over, you were done with me. That all you needed was the information I could provide. And then—" I choked on a sob, refusing to allow it to bubble to the surface along with my anger. "And then you kissed her, Matthias. Kissed her."

"Actually, she kissed me." It was jarringly straightforward. So like my monster.

"Then you faked your own death," I spat at him. Honestly, I was more pissed off about that than anything else. I couldn't kill or maim him for leaving me, but I could kill or maim that bitch for kissing him.

After I got Vas to give me her name.

Matthias took in a deep breath and let it out slowly. His face moved closer to mine, his palm cupping my cheek. He smelled so good. Pine and leather that evoked nothing but the feeling of safety and home.

His stormy eyes held mine, the turmoil in them stalling my own breathing. This was the most vulnerable I had ever seen him. The most open. He'd once said I was the chink in his armor. That he couldn't love me. Not the way I loved him.

His eyes told a different story.

"I don't regret that, Ava," he told me unapologetically. "I made a decision to protect you. To help you. My men were angry at me for not telling you the plan. For leaving you in the dark, but you needed to believe I was dead."

"Why did you make me *Pakhan*?" I asked. "Because Vas didn't want it?"

Matthias chuckled and shook his head. His face was so close that his nose brushed against mine. "No, little psycho," he breathed. "Because you were ready to be queen. You just needed a little push."

That was more than a little push. He'd practically shoved me into the deep end without a life jacket. Fuck, I still barely knew anything about our legitimate businesses.

"Are you going to take it all back?" I wondered. He could, by right. Everyone in the upper circle knew he was alive the entire time. Succession would revert to him since he hadn't really been blown to pieces.

"I thought we could do it together." The words surprised me. Before his sudden "death," he hadn't been interested in sharing anything. He never included me in meetings or kept me up to date. Then again, we'd spent a lot of time fucking or fighting. In some cases, both.

"No more secrets," I told him. "That's the deal."

Matthias smiled and my heart stuttered. Damn, he was gorgeous when he smiled. I'd almost forgotten.

"No more secrets," he agreed breathily, leaning in to kiss me.

"This doesn't mean I've forgiven you." Matthias smirked against my lips before he dove in, taking no prisoners. My fingers laced through the soft strands of his hair, gripping them tightly as his hot tongue slid between my lips, stealing my breath away. Warmth pooled between my legs. My nails scraped over his scalp, and he let out a soft groan of pleasure into my mouth.

This wasn't just a kiss; it was a claiming. Our mouths devoured one another, tongues dueling for control as we allowed ourselves to be consumed. Somehow, even amid our carnal desire, he was gentle with me. His hands caressed my body, kneading my flesh, massaging out the knots in my muscles as he lit my body on fire.

Matthias pulled back, and I whimpered at the loss of his body on mine. He leaned back on his knees and smirked down at me. Grabbing the hem of the long shirt I wore, he pulled it off me in one swoop. I moaned wantonly when he leaned back down, his mouth latching on to my breast, dragging his teeth across the nipple. Heat shot through me, zipping down between my thighs.

My hips bucked into his. I'd been completely bare beneath the shirt, and the feel of his jean-clad erection against my aching clit had my body wrapped in fire and begging for more. Groaning, he slid one hand between us, cupping my sex. His palm rubbed back and forth, a firm pressure against where I needed him most.

"Matthias." My head fell back against the pillows as I moaned his name. I arched into him, silently demanding more.

"So fucking ready for me," he growled, lowering his head to suck my nipple into his mouth. He slid two fingers inside me. I groaned at the pressure that filled me, threatening to send me over the edge before the party had even begun.

He drove me to the edge with his fingers. Alternating between fast and languid. Matthias didn't seem to be in any hurry to end what we started, but the fire burning between my thighs was raging.

"Fuck," I moaned. "Matthias, please," I begged as he brought me to the edge.

"Patience, *Krasnyy*." He trailed a line of soft kisses down my stomach. His fingers slipped out of me, pulling the wetness to my clit.

Matthias shoved my legs open as wide as they would go without hurting me. I could feel his breath on my clit. I rolled my hips in anticipation of his next move, but he didn't move to lick me. Instead, he bit the inside of my thigh.

I squealed, my hips coming off the bed slightly, and then suddenly his mouth was on me, teeth grazing my clit, and I fell right over the edge.

"Fuck." He licked at my clit before sucking it back into his mouth again. He let off and moaned like he had just had his best meal. "You taste so fucking good."

My chest was so fucking tight as I drew in breath after breath, struggling to remember how to breathe. I was still breathing harshly, the last remnants of stars dancing across my vision when he leaned down to suck at my mouth. I could taste myself on his lips and groaned at how erotic it was.

He freed my mouth and smiled down at me.

"I'm going to fuck you now, Ava." He stared down at me. "If it gets to be too much, just say *red*."

I licked my lips as he stood up from the bed and removed his clothing. God, it had really been too long. I let my gaze wander down his perfectly toned body that was covered in ink, not bothering to hide the heat behind my stare.

Matthias was mine.

"I'd like more orgasms now," I demanded haughtily when he didn't move. He had just been staring at my naked body as if he was trying to reacquaint himself with every inch. The purple bruising had mostly faded into a sickly yellow color, and some of the stitches over my cuts had already dissolved. I couldn't find it in myself to be self-conscious. Not with the way he stared at me like he was ready to devour me whole.

"Who are you to demand from me?" He quirked his eyebrow at me playfully.

I smirked. "Your queen," I told him. "And you have a lot to make up for."

He chuckled as he crawled back up the bed, his body covering mine.

"I guess I better get to work then."

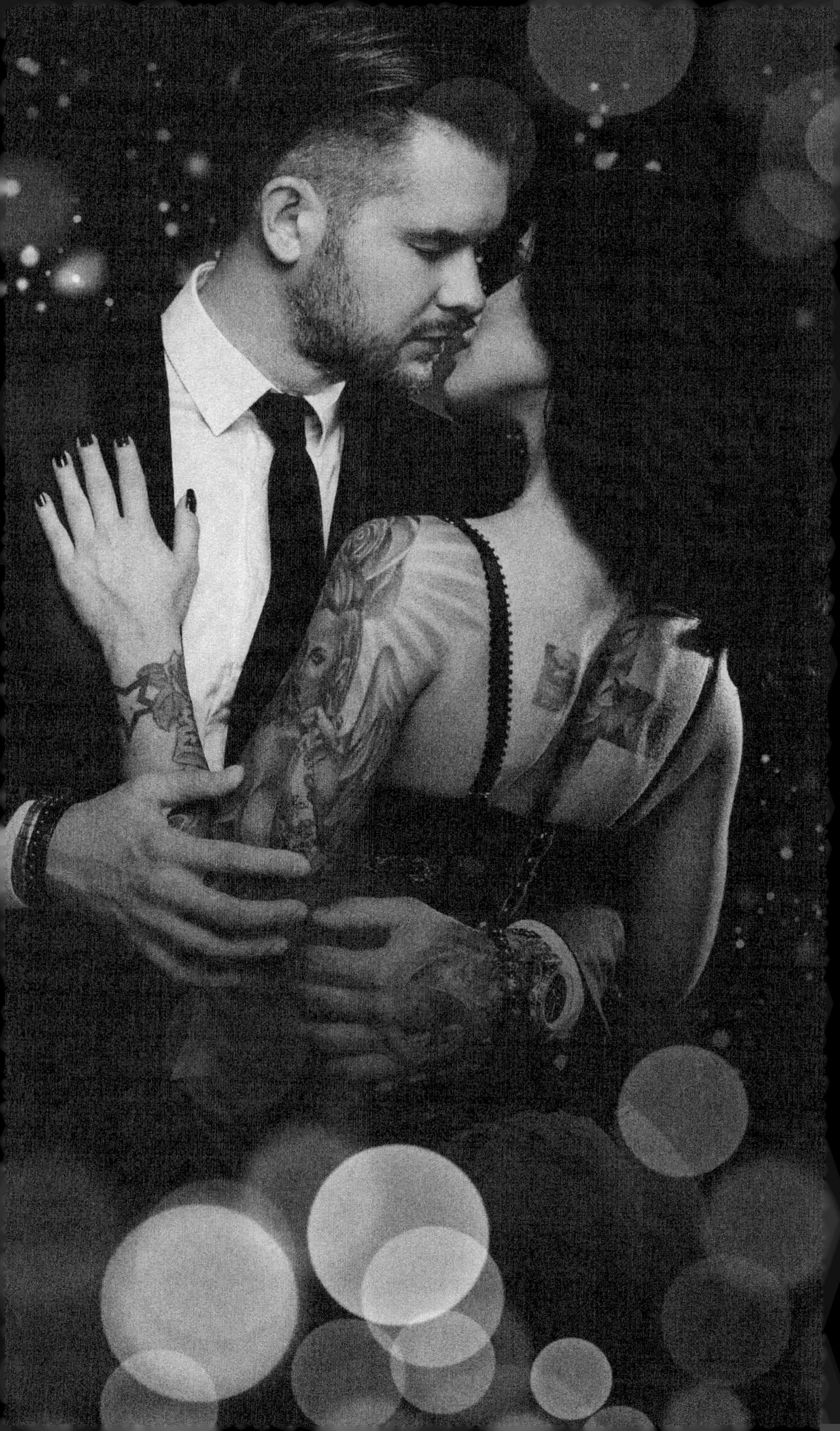

THIRTEEN

Matthias

Ava was spread out before me like a feast waiting to be devoured. My cock had been straining against my jeans as I'd lapped at her, and now that it was free, it wanted nothing more than to bury itself inside her sweet, wet cunt and make her mine.

I stared down at the ethereal beauty below me, noting every cut, slice, and bruise that marred her gorgeous skin. She would have her revenge. I would deliver the bastard on a silver platter and watch as she cut him to pieces.

Licking my lips, I thrust against her, the head of my cock bumping against her sensitive bundle of nerves. I brushed a knuckle over her nipple, my cock twitching when she responded with a sharp breath.

"So sensitive," I whispered. "Just for me."

"Just you," she breathed.

Palming her breast, I watched as her eyes fluttered, lips parting in a silent moan. "Good girl."

I leaned down, pressing my forehead against hers. "No more secrets, Red." I breathed my promise in her ear as I lined my cock up with her entrance. "No more pushing you away."

"Matthias," she gasped, arching her hips to try and force my cock into her tight hole. I pinned her hip down with one hand and grabbed a hold of her wrists with my other, pinning them above her head.

"You may be the queen, *Krasnyy*," I purred. "But I'm the one in charge here." Her body beneath me was tight with need. Slowly, I thrust with short strokes, never fully entering her.

"Matthias." This time my name on her lips was a warning. A low growl as she squirmed beneath me. When I only grinned at her, she attempted to free her hands from mine.

God, I loved it when she fought me.

My cock only hardened at her struggles to get me inside her. My balls ached.

I stilled above her, halting my short thrusts. "Who do you belong to, *moya lyubov'*?"

Ava turned her head away from me, her features set in a pout. Lowering my head, I bit her nipple.

"You," she shrieked. "I belong to you."

"*Khoroshaya Devoshka*." I slammed into her as hard as I could after calling her my good girl in Russian. A short, startled cry ripped from her mouth, and I didn't give her time to adjust before setting a relentless pace. One that had her quivering beneath me, a whimpering mess of pleasure.

My own release was tight on my heels, and I knew I wouldn't be able to hold out much longer. It had been far too long.

"Come for me, Ava." I growled the command. "Now."

Ava shattered beneath me with a scream, her body convulsing as her orgasm washed through her. Her pussy was clenching my cock so hard it triggered my climax, and with a few hard thrusts, I emptied myself inside her.

Pulling myself from inside her, I stood and walked to the bathroom. I ran a washcloth under warm water before striding back to the bed to clean her up. I washed her pretty pink pussy and kissed her clit. She mewled and shoved at my head. With a laugh, I threw the rag into the hamper before settling in next to her. I pulled Ava into my side until her head was resting tiredly on my chest.

"You will always be mine, Ava," I whispered to her. "You belong to me and always have."

I heard her yawn and looked down. Her eyes were heavy, fluttering open and closed. She was struggling to stay awake. She was the most beautiful woman in the world, and she was mine.

"Mine," I whispered into her hair as I closed my eyes, sinking into sleep. I could have sworn I heard her answer me.

"As long as you're mine."

AVA

When I woke, Matthias was gone. I sat up, stretching my muscles, groaning at how good it felt to move with minimal pain. My husband had been insatiable last night, keeping me up until the early hours of the morning, making good use of his tongue, his fingers, and his cock. How I had missed that. The vibrator I had purchased just wasn't the same.

Climbing out of bed, I walked to the bathroom, opening the faucets to start the shower while I brushed my teeth. I still needed to talk to him about what went on while he was away. Not to mention what he and my dad had been arguing about before I woke up.

Things were still far from being okay between my husband and me, but last night had helped ease some of the tension. I couldn't trust him not to change his mind again and decide I was too much of a liability to him and his empire. He'd changed his mind so many times before, and I would be a fool to trust him again so easily.

If he wanted me, then he needed to earn me. That was that.

After rinsing my mouth out, I stepped into the shower and let the warm water soak into my muscles, washing away the nightmares and pain of the past. Matthias was in for a surprise if he thought we were just going to pick up where we left off.

It wasn't that easy.

Slowly, I began to wash my body, careful of the still healing wounds. A smile formed on my lips as I took in the love bites he'd left all over my skin. One for each cut I'd suffered. Once I was done, I slipped out of the shower and dried myself, making sure to apply the ointment Dr. Radick had left for me.

I didn't see any clothes for me in the room, so I snagged a pair of Matthias's gray joggers and one of his T-shirts. The joggers were so large that I had to roll the legs up several times, as well as the waistband, to make them fit, but it was worth it. Those things were hella comfy.

Tying my hair up in a messy bun on the top of my head, I went in search of my family.

And coffee.

Lots of coffee.

It was pretty early in the morning, barely seven, so I knew they wouldn't be down at the bar yet. I took the elevator down a level to what I liked to call the *family floor*, which just meant that it housed the kitchen and living areas outside of the bedroom suites, which were on separate floors.

When I walked into the kitchen, Seamus and Kiernan were there to greet me with matching smiles.

"*Milis Deirfiúr*," they murmured, hugging me tight between them. *Sweet sister*. I nearly bawled at those two words.

"Thank you for coming for me," I whispered, my voice brimming with emotion. I'd always had Libby and Kenzi, but this bond was different. Just as special, but different, and I wouldn't trade it for anything.

"Always," they murmured at the same time, making me laugh. The two of them released me as my father strode forward with a cup of coffee in his hands.

Oh, thank the gods.

"Thank you," I mumbled before taking a sip. The simple notes of caramel and spice washed over my tongue. A week and a half without coffee had been the worst torture of all. My father kissed the top of my head and smiled down at me.

I looked around for my husband, but I didn't see him.

"He had an errand to run with Vas and Andrei," he told me. "Leon is having trouble with his father, and he went to give him some backup."

I nodded and took another sip of my coffee.

Yep, heaven.

My gaze caught on someone sitting at the table, brown locks tied back in a braid, shoulders taut as she scraped her fork along the plate in front of her. I'd know her anywhere, even with our time spent apart.

"What is she doing here?" I hissed, keeping my voice low so she wouldn't hear.

"Ava," my father scolded gently. "She's here because she is your sister."

I gave an unladylike snort. "My sister is dead."

"You can't harbor anger about something that never happened," he told me. Except, to me, it had happened. I'd watched her shoot the man I loved right in front of me and then taunt me about it. Saying that it should have been me. That she would make me pay. I had nightmares about that night for weeks.

"Did you invite her?" I asked.

My father shook his head. "No," he sighed. "She wanted to be here for you. Kenzi is one of the reasons the raid on the McDonough mansion went so well. Without her, it would have been a lot harder."

"Because she's a killer," I sneered.

"So are you."

My eyes fell shut, and I bit my bottom lip anxiously. Whose side was he on anyway? Even if he was right, he was my father, and he should take my side.

And I'm five.

Or I'm right.

Nope, definitely acting like a child.

Fine.

"Ugh," I groaned, stomping to the coffeepot to refill my

cup. If I was going to confront Kenzi, I was definitely going to need more magic mojo. I took a deep, measured breath before making my way to the dining room table where my sister waited.

I sat in the chair to her right. She didn't say anything or acknowledge me as I did. There was a brief beat of awkward silence before she pushed a plate of pancakes and a clean fork toward me. All right, then.

Picking up the fork, I dug into the fluffy pancakes. The sound of chewing and scraping forks filled the awkwardness. The only other sound came from the hushed voices of my family in the kitchen. We sat like that until the food on both of our plates was cleared and there was nothing else to distract from what was to come.

"I was so excited to go to London," Kenzi murmured brokenly, her eyes cast down at her plate, refusing to look at me. "I remember getting off the plane and heading out toward the car Father had arranged to take me to the college."

She took a shuddered breath, her bottom lip trembling. "There was a man waiting," she continued. "It didn't seem right. When I tried to turn away, he grabbed me. In broad daylight. And no one did a thing to stop him."

I kept quiet, letting her work through her story at her own pace. I'd never been known for my patience, but for Kenzi, I would make the effort. She was different from what I remembered. Not that I expected her to be the same. Even in the barn, I noticed just how little of the Kenzi I knew remained. There was a cold, calculated look in her eyes she didn't have before.

There wasn't any innocence left, because the world had gone and stolen it. Like it had been stolen from Libby.

From me.

Elias Ward had ruined us. Taken everything special. I'd let Dante take care of Kendra, but Christian was still out there somewhere, and he was mine. For taking Libby from me, the one who kept me believing in fairy tales. The most innocent of us all.

"They drugged me," she whispered after a few minutes, her gaze flitting to me. "I don't remember a lot, but it wasn't..." She paused. "They took me to a place—" She shook her head, trying to sort through the foggy memories. "A place where they trained us to seduce and kill. Cold-hearted assassins are what they tried to make us all into."

"Tried?" I cocked my head to the side and stared at her for a moment, taking in her pale face and blue eyes. "You looked pretty assassin-y to me back in that barn with all your kung-fu." Her lips twitched slightly.

"Not too bad yourself." She praised me sadly before letting out a long sigh etched with pain. "We're so screwed up."

Picking up my coffee cup, I leaned back in my chair and cuddled the warmth of the cup with my hands. "Yeah," I chuckled lightly. "But I think you're more screwed up."

She shot me a *what the fuck* look.

I shrugged. "Just saying." Taking a sip of my coffee, I smiled behind the mug.

"The fact that you can make a joke about it means you are so much more fucked up than me."

She had a point.

"What can you tell me about Madam Therese?" I asked her. Kenzi visibly shuddered, goose bumps erupting on her skin. She rubbed at her arms self-consciously and scowled at the plate in front of her.

"She was in charge of etiquette and recruitment," she

sneered. "Real piece of work, that one. She's the one who made a deal with our—*my*," she corrected herself, "father."

"They take people who won't be missed," Kenzi continued. "They don't discriminate. Men, women, children. They are all just bodies to be used by them. Those who are brought in are put through a test to see where they belong. Endurance, seduction, you name it and there is likely a test for them to measure it. Once you're done with the tests, they decide where to put you, and then your training begins."

"I don't understand," I whispered, guilt gnawing at me. "You weren't someone who wouldn't be missed."

Kenzi scoffed. "The only person who would have known I was missing would have been Libby." She gave me a pointed stare. "You ran away, and even if you hadn't, no one would have let you call me anyway. Christian and my"—she choked back a sob—"my mother were both in on it. The only person who would miss me was Libby, and she never bothered to call at all."

"Libby said she spoke to you every week," I insisted. "You would talk for hours on the phone about classes and friends you had made. She never believed anything was wrong."

"Did I ever send her a picture?" Kenzi raised a questioning brow at me. "Were there ever any texts with pictures of my dorm room? Or video chats? Did I ever text her out of the blue or answer any of her messages?"

She hadn't. Now that I look back at what Libby had told me, she hadn't once mentioned simply texting Kenzi or having any kind of video chats like they normally would when one of them was away. I couldn't believe we had both been so blind.

"What happened to her?" Kenzi bit the inside of her cheek nervously. "What really happened to Libby?"

"Matthias didn't tell you?" I would have thought he would have told her what happened that day, but Kenzi shook her head.

"He said it was your story to tell."

I tapped my fingers against my coffee mug. Its warmth had faded out over the time of our conversation, but it still gave me comfort. I imagined it was Matthias's warm hand wrapped in mine as I told her how Libby had been murdered by her own brother.

Because of me.

When I was done, she simply nodded, sadness and pain sweeping through her eyes as she stood abruptly from the table. "I need to go." That was all she said before she took off from the dining room, her steps barely making a sound on the wooden floor.

I took another sip of my coffee that was now lukewarm and tasted like ash in my mouth.

That was a first.

"She'll be back, lass," my father assured me as he took her empty seat. The maid was already busy cleaning up the dishes we'd finished with. "Just give her time to fully process everything."

"I spent so long being angry and wanting revenge that I never bothered to think about what she went through." A sob tore through me, my chest aching. "I can't imagine what she went through, and she did it all alone, thinking no one cared about her. She was—I failed her. I was supposed to look out for them, and I failed them. They shouldn't have..." I hiccupped. "I could have..." My father took the trembling coffee cup from my hands and set it on the table. He pulled me into him, my head resting on his shoulder as he rubbed my back in soothing circles.

"You couldn't have prevented what happened any more than I could have stopped what happened to your mother," he murmured in my ear, the voice of reason in unmitigated chaos. "We were manipulated and controlled by forces we never thought would be at work against us."

"She never got to say goodbye," I sobbed. "Kenzi never got to hear her voice again. Her laugh. We never even knew anything was wrong."

He didn't say anything after that because he knew there were no words that could soothe my battered soul. I'd taken hit after hit since being forced back from that little no-name town in Texas, and I just wanted it to end. For all of us.

Then it hit me.

Kendra was complicit in selling her daughter to the highest bidder. She'd known all along what had happened to her.

Pulling back from my father's embrace, I wiped at my eyes and straightened my shoulders.

"Where is Kendra?"

His brow furrowed at my question, but he didn't hesitate to tell me.

"She's been staying with Dante Romano, according to our sources."

I cursed under my breath.

"Why?"

"Christian may have been responsible for Libby's death directly." I stood up, pushing the chair back behind me, the legs scraping noisily on the floor. "But Kendra failed to protect her, just like she failed to protect Kenzi."

"You think she'll make a play for her?" he asked, following me out of the dining room. I nodded. "Christ. I'll call Matthias. He's with Dante, meeting Augustu La Rosa." Nodding, I grabbed a pair of my old shoes by the elevator and pressed the button for the parking garage.

"What are you planning to do once we get there?" my father asked as we stepped into the elevator. It jolted before moving. "She's got a considerable head start. Kendra might be dead already."

"Who said I was going to stop her from killing Kendra?" I winked at him and walked off the elevator. "I was going to hold her down while she pulled her hair."

"That sounds oddly specific." He looked at me askance.

"Lara Mesgrove was a bitch." I shrugged nonchalantly. "She had it coming."

My father shook his head, holding the door to his Porsche for me and closing it when I settled in my seat. During the girls' freshman year of high school, Libby tried out for the cheerleading squad, which Lara had been the captain of. After tryouts, Lara and her friends had cornered Libby and uttered every bad thing they could think of about her. Shoving at her and trying to tear at her clothes and her hair.

When Kenzi got word of what was happening, she took off like a shot. I'm pretty sure she got an offer from the football coach; that was how hard she had tackled Lara to the ground by her hair. I'd held her down while Kenzi wrote down every insult she had hurled at Libby on Lara's face in permanent marker.

The girls had been grounded, and I'd gotten a beating and two days in the shed, but it had been worth it. We protected each other, but I wondered briefly if I had protected them too much from the horrors of their own family.

Kenzi hadn't been as blind as Libby had been growing

up. She'd always been sharp, and I knew she saw more than she let on. Just like after I left. She'd grown curious at Elias's behavior.

Maybe if I had spoken up about how I was truly treated, she would have had a better chance at surviving.

But that was a lot of what-ifs, and it was too late for that now.

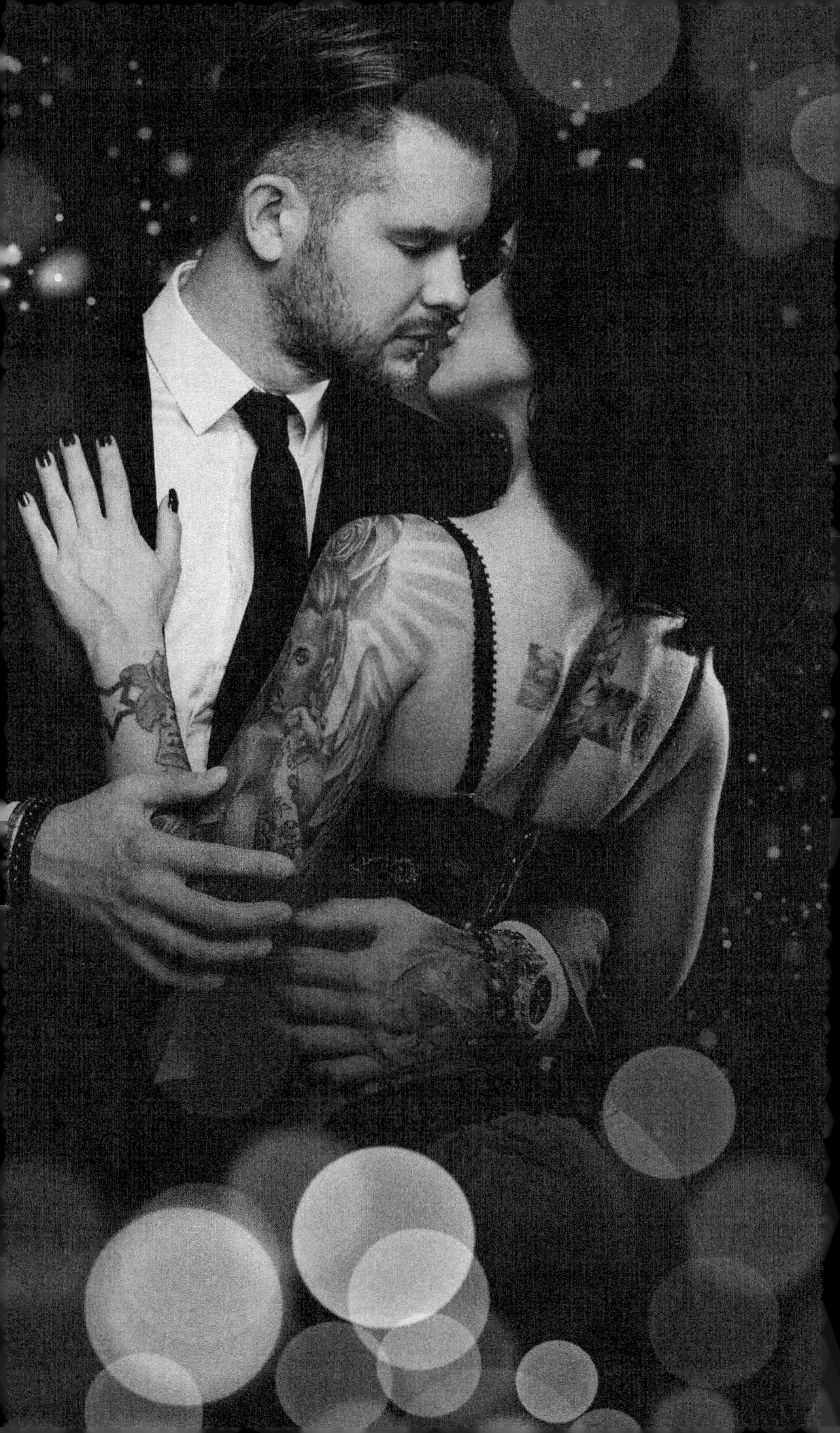

FOURTEEN

Matthias

I hated leaving my wife's side this morning. Her body was warm and snuggled up to mine. She'd thrown a leg over one of my own, one hand splayed over my heart possessively. This was what I wanted to wake up to every morning.

The sight of my wife lying beside me stirred something primal in my chest. We were nowhere close to being all right. Even though she clung to me during sex and sought out my embrace in the night as she slept, knowing I would keep her safe, there was still a long journey ahead of us.

My plan had been to take her with me to this meeting, but an unexpected visitor had shown up on Kavanaugh's doorstep. Kenzi looked worn and beaten down. For all her stoicism, she was still yet a child whose life had been taken from her too early. She had never gotten to experience what it was like to truly grow into an adult. Instead, she had been shoved into the deep end without a life jacket and expected to come out alive.

Currently, I was seated between Vas and Dante Romano at Augustu La Rosa's estate in West Seattle. I was fond of the estate. The house was large and modern, with big open windows and state-of-the-art appliances. I'd been searching for a place myself, but everything had come up lacking. This house fit my fancy and matched the modern design of the penthouse that had been blown to hell, but it wasn't Ava's style, and I wanted something that could fit both our personalities. A modern sort of bohemian vibe.

Bohemian. My skin crawled at the word, but the eclectic, soft tones and open décor made her happy, and that was all that mattered. There was a Queen Anne Victorian that had caught my eye. It was built in 2008 and had an old-world charm and modern subset that spoke to my soul and that I knew would speak to Ava's.

I personally knew the architect who had designed it and had already scheduled a tour. It was just on the edge of Columbia City, so the drive to the office wouldn't be terrible, and there were plenty of back roads to take. I was still waiting on the zoning commission to approve my proposal for rebuilding Dashkov Enterprises. No one other than the fire marshal was aware of what really caused the building to collapse.

The leading story the fire marshal had given the media was a gas explosion, and the secondary investigators all concurred. Still, they were dragging their feet for some reason, and I didn't like it. Arctic Security had plenty of room for me to work out of, but it didn't have the same capacity as the other building, which served multiple purposes.

"I don't care about what you want, you ungrateful

manello," Augustu spat at his son. "There will be no treaty between us unless my conditions are met."

Here we go.

Augustu La Rosa was after more territory than he could handle. His initial thought was to build an alliance through marriage, but as his last wife—and the three before that—had all mysteriously died, I wasn't willing to set that up. Neither was Dante Romano.

The man was a fool, which was why Leon had left. Well, he'd been kicked out when he was seventeen, but that wasn't how Augustu saw it. He'd given his son a choice, and according to him, he had chosen wrong.

I was inclined to disagree.

When I had heard through the underground that Leon La Rosa had forsaken his father and his right to be heir to the La Rosa name, I was intrigued. La Cosa Nostra was a lot of things, but I never imagined that someone like Leon existed within them.

Augustu had been best friends with Benedito Romano, Dante's father. The two had carved a bloody name for themselves in the city. They owned half of it and greedily sought to stretch their grasp beyond their borders. It led to an all-out war with the Irish, which is why Kavanaugh had not been invited to this meeting.

When Dante murdered his father, he cut all ties with Augustu and how he ran his business. Sex workers. Slaves. Bad dope. He'd built quite the reputation for himself, and not a good one. I'd taken more than half of his old territory when I entered the city. Territory that was rightfully mine since it had belonged to the *Bratva* leader before me. The one he had beheaded in the streets.

That was a news day for sure.

From what Leon had told me, his father was unhinged

and becoming increasingly so each day. Sitting before him now, I could see that.

"Why won't you help?" Leon questioned his father. "If the McDonoughs gain ground, it will do nothing but shove you out and kill you and all your men."

Augustu scoffed. "Let them try, eh?" He spat. "We Sicilians are built of stronger stuff than those Irish bastards. They will have nothing. Nada. You will see."

"This is a waste of time," Dante murmured from beside me. His voice was low enough that Augustu couldn't hear. "He either truly believes that they won't touch him, or he's in league with them."

"The McDonoughs don't seem like the kind people to make a deal with Augustu." I snuck a peek at the room. It was simple; barely any pictures on the wall and hardly any memorabilia. The house had been well kept, but there were obviously things missing. I doubted anyone in the household would be stupid enough to steal from Augustu, but I had heard rumors about his famous temper. He had most likely broken most of his things in fits of rage.

Whoever the McDonoughs were working for or whatever they were a part of would not risk making a deal with someone so unstable. One slip was all it would take.

My phone beeped in my hand. A missed call from Liam. My heart raced and anxiety dug through me at the thought of something having happened to Ava. I went to dial him back, not caring about Augustu, when a text message came through.

911 at Dante Romano's. Kenzi's after Kendra. Come quick.

"We are done here." I stood abruptly from my chair, passing the phone to Dante as I buttoned my jacket. "You are obviously not going to help and have very little self-preservation. So we will talk at a later time. Say goodbye, Leon."

Leon nodded at his father and turned toward the door

"That's right," Augustu sneered. "Follow after your master, you little *cagna*."

With a snarl, I lunged forward, ensnaring Augustu's shirt collar in my grasp, and yanked him toward me. He was sprawled over his desk, the angle forcing his head back. His face was red and splotchy as fury rolled through him.

At his furious scream, the door to the office flew open, his guards storming into the room, but we were ready. With my one hand still on Augustu's collar, I drew my Beretta from the small of my back and aimed it at the door. Dante and my men followed suit. My eyes never left the man in my grasp.

"Your son is ten times the man you will ever be," I growled at him, lips turned up in a vicious snarl. "Insult him again, and those will be the last words you ever utter. Understood?"

Augustu paled at my words but remained silent, defiance still sparking in his eyes.

"Understood?" I roared in his face, my hand tightening on his collar, choking him.

"Yes," he gasped, clawing at my hand. "I understand."

I tightened my grip, just a little, holding on to him for a few more seconds to make sure he got my point. Then I released him. The old man sputtered and choked as he righted himself. He glared at all of us but kept silent.

Good. If he uttered another word, I was liable to kill him, and that was not a headache I needed at the moment.

"Let us go," I commanded as I strode through the door. Augustu's men parted like the red sea as I moved past them, none of them wanting to risk drawing my ire. We'd already wasted precious time, and I was in a hurry to get to Dante's house. The extra time was worth it, however. It was my job to ensure my men knew I had their backs and would defend them.

"He's growing bold," Leon muttered as he opened the driver's side door to the Mercedes and climbed in. "It's going to be a problem," he predicted when I took my place in the passenger seat. Dante was in the car in front of us, and Vas was in the one trailing behind us.

Leon pulled out of his father's circular drive and sped down the suburban road toward the highway after Dante. Picking up my phone, I dialed Liam.

"Please tell me you're on your way," he whisper-shouted into the phone. I could hear yelling in the background and the sound of something shattering.

"We are getting on the freeway now," I told him. "Less than ten minutes."

Liam breathed a sigh of relief. "Might want to try and cut that in half," he warned. "I'm not sure if I can keep either one of the girls from shooting Kendra if she keeps running her mouth like she is."

"*Khristos*," I groaned, telling Leon to step on it. "What the hell are they even doing there?"

"One moment they were talking at the dining room table, and the next, Kenzi was rushing out and Ava was crying," Liam informed me. "The next thing I know, Ava's got this grand idea that Kenzi was going after Kendra, and she wasn't wrong. Bridget caught it a little late because the intrusion came from within our own building. Looks like Kenzi hacked into our database to find her location."

Rolling my eyes, I groaned, the frustration mounting. "Explains why she suddenly showed up this morning without an explanation."

"I was hoping it was to reconcile with Ava," I grumbled, wincing at the sudden pitch of the vehicle to the left as Dante took a sharp, sudden curb. "Fuck, he drives like a loony bin."

Leon chuckled.

"If it makes you feel better, I'm pretty sure they are reconciled," Liam coughed awkwardly. "It just might be over Kendra's dead body instead of a nice cup of coffee."

"You could put an end to it, you know," I pointed out. We were pulling into the Romano compound now.

Liam snorted. "I am not getting between an assassin and her target. Go for it."

Coward.

We watched as Dante threw his car into park in front of the house and dashed from the driver's seat and through the front door.

"I wonder what has a fire under his ass." Leon shifted the car into park, shutting off the engine before we both exited the vehicle. "You'd think he wouldn't have much care for a woman who sold one of his daughters and didn't do anything to protect the other."

I shrugged nonchalantly. It did not affect me. I was all for letting Kenzi and Ava shoot her. Kendra wasn't an innocent wife; she had been complicit in everything. The two women deserved a little payback.

Raised voices and the sound of a gunshot going off caught our attention. Someone screamed, and glass shattered. Leon and I exchanged a quick look before we took off into the house, the soles of our shoes sliding on the slick tile floor.

Kenzi was standing over Kendra, who was huddled in a ball on the floor at her feet, the barrel of her gun pressed against the top of her head. My wife stood slightly behind her sister, eyes trained on Kendra, cold and unfeeling. Fuck, that made me hot for her.

My little psycho queen.

"Put the gun down, Kenzi." Dante approached her from the right, his hands out in front of him as if he was surrendering. "You don't want to do this."

Kenzi let out a sharp laugh. "I've killed plenty of people," she hissed. "What's one more?"

Well, the woman had a point. I strode up behind Ava, pulling her back into my chest. I didn't want this to get messy, but if it did, I would make sure she wasn't harmed.

"She's your mother, Kenzi," Dante tried to reason with her.

More power to him.

Kenzi snorted in disbelief. "She was never a mother to me," she spat. "She let him sell me. Let Christian kill Libby. She isn't a mother. Mothers care about their children. They love their children unconditionally. I didn't offer her anything, so she chucked me aside and pretended like he had sent me off to college."

Her hand tightened on the gun, finger on the trigger inching infinitesimally.

"You won't just be killing her, Kenzi," Dante whispered urgently. "Kendra is pregnant."

"Good riddance to that," she snarled. "She and Elias don't need another spawn."

Except that math didn't add up. Kendra would be nearly five to six months pregnant, and she was barely showing, which meant—

"It is Dante's child, Kenzi," I told her. "Not Elias's, and even if it was, you do not want to kill someone that innocent. That child is not at fault for the sins of its parent. Neither are you."

Kenzi's eyes turned to Dante, wide and expressive. It was the most emotion she had shown in a long time. "How long have you two been...?" She trailed off, her gun wavering slightly as she processed everything.

"Since before you were born, *mio tesoro*," he admitted.

Kenzi stared at him, stunned, her mouth parted slightly, gun dropping to her side. Kendra did not dare move from her spot on the floor. She was still sobbing, apologizing, but it was too late now. The damage was done.

"I'm only going to ask you this once." Kenzi visibly swallowed, her fingers clenching and unclenching on the gun. "And I want an honest answer."

"Yes, *mio tesoro*," he answered her sadly. "I am your father."

Kenzi took in a deep breath before asking, "Christian?"

Dante shook his head. "He belongs to Elias."

"How long have you known?" Her brow furrowed, eyes narrowing at the man before her. "How long have you known that you were our father and never said anything?"

"Since the day you were born and I held you in my arms."

A choked sob left her lips, and her shoulders slumped forward slightly. "You let him..." Kenzi paled slightly as dark thoughts swirled in her mind, unbidden. "Did you let him..."

Ava rushed forward, her arms going around Kenzi, hugging her tightly to her chest, front to back. "He didn't know they'd sold you," she assured her sister. "He was in the dark, just like me. He didn't know. I promise. He didn't know."

The two sisters stood together, one behind the other, frozen in their own little world of quiet despair. In the time I had come to know Kenzi, I had never seen her break down. She hid behind her wit and charm. It cracked something inside me to see her utterly broken down, tears streaming in little rivulets down her face as Ava held her, whispering words of love in her ear. It had no doubt been a long time since Kenzi had been held and loved.

I snuck a glance at Vas, who was standing a few paces to my right. His eyes were pasted on Kenzi and washed with regret. He was no doubt thinking of Libby. I could not imagine how hard it must have been for him to see Kenzi. She was an exact copy of Libby on the surface, but if you looked beneath the dewy pale skin and brown hair to her cold blue eyes and tight, angular features, she was nothing like her sweet, docile sister.

Pain tightened his features. His shoulders were tense, and his hands were clenched into fists at his side. If I had any doubt about how he felt about Libby before, there was none now.

Dante looked defeated from where he stood watching them. His normally proud stature slumped in defeat. He hadn't cast even one glance at Kendra, who still sat sobbing on the floor, quietly now instead of the soap opera act she'd been giving earlier.

We all stood there. For how long, I had lost track, but soon, the scene changed. Kenzi shook her head, tears running dry, and she pulled herself from her sister's embrace.

"I can't," she whispered sorrowfully. "I can't do this."

Ava released a small sob of her own when her sister stalked away from her, back turned, gun still firmly in her grasp. She was a trained killer, after all.

A predator.

"Kenzi," Ava hollered after her, but her feet remained planted in place. "Kenzi, please."

But it was too late. Everyone had their breaking point, and even though I doubted Kenzi had reached hers, the predator in her sensed the oncoming weakness and did what a predator does best.

Squashed it.

Because a predator with a weakness easily became prey.

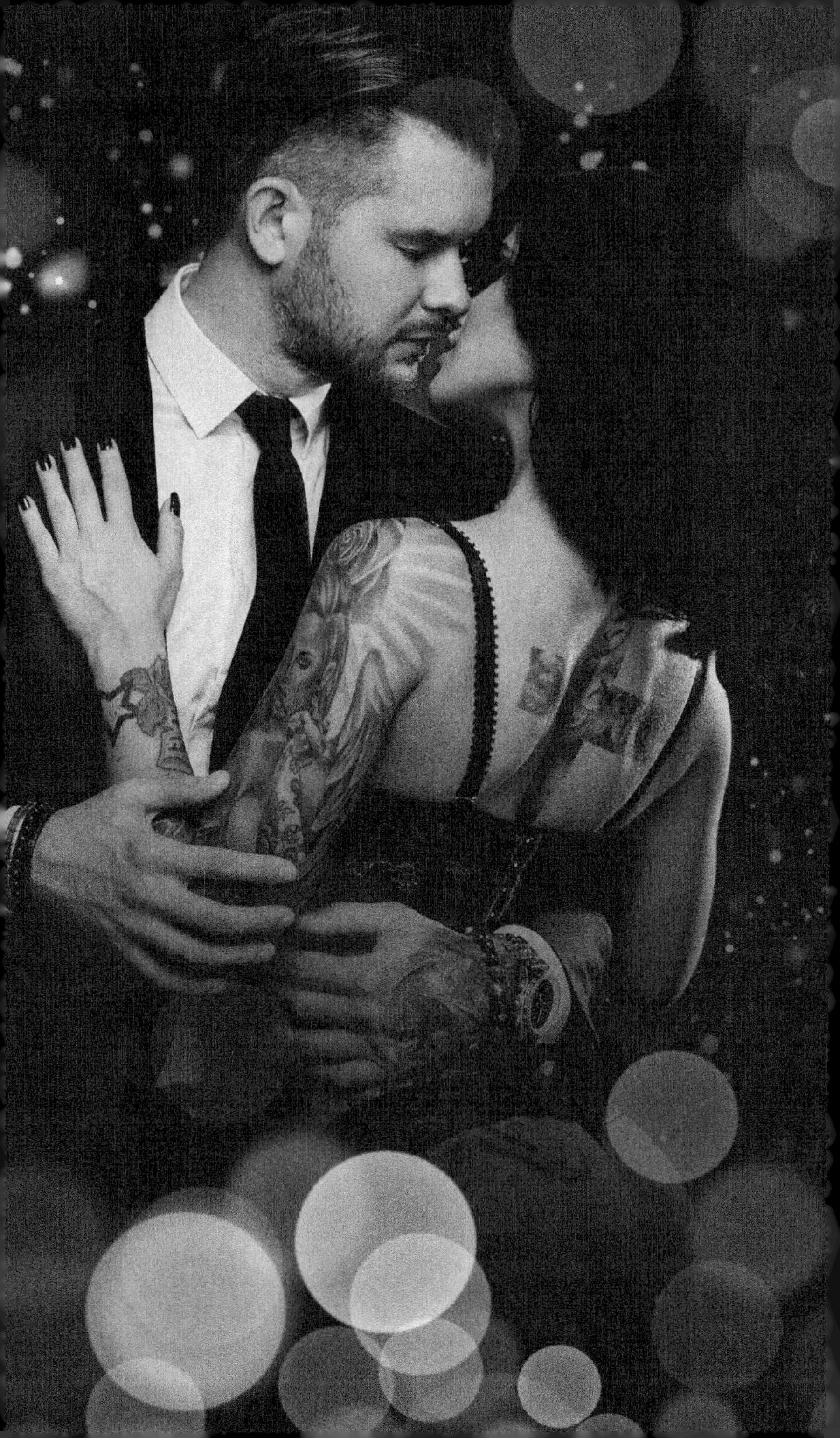

FIFTEEN

Ava

The acrid taste of fury was hot on my tongue as I glared after the silent footsteps of my sister. Seeing her cry, holding her in my arms, it felt almost wrong. Kenzi had always been the strong one between the three of us. The pillar. Now it felt as if she was a shell of the person she used to be, beaten down by the trauma she'd been subjected to.

I couldn't begin to imagine what she must have gone through while I thought she was away at college. There were no words of reassurance I could have offered her. No flowery platitudes or pretty prose meant to wash over the stains beneath the exterior. The minute Kenzi wrenched herself from my embrace, I knew she was shutting down. Matthias had done the exact same thing. She was protecting herself. Hiding her weakness beneath layers of stone so that

"Is she—" Kendra's voice filtered through the silence. "Is she gone?" The bitch's tone was soft and hesitant. She was playing at being the damsel in distress when she was nothing but a viper.

Growling, I bent down and grabbed the collar of her dress, dragging her up from the floor. Dante stepped forward to intervene, but the icy glare I cast his way froze him in place. I wouldn't hurt her, but that didn't mean I wouldn't give her a piece of my mind.

"You can quit with the act, Kendra," I snarled, shifting my hand to her hair and wrenching her neck back. Without her heels on, we were eye level with one another. "You aren't the victim here; you're the villain. The sex trafficker. And if you weren't pregnant with an innocent baby, I would gut you from stem to stern."

"I didn't—"

I yanked harder on her hair, cutting off any excuses she was about to offer me. "Fuck your excuses," I snarled. "You sold your daughter to become a fucking assassin. To learn how to seduce and kill people for a corrupt corporation you profited from. Don't pretend like you had no idea, because I have proof that you were complicit."

"You don't understand," she whined. "I didn't have a choice."

I laughed, the sound grating and devoid of warmth. "We all have choices, and you chose the wrong one. You should have protected her."

"Like you protected Libby?"

My breath stalled in my lungs as my gaze darkened.

"What did you just say to me?"

"Ava..." Dante warned from beside me. I ignored him.

"You blame me for not protecting Kenzi," she hissed at

me. The viper's fangs were starting to show. "But you did nothing to protect Libby. None of you did."

"Neither did you," I reminded her, my tone deathly low. "It was your son who had her murdered."

"And it was you who led him to it," she sneered. "You are just like your mother. Prancing around and ensnaring other people's husbands. Seducing them with your innocent smiles and big green eyes. You are both nothing but home-wrecking whores. If it wasn't for you, Kenzi would never have had to be sold and Christian wouldn't have been driven to kill Libby."

She spat at me.

"You led her down the wrong path. Seduced her to your side, and now she is dead," Kendra kept on, her face growing to be a plum shade of purple as her ire mounted. "Your mother is no better. It seems Ward men have a sickness when it comes to McDonough women."

Oh, this bitch was unhinged. She was still talking about my mother in the present tense, as if she were still here. Still seducing her husband. But she wasn't. She was dead, and Kendra knew it.

"My mother was a victim," I hissed. "Your husband stole her, she didn't seduce him, and she sure as hell didn't love him. The only one seducing other people's husbands is you." I shot Dante a cold look. The man at least had the decency to look ashamed.

Yeah, buddy, don't think I didn't guess that you and Kendra were hooking up while your late wife was still alive. Pathetic. If I ever found that Matthias had done that to me, I would cut his dick off and staple it to his forehead.

Limp dick leader would be his new name.

"Your mother is not a victim."

"Stop talking about her like she's still alive, you fucking bitch," I roared, my hand coming down on her face.

"Ava!" Dante surged forward to pull me away from Kendra, but Matthias intervened, holding him back.

"It is a small slap," Matthias grumbled. "She is fine."

Vas snorted. "For how long?"

"She won't hurt the baby," Matthias assured Dante. "Let her work this out. It has been a long time coming."

The slap had stung my hand, leaving a weak red handprint on Kendra's cheek. I let go of her hair in my rage, and she slumped back to the floor, holding her cheek with a shocked expression coating her face.

Then she looked up at me and smirked.

"I thought you would have figured that part out by now." She chuckled mirthlessly. "Ward men don't let anything go."

"What are you saying?"

My chest tightened painfully, breaths coming fast as my heart beat against my ribcage.

Thump. Thump. Thump.

It was all I could hear as I waited with bated breath for her next words. She couldn't mean what I thought she meant. There was no way. I'd seen the death certificate. The crime scene photos. The autopsy.

Kendra was lying.

She had to be.

Otherwise, she would have come for me. Her heart. Her star. She wouldn't have left me all alone.

"You honestly think my husband let her die?" Kendra scoffed. "No, your mother is very much alive." Then she shrugged. "Well, as alive as she can be anyway. Comas are a bit of a bitch."

My mother was alive.
My mother was alive.
My mother was alive.

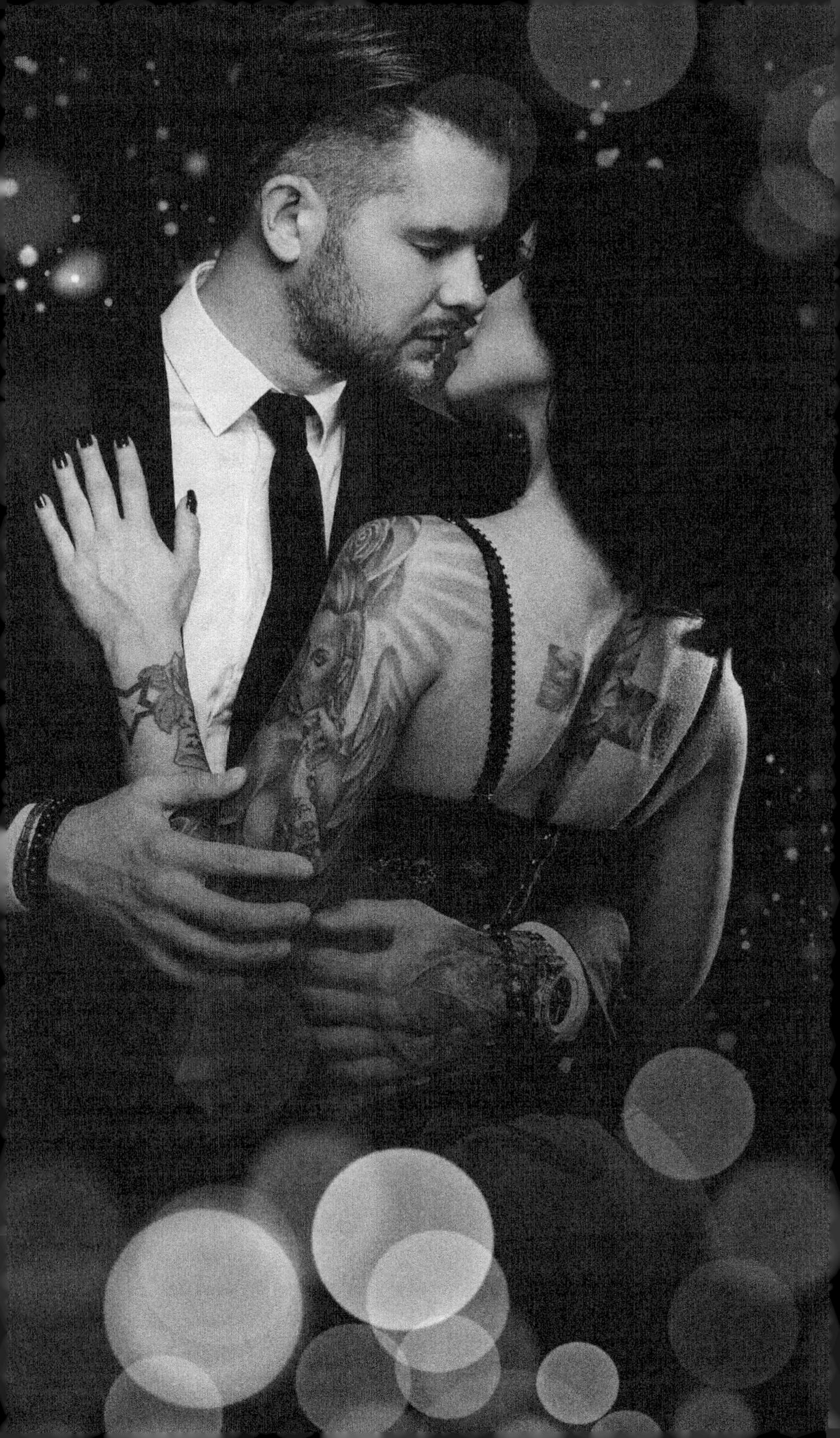

SIXTEEN

Ava

There was nothing that could have prepared me for this moment. Even in my wildest dreams, I could never have dreamed up the scene before me. She was lying there, arms at her sides, hooked up to wires and lines and tubes.

I pressed my hand against the cool viewing glass, yearning to be inside the room with her. Sitting by her side. There were a few things to take care of first, and I didn't want the darkness I was about to unleash to taint her sleep.

Dante had to feed Kendra some platitudes before she was willing to give up my mother's location. It was too bad she was pregnant. It would have been much more fun to hear her beg after I pummeled her plastic face.

. . .

JO MCCALL

"You honestly think he would have let her die?" she snarled. "Then you have no idea how far his obsession went. Just like Christian's obsession with you."

"Funny thing," I told her. "We haven't heard anything from your son. If he was truly obsessed, he would have been driven to pursue me, and since the bombing of the stables, he hasn't been heard from."

"Does a grand master voice his move before he strikes?"

Ugh, did she just compare her son to a grand master of chess?

"I'm not even going to dignify that with an answer." My nose scrunched in disgust. "Where is my mother?"

Kendra scoffed. "Do you honestly think I'm stupid enough to just give up what I know without any assurances?"

"You're alive," Liam hissed. "That's an assurance."

"And how long after I give birth to this baby will that last, hmm?" She looked at me and then Dante. "I will tell you what you want to know, under one condition."

I tapped my foot impatiently. "And what's that?"

"I want to be able to raise my baby after it's born."

And here I was thinking I could put a bullet between her eyes. I was mildly impressed that she hadn't just asked us to spare her life after she gave birth, but that she wanted to be part of her unborn child's life. That was growth.

"And I want enough money to support myself."

There it was.

"Why?" Dante asked coldly. "You won't be leaving this house for a very long time, Kendra. Everything you need, I will provide."

Kendra huffed. "I want my own income."

"Get a job then," I shrugged my shoulder. "I hear McDonalds hires washed-up trophy wife has-beens."

"I will not—"

"Take it or leave it, bitch," Dante snarled. The man had finally lost his patience with her. "I will allow you to live here and raise our child, but that is where my generosity ends. So choose. My generosity after our child is born or a bullet."

Kendra sniffed indignantly. "If those are my only two choices." She let out a dramatic sigh and rolled her shoulders. "He's had her at a small care facility on Mercer Island called Rejuvenation."

"She's been in a coma for over ten years?" Would she even have brain function? What was the likelihood of her recovering from something like that? Slim to none was my guess.

"Off and on," Kendra admitted. "He took her out of it a few times through the years for a month or two at a time."

"For what?" Matthias asked curiously. "Does she not need the life support to survive?"

Kendra shook her head. "The original hospital she was at in Portland kept her in a medically induced coma until her injuries had healed enough for her to cope with the trauma," she informed us. "I don't know why he took her in and out of the coma throughout the years. Elias was about punishment and control."

"Or he was hiding her," I breathed as realization dawned.

"Why?" Vas's brow furrowed.

"Succession," my father growled. "If Marianne is truly Katherine's twin—" I shot him a scathing glare. He held up his hands placatingly. "I'm not doubting you, but you have to admit that Sheila could be manipulating the facts. Instead of twins, they could simply be half siblings."

That was a good point. If Marianne wasn't my mother's

twin, she didn't have a strong enough claim as heir. She was still a McDonough, though. But there was nothing to prove that. Right? I would have assumed Seamus and my great-grandmother would have removed all knowledge of a second baby being born.

This shit was giving me a headache.

That headache wasn't going away anytime soon.

I looked down at the doctor Matthias had put on his knees in the lobby. The clinic or whatever they called it was remote and only contained a handful of patients. Mostly women who had been prostituted and addicted to drugs. We released the ones who were obviously sober and being held against their will. Vas was taking care of how to get them where they needed to go. We kept the ones that were still strung out locked in their rooms until we could transport them to another facility. One that didn't hold them against their will.

"What is your name?" My gaze was cold and expressionless, head cocked to the side.

"Peterson," he stuttered. "Derek Peterson."

"How long have you been attending the woman in room eight?"

The doctor fidgeted nervously. "Um—" His Adam's apple bobbed in his throat and sweat had begun to collect on his brow. "Three years."

"And who attended to her before then?"

"Dr. Williams," he told me without hesitation.

"Anyone before him?"

The doctor shook his head.

"Where is he now?"

His eyes darted to the room where my mother lay in a coma before they settled back on me.

"She strangled him with one of the cords from the monitor."

Badass.

"When was the last time she was awake?" my father questioned harshly.

The doctor licked his lips. "Three years ago."

Elias must have put her back under as punishment. I couldn't believe she had been awake just three years ago. She'd been here this whole time, right under my nose, and I didn't know it. It broke my heart to see what Elias had been doing to her. The medical records were detailed. There were times when she wasn't fully unconscious. When she could hear and feel everything that Elias did or said. If that fucker wasn't already dead...

The whir of a helicopter met my ears.

Dr. Radick had arrived.

It took several more minutes for the copter to shut down, but soon Dr. Radick and his team were pushing through the clinic's door with a gurney in tow.

"I take it this is the *sukin syn* who's been keeping your mother in a coma?" Disgust and contempt rolled off the Russian doctor in waves as he glared down at the man on his knees.

"One of them," I told him. "The other one is dead."

"*Khoroshiy.*" *Good.* "I looked over the reports, and despite the flagrant disregard for human rights, she is in good health."

"She's in a coma," my father deadpanned.

"That is right," Radick nodded sympathetically. "But she has been receiving not only daily physical therapy but also Botox injections to help maintain muscular efficiency."

"Should we applaud the good doctor?"

"I'd shoot him." Radick shrugged. "But that's not really my decision."

I couldn't help but chuckle at his humor.

"They've been using a pretty heavy cocktail of propofol, phenobarbital, and thiopental," Radick explained. "These drugs have a continuous effect on the patient, keeping them in a sustained state of unconsciousness for as long as the drugs are flowing."

"What should I be worried about?" I asked hesitantly. There was bound to be some problems once we took her off the medications.

"Addiction is one of them," Radick informed me honestly. "We will have to wean her off the drugs little by little so her body doesn't go into withdrawal and stop her heart."

Wonderful.

"Once we start weaning her off the drugs, she'll slowly start to gain consciousness," he continued while he glanced at the paperwork in his hand. "She'll come off the tube once she starts breathing on her own. Her vocality will be limited, but with some speech therapy, that too can be resolved."

"Okay," I whispered. Dr. Radick focused his full attention on me. His brown eyes were a calming moment in a stormy sea. He was a good doctor. Patient and understanding. I wouldn't be alive if it wasn't for him and his team. I trusted him.

"We'll get her set up at my clinic and keep you informed every step of the way," he assured me. "I will give her the utmost care. I promise."

Swallowing back the lump of emotion welling in my throat, I nodded, afraid that if I spoke, I would cry.

He gave me a sharp nod and then directed his team through my mother's door.

She was safe now, and that was all that mattered. Everything else would fall into place, and I would be there every step of the way.

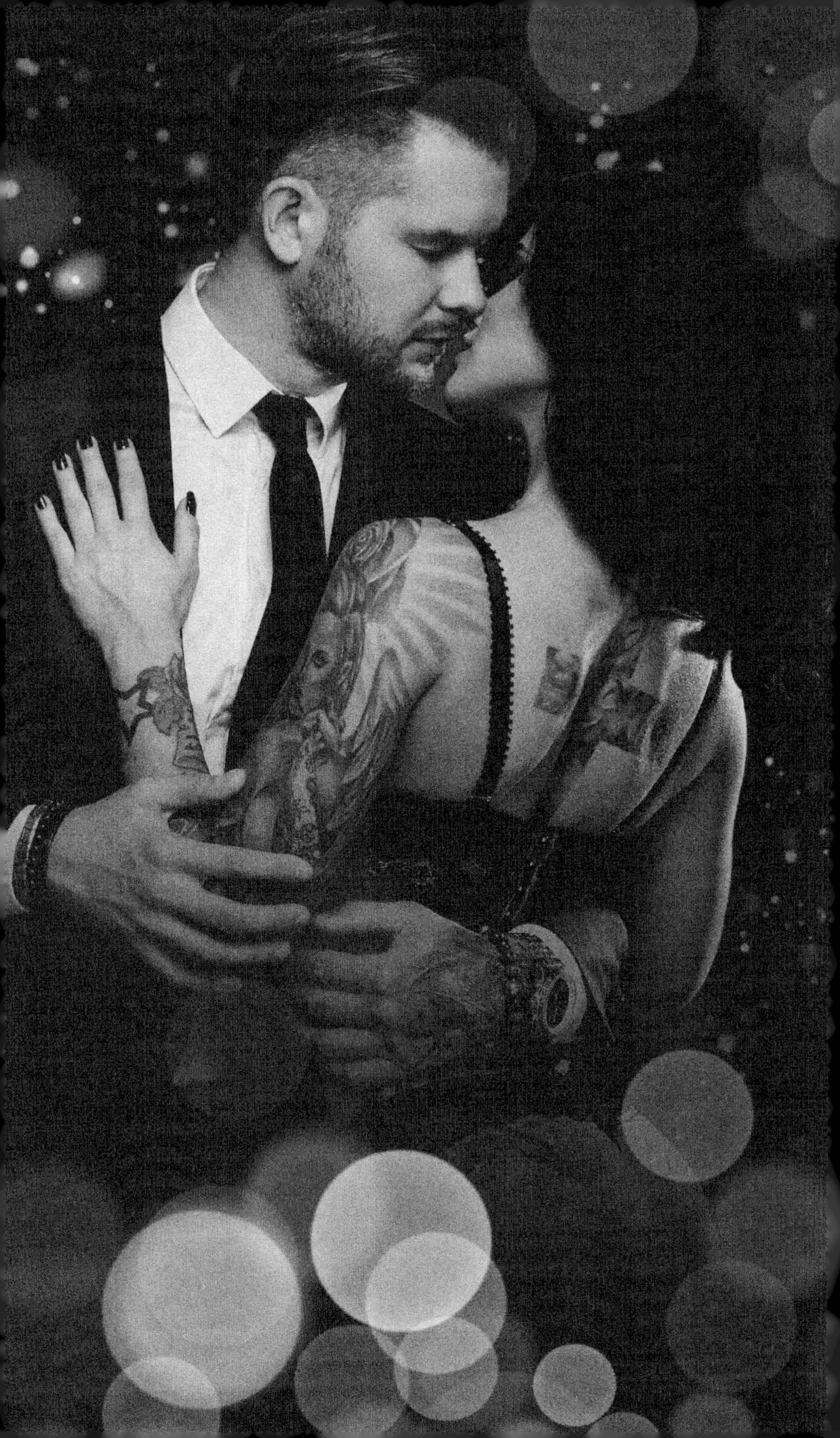

SEVENTEEN

Ava

Arctic Security was nothing like I imagined. It was huge. There were forty-two floors in total. Ten subfloors, twenty floors dedicated to the security business, and the top twelve were part of the consulting and legal firm.

Matthias had been at the office for the last few days, barely getting away except to sleep for a few hours. Then he would go right back. For the most part, he had taken over the *Bratva* again, but I was fine with that. He wasn't leaving me out of the loop; he was simply more efficient at running the operation.

I'd come in with little knowledge of how to run the mafia, and most of my time as *Pakhan*, a title I still held, was spent searching for answers and revenge. Matthias was planning on teaching me everything he knew so we could truly rule as partners, but right now, he had a mole to find, and I was busy searching for my traitorous family.

When it came to the security company, we didn't involve the operatives in mafia hits. The men and woman who made up Arctic Security were all legit, and Matthias didn't want to taint that. He did, however, run a black ops cyber unit that tied in with the more criminal side of his empire. Mark would be so pissed at me if he knew where I was right now.

"We have more than fifteen satellites circling the globe at any one time," Maksim informed me. "Our team has created back doors into the local law enforcement, the CIA, FBI, NSA, ATF...you get the point."

Wow. That was scary impressive.

"The legit side of our black ops unit surveys security threats for other corporations. Social media monitoring, and so on," he continued as he led me down the corridor. "We have trained analysts who search for keywords, photos, hashtags, videos and the like to remove all evidence of the *Bratva*."

"Is that why Matthias is able to run a corporation so legitimately without any problems?" I'd wondered how he managed to be the face of Dashkov Enterprises and Arctic Security.

"For the most part," Maksim offered. "A good amount of our clients know who Matthias is, but those clients work in the underground. They're just as shady." He smirked. "Even the government contracts with us. They suspect who Matthias is, but when it comes down to it, they don't care. There are bigger fish out there to fry. As long as we aren't moving humans, the US government turns its head away."

"That is a little worrisome."

"Why is that?"

"I mean—" I ran it over in my head a few times to make sure I was wording it correctly. "We're still running drugs and weapons. Drugs that cause overdoses. Guns that kill people. Isn't the government supposed to be all about shutting that down?"

Maksim stopped so suddenly I nearly toppled into him. He didn't look angry, but the air around us had certainly shifted.

"That is true," he admitted. "But let's look at it this way. We may sell the drugs, but we don't put the needle in their arm. We aren't responsible for what people do with the drugs we sell them." I scoffed at his simple way of looking at the situation but remained silent. "We may sell weapons, but our guns don't kill people, Ava. People kill people. We can't help that."

"Then why sell them at all?" I was curious. If their legit businesses were doing so well, why have the criminal element in the first place?

"Sure." He shrugged and continued walking. "We could go completely legit, but then we couldn't afford to employ nearly half the people we do. The compound would cease to exist, and the people we've helped would have nowhere to go. We wouldn't have the resources to save the women like we did at the docks. Not to mention, we may sell drugs, but we don't cut them with rat poison or fentanyl. They are clean and safe."

I shot him a dubious look. He smirked. "As safe as drugs can be anyway," he admitted. "If we didn't sell guns, someone else would. Yes, we do what society considers, criminal and bad, but there are people much worse than us out there. We have morals and standards. Can you say the same about Ward? Or the McDonoughs?"

There was a part of me that wished I could disagree, but

he had a point. Despite their illegal activities and looser than normal moral codes, for criminals, they were well above par. Sure, they killed...no, *we* killed people and threatened them, but it was never just to watch them die.

What did Sansa say in *Game of Thrones*? "It isn't what I want, but what honor demands?"

"You're right," I admitted. "I was looking at it from the wrong perspective."

Maksim smiled down at me as we stopped in front of a heavy metal door. "The fact that you can admit that shows you will be a great leader, Ava," he said proudly. "Remember that there are two sides to every coin. Sacrifices that must be made. You want to save women like your mom and Kenzi? Then you need to play outside the law. It's not cheap to do what we do."

I smiled up at him and nodded as excitement bubbled up inside me.

"I get that," I told him honestly as I bounced on my feet. "Now can we go inside? Mark is going to die when he finds out I was in here first."

Maksim grunted. "That kid will never be allowed in this place if I have anything to say about it," he grumbled. "The damage that hellion could do."

"You know he already has his own access to almost everything, right?" That included the Dashkov satellites, although he was highly monitored and only given access in dire circumstances.

"Don't remind me." He opened a small black box to the right of the door that was painted the same black as the door itself. If he hadn't opened it, I wouldn't have guessed it was there. "Just like the vault at the Dashkov Building, every designated person has their own individual code that rotates at the end of every week."

"Who are the designated people?"

Maksim's smile widened. "Matthias and Vas, obviously," he told me. "Dima and me because we share duties as head of *Bratva* enforcers, the six people who rotate shifts in that room, and you."

I thought about that for a moment. "What about Nicolai and Leon? Wouldn't they have access as well since they are part of the upper cadre?"

Maksim shook his head. "Nicolai's and Leon's duties have nothing to do with our cyber security unit. Nicolai, as *Obshchak* deals in money and businesses. His responsibility is managing the smaller businesses such as the nightclubs, restaurants, and strip joints we launder our money through."

"And Leon?"

The giant Russian winked at me. "Leon the liaison is what we call him," Maksim chuckled. "He is the face of most of our businesses. Matthias may be the CEO, but Leon is the one everyone sees. Press meetings, marketing, all of that is him and our PR coordinator Melanie."

"I feel like I should have known this already," I mumbled petulantly, embarrassed at my lack of knowledge on the inner workings of my own...empire? Yeah, empire sounded perfect and badass.

"Honor demanded vengeance," Maksim assured me softly. "That is why you have us. You'll learn as you go. Matthias had years to be trained by Tomas to be *Pakhan*. You weren't even given a how-to manual."

Ugh, the amount of wisdom this man had in his head was maddening. Once again, he hit the nail on the head. Fuck. Maksim entered his passcode into the silver keypad and tilted his head back slightly for the retinal scanner.

With a small beep, it granted him access, the lock on the

door disengaging. Cool air wafted into the warm corridor, causing goose bumps to break out over my exposed skin. Maksim waved me inside, closing the door tightly behind us. Funny thing about this room was that you had to use your code and retina scan to leave as well.

The room was painted in a light cream color. I had been imagining something much darker, like a hovel of some kind where they were all hunkered down and saw very little light. That wasn't the case since my imagination wasn't conducive to a good work environment and would probably make vampires out of everyone being unable to see the sunlight.

Which they couldn't, but the walls had artificial windows with digital landscapes inside them. The lights in the room produced a type of artificial sunlight. It was genius really. This had to be the best room in Washington, where seasonal depression was a huge thing because of how little the sun shone throughout the fall and winter months.

There were no individual desks or offices in the room, save one that was used during an active op. The analysts in charge of the mission could use the room without being disturbed or crossing channels with anyone else in the comms center. Otherwise, the desks were shoved together in the middle of the room with obvious stations set up, but there were no boundaries or dividers.

"They don't have separate workspaces because most of the time they aren't working alone but as a team, and the teams change." Maksim read my mind. "This allows them to switch up where they sit and who they sit with to better accommodate their needs."

Some of the analysts looked up from their laptops, interest sliding into their gazes as we walked farther into the room.

"Great," one of the analysts muttered. "Another one to babysit." The girl across from him ducked her head, cheeks burning hot with embarrassment at his less than subtle jab at her. Clove was her name, if I remembered correctly. Maksim had given me a dossier on each of the analysts in the room. She was the only female, but her skills and credentials were far more impressive than most of her male counterparts.

Especially this one.

"Travis," I looked down my nose at the man. "Isn't it?"

He glared up at me, nose wrinkled in disdain. "Yeah? Want a cookie or something for knowing my name, princess?"

Next to me, Maksim growled at his insult but stayed quiet. I smirked at the dark-haired man before me whose obvious dislike of his coworker and immediate distaste for me spoke volumes about his character. He was smart, for sure. Off the charts. But his background held a large history of misogyny, and his current projects were somewhat lacking. As if a newbie was doing his workload on top of their own. He had a history of having other people do his work, using his power over others to get ahead, and skimping out on his own duties.

When I pointed this out to Maksim this morning, he had been livid at having missed the signs. I couldn't blame him, though; he was stretched thin. The problem was that Matthias had his men trying to run both the criminal side and the legal side of the businesses. It wasn't to say that they couldn't do it, but that was how things like this slipped through the cracks.

"Travis Dorchester, born March 18, 1990," I recited his information. "Lived with his mother and father until two years ago when they finally kicked him out on his ass." The man before me paled. "Resigned from his last few jobs because he said they weren't working out. Only, come to find out, you were forced to resign due to complications with your coworkers. Specifically of the female variety. Making them do the work that was assigned to you. Taking the credit where it didn't belong. Applied under the last name Crenshaw so that no one would put two and two together."

"I don't..." He stuttered and tried to come up with a believable lie. Wasn't going to work for me.

"You don't what?" I asked, eyes narrowed at him. "Don't know why you did it? Don't know what I'm talking about? Don't care?"

"What? No..."

I didn't let him finish. "Good," I smiled at him, condescension dripping from my tone, "because you have two options. I can either fire you, or you can take a pay cut and a demotion until you prove you can do the work on your own without the assistance of those around you."

"What?" He jumped his feet, the chair beneath him falling to the floor with a dull thud. "You can't do that. You aren't my boss!" Travis's gaze slid over to Maksim in disbelief. "Are you really going to let her do this, man?"

Maksim raised his eyebrows, his shoulders shrugging, mouth tugged downward.

"Sit back down," Maksim ordered. Travis immediately obeyed, straightening his chair before he took a seat. "I'm not the boss here." Maksim raised an eyebrow at him and jerked his head toward me. "She is." Everyone in the room sat straighter in their chairs, except Travis, who was staring at me with his mouth open in shock.

"For those of you in this room who don't know who I

am," I spoke to the entire room, my head high, "my name is Avaleigh Dashkov, and from here on, I am the CEO of Arctic Security and Associates. That means you all answer to me. Anyone got a problem with that?"

Everyone but Travis the bigot shook their heads.

Inclining my head, I looked him over. The way his eyes shifted nervously and the sweat clinging to his brow. He was nervous, but about what? Getting found out? The embarrassment I caused him? Or was it something deeper? We had a mole in the division somewhere. Only a handful of people at Arctic knew about the detonation sequence, and most of them were in this room.

Which is why it was time to set up the game.

"We have a mole in one of the departments," I told them. "Someone with access to classified information on the construction of the Dashkov building leaked the codes and blueprints to our enemies. They hacked into the mainframe of the building and downloaded a code-sensitive virus that triggered the building's self-destruct."

"That shouldn't even be possible." One of the analysts spoke up. Sam, I believed his name was. He was a promising analyst who once worked with the CIA before they burned him. "The self-destruct sequence is on its own separate server. To download a virus, you must be directly linked to the server as a hardline. You can't do it remotely."

"Exactly," I smirked at him. "And the only people who have direct access to the servers are in this building."

"Including us," Travis pointed out. "Are you accusing one of us of sabotage?"

"No," I told him honestly. "I'm accusing you of murder and espionage."

A terrified silence fell through the room. They were

each waiting for the gavel to come down on them, but it wouldn't. Not yet.

"Your job is to find me the mole." My gaze swept over each one of them, taking in every minute facial expression. They all twitched nervously. Their hands twisting in their laps, chests rising and falling rapidly. They were all signs of anxiety, but not necessarily guilt.

Yet.

"Mr. Crenshaw or Dorchester or whatever you're called." The analyst clenched his jaw but kept quiet. "You've got janitor duty for the next month. Then we'll talk."

"Are you kidding me?" he asked incredulously. "A janitor? What is that supposed to do?"

I smirked. "Teach you some humility." I shrugged nonchalantly. "Also, good luck with trying to get those men to do your work for you. They're some mean bastards." I pointed toward the door. "You can start now. Your access to this floor will be restricted. Have fun."

The room snickered quietly when he all but stormed out of it, slamming the heavy door behind him. "I'll make sure his access is revoked," Sam told me. I smiled at him and nodded before turning to leave.

"Um, ma'am." Clove held up her hand from her station nervously. I turned back toward her.

"Ava is fine, Clove," I informed her. "I'm not big on titles or formalities." Plus, being called ma'am by someone who was my age made me feel old.

She cleared her throat and bit her lip before nodding at her computer screen. "You might want to see this." There was a guilty look on her face, as if she had been caught with her hand in the cookie jar.

I walked past the analysts at the head of the table and stopped when I'd reached her.

"Travis had me monitoring his floor today, which is the main office between Arctic and the associates," she rambled quickly. "None of the offices have cameras, but the hallways, stairwells, and elevators do, you see." She pointed at her laptop screen, where the security footage showed Matthias coming out of the elevator with a woman on his arm. He wasn't smiling, in fact, he looked downright pissed. The woman had his arm wrapped in both of hers, a dewy smile on her face as she stared up at him. She was wearing a contoured body dress and fuck-me heels.

Serena.

That bitch.

Matthias telling me why he had taken Serena to the gala hadn't eased the betrayal I felt that night. He did it to get information about his mother's grave since her father had been the one to bury her that night on Kirill's orders. In return, he'd promised to pay off the suitor her father had lined up for her. I wasn't sure who he was, but he didn't sound pleasant.

He'd wanted Serena as his fourth wife.

I was afraid to ask what happened to his other three.

Matthias told me he terminated things with her after that night, but that she'd been trying to get him alone since she found out he'd returned, telling him that their deal wasn't fulfilled.

Bitch didn't know how to take a hint.

"Get me everything you have on her and send it to my tablet," I ordered her, my voice slightly rougher than I wanted it to be. "Please," I amended softly. Clove nodded, her fingers flying across the keyboard lightning fast.

Snarling, I stalked toward the door and waited for Maksim to open it since I didn't have a passcode yet.

"Where are you going?" he asked with a frown as I stormed down the hallway toward the elevator.

"To skin a bitch."

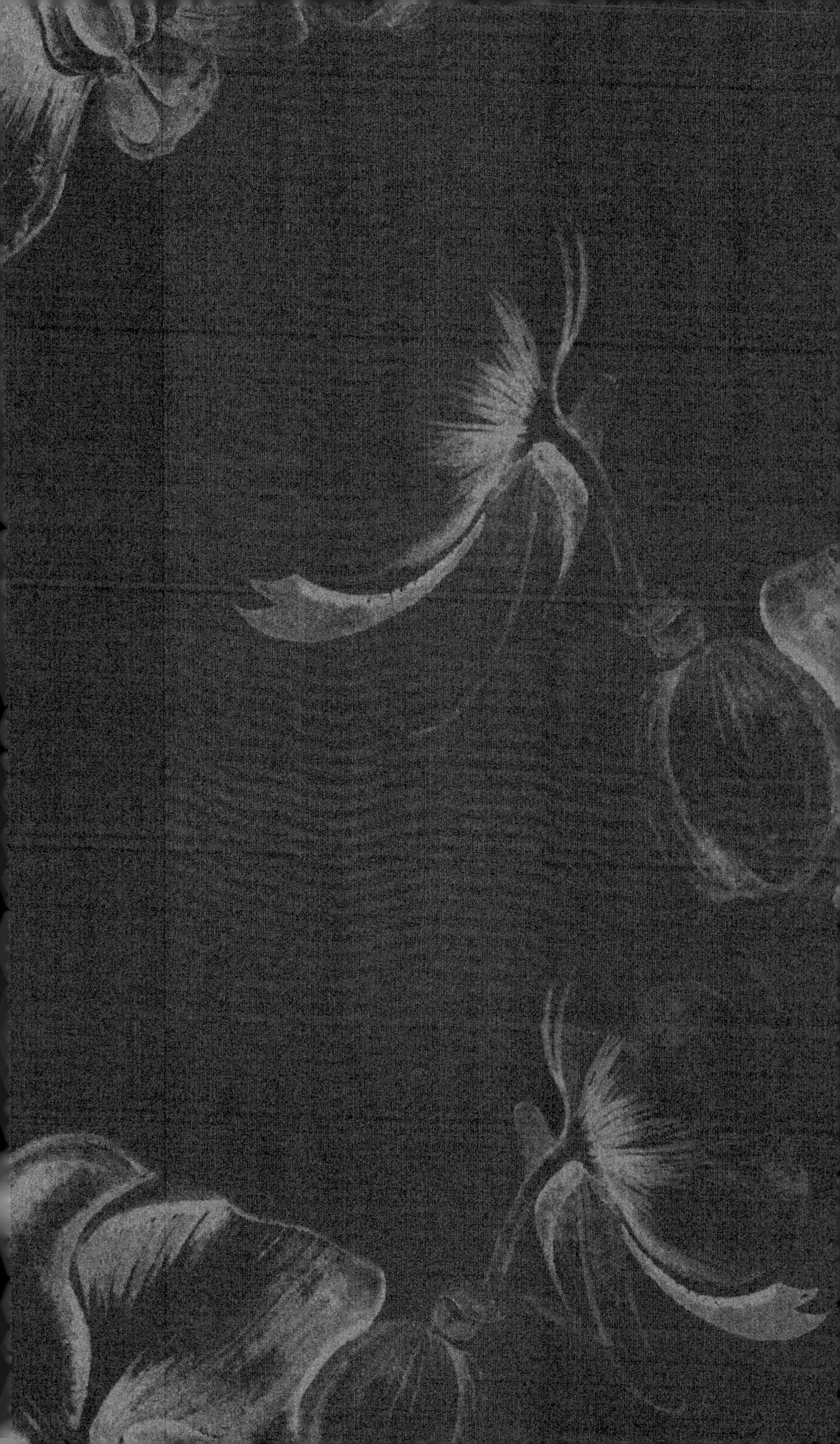

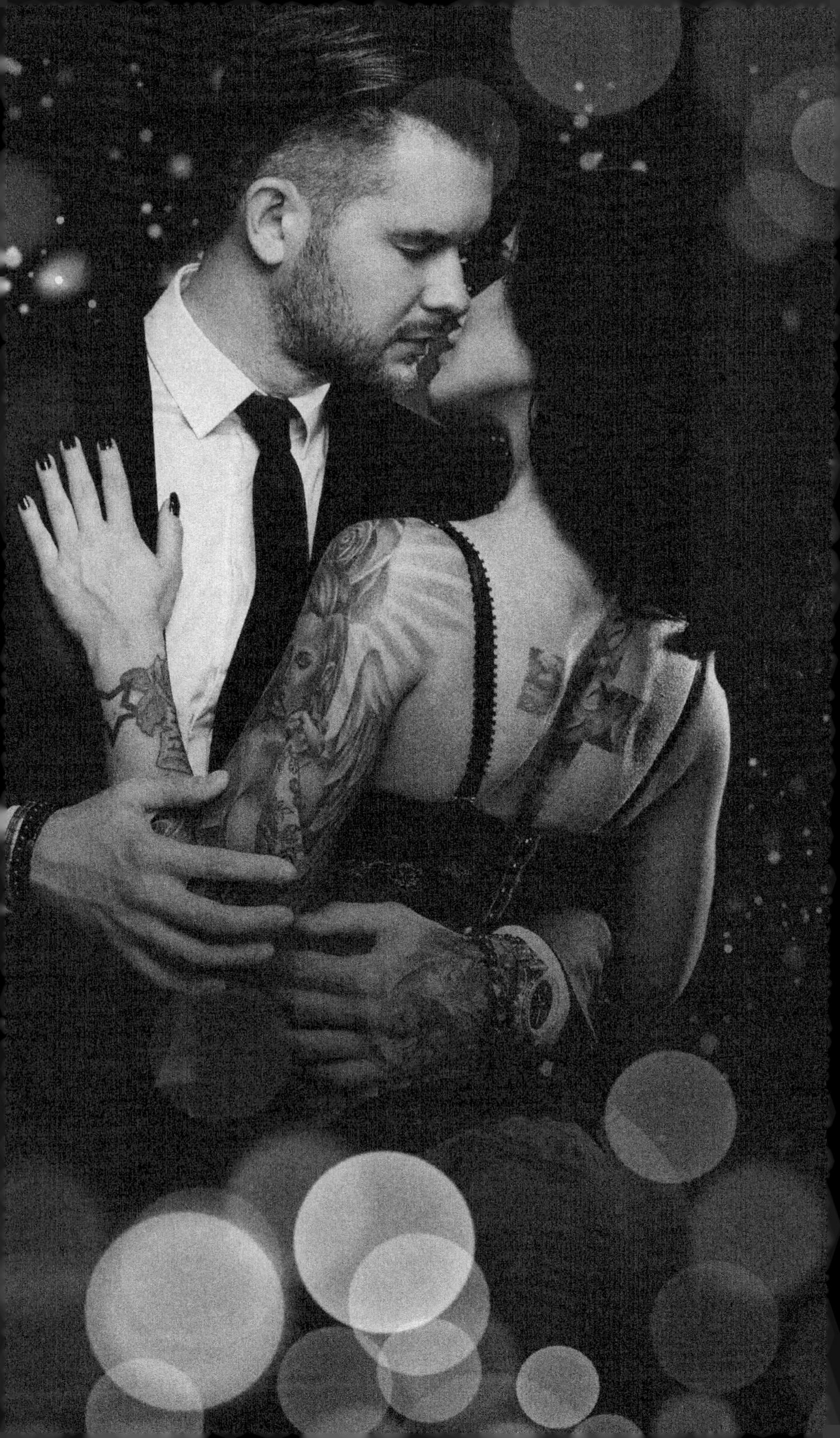

EIGHTEEN

Matthias

Serena clung to me like a second skin as we stepped off the elevator and headed to my office. Her big brown eyes stared up at me and she fluttered her eyelashes flirtatiously, thinking it might endear me to her. The only thing it made me want to do is rip the fake eyelashes off and shove her out the nearest windows.

Unfortunately, that would be a PR nightmare.

"You owe me that information, Serena," I reminded her coldly, peeling her off my arm. "I did exactly as you asked, and I compensated your father to keep him from arranging any future marriage deals."

Serena sneered as I led her into my office. I went straight for the top-shelf whiskey and filled one of the crystal glasses from the bar with as much of the amber liquid as it could handle. "You honestly think that is going to stop my father from going behind your back and trying to do it again?" She ran a hand through her lengthy black hair and sighed, leaning her frame against the side of my desk. "We both know that he will burn through that cash by the end of the year, and I will be back where I started."

"That is not my problem." And it wasn't. I'd been generous with the money I gave her father. He was a leading power player in corporate politics. He'd been trying to sell Serena to the highest bidder, who happened to be Augustu La Rosa. She'd been begging Leon for help, but he'd refused, directing her my way instead. He knew I needed something from her father, and she was the only one who would be able to get it.

My mother's gravesite back in Russia.

Edrik Mickelson had been a low-level thug for Kirill before he came to the states. I remembered his face and the times he paid Kirill so he could fuck my mother and make her scream. It was a running tally I had in my head on how I was going to make him pay. It was why I went with Serena to the gala and made him an offer he couldn't refuse. Serena had the time I was away to collect the information I needed, and now she was trying to bleed me for more.

It wasn't going to happen.

She was a means to an end, and if she proved to be difficult, I would make her life a living hell.

Or Ava would.

"It is if you want the information on where your mother is buried," she threatened me. I growled.

"Do not make idle threats, Serena," I warned her, my lips curled into a snarl, teeth bared. "I am not a man you want to cross."

Serena laughed, oblivious to the hole she was digging for herself twice over. "You think I don't know that?" She tilted her head slightly and batted her eyes at me. It was something that would have been cute on Ava, but on her, it was just desperate. "I have something you want, and there is only one way you're going to get it."

"And how is that?"

Serena grinned up at me like the cat that ate the canary. "You and I are going to get married."

The laugh that rumbled out of me pissed her off. Her dark eyes looked at me askance. She did not like being mocked.

"I am serious, Matthias," she hissed. "We get married, or I don't give you the information you're looking for, and I tell my father who you are."

I shrugged a shoulder. Killing Edrik was at the top of my list of things to do anyway, so if she told him, it would not be such a loss. Kirill was dead, so Edrik finding out my identity was not of any consequence anymore.

"Go ahead." My gaze met hers calmly. "Then I kill him and you. Win-win."

Her face paled for a moment, eyes wide as the cogs in her mind turned, wondering if my threat was real.

"You—you wouldn't," she sputtered. "You don't kill women."

"Eh." I tipped my hand back and forth slightly. "There are exceptions to every rule." The ding of the elevator caught my attention, and I bit back a broad smile. I'd wondered how long it would take my wife to find her way up here. She'd been on the ops floor for the last half an hour, and she was bound to see me getting off the elevator with Serena and come find us, claws bared.

She didn't disappoint.

"Matthias." Serena captured my attention again. She leaned back against the desk, her legs splayed open slightly, giving me a glimpse between her thighs that I had no interest in seeing. One hand rested on the sturdy oak of my desk while the other lightly trailed down the middle of her chest. Not even Valerie's girls were this desperate-looking. "I'm sure I could make it worth your while."

"Not interested," I deadpanned, scrunching my nose, and waving her off.

"If you would just—" Serena was suddenly cut off by the sound of the door opening.

"Well," Ava's sweet voice was music to my ears. "This is a surprise."

Now it was time to play.

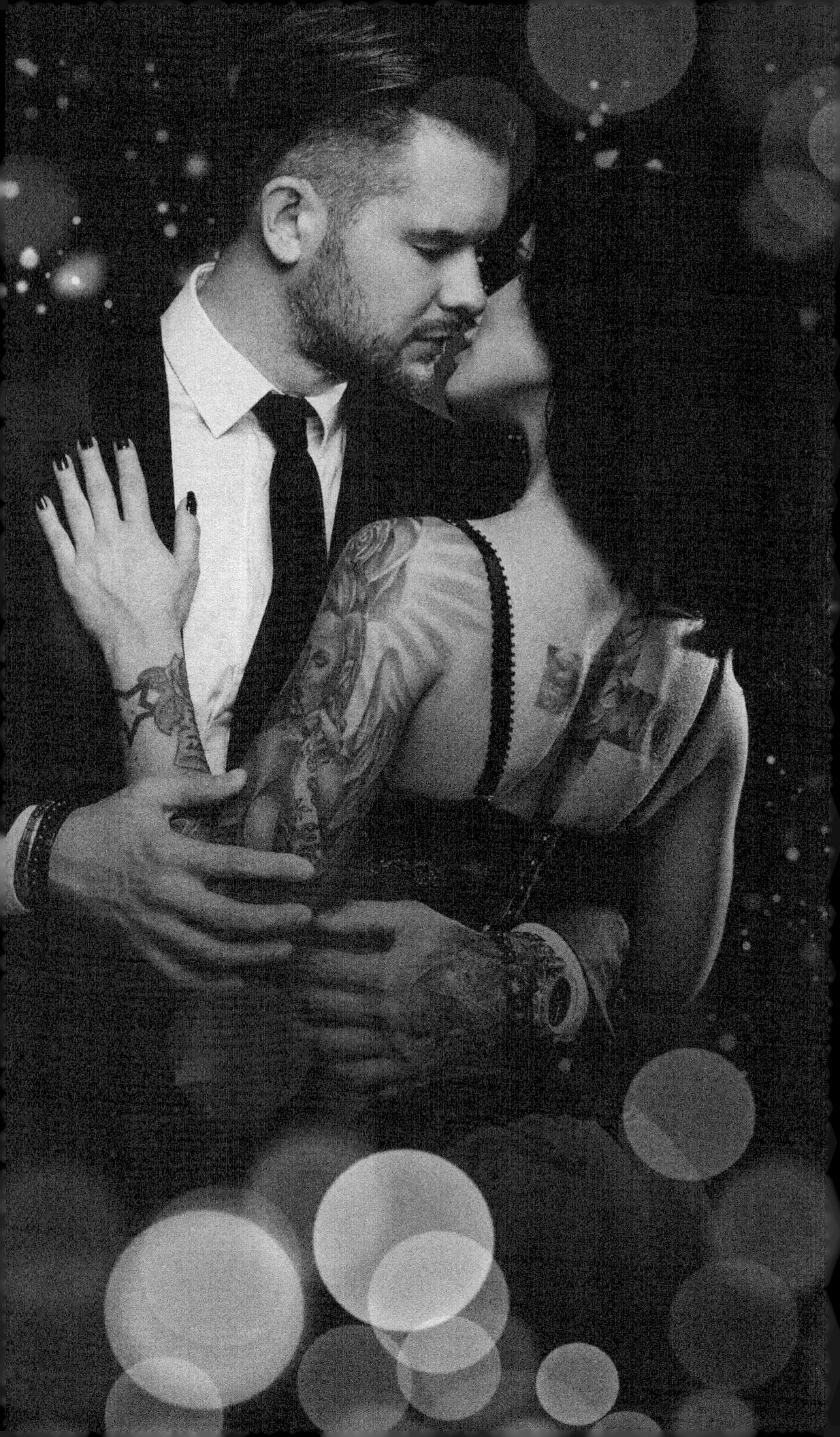

NINETEEN

Ava

She was leaning against his desk, her Raven hair tossed over her shoulders as she pushed her fake water wigglers out in a desperate attempt to catch my husband's attention. The dress she wore barely covered her liposuctioned ass. Matthias stood a few feet away from her, a heavy crystal glass in one hand that was nearly empty, and his hardened gaze fixed on her overly scalpeled face.

"I didn't realize we employed whores when the sun was out." Matthias turned toward me as I strode into his office. He wasn't the least bit surprised to see me.

Serena sneered at me, her eyes narrowed, but then it was gone, replaced by a fake smile and taunting eyes.

"And you are?" The question would have been innocent if we hadn't already met. If she hadn't put her lips on my husband at the gala.

"My wife," Matthias told her before I got the chance. "The one I was just telling you about."

"Oh?" Serena's mouth dropped open slightly, eyes wide. The perfect picture of innocence. "I don't remember you saying you had a wife."

She was good, I would give her that, but my husband was a master of facial expressions. A human lie detector test, and I had picked up on a few things here and there. I knew full well he had told her we were married the night of the gala.

"Wow, you're good," I applauded her mockingly. "But not that good. Your left shoulder shrugs a bit when you lie."

Serena huffed, dropping her façade, and stood straighter, shoulders rolling back as she transformed before my eyes into the woman I had seen the night of the gala. Cold and calculating.

"Perceptive little bitch, I see," she snarled. Matthias growled at the insult, but I was one step ahead of him. I sprang forward, my hand snatching up her perfectly placed locks, ensnaring them in my gasp. Serena gasped in pain when I wrenched her head down. Her back was arched uncomfortably, acrylic claws digging into my arm as I all but dragged her toward the open balcony.

Swinging her around to face me, I dropped the hand from her hair in favor of her neck and pushed her body against the metal railing of the balcony until her feet came off the ground and stark fear crawled onto her face.

"Let's get one thing straight, Serena." My voice was calm and steady, as if I was talking to a friend instead of hanging a whore partway off a railing thirty flights up. "I'm not a bitch. Or a whore. Or any of the other colorful names you are probably calling me in your head right now. My name is Avaleigh Dashkov, *Pakhan* of the Seattle *Bratva*, wife of Matthias Dashkov, and I want you to remember that when you address me."

"I—" I tightened my hand around her throat.

"I'm still talking." She quieted immediately. "I am well aware of how you tried to blackmail Matthias at the gala for the information you have on where his mother is buried, and I have no doubt you were trying to be just as salacious in his office a minute ago."

She shook her head, panic seizing her features as she tried to deny it.

"I really do hate liars," I scolded and shoved her a little farther up the railing.

"No!" she cried out, her feet swinging wildly as she clawed at my hand around her throat viciously. "Please. You don't know who my father is."

I scoffed. "And I don't give a fuck," I told her. "You are going to give my husband the information he asked for. He paid his debt when he redirected your unwanted suitor. If you try this seduction act again or try and retaliate, I will send you back to your father piece by piece." I paused. "Or maybe I'll drop you off on the doorstep of that suitor you seem so afraid of."

Serena froze, chest rising and falling rapidly as she struggled to breathe. "Please," she begged, tears streaming down her perfectly made-up face. Ouch, mascara lines were a bitch to clean up. "Please don't. I—I promise."

"Promise what, Serena?"

"I promise I'll leave him alone!" she screamed. "Just please don't let him take me."

Shouldn't I have felt pity for her predicament?

I didn't. Not at all.

"You should have thought about that before you came in here with your seduction and your threats," I bit out. Tightening my hold on her neck a little more to get the point across, I let her hang there for a moment longer. Once I saw the fear crawl fully into her eyes, I dragged her away from the edge. She hit the concrete with a harsh cry.

"Where is my mother's grave?" Matthias stared down at her, his eyes cold and unfeeling. This woman had used up all her chances with him.

"*Kuz'minskoye Kladbishche*," Serena whispered. "That was where Kirill ordered my father to bury your mother. He buried her in another grave so no one would find her."

"What was the name on the gravestone?"

"Uh," she stalled for a second as she thought about it. "Anya Levchenko or something like that. She's in sector D4. I looked it up."

I looked to Matthias for direction, and he nodded. She wasn't showing any signs of lying.

"Get the fuck out of here," I hissed at her. "If I ever see you near my husband again, your father and unwanted suitor will be the least of your problems, I guarantee it." Serena didn't bother to acknowledge my threat before she took off toward the elevator as fast as she could go in her scuffed-up Jimmy-Choos.

Clearing my throat, I brushed off my skirt and strode back into his office with my head held high. Matthias didn't say a word to me. He just walked to the door, shutting it and locking it behind him. He closed the blinds next and dimmed the lights slightly.

"Turn around, Red," he ordered as he stalked toward me, a deep hunger echoing in his stormy eyes. Licking my lips, I immediately obeyed, bending myself over in the exact spot Serena had tried seducing him. A shiver of excitement ran through me when one hand skated up my inner thigh.

He parted my legs with his knee and yanked my skirt up, exposing my ass.

"That was hot, *moya koroleva*," Matthias whispered in my ear. I moaned when he slapped my ass, the stark sound reverberating through the quiet office. Matthias chuckled. "Such a dirty girl for me, Ava." He pushed down my underwear until they were resting at my ankles.

"Fuck," I moaned again, satisfaction brimming through me when he pushed two fingers inside me.

"So wet for me already," he groaned. "Did threatening Serena turn you on? Does violence make you horny and wet for me, my little psycho?"

He slapped my ass harder when I didn't answer, the action shoving me tighter against the desk, the edge digging into my waist.

"I asked you a question."

"Yes," I breathed, pushing back against his fingers. "Putting that bitch in her place made me horny for you."

"Good girl." Fuck, I clamped down on his fingers when he said those words. The bastard chuckled. Fabric rustled behind me, and I turned my head to look at what he was doing. A small yelp burst from my lips as his hand tangled in my hair and he wrenched my head back, preventing me from looking anywhere but in front of me. "Eyes front, Ava."

He let go of my hair when I did as I was told and trained my eyes on the small picture of me on his desk. Tears sprang to my eyes when I saw it, an emotion I didn't want to name burrowing into my heart. The photo was of my first day teaching at the compound. I was smiling, hair up in a messy bun. I don't remember anyone taking a picture.

Soft silk slid around my neck. His tie. Matthias pulled,

the silk going taut against my throat, forcing me to arch my back to keep it from strangling me.

"Let's play," he whispered, his voice low and husky. He pulled his fingers out of my pussy to open his zipper. My body trembled in anticipation at the sound. I felt the hard length of him rubbing against my folds, coating it in my juices. I was a hot dripping mess down there.

"Matthias." In one swift motion, he filled me up, burying himself to the hilt. The cinch of the tie around my neck and the feel of the edge of the desk grinding against my clit had my nerve endings lit up like Times Square on New Year's Eve.

"Fuck, *Krasnyy*," he groaned. "I could stay buried in you forever." Removing his cock until just the tip remained, he slammed into me again, the desk sliding along the floor a few inches.

"Jesus," I cursed as he did this a few more times, pulling nearly all the way out before aggressively shoving himself back inside of me. The tie around my neck remained just tight enough to make it hard to breathe but not enough to cut off my air supply. Not that I would have cared at this moment. I was riding high on cloud nine.

"You want to come, good girl?"

I could only nod, the cresting wave of pleasure too much for my addled brain to formulate words.

"Please," I begged as the coil in my stomach tightened further and further. It was almost there, ready to release and make me fly. If only—

"No," I cried out desperately when he suddenly stopped. Matthias chuckled darkly.

"Not yet."

"I'm going to claw your eyes out," I snarled and pushed back against him. If he wasn't going to fuck me, then I would fuck him. And it worked, for like two seconds. Then he tightened his hold on the tie and pounded into me earnestly.

"Is this what you wanted, my little psycho?" he asked me as he pounded into me over and over again. My pussy clamped down around his cock, my back arched, welcoming the rough touch he bestowed on me. "You wanted to be owned? To be fucked like the little whore you are?"

He reached between us with his free hand, finding my swollen clit. "But you're my little whore, aren't you, Red?" He pinched my clit and waited until I was gasping and writhing from the fresh pain. Matthias gave me no reprieve as he kept up his zealous rhythm.

"Matthias," I moaned, pushing back against him, trying to meet every rabid thrust, aching for the next.

"Good girl." He thrust harder, forcing my hips into the desk. "Fuck, Ava," he growled, his hips stuttering slightly and his thrusts becoming more erratic. "Beg me to let you come."

I shook my head. Fuck no, I wasn't. He slapped my ass hard and pulled on his tie. My eyes widened as my throat became completely restricted. What the fuck? Shit. I was pretty sure I just geysered even more wetness between my thighs.

"Beg me to come," he snarled dangerously, not allowing me room to breathe or pull back.

"Please let me come!"

"Not enough," he growled. "Beg."

"Matthias." My body was tightening, preparing for the crash of bliss that was just out of reach. "Dammit. Please, sir, let me come. I need to—"

He pushed forward one last time, stealing the breath from my lungs when his fingers pinched my clit hard, and I suddenly unraveled. My scream was hoarse, lungs begging for air as he fucked me even harder through every roll of pleasure. His balls slapped against me, cock plowing deeper and harder into my heated pussy.

With a roar, Matthias emptied himself into me, deftly undoing the tie around my throat as he did. Panting, he leaned over, bracing himself on either side of me, hands on the desk. His teeth bit into the curve of my neck, and I arched into him, moaning his name once again.

"*Ya lyublyu tyebya, Krasnyy,*" he hummed in my ear.

"I love you, too."

And I did. I just hoped that my loving him didn't end in disappointment.

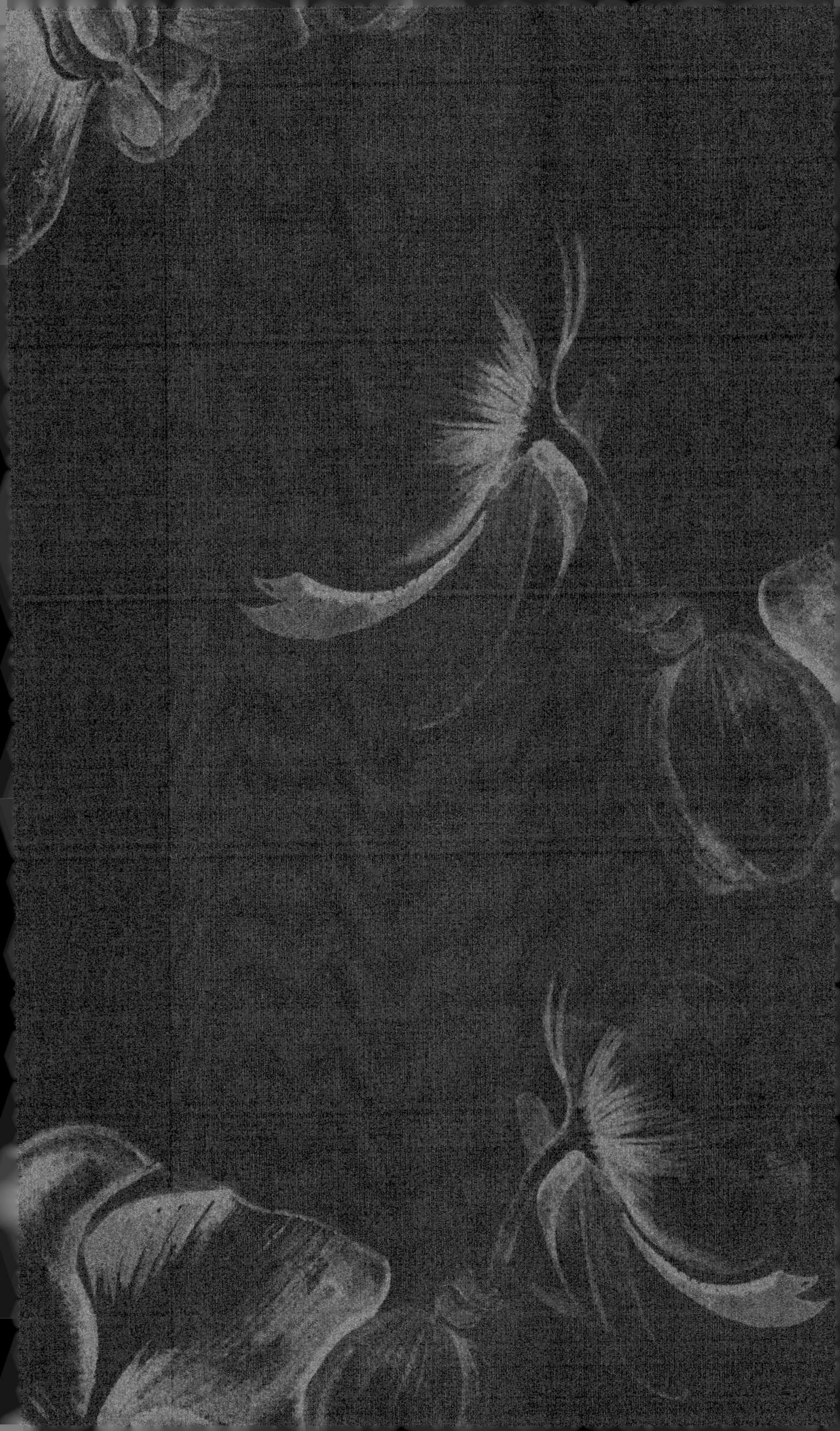

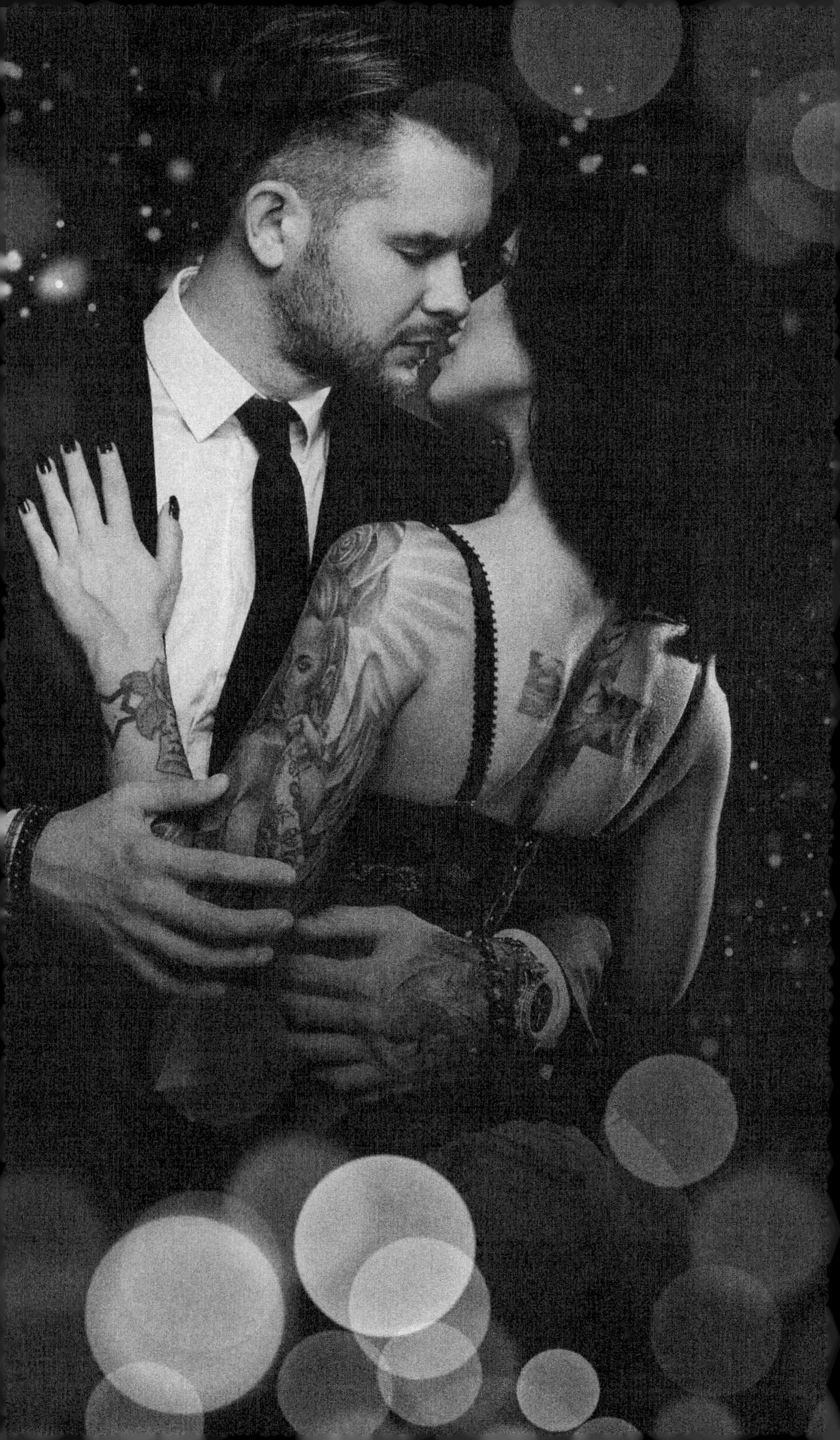

TWENTY

Ava

I stood nervously outside her new room. She couldn't see me through the one-way mirror, but from the way she tilted her head and stared at it, I had no doubt she knew I was there. Her hands were folded neatly on her lap as she waited patiently in the room while the nurse looked over her vitals and gently murmured at her, asking her questions and testing her memory and awareness.

My mother looked frail and thin sitting up in the hospital bed. Even with the Botox injections and daily stretching, her muscles had atrophied with the passing of time. Dr. Radick explained that she would need extensive physical and speech therapy in order to recover fully from her ordeal. But the prognosis was good, and that was all that mattered.

Time was no object anymore.

Even with the threat of Sheila and Remus out there.

"She won't be able to say much for a little while," Radick informed me. "Her voice box is slightly damaged from all the endotracheal tubes she had to endure over the years and also from disuse. The propofol might have messed with her memory slightly, so do not be surprised if there are gaps. It is all right if you fill her in, but if you can, try to let her remember them on her own. Guide her, but don't force her. Yes?"

I nodded at him numbly, my eyes still not believing that she was awake. She had a slight smile on her face as she continued to stare straight at me, sensing me as she always did when I was a child.

"Can I see her now?"

Dr. Radick gave me a broad smile and nodded toward the door. "After you."

Without a backward glance, I rushed through the door and to her side. It took everything in me not to throw myself into her embrace and weep like I was a child again. I knew she couldn't take that, but it didn't stop the river of tears from sliding out of my eyes.

And I was going to be so put together for her.

She smiled up at me, her eyes shining brightly.

"*M..mo...ch..roi.*"

My heart.

"Mama," my lower lip trembled, and I gently took her hand in mine. It was cold and listless, but it wouldn't be that way for long.

"Sit, Red." Matthias pulled up a chair next to the bed and guided me to sit. I didn't protest. My mother's eyes glanced up at him with interest before settling back on me.

"She's been awake for almost three hours now," Dr.

Radick told me with pride in his voice. "Your mother is a fighter."

"My wife had to get it from somewhere." Matthias smirked. At the word wife, my mother's eyebrows buried themselves in her hairline. My husband grimaced. "Sorry, *Krasnyy*." Guilt washed over him, but I waved it away. There would be no hiding anything from her.

"It's okay." I dragged my gaze away from my mother to smile up at him. "No secrets." Matthias nodded, repeating the phrase that had become a staple since he'd returned from the dead.

"A...a..." My mother's eyes misted over as she stared at me longingly.

"It's okay, Mama," I whispered, placing her hand against my warm cheek. "Everything is going to be okay now. I am so sorry for everything."

Then the gates holding back the flood opened. "I can't believe you were alive this whole time." I sobbed earnestly, clutching her hand to me like a lifeline, afraid that if I let go, she would disappear. Tears tracked down her face, sorrow imprinting itself in every fine line. The nurse gently wiped at my mother's cheeks, but the moisture kept pooling.

"How long will the listlessness last?" Matthias asked Radick as I wept.

"She still has a good amount of the cocktail in her system," he said. "Propofol, which is the most recent drug the facility was using, has a short half-life, but since she has been receiving it continually for so long, it could take up to twenty-four hours for it to completely clear her body."

"And the other drugs?"

Radick waved it off. "Minimal," he assured us. "It looks like whenever she started to wake or build a tolerance to one of the drugs used to induce comas, they would shift to another one."

Sniffling, I asked, "Isn't that dangerous?"

Radick nodded. "Extremely."

"How long before I can take her home?"

Radick smiled at me. "If everything goes well and we see an upward projection in her ability to stay conscious and we don't find anything alarming on the MRI or CT, and she takes to physical therapy, she can go home in about two weeks."

"That's so long," I argued. Matthias shot me a look, and I flushed. Out of the corner of my eye, I could see my mother watching us. Even now, she was sensing the situation and compiling information. From the way my husband's lips turned up at the edges when he looked at her, he could see it too.

Radick chuckled. "Trust me; it will go by fast," he assured me. "But let's give the patient some time to rest, and you can come back tomorrow." I frowned at him. My eyes flickered over to my mother, whose face was drawn and pale, her eyes growing heavy with sleep, and I knew he was right.

"I'll be back tomorrow, Mama." I leaned over her bed and planted a soft kiss on her temple. I didn't want to leave her. What if someone came to take her away again?

The frightened little girl inside me made an appearance after so many years, casting doubt and fear in my mind. Elias was dead, but someone had to have been paying the doctor. It had been months since his death. Surely the money would have run out.

"Something doesn't feel right," I told my husband as we settled into the back seat of the car. Matthias looked over at me.

"What do you mean?"

I rubbed at my temples, staving off the mounting migraine. "Who's been paying the clinic since Elias's death? Actually, the Ward assets were frozen a month prior to Christian murdering him, so..." I trailed off, twisting my hands in my lap. "Maybe there is another player we don't know about? Or—"

"Ava." Matthias stilled my hands, bringing them up to his mouth and kissing them gently. "No one other than Elias was paying the clinic," he assured me softly. "According to the financial records, Elias paid one giant sum of money toward the clinic every three years and provided a host of other incentives that were somewhat disreputable to keep the clinic busy and the staff fairly rich."

"Oh." The breath in my lungs whooshed out. I hadn't even known I'd been holding it in.

Matthias smiled. Jesus, he was all smiles and gentle whispers nowadays. As much as it made me swoon and made my panties dampen, his surly, growly demeanor had me wetter than a Texas whorehouse.

"Mark has been digging into everything since the night of your mother's *murder*," he relayed. "We think Elias knew Remus and Sheila were looking for her. Even though she had disappeared, your mother was still an obstacle they needed to get rid of."

"So they sent Marianne to do the job?" I remembered that, in her journal, Libby said that she had overheard the conversation between Remus and Elias.

"I sent the woman to deal with your obsession years ago..."

I relayed what I had read to Matthias.

"I'll have Mark track Elias's movements on the days leading up to the event," he assured me. "I wonder if he followed her, waited for her to leave, and then stepped in. That would also explain why it took them so long to find you."

I furrowed my brow. "What do you mean?"

"From your own memories, it sounded like everything was practically cleaned up by the time that officer found you in your hiding spot," Matthias pointed out. I didn't see how that mattered, and I told him so. "You said the officer told you the phrase your mother taught you to listen to. Correct?"

I nodded. *A chroí.* Heart. It had been our codeword for as long as I could recall.

"I think the officer knew where you were all along." The car pulled into my father's parking garage. "He had to wait until anyone who wasn't on Sully's father's payroll had left to keep you secure. He would have known about the cleanup."

I shook my head. "But Elias still found me."

"The social worker was most likely a plant," Matthias offered. "He went to do the right thing but got stabbed in the back for it. Otherwise, you might have grown up with him and his wife. He had filed a petition for custody, stating familial ties. It probably tipped off whoever worked for Elias."

"Fuck." I could have grown up in Portland with a loving family instead of in the hellhole Elias created for me every day. Love and comfort. Sighing, I set those thoughts aside. What-ifs would get me nowhere, and thinking about what could have been would only lead me down a road I didn't want to go.

This was where I was today, and I wouldn't change it for the world. My path led me to Matthias and Vas.

To my father and my siblings.

It led me back to my mother.

These were things I never would have had if it wasn't for Elias.

I couldn't be bitter about the past when it had brought me to this point, and I could only hope that the future would keep getting better.

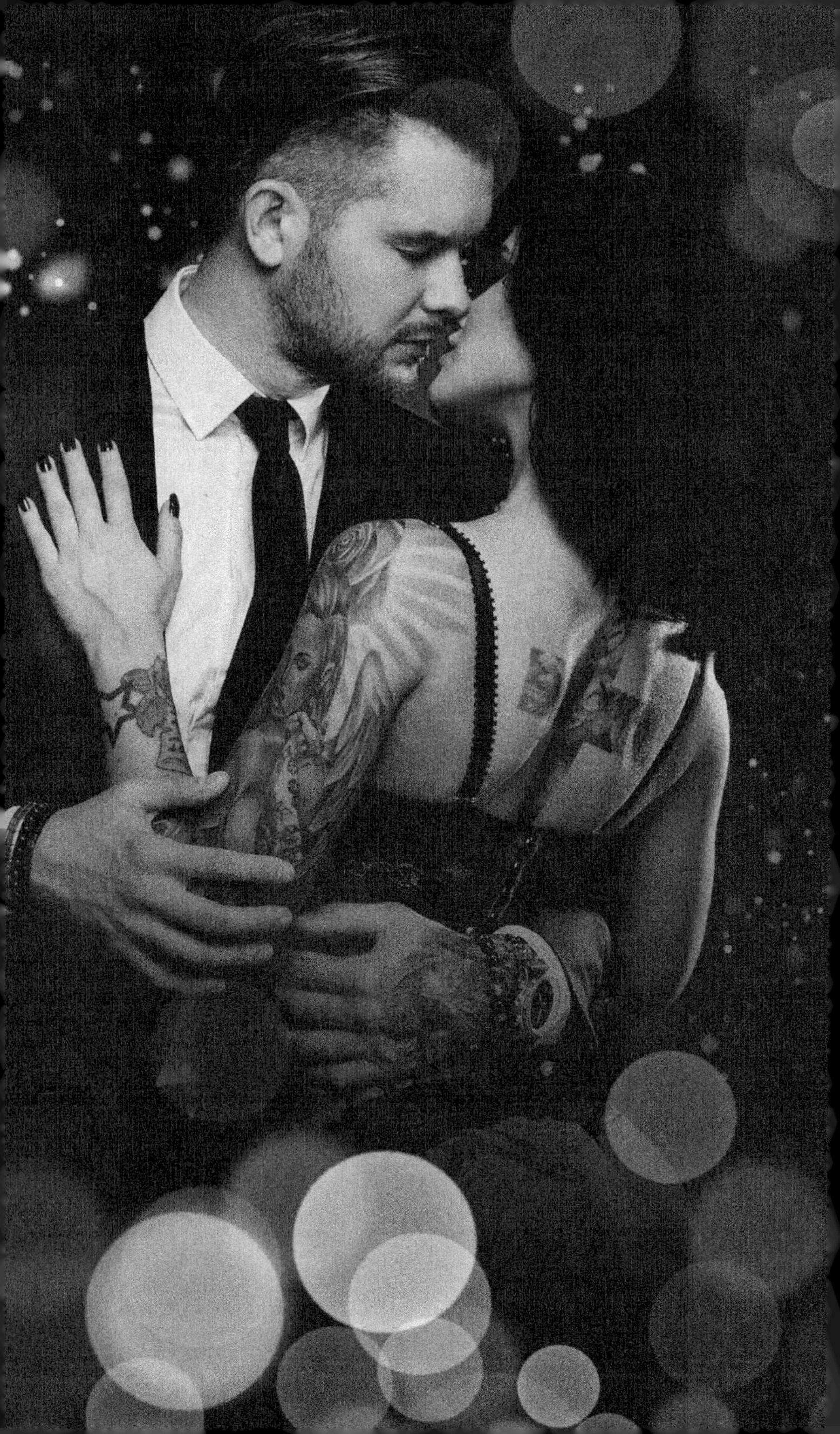

TWENTY-ONE

Matthias

Ava had been restless all night. Barely sleeping, even in the secure warmth of my embrace. We were all exhausted in the morning. Vas, Liam, Ava. Even the twins wore haggard expressions when they sat down at the dining room table that morning.

My little wife was quietly thinking to herself, her cup of coffee held tightly to her chest. I had come to realize that it was a form of security for her when she was out of sorts or contemplating something. She would drag the warmth of the cup into her and concentrate on the peace it brought her in that moment. It centered her.

Her leg bounced anxiously beneath the table, and she was biting her lip. I couldn't help but smile at how she was chomping at the bit to see her mother again. Radick had informed us, however, that we should wait until the afternoon to visit so her mother could have enough rest.

Liam had his chin in his hand, elbow braced on the table, eyes cast down in thought. I could only imagine what he was going through, finding out that the woman meant to be his wife was alive and well and that it was his current wife that had tried to murder her. It had been unanimously decided that we would wait until it was time for Katherine's discharge to include Liam in everything. Unless she asked for him, but I had a feeling that she wouldn't.

"Any news on Christian?" Ava asked me once I had kissed her good morning. I nodded.

"Mark has been monitoring internet chatter with Bridget," I said. "But your brothers have been coming up with a plan to draw him out."

Ava raised her brows in surprise and glanced over at the twins. "Ooh." She grinned excitedly. "Do tell."

"You're gonna be bait." Seamus grinned at her. I growled quietly next to my wife with my arms crossed against my chest, glaring at the smug bastard.

This was the part of the plan I didn't like. There was no mistaking that Ava had become well trained while we had been separated, but she was nowhere near master level. She was small and slight, which gave her an advantage, but if her opponent got her in a compromised position, she could have a hard time getting out of it. Especially if it were a man twice her size.

"I do make good bait," she teased, her eyes twinkling mischievously when they flickered my way before she glanced back to her brother.

"He's been following you," Kiernan sneered. "The fucking cockroach has had you under surveillance this entire time, and we barely caught on to it."

"How?" she wondered. How indeed.

"We thought the hack into the Dashkov building was

planting the virus that triggered the explosion," I told her. And we were fucking wrong about that. "It wasn't." I continued. "The hack spread a virus through our entire system that was searching for one thing only. You."

"Umm." Ava shifted in her seat uncomfortably. "What do you mean searching for me?"

"Keywords mostly," Seamus explained. "We believe that whoever set the virus in motion before the explosion has our information being filtered through a program that searches out specific keywords."

Ava still looked confused.

"It's similar to putting words into a search engine," I explained to her. "Like 'red hair' or 'Dashkov.' Any time their program picked up keywords they entered into their parameter filters, it would alert them."

"That's not creepy." She wrinkled her nose. "Wait," she looked around, "are they watching us?" She turned a fresh shade of red. "Like in your office or…" The twins exchanged mirrored looks of amusement and disgust.

"No, Red," I assured her. "My office doesn't have cameras, and your father's system is completely separate from ours."

"But," Kiernan chimed in, "we believe they've been tracking you using CCTV footage as well."

Ava's mouth parted slightly. "This is like a spy movie or some shit," she murmured. "Except I'm not James Bond." She pouted slightly at that, and I couldn't help but smile a little.

"So how do we use me as bait?" she asked.

"You've had a guard or one of us with you since we rescued you from the McDonough mansion," I told her. Ava let out a dramatic sigh.

"Is there a point to this somewhere?"

Her father chuckled. "They're going to make it look like you're alone, lass," he explained. "Make it seem like he got the drop on us while our guard was down."

"Great," she agreed. "How are we going to do that?"

Liam leaned back in his chair. "Christian doesn't know that Kenzi isn't playing his game," he told her. "He thinks she's on his side."

"That is where she's been?"

I shrugged. "Sort of."

Ava shot me a quizzical look. "If she is 'sort of' with him, then why doesn't she just kill him?"

"Because she's in contact with him, but not in person," I explained. "Paranoid motherfucker."

Ava took a deep breath and let it out. "All right." She leaned forward in her chair slightly. "Break it down for me."

I dropped Ava off at the clinic later that afternoon after we went through our plan on how to corner Christian. Kenzi would float her own plan to her brother about luring Ava away to meet her and reconcile over the past. Some undisclosed spot she would mention to him. He would be hiding with his men, and so would we.

My focus now was on finding Sheila and Remus. The pair had managed to somehow slip under the radar. Whoever they worked for had skills and deep pockets. Not even the dark web had been able to pick up a trace of them. I had thought that the organization started and stopped with Sheila, but my gut told me she was just another pawn in a game no one knew the rules to.

"From what I can find, Sheila McDonough was born Sheila Islandier, a native born Irish," Bridget told me. She'd been leading the charge on Sheila and Remus McDonough, while Mark was set on finding the mole and Christian. "On paper, she was born in the late 1950s, lived and studied in Cork, and met Seamus McDonough at age eighteen. Had Katherine McDonough less than nine months later."

"That is rather suspicious," I sighed. "And what do you mean by 'on paper'?"

Bridget clicked her tongue and shoved the small screen aside for another one.

"I mean that Sheila Islandier never existed." Jesus, this family was complicated. "There is no proper birth record for her. The one on file is a fake and the worst but, it was the fifties, so." Bridget shrugged.

"Who is she then?"

"Well." Bridget blew out her cheeks. "When you told me about the creepy-ass human barn in Portland where you believe Marianne was kept, I did a little digging." She paused to swipe left. "A lot of digging, actually, and there are things I cannot unlearn."

"Like?" I was beginning to get impatient.

"A girl fitting Sheila's description was reported missing by her family." Bridget sniffed in disdain. "Except that they reported her missing a week after the authorities believe she was taken. Now, local police couldn't tie anything back to the prominent family."

"How prominent?" I asked, eyes narrowed at the screen.

"A senator with a very large gambling debt."

Just like Senator Crowe. Except the daughter he had tried to sell was not his.

"Sounds like a theme."

Bridget snickered. "Well, I did say to myself, 'Bridg, if one disgusting baldheaded Senator sold his daughter for money, how many others did as well?' And you know what I found?"

"The jackpot?"

"The jackpot," she confirmed.

"Why am I not surprised?"

"You shouldn't be," Bridget teased. "I'm amazing."

"It would be amazing if you got to the information I need."

"Pfft," she snorted. "Spoilsport."

This girl was going to be the death of me.

"I did a facial match on the current Sheila to the girl in the photo the Senator and his wife provided to the police," she told me. "Let me tell you. The 1950s sucked. Luckily, most of the precincts nowadays are scanning everything into the system, otherwise I would have had to dig through the newspaper archives, and those archives are so messy, and you can't really find anything because they don't—"

"Bridget!"

"Right." She coughed awkwardly. "Sheila's real name is Margaret Melozzi, Italian. Born to Greg and Jane Melozzi in 1958 in Portland, Oregon. Went missing when she was three. Police chalked it up to a kidnapping, but the timeline didn't match up."

"Where are they now?" I asked.

"Dead. Died in a house fire in 1976."

"The same year she married Seamus McDonough."

Bridget nodded.

"Funny thing is," she clicked over to another screen, "there are more than five dozen cases of missing children, mostly girls, in the last sixty years."

"That can't be a coincidence."

Bridget shook her head. "It isn't," she agreed. "Especially since the one thing that links all of those children is the fact that their parents were killed on their eighteenth birthday."

I cursed under my breath. This was much bigger than anyone thought.

"What else can you tell me?"

Bridget rolled her shoulders. Her fingers flew across the neon keyboard like a rocket. Soon, the screen was filled with images, documents, and video footage. Fuck.

"Now that I know the link, I went searching for the missing children using a combination of an age progression matrix and significant facial structures that remain the same over time, like eye color, hair color, etc."

"The problem is that even though CCTV was invented in 1929, the ability to record said footage didn't come around until the 1970s when VCRs were invented," she rambled. "So anything before that is pretty done for, and honestly, most places don't store CCTV for longer than a few days after the incident unless a crime was committed or something."

"Back to the point." I guided her back toward the topic. Liam warned me she was a bit squirrely with her thoughts and often went off on tangents.

"Right." She nodded. "I dug through years' worth of newspaper articles, wedding and death announcements, funeral photos...well, my program did. I just sorted through the possibilities once it made possible matches and found several of the missing children from before the 1980s. Everyone between 1920 and the late 1940s is dead, but damn, they were some popular names."

"Anyone I would know?"

"One disappeared circumnavigating the globe."

Blyad'.

"Every heard of the Glastonbury Mountain?" she asked.

I nodded. "It was dubbed the Bennington Triangle, and from 1920 to 1950, more than ten people disappeared there. All but two of the pictures of the missing people are a direct match for the missing kids. The two that didn't match were anomalies. A college student and an eight-year-old boy."

"Could have come across something you weren't supposed to."

"I mean, the list goes on and on all the way up to five days ago when tech billionaire John Rosentry died in a penthouse fire. His daughter went missing when she was ten."

That was another anomaly.

"Don't most of the children go missing when they're toddlers?"

Bridget nodded. "It makes more sense that way. The younger the child, the easier to manipulate and retrain."

"But she was taken at ten," I mused, scratching my bearded chin. I hadn't had time to shave in the last few days, and Ava had shown her pleasure for it when I ate out her cunt this morning. "Kenzi was sold at seventeen. Crowe tried to sell Bailey at twenty-four. Why the change?"

"What if it wasn't a change?" Bridget swiveled her chair around to face me. My brow creased as I stared down at her.

"What do you mean?"

"Were operating under the assumption that whoever took those children are the same people who are buying up women, right?" I nodded. "What if they're a hydra?"

"What does a mythological creature have to do with this?"

Bridget snorted. "Not the creature itself," she chuckled. "The hydra has one main body and several heads that can easily be regenerated. Some even say that when you cut one head off, two take its place. So, what if taking children is one head of the total body, acting on its own independence from the other heads?"

Woman had a point. A good one too, especially in this day and age. If Bridget's theory was correct, it meant that there were far more working parts out there than we realized. We knew that Sheila and Remus worked for some type of secret society that spanned generations. Was it old enough to have been responsible for the missing children in the 1920s, or was the society simply another head?

"Did you find anything on Remus McDonough?" I asked while we were on the topic. Bridget nodded and turned back to her laptop.

"Once you told me that they were removing twins at birth, I traced the steps of Ava's grandmother and found that she gave birth at Dublin Memorial," she told me. "The hospital recorded five live births that day, but only four birth certificates were issued."

"Remus."

"I tracked his progress and digital footprints through the years," she told me. "Luckily Ireland is very paranoid about domestic terrorism and the resurgence of the IRA, so they store footage for decades."

She pulled up a picture of a man I recognized to be Seamus McDonough. But it wasn't. The eyes were slightly off in the photo, colder than the ones Kavanaugh had shown me. His nose was crooked, most likely from being broken several times, and there were several symbolistic tattoos I didn't recognize.

"His name is Remus O'Connor," Bridget told me. "Once I found a slightly modern photo of him, it became a lot easier to track his childhood. He was adopted by the O'Connor family when he was four years old. Where he was before that, I have no idea, but I have a sneaking suspicion it was in a place like the Portland barn. A sort of... waiting place for women and children to be trained or kept until they're needed.

"The O'Connors weren't good people, Matthias. They were heavily involved in the IRA until they were killed in a bombing in 1997, two days before the cease-fire. From what I can tell, it was a setup by this ghost organization. Events like Bloody Sunday and the Belfast bombings, those were all setups by the O'Connors to keep the war going. To profit off it."

"I'm assuming, then, that their deaths led to the cease-fire."

"Bingo."

The question was what did whoever was running the heads of the hydra have to gain from an Irish civil war? If they planted a four-year-old Remus within the family of the ranking IRA members, why did they wait to have them killed?

Unless Remus went rogue at some point. But when?

Bailey had mentioned that Madam Therese made the comment that two of her assets had gone rogue. We assumed one of those assets had been Kenzi, but now that I looked back, it didn't make sense because we hadn't broken her cover yet. What if she had been talking about Sheila and Marianne?

We knew that Remus was Katherine and Marianne's biological father. We also knew that sometime between Katherine's graduation and her kidnapping, Seamus was murdered and replaced by Remus. Had it been so well organized that even the people who controlled their assets hadn't known about the replacement?

Fuck, this mystery was getting more tangled by the

second, and I wondered if there would ever be a time we would unravel it, or if our lives would continue to be caught up in a web we'd never escape from.

"How is she doing?" I stood in the hallway just outside Katherine's medical suite, hands in my pockets, as I watched the woman gently stroke her daughter's hair. At some point, Ava had fallen asleep in her chair, slumped over, her head resting on her arms at the edge of her mother's bed. The woman had a content smile on her face as she gazed lovingly down at the daughter she had sacrificed so much for.

"I'm impressed with the progress she has made already," Radick admitted proudly. "Then again, she has gone through this several times in the past, so it's not too surprising. She still doesn't have much vocal capability, but she's been practicing by saying Ava's name all day."

"Good." I nodded. As I stared through the window, I wondered how much Katherine McDonough knew about her family. Had she known about Marianne prior to the night of her supposed murder? How long had she known Remus had been masquerading around as Seamus?

"I am slightly concerned about her mental well-being, however."

My head turned toward the good doctor. "What do you mean?"

"Katherine has been through some significantly traumatizing experiences," he elaborated and gestured to her chart. "The doctor who had been taking care of her left extensive medical notes documenting every time Elias came to visit her."

"While she was awake, of course."

Radick visibly swallowed.

"No." His jaw clenched angrily. "I wish I could say that any doctor wouldn't allow for such an abhorrent breach of medical conduct, but I'm afraid that isn't the case here."

There was not much that could turn my stomach, but what the doctor was implying churned my insides, bilious and sour.

"How many times?" Fuck, I didn't want to know the answer, but I asked it anyway.

"Once or twice a month for years, and that isn't counting whatever he did to her while she was awake."

My teeth ground together, jaw aching as I struggled to keep from being sick. There were times when such things were appropriate under consensual role playing, but this was not one of them. As soon as I was done here, that doctor was going to find out what it meant to feel real pain.

"Any lasting damage?"

"She won't be able to have any more children." Radick huffed out a breath. "It looks like her ovaries were damaged during the original incident, but as far as I can see, there is no lasting physical damage from the extra involuntary proclivities." He spat the last few words out angrily.

Blyad'.

"I suggest a therapist," Radick continued. "Once or twice a week to start, and the schedule can adjust from there. Maybe some antidepressants."

I nodded my head to let him know I heard him, but I wouldn't agree to medicating Katherine without her permission. She had already been violated without her consent. I wouldn't allow that to happen again, even on something like this.

"Thank you, doctor," I told him sincerely before striding

into Katherine's room. "Hello, Katherine." I spoke softly so I wouldn't disturb my slumbering wife. Walking over to her, I bent down to pick her up in my arms when a hand slapped against my wrist.

Startled, I looked up into the cold, lush emerald eyes of her mother, which were narrowed at me in warning. There was a storm on her face as she looked at me in a silent warning. Radick hadn't been exaggerating about her improvements. Her grip, although still weak, held more weight than it had last night when she'd barely been able to move it.

"It is all right," I whispered to her calmly. "I am only going to move her to the bed. She will have a neck cramp and a backache tomorrow if she stays like this."

Katherine eyed me suspiciously for a moment, and I realized that Ava must have told her mother everything about us. Sure as hell wasn't going to earn me any brownie points. She glared at me a few more seconds before releasing my hand and looking mildly ashamed when I laid Ava down on the large bed beside her.

Straightening up, I looked Katherine in the eye.

"No one will ever tear you two apart again. I promise you that."

She closed her eyes, a tear escaping down her pale face. When she opened them again, they were clearer and full of gratitude I didn't deserve.

"Thank..." She paused to take a slow breath. "...you."

"You don't need to thank me, Katherine," I told her softly. "I always protect my family."

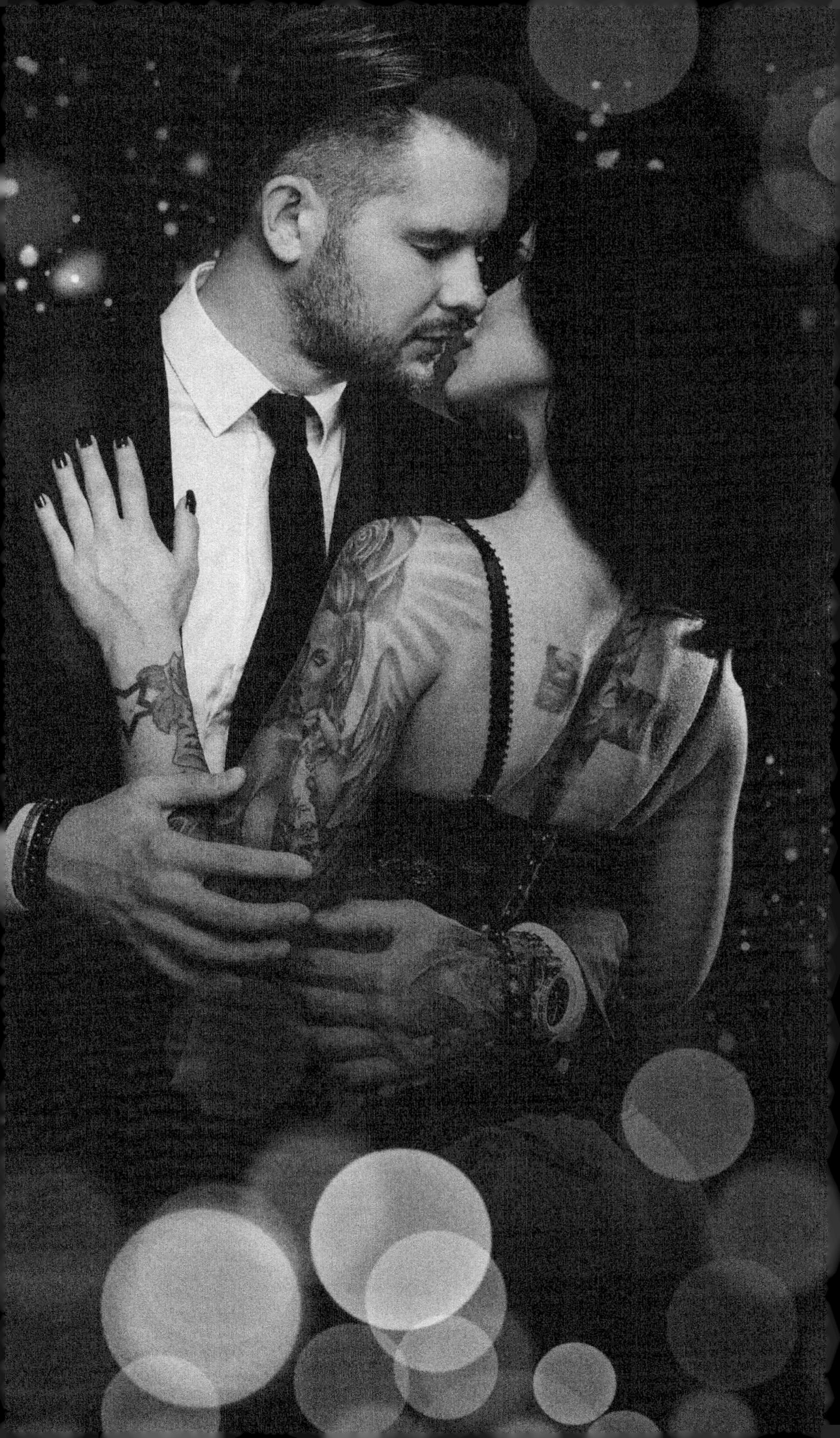

TWENTY-TWO

Liam

I paced nervously around the entertainment room, waiting for their arrival. It had been nearly a month since Katherine had woken up, and today was the day she was being discharged from the hospital. I'd prepared her room across from mine. It was the only one I was able to modify to fit her accommodations.

Katherine was still weak, mostly using a cane to get around for short distances, but anything past that required a wheelchair. The bathroom was also the only one that had a walk-in shower instead of a tub. I had outfitted it for my mother several years ago, in case something was ever to happen. She'd cursed me out and thrown several rags at my face, calling me an ungrateful son and that she was fresh as a spring chicken.

Since everything had gone down with Marianne, I was adamantly avoiding the house we had shared together. Not that I had ever been there much to begin with. It was always too ostentatious for me, but Marianne insisted on a large, opulent home for entertaining.

"I can walk perfectly fine, you know." Katherine's voice drifted through the space. The elevator doors opened on a ding, but I had been too immersed in my thoughts to hear it.

"I know, Mama." Avaleigh sighed dramatically. "We're just trying to make sure you don't tire yourself out too fast."

Katherine snorted dismissively. "I'll have you know... Liam." Her gaze had caught me lingering in the doorway, and she'd left her sentence unfinished. I hadn't laid eyes on Katherine McDonough in nearly twenty-four years, but seeing her again, even after all this time, still took my breath away. She was just as gorgeous today as she was the day I met her.

Her ginger hair was set on top of her head in a messy bun. Avaleigh's signature look. Her lush emerald eyes were still bright and full of life, but there was a strip of sorrow there that I had never seen before.

"Hello, Kat." I breathed her name, my voice low and husky, as I took in her lithe form. Katherine had always been shapely, with solid hips and muscular thighs that squeezed me tight when I pounded into her sweet cunt. Now, her body was thinner, less defined from years upon years of tube-fed nutrients.

The gorgeous minx stood from her chair, hands and legs shaking slightly with the effort to stand. Ava handed her the wooden handcrafted cane I had designed specifically for her discharge. She took several shaky steps toward me and stopped when we were nearly toe to toe.

I breathed in her scent.

Sweet honeysuckle.

Slap.

Avaleigh gasped in horror behind her mother, whose aim was still spot on. Stretching my jaw to ease the pain, I brought my hand up to massage the area, chuckling beneath my breath.

"Haven't lost your power behind that swing, I see."

She didn't say anything, just stared up at me with tears of anger in her eyes. I doubted they were tears of happiness and joy. We definitely wouldn't be falling into old times together anytime soon, as much as my dick jumped at the thought.

"Do it again!" one of the boys shouted from behind me. I let out a long sigh, my eyes falling closed as I counted to ten. "We would love to get a video of that for our TikTok."

Startled, Katherine stepped back, eyes wide as she took in my twin sons, who were only months younger than their sister. Funny thing was, they didn't look anything like Marianne with their ginger locks and green eyes. The only thing they seemed to inherit was her ability to turn up at the worst possible moment.

"I..."

Seamus strolled up next to me and smiled down at her. His charming smile disarmed her for a moment, and she simply stared at him, mouth parted slightly in surprise. "Hi." He held out his hand for her to shake. "I'm Seamus, the better-looking twin, as you can clearly see."

Katherine barked a laugh, her body jumping slightly, as if she was surprised by her reaction. Gingerly, she took his hand and gave him a weary smile.

"Katherine."

"Oh, we know who you are." Kiernan smirked next to his brother.

"Our da has been telling us stories about you since we were in diapers." Seamus chuckled.

"Like about the time you put Mentos in his toilet before he sat down to take a shit." He grinned. "Or the time you dragged his air mattress out to the lake, and he woke up the next morning in the middle of it."

Ava was nervously biting her lip behind her mother, afraid of the reaction she might have to the sudden bombardment of memories and my oldest sons—Marianne's oldest sons. None of us had bothered to factor them in to the equation when we built out the plan to bring her here. To bring her home.

Her face was drawn in sorrow as she stared at my sons, but I could see a glimmer of affection sitting just beneath the surface. These may be the children of the woman who nearly murdered her, but unlike her...sister—Jaysus, that was still odd to say—there was no hostility to be found.

Tears pricked at the corners of her eyes, and I went to shoo the two boys away, but someone beat me to it.

"Seamus and Kiernan Kavanaugh, what in blazes do you think you're doing?" My mam hustled her way into the entertainment room, hands on her hips, staring at her grandsons. "Honestly, making such a ruckus when she just arrived. The poor girl will think you were raised in a barn."

"Technically, the compound was an old barn, so..."

"Get out with you." My mother snapped her towel at the two as she stomped our way. "Out. Out." Seamus laughed wildly, winking at Katherine before he and Kiernan hopped off to meet their girlfriend.

My mother shook her head in disbelief as she stared after the twins. "Honestly, now." She sighed and turned toward us. Her smile brightened when she saw Katherine, eyes brimming with raw emotion as she gazed at the woman before her. "Well," she took a quick breath, "you're just as beautiful as the last day I saw you." My mother opened her arms. "Welcome home, *iníon*."

At the word, daughter, the tears Katherine had been holding back fell from her eyes like a dam breaking. She fell forward into Mam's warm embrace, crying into her shoulder, while my mother whispered into her hair.

"It's all right now, love," she cooed at her, running a hand up and down her back. "You're home. You're safe, and you're family."

It was at that moment right there that I decided I would slay every last one of Katherine's demons, no matter the cost. Even if it never made things completely right between us again.

I had to at least try.

She didn't know it yet, but Katherine McDonough was mine.

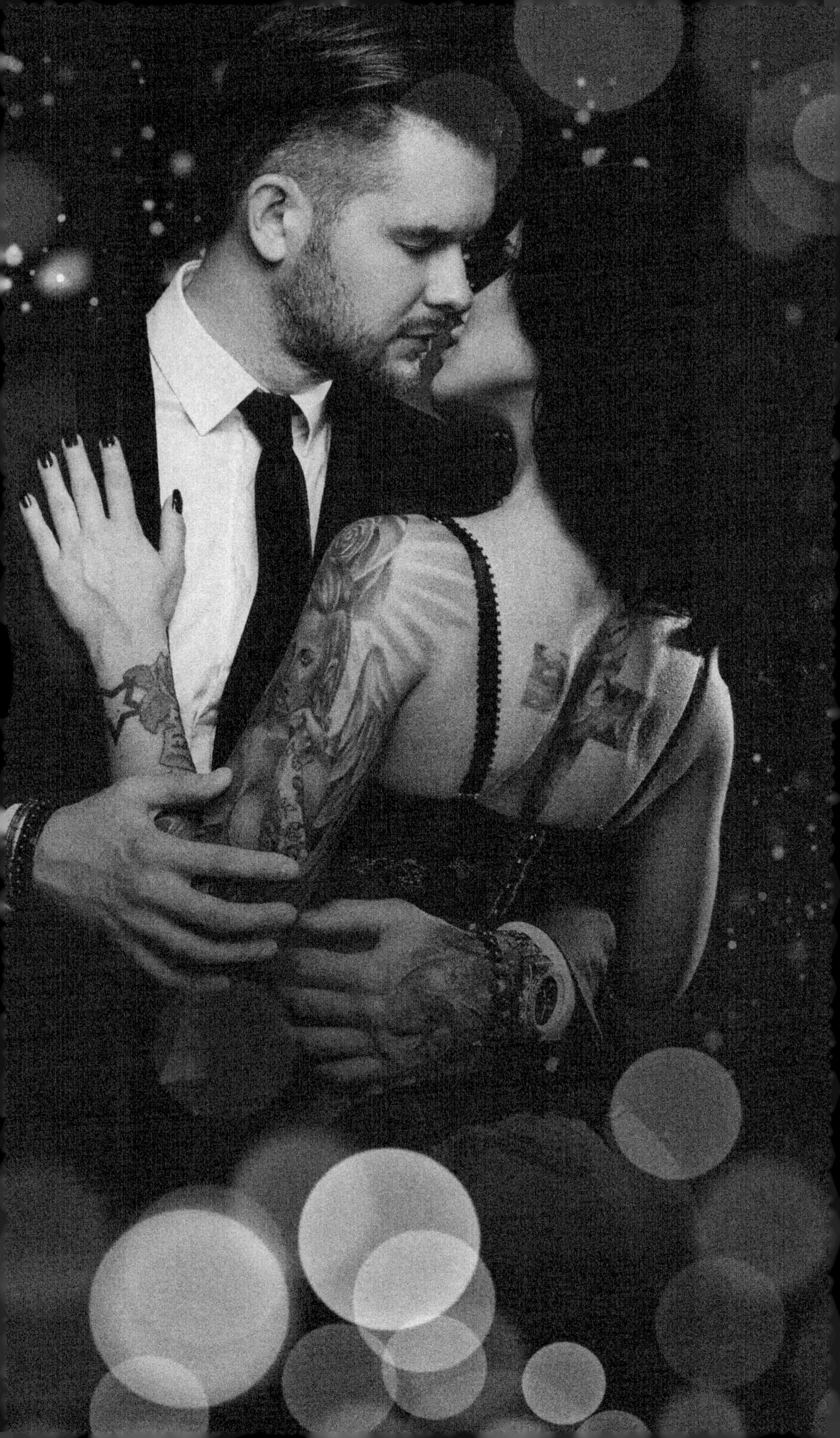

TWENTY-THREE

Matthias

Things had become uncharacteristically quiet over the past few weeks. There had been no sign of Christian. Even Kenzi hadn't heard from him, and that made the hairs on the back of my neck stand on end.

A storm was brewing, and we needed to be prepared for what was going to bring. The cleanup of the Dashkov building had commenced over a month ago and was nearly finished. Soon, we could start on the new construction. An eco-friendly high-rise without the added explosives.

It was a waste if you asked me, but Ava had been adamant about not having any type of self-destruct mechanism this time. She had told me we would just have to come up with a less dramatic way of keeping our secrets from getting into the wrong hands.

Boring.

"What about acid?" Dima questioned. "Have a vat of it

in the basement to dispense with what we wanted to get rid of."

Andrei shot him a look that clearly said *what the fuck man?* I chuckled.

"And how would you get everything down there by the time the FBI showed up to your doorstep?" he asked with an edge of condescension dripping into his voice.

"Laundry chutes on each floor that lead directly down to the basement and into the tub of acid." Dima winked at him playfully. "Duh."

Andrei's lips turned down in distaste, and he shook his head. "And you call yourself a made man."

Dima splayed his palm across his chest dramatically, a scandalized look of shock splashed across his face. "I will have you know I am a very well-made man."

I groaned. This was why we could not have people over. "Don't you have things to be doing?" I asked him. Dima shrugged.

"Everything is set to go," he assured me confidently. "I've got guns hiding in plants, under tables, inside cabinets, behind cushions. You name it, and there is a gun there to be found."

"Good," I praised him. "Now go do your rounds and stop mucking about." Dima got to his feet and gave me a half-assed salute.

"Sir," he winked, "yes, sir."

"Cheeky fucking bastard," I muttered under my breath as he strode from the room. "One day I might still drown in him in a vat of acid."

Andrei chuckled. "Just dump him down the chute."

The two of us laughed easily together.

"How is Ivan doing in London?" I asked curiously.

Since leaving him there to establish his reign as *Pakhan*, I hadn't heard from him much. Andrei smiled.

"He is doing well," he told me. "Ivan was born to be a leader." He paused, his gray eyes meeting mine. "Just like you."

I shrugged nonchalantly. "I would not be where I am today without Tomas," I admitted humbly. "He took me in and saw potential."

"I thought it somewhat unconventional that his son, Vasily, is your *Sovietnik*." He laughed.

"Vas is rather unconventional himself," I admitted with a fond smile. "I couldn't ask for a better second."

Andrei nodded his head. "I must admit that your entire operation here is much different from most," he mused. "Tomas himself had always had grand ideas that were outside the norm, though, so it isn't surprising."

"There was a lot of pushback at first." I took the last few sips of my whiskey. "Those who didn't agree with it left, and those who were willing to follow me were rewarded. They may be soldiers, but they are also family, and I try to treat them as such."

Pride shone in my father's eyes as he stared at me.

"A leader is only as good as the men who stand behind him."

That was something we both agreed on.

"Any news on mother's grave?" I asked curiously. I'd forwarded all the information Serena gave me to him, knowing he had the better resources to bring her home.

Andrei bit his lip. "The cemetery is a big place." He sighed. "But I have my best men working on it."

"If it helps, I can have one of my analysts move our satellite in that region," I offered. "Maybe we can try some thermal scans or even Lidar to map out one section at a time. I doubt there are many graves with two bodies in them."

Andrei hummed thoughtfully and inclined his head. "Thank you. I would like that."

"There isn't any reason to thank me," I told him mournfully. "She was my mother, and I failed to protect her."

It was something that had always weighed on my heart. I had let Kirill murder my mother without fighting back. He took her from me, and I had done nothing. Sometimes, she still haunted my dreams, her pale face peeking up from the dark alongside the brother I had been forced to kill. If only I had been stronger, a better fighter. If only—

"Stop berating yourself, Matthias," he reprimanded me. Andrei leaned forward in his chair, elbows resting on his knees, his stormy eyes roaming my tormented face. "You know she named you after her father. Matthias Belov was your grandfather. He was a hardworking man who moved to America with his only daughter, your mother, after his wife died. Your grandfather and your mother had a relationship most would dream to have. He was loving and supportive. When I came in and took her away, he was happy for her despite her choice in men."

"Did she know you were heir to the *Bratva*?" I snorted.

"She did." He chuckled lightly. "We never told her father, though. I wanted to keep my life." The two of us laughed. "My point is, you were only a boy, Matthias, and you did the best you could with what you were given. Amalia did the same for you."

I sighed, running a hand through my mussed hair.

"I don't have any ill will toward you, my son," Andrei murmured. His gray eyes were glassy as he stared at me. "What happened with your mother and Antony was not your fault. It was Kirill and my blindness that led to their deaths."

Pursing my lips, I shook my head.

"You could never have known, Father, that he would betray you."

He blew out a breath. "Kirill had always been someone to seek what was best for him first," he admitted. "And I should have seen that. But none of that matters now because it led us here. You never would have made the connections you made or forged the bond you have here with your brothers if it hadn't been for his treachery. We may have lost people, but we gained so many as well."

My father stood from his chair, placing his empty tumbler on the table to his right.

"I learned a lot over the years," he admitted sadly. "After Ivan left me, I was lost, drowning in a black pit of despair because I had nothing left. It took me a long time to realize that if I kept looking at the past and imagining what could have been, I would never have a future."

"Goodnight, *otets*." I smiled up at him.

"Goodnight, *syn*."

I sat at my laptop for a few more hours, running through weekly reports from my men. Despite everything that was going on, I still had a *Bratva* to run, as well as some of my other businesses. Nicolai took care of most of the clubs and bars, but he still reported to me and kept me in the loop. Ava had taken over running Arctic Security so that Leon could step down from the more public eye. He never liked being the face of most of our companies. He liked to get his hands dirty too much.

Setting my laptop aside, I stood from the chair and stretched, my sore muscles groaning in protest at the movement. Fuck, I was getting old. Taking the elevator up to the residential floor, I quietly entered the room we'd been staying in while the house I bought was being renovated. It didn't need much renovation, honestly, since it was fairly new construction, but there were safety features I wanted added, and the houses next door were being torn down to make room for a larger lawn.

"Not again," I muttered under my breath when I found our bed empty and still made. It was nearly midnight, and she still hadn't come back to the room. I was all for motherly bonding time, but this was getting ridiculous.

Shaking my head, I exited the room, leaving the door open slightly for when I came back, and took the elevator up one more floor to where Liam had housed Katherine in the suite across from his. I turned the doorknob and quietly padded across the living room carpet and through the open bedroom door.

There my wife was, cuddled into her mother's side like a kitten, on top of the covers while her mother slept peacefully beside her. Stepping up to the bed, I leaned over and drew Ava into my arms. She whimpered as I pulled her away and into my chest.

"No," she whispered grumpily, her eyes still half closed. "I want to stay."

I shook my head. "Not tonight, Red," I told her. "You are my wife, and you will be in my bed."

Her cute face twisted into a scowl, the sleep washing from her eyes as she glared up at me, her nose scrunched angrily. Damn, why did that make my dick twitch?

"She needs me," Ava insisted haughtily.

I stared down at her as I walked us out of the room and

into the elevator. "And I need my wife," I told her. "You can't use your mother to put distance between us, *Krasnyy*." Ava bit her lower lip guiltily. Yes, I knew exactly what she had been doing, and I was not going to stand for it. "How am I supposed to show you that what we have is real if you don't allow me to? I have given you time to spend with your mother to remold the bond you lost, but now it is time to give her some distance."

"But she shouldn't be alone," Ava whispered, her eyes growing sad. Shit, I hope she didn't cry. I never did well when she cried.

"Ava." I nudged the door open to our room with my foot and let it slide fully closed. Carrying her to our room, I set her gently down on the bed and crawled over her, bracing my arms on either side of her head. Instantly, her body relaxed, feeling my heat and the weight of me pressed down on her. "This is going to be hard for you to hear, *malyshka*, but she has been alone for a very long time. Did you ever think that maybe you are overstimulating her by spending every moment with her?"

From the way her mouth shifted and her cheeks heated, she hadn't.

"My sweet little psycho," I whispered into her hair.

"I just want her to know she isn't alone anymore," Ava hiccuped. Her legs came around my waist, and she held herself tight to my body.

"And she will know that for the rest of her life, baby," I assured her. "I promise you that, but you need to give her some room to find her own way."

Ava frowned slightly, the wheels in her mind turning, processing what I was telling her. I didn't tell her any of this to be cruel or to earn more of her attention. There was no need to when I could simply take it. But I needed her to understand that if she didn't let up a little on her mother, she might do unintentional damage. It was easy to see that Katherine loved and adored her daughter, but there were times that her face would twist with frustration, quickly followed by regret whenever Ava plastered herself to her mother's side.

My little wife was excited to have her mother back, and there was nothing wrong with her enthusiasm, but the last time Katherine had seen her daughter was when she was eleven. The woman had been on her own since then, surviving abuse that no woman should have to endure. It didn't surprise me that Ava's excitedness rubbed at her.

Ava's chin quivered as she nodded. She understood what I was saying, but it was hard for her. She'd spent nearly her whole life fantasizing about her mother being alive, and now that wish had come true, and she wanted to hold on to it for dear life. Bringing her hand to my jaw, she uttered the three words I would never tire of hearing. "I love you."

"No more hiding." I glared down at her playfully, and she smirked, mischief lighting up her emerald eyes.

"Promise," she whispered, and with a wicked grin, she began tugging up my white shirt. I swept it over my head and watched her eyes trail hungrily over my chest and abs. Licking her lips, she reached out and ran her fingers over my muscles. Closing my eyes, I relished the feel of her warm hands caressing my skin. I could feel her tracing over my tattoos. The Vor stars on my shoulders that signified that I was a made man and bowed to no one, the color spectrum of Russian prison tattoos I'd gotten during my stint in lockup. I was fourteen at the time and served six months for armed robbery.

Rising to my knees, I straddled her and sat back on my

heels while my hands drifted beneath her nightshirt. I peeled it away, slowly revealing the creamy expanse of her skin, until every inch of her was exposed to me.

"So beautiful," I murmured, throwing the fabric aside to join my shirt on the floor. Reaching down, I cupped her pussy and pushed two fingers inside her heat. Damn, so tight and wet. How had I gotten so lucky? Ava moaned, her hips shifting off the bed to thrust my fingers deeper inside of her. I pressed my thumb to her clit, rubbing slow circles around the bundle of nerves.

"You like this, Red?" I whispered huskily. Her eyes met mine, molten pools of hot desire, and nodded. "Do you want to come on my fingers, good girl?"

Her light blush was barely visible in the darkened room, but I could see it tinting her cheeks as she bit her lip shyly and shook her head.

"I'm not going to do anything unless you tell what you want, Ava." She bit her lip harder as her breathing grew more rapid when I increased my strokes inside her cunt. "Come on, baby. Tell me what you want."

When she still didn't respond, I removed my fingers from inside her. Ava mewled in disappointment, her eyes following my fingers, wet with her arousal.

"Suck," I growled, bringing the fingers to her mouth. Ava opened her mouth obediently and sucked on my fingers, swirling her tongue around them like she would my cock.

"Please," she whispered with my fingers still stuffed in her mouth. "I need you." Her words, dripping with wanton desire, did something to me. I rumbled low in my throat and rolled onto my back so Ava was straddling me.

I quickly dropped my sweatpants down to my knees,

shoved her panties aside, and speared the redheaded minx on my cock.

"Matthias!" she screamed in pleasure when I buried myself balls deep inside her. "Fuck."

"Ride me, baby." I licked my lips and stared up at her, hands resting lazily on her hips. Ava wiggled around, setting herself where she wanted to be. She planted her hands on my chest, using them and the power of her thick thighs to bounce herself up and down on my hardened cock.

"That's it, baby," I moaned, throwing my head back into the pillow. "Just like that." Fuck, she felt so good I wouldn't be able to hold on for long. Ava rode me like it was her job, ass slapping against my balls, her arousal drenching me. The sounds of our lovemaking filled the room, and it was then I realized I must have been in heaven.

This was heaven, and she was my angel.

"Jesus." I sat up, lifting her off my cock despite her protests, and turned her around so she was facing away from me. Ramming her back down on my cock, I took control. The view of her ass bouncing before my eyes made my dick grow harder and my balls ache. "You're perfect, baby," I whispered to her. "So fucking tight around me. Choking my dick like a fucking champ. Beg me to make you come."

This time, she didn't hesitate before pleading with me to let her come.

"Make me come on your cock," she moaned. "Please, I need to come."

Smirking, I slapped one ass cheek, then the other before running my thumb through the arousal leaking onto my stomach. She was still riding me hard, and I was thrusting up to meet her every time.

"Good girl," I grunted and shoved my thumb into her ass.

"Oh, god," she screamed as she clenched tightly down on my cock. I fucked her hard through her orgasm, my thumb still buried in her ass, plunging in and out in time with my dick.

"Shit, you clamp so hard on my dick when you come," I breathed. My rhythm faltered as my pending release grew closer, and it wasn't long before I buried my cock deep inside her and let the waves of euphoria sweep over me.

Fuck, this was indeed heaven.

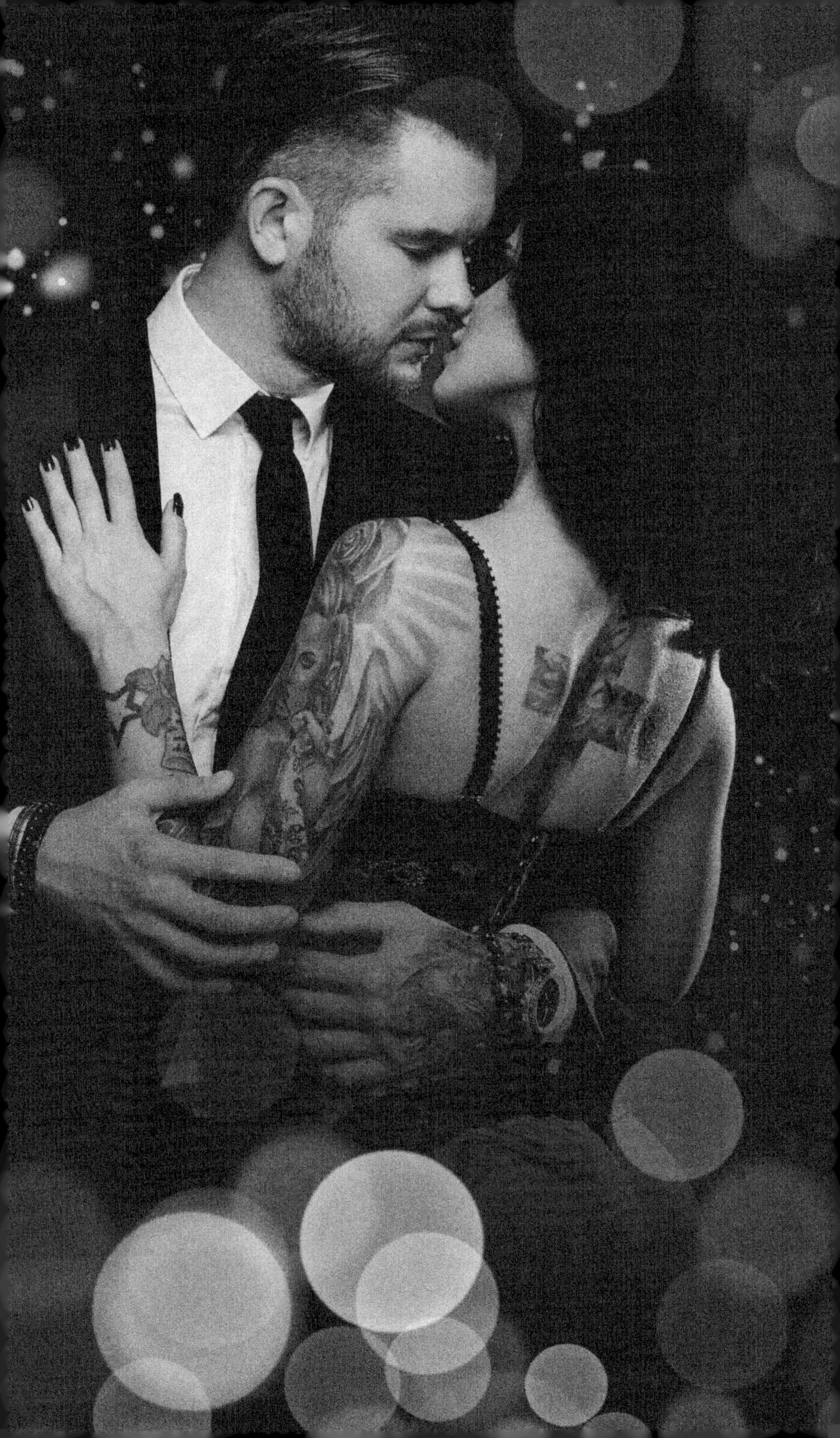

TWENTY-FOUR

Ava

It was early when I woke. The sun barely peeked over the tops of the buildings. Matthias was already gone, his side of the bed still warm. It was expected, though. He had an early morning appointment with one of the suppliers on the East Coast. Some of the shipments had been hijacked en route, and it wasn't looking good.

I showered quickly and dressed, not wasting time washing on my hair. A bun would do just fine, and since I was spending most of the day at the bar, I opted for a pair of black jeans and a gray off the shoulder sweater with simple black flats.

Since it was only around five, I took the elevator down to the bar instead of the family floor. The kitchen staff would be prepping for lunch, and a hot carafe of coffee would already be made. Maybe I could convince the chef to whip me up some eggs, too.

Stepping off the elevator, I strode into the main dining area and toward the bar. The stench of copper filled the air, and it was unusually quiet. Where was everyone? Normally, you could hear the clanking of pots and pans through the service door and the chef yelling obscenities like an Irish Gordon Ramsey knockoff.

"I'd stop right there if I were you." A voice drifted through the empty bar as I approached the kitchen doors. Then there was the click of a gun. Fuck, the bitch couldn't let me have my coffee first?

"Marianne," I drawled her name in a bored tone as she stepped out from behind the service doors and the bar, her gun level with my face. "You look like shit."

Her strawberry blond hair was slicked back in a ponytail, and her eyes were tear-stained and puffy. She'd collected quite a few bruises since I had seen her last. They snaked up her arms, and the ones on her throat had begun to turn a sickly yellow.

Whoever had done that to her wasn't a happy person.

"Shut up," she snapped. Her grip tightened on the small revolver in her hand—a .38 lady. Nothing special, but it would suck if I got shot with it. "You ruined everything," she hissed at me. "Everything. Just like your whore of a mother."

Shrugging my shoulders, I yawned, already bored with where this conversation was heading. She was spewing the same old shit.

"Is that what you told my mother the night you killed her?" I asked, knowing full well it wouldn't be long before my father or one of the twins came downstairs for their own cup of morning coffee. Marianne sneered at me. "Oh, come on. Just between us girls. You can tell me anything, I promise."

Her lips were shut tighter than Fort Knox.

"Why don't you tell me about how you screamed at her that Liam was yours," I taunted. "That she took everything from you. How you were never her friend and whispered your secrets in her ear before you left her to die."

Marianne let out a sharp, mocking laugh. "What are you trying to do, little girl?" she asked, her lips splitting into a demented smile, showcasing her pearly white teeth. "Get me to confess to something I never did to make your story more plausible? I never hurt your mother. I was her best friend. *You* are the one who orchestrated all of this. *You* are the puppeteer. So jealous of what we had here that you had to go and try to tear it apart."

Huh? "What are you talking about?"

"Don't be stupid, little girl," she spat venomously. "You want your father all to yourself. Admit it. Want to take everything you didn't have. What doesn't belong to you. Don't play stupid."

My god, the bitch was unhinged.

Which, of course, naturally meant I was going to poke her with a stick.

"I think someone is projecting, don't you?" I held my hands up in front of me and shrugged. "I mean, you did take everything that was meant for my mother, after all."

"This is *my* family," she screamed. Yep, that ought to wake the neighbors. "Mine. Not yours. Not your mother's. Mine. Your grandmother took everything from me." She brandished the gun at me, taking a few steps closer. "Everything, you hear me? She deserved what she got just like your..."

"Mom?" Seamus stepped into the bar, his green eyes on his mother, brow creased with concern. Or maybe suspicion. It was hard to tell. Meanwhile, Kiernan, who was a few short steps behind him, looked downright hostile with his cold, dark eyes glaring daggers at the woman who gave birth to him.

Kiernan was a naturally suspicious person. Unlike Seamus, who was open and trusting, he had seen Marianne's treachery early on in his childhood. It wasn't that his twin was blind to their mother's actions, but I think, in a lot of ways, he was like I had been with Elias. Hoping that one day she would show him the parental love he had always wanted from her.

I snorted internally at the thought. Fat chance of that. The woman was a pure narcissistic sociopath.

"Seamus," she breathed.

"What are you doing?" He frowned at the gun in her hand. Marianne's face fell as she looked at her son.

"What do you mean?" she asked innocently. "Your sister has been manipulating you. Poisoning your mind against me."

Rolling my eyes, I blew out my cheeks. "Yep, that was exactly what I had been doing. Caught me. Criminal mastermind of my own making."

Marianne scowled at me.

"Put down the gun, Mother," Kiernan hissed at her, his hand going to the back of his pants.

"You don't tell your mother what to do, boy," she hissed at him, dropping the innocent face she'd been sporting seconds ago. "This is my house."

"Actually, it's mine," my father's voice boomed. Taken off guard by his sudden entrance, Marianne seized my moment of weakness and pounced. Her long nails scratched at my scalp when she grabbed a handful of my hair, wrenching me to her. With my back to her front, she placed the barrel of her gun against my temple and snarled.

"This has to end," she cried. "She's tricked you. Manipulated you. Why can none of you see it?" She dug the barrel into my temple, and I winced. That was going to leave a bruise.

"Put the gun down, Marianne," my father growled.

"I didn't do anything!" the lying bitch screamed. "It was all her. She did this to take you away from me." Now she was growing agitated, her grip on my hair harsh enough that I could feel some of the strands detaching from my scalp.

I better not end up with a bald spot.

"Oh yeah," I snorted. "I'm the criminal mastermind here. You figured out my master plan. Oh no."

I heard one of the twins snort a laugh. Seamus, most likely, but my current view only allowed me to see my father's thunderous face. Oops. Not a fan of my nervous, under pressure comedic prowess, apparently.

"Not helping." He shook his head and sighed. "Marianne, let her go and let's talk about this."

That wasn't going to happen.

"Do you think I'm stupid, Liam?" she growled. "The minute I let go of her, I'm a dead woman."

Maybe she wasn't that stupid after all.

"Whatever is going on," he held his hands out toward her, "we can figure it out."

Scoff. Once she was buried in a deep, deep grave, we could.

Damn, I really needed to take some meditation classes or something. Shit was getting dark in my head.

"She did this," Marianne screamed. "Why can't you see it? All of this has been just an elaborate setup to take everything I have. To take what I love most in the world from me. Just like Katherine."

"Keep her name out of your mouth, bitch," I snarled at

her. "The only thing you love in this world is yourself. Money and power are the two things you crave. That is it. Don't drag my mother into this unless you want me to air your dirty secrets to the world."

"I'm not the one with dirty secrets," she hissed. "Tell them how you killed your mother, little Ava. It was all you. Everything was you."

What the fuck was going on? Was this chick for real?

"They told me," Marianne insisted, turning her gaze on Liam, her eyes pleading. "Sheila and Seamus have been looking into Katherine's death, and everything points back to her." She shook the hand she had clutching my hair, pulling it at the roots, and I couldn't help the small cry that fell from my lips.

"Stop the lies, Mom," Seamus hissed. "We know everything."

Marianne scoffed. "You don't know anything," she dismissed him. "You can't even do what you're told. Look at everything now. Building alliances with motorcycle scum and putting a target on our backs because the two of you couldn't keep it in your pants. You're a disappointment."

"Enough!" Liam roared. "You will not talk to my sons that way, Marianne." Usually that tone of voice was enough to make the woman holding me in her grasp cower a bit. Or at least cow her. But this time, his warning didn't work. Something else was at play here. There was no way in hell Marianne would be this brave if she was alone.

Suddenly, the whole scenario made more sense.

Marianne wasn't trying to convince them I was guilty. She was biding her time. The question was, where were the people who were making her so bold?

"Why are you really here, Marianne?" I questioned through gritted teeth, the pain in my scalp becoming unbearable. It was more fun when it was Matthias pulling my hair. "What are you waiting for?"

"I want you to tell them the truth." Her cold eyes turned to mine. "Tell them what you did."

"Why should my daughter confess to your sins?"

All eyes turned toward my mother, who had maneuvered herself between Seamus and Kiernan. Marianne's mouth fell open, her face paling and her eyes going wide as she gaped at the ghost before her.

"That's..." Marianne stuttered, her hand loosening its hold on my hair. "You're..."

"Dead?" my mother finished. "One would think so after the damage you did." My mother flicked the cane in her hand, twirling it in a circle. "With this."

Where the fuck had my mother gotten that? In her hand, she was holding a silver crossed cane. The lacquer on the wood was peeling, and the cross was bent at an odd angle.

"Jesus," I whispered under my breath.

"I've never seen that before." Her left eye twitched at the lie. My mother raised a brow in disbelief.

"Really?" she mocked. "You don't remember the tool you used to nearly beat me to death all those years ago? How odd."

"I didn't have anything to do with that," Marianne insisted. "I was here. Working the bar."

Liam shook his head. "Except you weren't," he said. "You should know by now how thorough I am with keeping track of things, Marianne. No one saw you during the lunch rush. In fact, no one saw you until closing."

"My timecard..." She trailed off helplessly.

"You mean the one you had Eduardo clock you in with?"

Marianne visibly swallowed as fear shone in her eyes. "You don't understand."

"Understand what?" my mother asked calmly. "That you took everything I ever loved away from me? Do you know what Elias did to me, Marianne? Night after night, day after day, and that was before he found me half dead in my own house just feet away from my daughter's hiding place."

"You didn't deserve what you had," Marianne snarled. "You were nothing more than a spoiled Irish princess with a silver spoon in her fucking mouth. Did you ever think about what I went through growing up? What they did to me?" She shook her head wildly. "No, of course you didn't. Too busy fucking Liam in your ivory tower."

"I didn't even know you existed, Marianne," my mother told her softly. "Not until you sold me out to Elias for the second time. You were never a thought in my mind until the day we met when we were thirteen and became best friends."

Marianne scoffed. "Please." Her lips twisted into a cruel snarl. "We were never best friends, and you know it. You didn't give a fuck about what was happening in my life."

"I did," my mother assured her. "If you had only told me before I became suspicious myself, then maybe it wouldn't have come to this. I had always felt like something was missing in my life, and when you came along, I felt like that hole was filled. I just didn't know why. But you burned that bridge when you conspired to have me killed. Fuck, it hadn't crossed my mind that you would have betrayed me like that, but now I can see the whole picture."

"And what are you going to do about it?" Marianne derided with a sneer. "Kill me? Liam won't let you do that. I'm the mother of his children."

"I wouldn't be so sure," Kiernan muttered and glared at Seamus, who had elbowed him in the side.

"No, Marianne," my mother sighed. "I wouldn't take away their mother like you tried to Ava's away from hers, but you will be going away for a very long time."

"You see," Liam stepped forward, "the Irish clan council has been informed of the treachery within the McDonough clan, and they are less than pleased."

"Pfft," Marianne dismissed. "The clan has no say in what goes on here." Liam shook his head, eyes full of sorrow and regret.

"If you had bothered to pay attention to more than just your phone and vendetta," he told her, "you would have known that every Irish clan answers to the council. They are the ones who ensure we don't fight among ourselves or repeat the sins of the past."

"Murdering my father—" My mother's hand tightened on the cane she was holding. "Putting someone else in his place. Selling women and children. Those are things the council frowns upon. You will all be held accountable."

"He wasn't even your father."

"He was to me," mother breathed sadly. "And that is all that matters."

The hand that had loosened on my hair tightened again, pulling me back into Marianne's chest. She began walking us backward toward the kitchen doors, the gun in her hand moving from my temple to my mother.

"If you think for one second that I am going to allow you to take me in like some kind of criminal," she hissed, "you're wrong. I told you this once already, *sister*," she spat out the word as if it were something bitter coating her tongue. "I'm a goddess, and they named me Hera."

Movement caught my attention out of the corner of my

eye. A sharp scream tore through my throat as I watched Marianne's finger tighten on the trigger. I didn't need to think about what I did next. The moment I saw her finger tighten on the trigger, I slammed my head as hard as I could into the hand holding the revolver.

The shot meant for my mother went wide, the bullet landing somewhere in the far wall.

That was when all hell broke loose.

Glass shattered on all sides, and smoke began to fill the room as chaos erupted.

"Everyone, get down," my father shouted. "Seamus, secure Katherine."

Marianne was barely fazed by the sudden onslaught of gunfire and smoke. Her grip on my hair tightened even further as she dragged me into the kitchen, the gun at my temple again.

"Fucking have to ruin everything, you stupid bitch," she hurled under her breath. "Lucky that bastard wants you alive, or I would just stick a bullet in your skull."

Who wanted me alive?

Dread washed through me as I eyed the bodies of the kitchen staff. There was no way Marianne had killed them. My heart beat in my chest at a rapid-fire pace, bouncing against my rib cage.

Thump. Thump. Thump. Thump.

Was she returning me to Kellan? The scars he'd left on my body ached at the thought of being at his mercy again. I'd narrowly avoided being raped by him. I wouldn't survive him like my mother had survived Elias. I wasn't that strong.

"Finally. Took you long enough."

Ugh. I was trying to decide whether this was a better or worse predicament than I imagined. Brightside, it wasn't Kellan. Instead, Christian waited for us as we exited the heavy metal door that led to the alley between the buildings. He was lounging against the wrought-iron fence that kept the homeless out at night, looking pleased with himself.

"Things got chatty in there," Marianne told him as she shoved me into his waiting arms. "Hopefully, your men are good at pest control."

Christian smirked. "They're excellent."

I may have snorted at that statement.

He glared down at me dispassionately but turned his attention quickly back to Marianne. "Everything has been transferred. There is a private jet waiting to take you wherever you want to go."

Marianne nodded, her cold eyes shifting to mine. It looked like she wanted to say something, but instead chose to bite her lip and run off like the coward she was. If she thought she could hide, she had another thing coming.

"Let's go," Christian commanded, taking my wrist in a bruising grip. Fuck that. I had learned a lot since my time with him, and I wasn't about to be his fucking bitch anymore. I took a small step back, keeping some distance between us, and twisted my arm to the inside before shoving it forward and catching him off guard. Christian faltered, stumbling backward slightly, giving me just enough room to bring my foot up to connect with his groin.

Growling, he pivoted at the last second, and my foot caught the inside of his thigh instead. His hand caught my ankle and pulled. The breath whooshed from my lungs when I hit the concrete, and I struggled to take in air.

"Fucking bitch." He got to his feet and towered over me. "Still haven't learned your fucking lesson."

"Fuck you." The words came out slightly croaked, but it got my sentiment across. Christian laughed cruelly.

"Oh, I'm going to, little lamb," he taunted. "You just wait."

Movement behind him caught my attention. It was a lithe figure clad in black, stealthily moving among the shadows. Christian was a fool to be out here by himself with no backup. Not that it mattered. No one could stop what was coming, and god help anyone who tried.

I let out a breathy laugh and waited.

"You think this is funny?" he snapped, his hand coming down to slap me across the face. Christian never saw it coming. The knife slid across his throat like butter on toast. His eyes bulged from his head, hands clutching at his bleeding throat as he sank to his knees. It didn't take long for him to bleed out, his body hitting the ground with a cold thump.

"Certainly funny now."

A gloved hand entered my vision, and I took it, groaning as it assisted me to my feet. Shaking my hair from my face, I stared into the azure eyes of my sister.

"You always find yourself in the worst predicaments," she teased. I scoffed and waved my hand dismissively.

"I don't know what you're talking about," I said primly. "Unlike you, I am not some badass ninja."

"Assassin," she corrected.

I shrugged. "Same thing." We laughed, the sound pure and untainted, even with Christian's blood seeping into the cracks of the alley. "What are we going to do about him?"

"Bonfire?" Kenzi suggested. "I read about a lady who roasted marshmallows over the man who tortured her."

What the fuck? That was the look I sent her too.

"Is this a real lady or one of your imaginary friends?" I questioned. Kenzi shot me a glare.

"It was in a book I read."

"So an imaginary friend."

"Where do you get imaginary from?"

I snorted a laugh as we left Christian's corpse behind, walking back through the kitchen. Shit. My dad was going to be pissed that all his kitchen staff was dead. The people who worked here were like family to him and the boys.

"When you were younger, you used to play act with your imaginary friends from the books you read."

"No, I didn't," she denied vehemently.

"Yeah, you did," I told her. "Thank god you stopped doing that before *Twilight* came out. Shit would have gotten weird."

Kenzi blew out her lips. "Never fucking read *Twilight*."

"Say that to the journal decorated in Team Jacob stickers you used to hide under your bed."

Kenzi shot me a colorful string of swear words that would have a sailor blushing. "I knew someone read it."

"Oh, Jacob." I threw my hand up on my forehead and dramatically swooned. "You can take me like an animal."

"Gross." Kenzi stuck her tongue out at me. "I did not say that."

"Did too."

"Did not."

"Did—"

"Girls!" My father's voice boomed from the bar lobby. "Do you mind having some sense of awareness here? What if there were still hostiles? You two arguing over sparkling vampires would have easily given you away."

Kenzi and I exchanged a contrite look.

"I was just following the assassin."

Threw her right under the bus.

Kenzi gasped. Drama queen. Ninjas don't gasp like that.

"Ava got herself snatched again."

Traitor.

I pointed my finger in her face. "She knifed someone in the alley."

"And I'm about to ground both of you."

That shut us up.

Not that he could actually ground us, but it would be fun to watch him try.

Kenzi shot me a sly smile, her eyes sparkling. I had been worried that I lost the sister I had grown up with. The one who was always full of smiles and sass. Maybe I didn't lose her. Maybe there was hope after all.

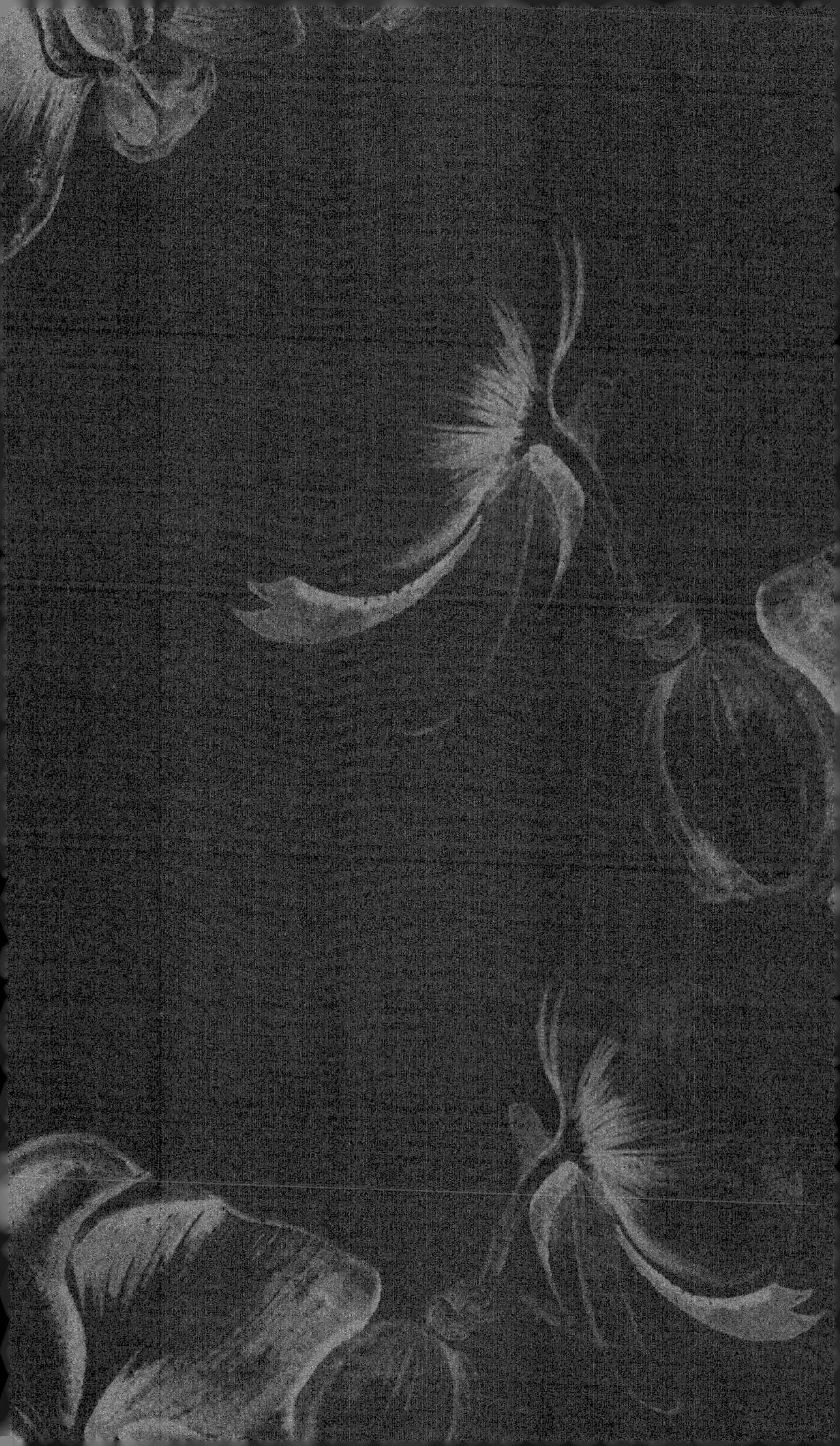

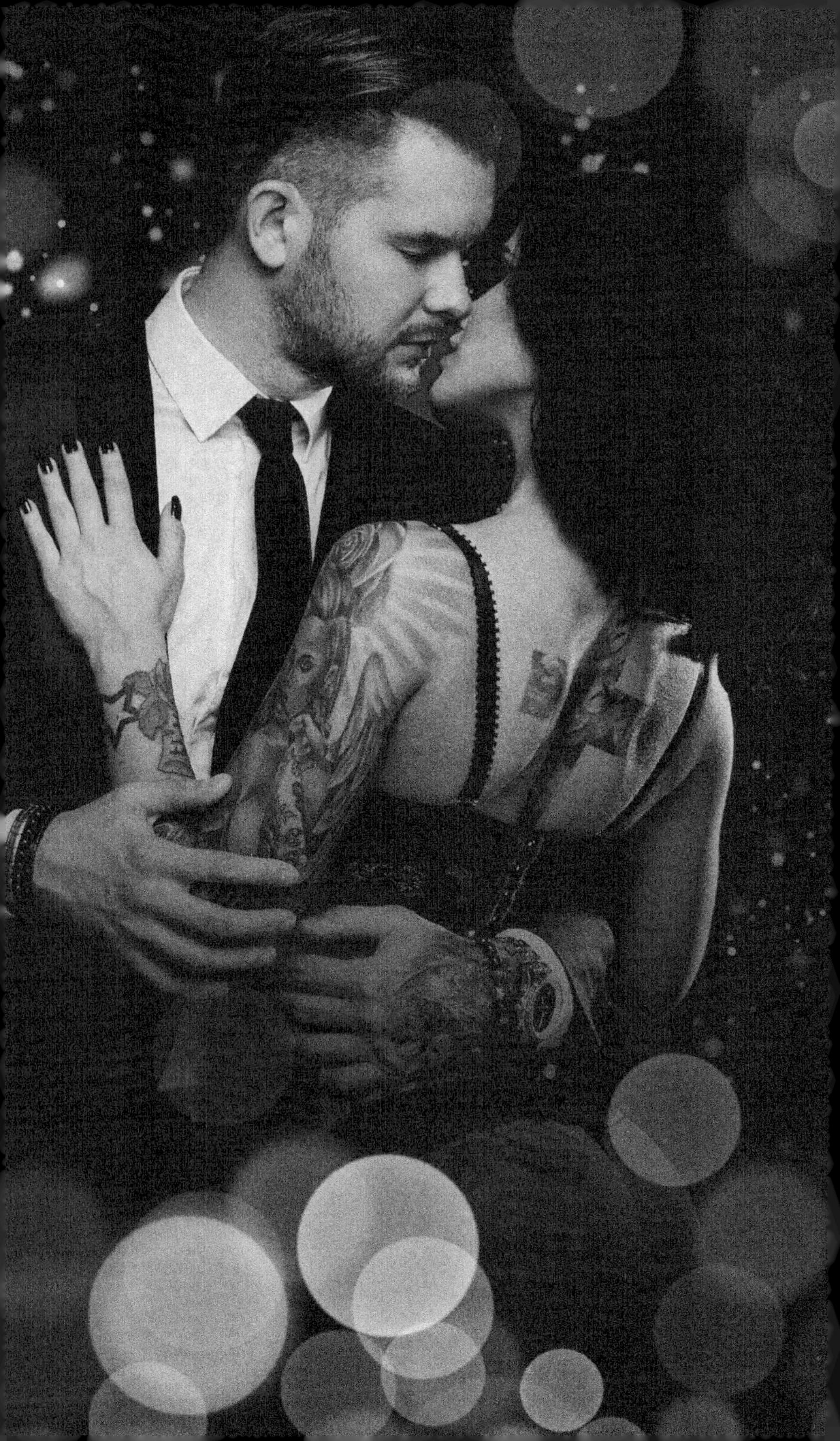

TWENTY-FIVE

Matthias

"Why does this feel like a fucking set up?" I breathed as we walked into my office at Cataclysm, one of the kinkier clubs I owned in Seattle. "We've never had a problem with any of our shipments from Maine before, but now three in less than a month? Something is not right."

Vas hummed his agreement as he assembled his FN PS90. It was standard carry for my people when performing ambushes or raids. It was smaller and more compact than an AK-47 or AR-15. It was also more reliable. It allowed for a thirty-round magazine, and the bullet was lighter than a 115 grain 9mm and traveled nearly twice as far.

"Do you think Ricardo is in on it?" he wondered, passing one of the magazines to Maksim. That was a fair question. We had been using Ricardo as our supplier for years, and he had never fucked up before, but that didn't mean he couldn't be bought. If someone offered the proper incentive, I wouldn't be surprised if he turned on me. I just hope I was wrong.

"Anything is possible."

The door to my office opened, and in walked Nicolai.

"Everyone is ready," he told me, strapping on one of the vests from the table. "We have two teams hitting the airport and another hitting a warehouse listed under the name Remus Islandier. Your father found it buried beneath a stack of horribly organized paperwork at the mansion."

He had taken over the mansion, digging through the piles and piles of paperwork that were left carelessly behind. He'd be leaving for Russia in a few weeks and wanted to have the place in shape for when he came back to visit me.

Maksim snickered. "That was too easy to find," he boasted. "Although I suppose they never expected anyone to find out who either of them truly was."

Nicolai grunted. "Still could have made it slightly more of a challenge."

Dima laughed over the comm line. "Seriously?" he crowed. "We've been looking for these assholes for over a month, and you're complaining-they didn't give you a challenge?"

I laughed. Fucker had a point.

"We could let them escape again," I suggested with a shrug. "Send you after them like a hound on a fox's trail."

"I'm good," Nicolai mumbled. "Promise." We all roared with laughter. If there was one thing my *Obshchak* hated, it was traveling.

"Dima." I drew his attention back to me. "You are clear to breach whenever the urge arises."

Dima chuckled darkly. "Lock and load boys." I didn't

have time to correct him on how to address his men properly before the alarm of the club signaled a security breach.

"Hell yeah," Maksim bellowed, shoving his fist in the air. "*Ura!*"

Vas shook his head as he followed after Maksim, who had bolted out the office door. "Fucking Soviet war cry," he sneered. "Couldn't pick something better? More poetic? It's just a fucking noise. Not even a real word."

"They are attempting to get in the front door." Maksim's smug voice filtered through the comm line. Fucker was fast if he had already made it to the front. "Stupid idea, really. The best access point is through the dumpster chute."

Vas snorted. "Let's not give them any ideas, hmm?"

"I'm getting too old for this," Nicolai huffed, running a hand through his beard. I jabbed his side with my elbow.

"Don't worry," I teased. "We have a great senior citizen plan."

He took a swipe at me. "Fuck you." I laughed. There was no heat behind his tone. If he were anyone else, I would have killed him on the spot. This time, I would let it slide, I supposed.

"Back. Back. Back." We had reached the bottom of the last set of stairs that led into the lobby of the club when Maksim and Vas came running toward us. I couldn't remember the last time I had seen either of them run like that. It was as if their asses were on fire.

"Grenade!" Maksim and Vas launched themselves over the bar to relative safety. I stared after them for a moment before his words sank in.

"Shit," I hissed and pushed Nikolai into the small hallway to the right of the stairs we'd just exited. The explosion shook the ground beneath our feet, dust and debris flying every which way. Smart, but now they had given us the perfect cover.

Maksim cackled as he popped up from behind the bar top, opening fire like Rambo on the enemy as they swarmed inside. All hell broke loose as we took out man after man who breached through our doors. Fucking Ricardo better be dead, because if he wasn't, I was going to make his last few breaths utter hell.

Luckily, we had chosen a club I wasn't too fond of.

"Shit." I ducked behind a concrete pillar as more men came streaming through the door. That fucker had been made of steel. Grenade my ass. The fuckers probably used a rocket launcher. "Mark, I need eyes on Cataclysm."

"Got it, boss." Mark went silent for a moment as he worked his magic. "I hope you have more men with you because you've got a small army coming at you through the parking lot."

"How small is small?" I asked impatiently, flinging my knife at one of the men sneaking up on Nicolai. It hit him between the eyes. Dead fucker now.

"Well, it's not quite the Roman Legion..."

"Mark!" I gritted my teeth as I took out another two men with my gun.

"Forty or so." He didn't sound so confident in those numbers.

"Or so?" Maksim sneered. "Or so!"

"Well, we're fucked," Nicolai laughed dryly. "Wave the white flag, boys. We are going down with the ship."

"The white flag means surrender, dumbass," Dima's voice interrupted through the chatter. "We're done over here, boss. Nothing special to report."

Shit.

"No sign of the McDonoughs?"

"Nope," Dima popped. "Just a whole bunch of now dead men and some cash."

I grumbled.

"Could use some help over here," Vas grunted as he headbutted a guy in the face. "I'm almost out of ammo."

"We're on our way."

Great. Just great.

"Hey, boss, you've got more company rolling in."

And this was not going the way I had planned it.

"How much company?" I honestly did not think I wanted to know.

"A few trucks full."

Blyad'.

"Well, it was nice knowing you all," Maksim grunted, shoving a machete straight through a man's neck. Where the fuck had he gotten that?

"We're not dead yet, idiot," Vas sneered. "Feel free to fall on your sword for us, though."

That got a laugh.

"You do know how fucked up you all are, right?" Mark asked, astonished. "Most people don't have this conversation while fighting for their lives."

We all gave half shrugs. "Eh, you learn to see the humor in things. Even death."

"Not dying would be great, *Russo idiot*." A smooth Italian accent drifted over the comm line.

That was not something I was expecting.

"If fake dying sent Ava on a rampage, I don't want to know what she would do if you actually died."

Vas snickered. "Bury him with his balls in his mouth."

Dante laughed. "We're coming in," he told us. "My men are the one wearing the striped caps. Don't shoot them, please."

"No promises," I muttered petulantly. Fucking Italian was never going to let me live this down. Within minutes, his men had stormed the parking lot and poured into the club. Fucking perfect. It didn't take long for us to clear out the rest of the enemy combatants.

"Fuck." Vas wiped at his forehead, trying to keep the blood from pouring down his sweat-covered face and into his eyes. "That was a workout."

We all stood in the middle of the club, surrounded by a sea of dead men. None of whom I recognized.

"Who the fuck are they?" Maksim voiced the question rattling through my brain. "They don't have any tags. No gang signs or insignia."

It was disturbing to know that we had no way of identifying who had sent the men. At first, I believed that they had been sent by Sheila and Remus McDonough, but now, I was beginning to question that. So were my men.

"Can we all agree that these soldiers aren't McDonough soldiers?" Vas sighed. We all nodded. Even Dante didn't believe they could have done this. There were too many men, and they were too well trained. The men at the mansion when we had rescued Ava were mafioso type. Most likely those who came with them from Boston.

The men who surrounded us now were specially trained. Former soldiers and black ops from every nationality laid dead across the floor of my club.

"You think it's them?" Nicolai asked. "That secret society or whatever."

Gritting my teeth, I nodded, accepting that it was the only thing that made sense. They'd attacked us in broad daylight at a public venue. Whoever they were, they weren't messing around.

"Hey, boss," Mark called frantically over the comms. "The bar's silent alarm was just tripped."

Fuck. If the same people who attacked us were also hitting McDonoughs, they wouldn't stand a chance. We'd gotten lucky that Dante had been monitoring our comm frequency like the paranoid Italian don he was. Something we would be talking about in detail later, but for now, I was just grateful for the backup.

"My men will stay here and work on cleanup," Dante assured me. I nodded as we piled into one of the SUVs.

Fuck all if I was going to lose Ava.

Not when things had been going so well.

Taking out my phone, I dialed the one person I knew could save her if I couldn't be there in time.

"Ava's in trouble, Kenzi." I didn't bother with pleasantries. "McDonoughs."

That was all I managed to say, and then the line went dead.

Hold on, Red. We're coming for you.

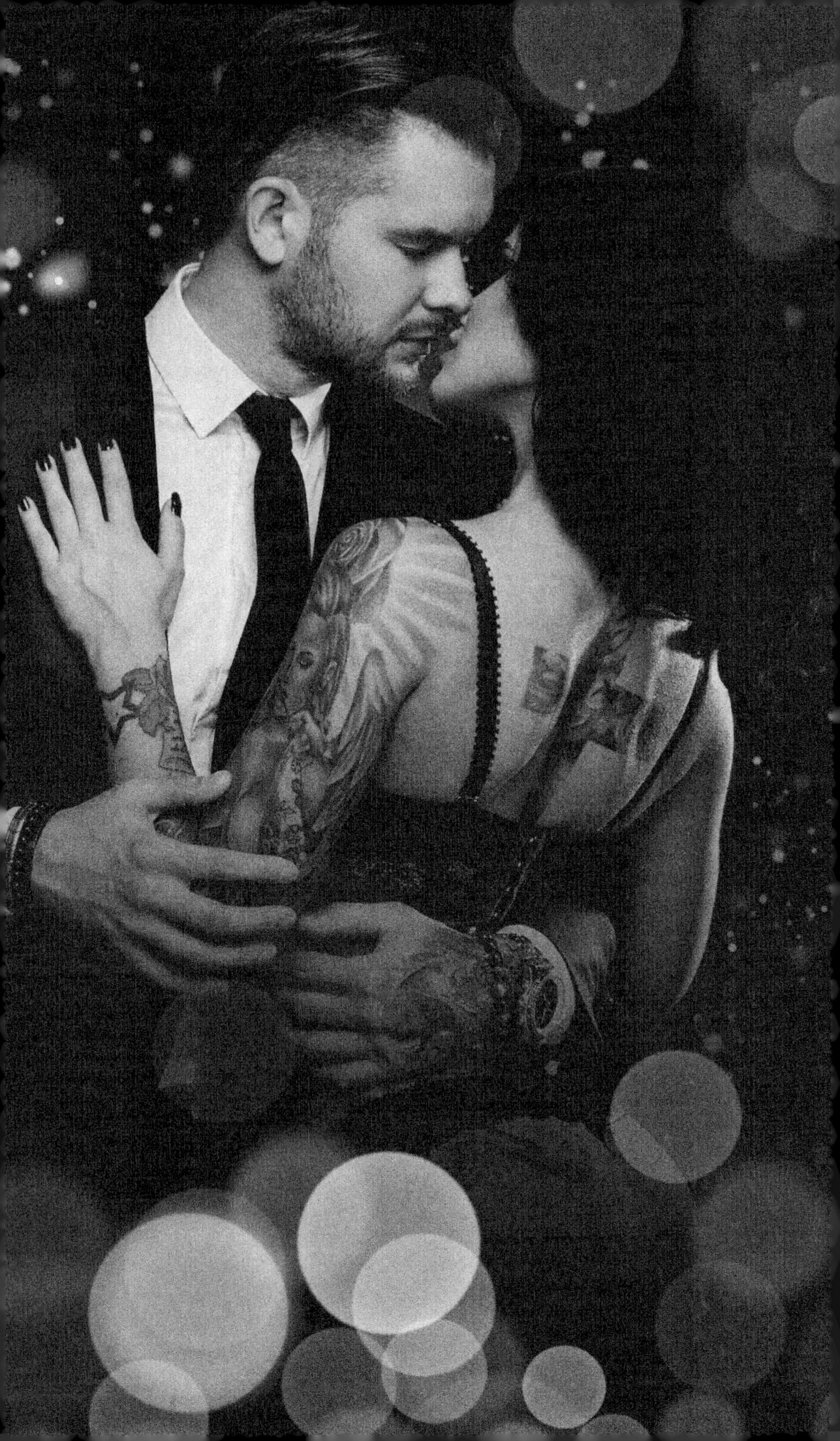

TWENTY-SIX

Ava

"You didn't, by chance, happen to keep any of the fuckers alive, did you?" I asked my father as I helped him dispose of the unwanted trash in the back of one of the vans. He just grunted, which I took to mean, no, he hadn't. "Would have been nice if you did."

"You could have kept Christian alive."

"Pfft," I dismissed that real quick. "He would have been useless. Plus, that was all Kenzi."

My sister rolled her eyes at me. "Save your life, and how do you thank me? By throwing me under the bus."

I shrugged. "I'm not taking the blame for you. Plus, I already said thank you."

"Could have said thank you by not making me help you carry dead bodies."

My father chuckled. "Got to learn to clean up after yourself, kiddo." Kenzi made a noise of disagreement.

"I don't clean up bodies," she deadpanned. "I leave them."

"She never picked up her toys as a kid either," I whispered loudly to my father. "Always made me or Libby do it."

Another eye roll.

"Ava!" My ears perked up at the sound of someone yelling my name rather frantically. "Red!"

It was Matthias.

I walked into the kitchen from the alley, following the sounds of his voice. The bodies of the staff had already been taken to the local mortuary, and the families had been notified by the twins. I shivered. I'd rather clean up the dead bodies than talk to any family members. I barely made it past the bar top when my husband scooped me up into his arms, crushing me tight against his chest.

"Matthias," I choked out. Jesus, he was crushing me. Death by Russian hug. Wouldn't be the worst way to go. "I can't breathe."

"Shit," he cursed, loosening his hold on me enough to allow my lungs to expand but not enough to squirm out of his hold. After a few moments, he set me back on my feet, his hands roaming my body diligently. He was clinical with his touch, which was probably good since we were in the middle of the bar with everyone watching.

"Are you okay?" I eyed the blood covering him from nearly head to toe. In fact, I looked around at Maksim, Vas, and Nicolai. They were all covered in blood. The only one who managed to come out barely scathed was Dante. "What happened?"

He looked down at me with a knowing smirk. His hand, covered in dried blood, cupped my cheek gently. "Worried about me, Red?"

Feigning nonchalance, I shrugged. "I just don't want to hear Vas bitch and moan about you being dead again, and funerals are a pain in the ass to plan."

My father laughed from somewhere behind me. "That's my girl."

Matthias's chest rumbled possessively, and it made my core clench like a seasoned hoe. The man had fucking ruined me for anyone else. He tore his eyes from mine reluctantly and gazed around the room. His forehead puckered, eyes narrowing at the scene before him.

"What the hell happened here?" he asked my father, who rolled his eyes as if it was obvious.

"We were attacked," he deadpanned. "And do you mind? You're getting blood everywhere." Matthias looked down at the blood-stained wooden floor, then back at my father, eyebrow raised.

"Really?"

My father shrugged. "I'm assuming you were hit by the same people?" he looked Matthias and his men up and down.

"That was my thought, but it seems like they sent considerably fewer men after you."

Inclining my head, I stared up at him quizzically. "What do you mean?"

"We were ambushed by nearly four dozen men," he frowned. "Highly trained operatives." Matthias bent down to pick up one of the smoke grenades that had been thrown through the front windows of the bar. "This is an $M18$ smoke grenade. Simple but effective. However, it's not high tech and provides little cover.

"The smoke grenades that were used at the club were $M106$. Obscurant type. It provides quick and fast cover, but also messes with infrared. Mark had a hard time identifying how many men there were because of it." Matthias paused and turned toward my father. "Where are the men who attacked you?"

My father shoved his thumb toward the kitchen doors. "Out back in the alley, being loaded into a van." Matthias nodded and stalked toward the service doors.

"You couldn't change first?" My father groaned as we all followed behind my husband, who appeared to be on a mission.

Matthias flipped him off over his shoulder. "Bill me."

Father laughed.

We stepped into the alley where Ioan, one of my father's lieutenants, and Kenzi were casually tossing the rest of the dead bodies into the back. It was going to be a full load. They stopped when they saw us.

"These aren't the men who attacked us," Matthias muttered and turned to Vas, who nodded in agreement.

"They appear to be McDonough's men." Vas leaned in closer to get a look and pointed toward the bottom of the pile. "Is that Ward?"

Kenzi smirked. "Sure is."

Vas beamed with pride. "Nice."

"Slit his throat," she bragged. "Ear to ear."

"What was he doing here?" Matthias questioned.

"Trying to get his hands on your wife," Kenzi muttered. "Again."

My husband's stormy eyes turned to me, and I just shrugged.

"Don't look at me." I held my hands up innocently. "This was all Marianne's doing."

"She was here too?" Matthias closed his eyes and took a deep breath. I wondered if he was going to have a stroke or something. With the way the vein in his temple was throbbing, I wouldn't doubt that one was near.

"Take a chill pill, caveman," Kenzi snorted. "Everything went fine. Christian's dead. All their men are dead. Marianne escaped somewhere."

I groaned, then thought about it for a moment.

"Wait." If it wasn't my grandparents' men who attacked Matthias, then who did? "Who were the men who attacked the club?"

"We haven't been able to figure that out," Dante admitted with a shake of his head.

"They had no identifying marks or tattoos," Vas informed us. "They were special forces and black-ops trained, that is for sure. High-grade explosives and smoke screens. Their moves were practiced and precise. We never saw them coming."

That didn't make any sense. "Wasn't Mark monitoring radio chatter around the club?" I asked. "He should have been able to give you a heads-up."

Maksim snorted from where he leaned against the metal doorframe between the alley and the kitchen. "Except there was no radio chatter. It was completely silent until the alarm was tripped, and the one fucker who had managed to barely survive didn't say shit. Silent as a fucking mime."

"Or a mute."

We all turned to look at Kenzi, who was washing her blood-covered hands off under the spigot on the wall.

"What do you mean mute?"

Kenzi snorted. "You know, like can't talk? Silent. Suppressed. Quiet. Take your pick."

"Why the fuck would you think they're mute?" Vas eyed her skeptically.

Shutting off the spigot, Kenzi whirled around to face

the tall Russian, hands on her hips. "Did they make any noise at all? Did you hear them shout out orders to each other or scream when they were hit?"

"Well," Vas stuttered slightly before looking defeated. "No."

"That's what I thought," she reprimanded him before turning to Matthias. "Did you look inside their mouths?"

Vas sneered. "Why the fuck would we do that?"

Kenzi ignored him, focusing her attention on Matthias, who shook his head.

"What about radio chatter?" she continued. "You said Mark didn't hear any, but was that just words or was he listening for anything else?"

"Like what?" Matthias questioned.

"Knocks. Tics. Tones," she explained. "Anything like that."

Matthias eyed his men, who all shook their heads.

"I'm not sure."

"Great," Kenzi huffed. She grabbed her phone from her pocket and hit speed dial.

"What's up, Kenzi?" Mark's voice filled the alleyway on her speakerphone. "Kinda busy."

"Aren't we all," she drawled. "When you were motoring the comm lines near the club, did you pick up on anything?"

"Nah," Mark denied. "There wasn't any chatter on any frequencies in the area. Just the hangar and the bar. Why?"

"You're sure you didn't hear anything at all?" Kenzi questioned further. "Not just voices. Any kind of tapping or tones that didn't quite make sense?"

Mark's silence was all the confirmation we needed.

"Well, there was this kind of...beeping sound that was embedded in the radio frequency, but it was random. Or sounded like it anyway."

"Did it sound a little like Morse code?" she asked him. "Long beeps and short beeps."

"Yeah, a bit, but I thought it was just static," he told her. "I thought it could have been Morse code at first, but none of the words would have made any sense."

"Perfect. Thank you for your help."

"Wait—" She hung up on him.

"They're called Timbres," she breathed, one hand white knuckled her cell phone while her empty hand clenched and unclenched at her side. Kenzi was scared. "I don't know much about them, just that they're deadly. Rumors floated around that they've wiped out whole corporations in bloody massacres, leaving no trace behind."

"So what?" Vas scoffed. "Only mutes can apply? That doesn't make any sense."

"Those soldiers aren't born mute, idiot." Kenzi's eyes darkened, lips turning up in a sneer. "Their tongues are cut out when they're recruited."

"By choice?" Maksim balked, licking his lower lip.

Kenzi bobbed her head. "Some of them," she conceded. "Others are forced into recruitment depending on their skills evaluation."

"But why cut out their tongues?"

"When a secret is revealed, it is the fault of the man who confided it," Kenzi recited.

Dante smiled down at his daughter. "Jean de LaBruyère."

"I am so confused right now," Vas admitted.

"It means that whoever employed them ensured they wouldn't be able to spill their secrets," Dante explained. "That must be why Mark heard the beeping sound over the comm frequency. It's how they communicate."

"I'm not sure what it is, but Mark was right when he said it wasn't Morse code."

Matthias shrugged. "Morse code can be easily changed to meet someone else's needs as long as the people who are receiving it know it as well."

"Great," Maksim grumbled. "Now we have to worry about someone powerful enough to send deadly mute assassins after us. Just what we need."

"What you all need right now is to shower." My father shook his head. "We can discuss everything later. These bodies need to get taken down to the funeral home to be burned, and I need to get boards up over the windows in the front before the homeless decide to invade."

"Come, Ava." Matthias took my hand and pulled me along beside him toward the door that led to the kitchens.

"Jaysus," my father hollered. "Can't you take the back stairs and not track blood through my bar?"

"Bill me for it, old man," Matthias hollered back, but I didn't miss how he veered off to the left toward the back stairwell.

It was a short trip up to the residential floor and into our suite. I was nearly running to keep up with my husband with his long, hurried strides.

Matthias pulled us into the bathroom, and all I did was stand and watch him as he opened the faucets. Steam filled the large space within minutes. I stood there waiting for him, not moving to remove my clothes until he was ready. I'd heard the way he had called my name through the bar. It had been suffused with panic and raw fear. He needed to be in control right now. To ensure I wasn't hurt.

Reaching out, he pulled my sweater off me. He kept going until I was stark naked, and then he stripped off his own clothes, which were covered in dirt and blood. I breathed a sigh of relief when I noticed none of it appeared to be his.

I licked my lips as I watched him reveal his body inch by inch, my pussy already pulsing at the thought of what he could do to me with it. He was a machine. A powerhouse. Every inch of him solid perfection crafted from hours of hard, torturous work.

He tilted his head toward the shower, smirking when I shook my head to clear out the daze his statue of a body created. He stepped in behind me, closing the door, and yanked my body to his. I melted against him; his arms wrapped tightly around me. He ran his hands along both of my arms, categorizing each bruise and scrape. There weren't that many since Marianne had gone for my hair, and my clothes had taken the brunt of the force when I hit the concrete.

A few scraped knees and elbows were far better than my previous encounter with either of them.

He growled when I winced at his hands in my hair. He'd lathered them up with shampoo and had managed to hit the large knot on the side of my head where I had head-butted Marianne's gun. Not my smartest idea, but it had worked.

"I'm going to kill her when I find her," he snarled, gently avoiding the injured area.

"Not if I get to her first," I grumbled. "Or my mom."

Matthias let out a low laugh as he tipped my head back under the warm spray to rinse my hair out. "That would be a sight to see, my little psycho."

I hummed delightfully as I poured a good amount of bodywash into my open palm. "I love it when you call me that," I admitted. Lathering up my hands, I glided them along his body, remapping every hard inch of him like I had so many times before.

We'd grown closer since his miraculous return from the dead, but we were still working every day to make things work between us. He was still a controlling asshole most of the time, but I wasn't going back to being that meek, quiet girl he had forced to marry him.

Not that he seemed to mind that I had changed. If anything, he encouraged it. Except in the bedroom. That was when he made sure to be fully in control. I sure as fuck didn't mind that at all.

Matthias groaned when I took his hot, hard length in my soapy hand, rubbing him with long, sweeping motions. I brushed my thumb over his tip each time I passed it, applying just enough pressure to see his knees shaking slightly. And they say women don't have any power over men. Holding him now, hard as stone in my hand, I held all the power, and we both knew it.

"Fuck, Red," he breathed, leaning his head back against the tile with a dull thud. "Your hand feels like heaven." Urged on by his strained moans, I quickened my pace when he bucked into my hand, seeking more.

One arm wrapped around my waist, he dragged me closer, his other hand slipping down between us to rub at my clit. Jesus. I'd read that most men couldn't find that sensitive bundle of nerves with a magnifying glass, but here he was, latching on to it with his fingers like a heat-seeking missile since day one.

Man was a sex god.

Matthias jerked suddenly, switching our positions. He shoved me up against the tiles, and his mouth crashed down on mine. Fireworks danced behind my eyes as he rubbed his hand vigorously against my swollen clit. Fuck me, how did he do that so well? His tongue drove into my mouth, and all my thoughts went right out the window.

There was nothing but fiery heat between us. A blazing inferno of lust and desire fueled by a need to stave off the darkness that only the other person seemed to keep at bay. He was everything to me, despite the heartache and the pain.

Hell, if he kept giving me orgasms like he had been, I sure as fuck would forgive him a lot faster than I planned. I whimpered in protest when Matthias's fingers left my pleasure center in favor of lifting me up against his body.

He pinned me to the wall, and I wrapped my legs tightly around him.

"Matthias." I moaned his name when I felt his hard cock press against my soaked core.

Hell yes.

Matthias leaned in, kissing me, his tongue filling my mouth and dominating me. He nipped at my bottom lip harshly, and I groaned at the pain before he soothed the wound with his tongue. One hand came up to palm my right breast. I shivered as he brushed his thumb over the nipple. With his stormy eyes on mine, he bent his head down and brought his mouth to the opposite nipple and sucked.

The sweet sensation sent a jolt straight to my core, causing it to clench with need. Suddenly, his teeth bit down on my left nipple while he pinched the opposite one at the same time, causing a jolt of electricity to surge through me and stars to burst behind my eyelids, which had fallen closed at his ministrations.

"Please, Matthias," I begged, my voice husky with desire. "I need you."

Mathias let out a low chuckle as he released my nipple with a pop.

"What do you need from me, *malyshka*?" he breathed in my ear. "Tell me what you want."

"I need you inside me," I pleaded desperately, clawing at his back as he thrust his hard length against me.

"You want me to fuck you?" he asked.

What kind of stupid question was that? Of course I wanted him to fuck me.

I nodded my head vigorously and bucked my hips, trying to urge him inside me.

He made a tsking noise and shook his head in mock disappointment.

"Remember, *Krasnyy*, you don't control this. I do."

Torturously slow, he began to rub his cock against my sensitive bundle of nerves, his gray eyes sparkling mischievously. A slow smirk stretched across his face.

"Are you going to beg me, my little psycho?" he goaded. "Are you going to beg me to fuck you against the shower wall?" A burst of air exploded from my lips, and I dug my nails into his shoulders as he continued his torturous ministrations against my clit.

Wave after wave of delicious tingles crashed over me, the coil in my belly tightening inch by inch until it was ready to snap.

When he didn't hear me begging, his movement came to a sudden halt. I let out a frustrated groan. I was going to murder him. There were no ifs, ands, or buts about it.

"Fuck you," I growled at him, but there was no heat behind my words. Matthias's smirk deepened.

"That's what I'm trying to do, baby," he teased. "You're the one not telling me how badly you want my cock."

Holy hell.

Since he'd suddenly been resurrected, he'd gotten a mouth on him. Then again, as much fun as sex had been before, we never had much of a connection. Not like we did now.

His filthy words did something to me I hadn't expected. He had called me his whore before, and there was no denying it had certainly turned me on, but there was always a niggle of doubt in my mind that it was how he saw me. As nothing more than the whores he had fucked before me.

"So." He quirked an eyebrow at me. "How badly do you want me to fuck you, Red?"

I looked up at him from beneath heavily lidded lashes, a coy smile stretching across my swollen lips, and purred, "Fuck me, Matthias. I need your cock. Only your cock."

Heat flared in his gaze, and he thrust hard against my clit one more time before notching himself at my entrance, where I was wet and ready for him. With a powerful thrust, he filled me, burying himself to the hilt.

A cry exploded from me at his forceful thrust, the pain edging with the pleasure. A satisfied groan pulled from his chest, and his mouth claimed mine in a brutal, domineering kiss. Matthias moved hard and fast against me. His pace was relentless as he fucked me hard and dirty, like an animal on the rut. I had no control, and I simply let myself be devoured by my protector. My lover. My husband. The man I'd spend the rest of my life living for and dying for, if it came down to it.

My body quaked and trembled beneath him, with every thrust sending me toward oblivion. Cries and moans spilled from my lips and echoed around us, bouncing off the tiled wall. My hands dug into his hair, holding on for dear life as he continued his brutal pace.

"God," I whimpered into his neck. My lips caressed the

skin down to the juncture of where his neck met his shoulder, and I bit down. Hard. Matthias groaned loudly, his hips stuttering slightly before he picked up his already rapid pace.

My body strained for release, my hips bucking up to meet his thrusts.

"Come, *Krasnyy*," he ordered, his voice rough and gravelly. "Come on your husband's cock." My body obeyed, and I unraveled faster than a bullet train. I buried my head in the crook of his neck as I came apart around him. The ecstasy that seized me was overpowering, and I was nothing but a slave to its will.

I couldn't breathe. I couldn't think.

There was nothing except the galaxy of pure, unadulterated pleasure washing through me.

"Ava," Matthias hissed through clenched teeth. "So, fucking tight, baby. So, fucking hot." His body jerked, and he pushed farther inside me. With a long, satisfied groan, Matthias's release hit him, triggering another one of my own. A sob spilled from my lips even as he slowed his pace as I crested again, this one shorter but just as strong, and I felt slightly lost from reality.

I could hear the water shutting off somewhere in the distance and feel movement beneath me.

"Such a good girl," Matthias whispered in my ear. "Always such a good girl for me."

My eyes fluttered as I was cocooned in warmth. "Your good girl," I whispered, unable to keep my eyes open any longer. Strong arms came around me, anchoring me to a strong, broad chest.

"That's right," he chuckled lowly. "Sleep now, my good girl."

My body obeyed his command, just like it always did.

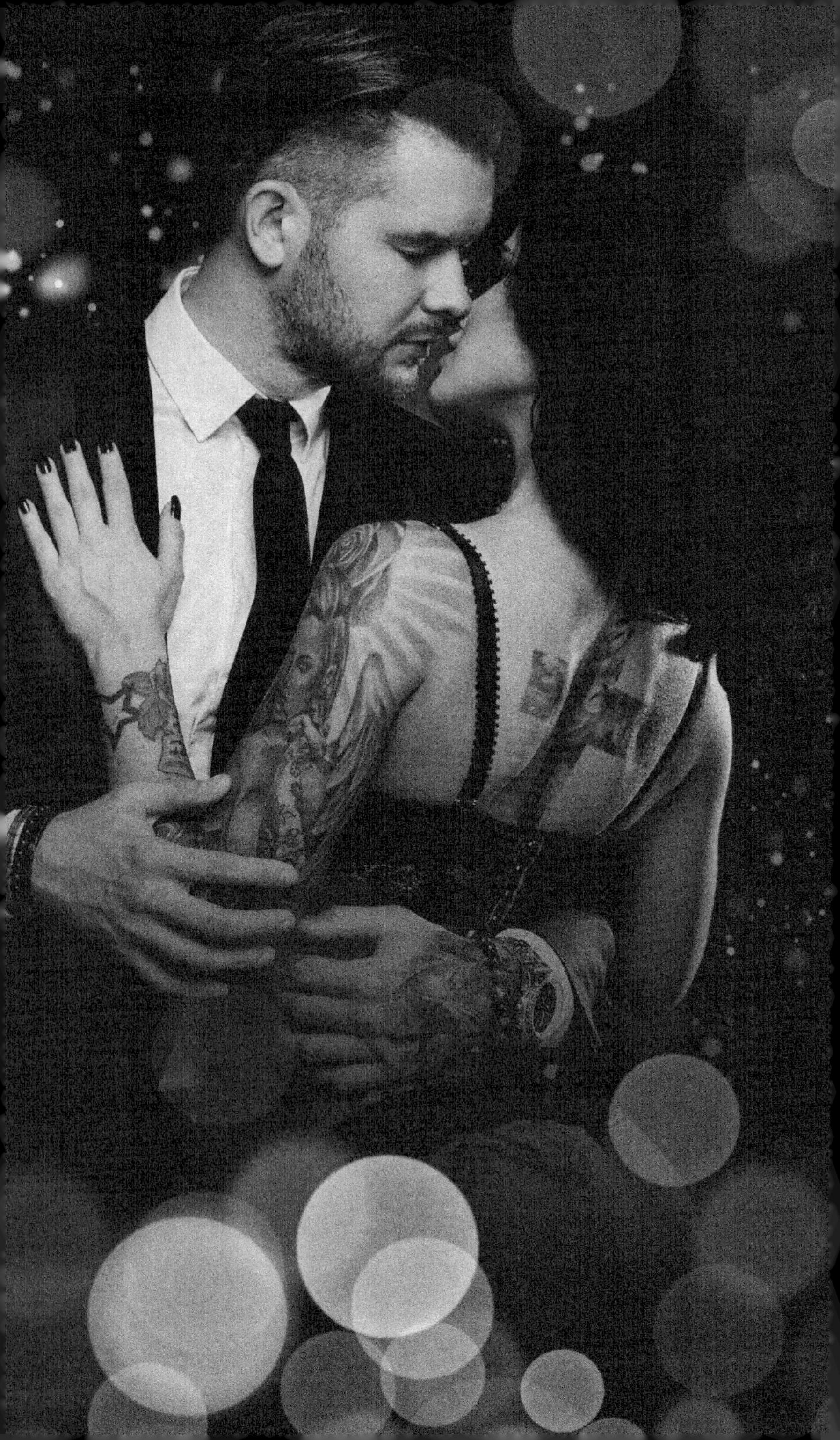

TWENTY-SEVEN

Matthias

We had slept most of the day away. It was dinnertime before we found ourselves downstairs, still utterly exhausted.

I may have woken her up a few times with my head between her thighs.

"What do you mean you can't find them?" I growled at Mark and Bridget. We were sitting at the family dining room table going over everything we had learned and collected. My father had managed to find some documents at the McDonough mansion that helped to piece together some of the puzzle, but it also opened up a lot more questions.

"I mean, one minute we had a location on them, and the next, they were gone."

"Gone?"

"Yeah." He stared at me like I was an idiot speaking Chinese. "You know, gone? Poof? Adios? Not to be found?"

"Your body won't be found if you don't quit," I growled.

Mark blew out between his lips. "I thought sex was supposed to give you endorphins and make you happy."

Everyone but Liam and me roared with laughter. Not even my glare could silence them. Fuckers.

"As you were saying, Mark," Liam drawled. The hacker snickered before clicking something on his tablet. The portable projector he brought came to life, emitting a soft light over the blank cream wall just ahead of me.

"We sent Dima to the airstrip because that was where chatter said they were going to be," Mark explained. "It was supposed to be a foolproof plan."

"Except," Dima butted in, "the only people there were their guards."

"But no Remus or Sheila." Mark tapped his screen again to show video footage of Sheila and Remus getting into the exact car that Dima had ambushed at the hangar.

"Was it a decoy?" Andrei wondered. "Maybe they knew you would be monitoring them."

I shrugged. "That is a possibility."

Andrei turned his attention to Ava's mother, who was sitting silently next to her daughter, her green eyes fixed sadly on the grainy image of her mother. "What do you know about that cane you found?" my father asked her. Katherine's gaze shot over to him.

"Other than it was used to beat me nearly to death?" She let out a dry, humorless chuckle. "Not much. But it was the first thing I noticed was different about my father."

"How so?" Ava asked softly next to her. Katherine looked over at her, eyes softening.

"I remember that one day he wasn't carrying it and then

suddenly he was," she recalled. "It was my sophomore year of high school. I asked him about it, and he said that he had twisted his knee coming off a step wrong.

"There was nothing suspicious about it at first, and I shrugged it off easily. Then a week later, it was gone again. I joked and said how I was surprised such an old man was healing so fast, and he stared down at me and asked me what I was talking about. 'You hurt your knee,' I had reminded him. "I saw you walking with a cane, remember?" My father had shaken his head and said he hadn't injured his knee at all. In fact, he hadn't even been home all week. He had been in Aspen with his CFO."

"Did you say anything to him about it?" Andrei questioned lightly. Katherine nodded.

"I tried," she admitted. "But he said I must have either dreamed it or mistaken one of the staff members for him."

"That seems a bit...convenient."

And it did.

"After that, I kept a closer eye on him," Katherine admitted. "By the time graduation came around, I had compiled a laundry list of moments that seemed inaccurate. The day Liam and I left for college, I emailed him everything I had over a secure server. Our relationship toward the end had become strained and rocky. I have a feeling my mother was the cause of that."

"Why do you say that?" Ava asked. "Besides the fact that she turned out to be a psycho."

Katherine smiled at her daughter. "It is true that your grandmother never held any love for me, and now I know why."

"Still doesn't make it right," Ava muttered petulantly. "You were still her daughter."

"That's true." Katherine smiled sadly. "But I don't

believe that Sheila was capable of loving me or Marianne. We were simply tools to be used and discarded when necessary. Even Marianne. Otherwise, she would have been with them instead of begging that Ward boy for a ticket to her freedom.

"I believe that she grew suspicious of when I started asking questions, but at the time, I never would have thought the woman who raised me would betray me so deeply. There is no doubt in my mind that she was spewing lies to my father to create a gap between us so that he wouldn't believe my evidence when the time came."

"But he did," Andrei smiled. "I remember him reaching out to me after you went off to college." Katherine stared at him across the table in surprise.

"He did?"

Andrei nodded. "He was proud of you," he told her. "Talked about how you were going to be the one to lead them into a new generation. A new tradition. Unfortunately, he never got the chance to tell me what he needed help with. When I called back a week later, as we discussed, he blew me off, stating he no longer needed or wanted my help."

"Remus," Ava snarled. Andrei nodded.

"No doubt, little one."

Ava beamed at his nickname for her. The two had formed a bond since he'd helped rescue her, and it warmed the cold, dead spaces of my heart. I never knew what I was missing before. Vas and my men would always be my family. My brothers. Tomas would always be the man who raised me and sheltered me and nurtured me into the man I am today. But having him here with her was something I never knew I needed.

"Tell us what happened, Kat," Liam begged. Her

mother took a sharp intake of breath, but she didn't run like I expected her to. I could see her knuckles whitening on the chair arms beneath her, but she remained strong.

"Marianne and I had been rooming together in an apartment just off campus," Katherine began, her voice soft and her eyes drawing in a faraway look. She was dissociating. It was a common tactic among survivors. "Liam went out of town on an errand for my father, but it didn't feel right. I warned him but..." She trailed off. "I knew she had been hiding things, so I tore the apartment apart while she was supposed to be in one of her lectures. Inch by inch, I searched every nook, hole, and cranny until I found what I was looking for."

"The cane?" Ava asked. Her mother shook her head.

"Her birth certificate," Katherine corrected her. "I'd only ever known her as Marianne McAllister. Liam and I had met her parents on a few occasions, but like our own parents, they traveled a lot for business. I remember wondering if they had adopted her because she looked nothing like them, but I never brought it up in case Marianne didn't know.

"My mother came down a few weeks after I settled into the apartment. I took her out for lunch, and we ran into Marianne while she was out with a few friends from class."

"You saw it." Ava bit her lip nervously. "How similar they were to one another."

Katherine nodded. "They were so strikingly similar that it was almost scary, and when I pointed it out, they both became cold and frigid. Later, Marianne laughed it off that they were doppelgängers, but when I looked back at how many times I had seen Marianne with my mother, it was only once. One time, when we were first introduced, and that was it. I was thirteen at the time, so I doubt I would have noticed the similarities then."

"Then you went digging," Liam stated the obvious.

"Using my own funds, I traveled back to Boston to the hospital where I was born," she admitted. "The records were off."

"More births recorded than birth certificates issued," I said. Katherine smirked.

"Someone has been doing their homework," she praised, and we all chuckled. "I managed to track down one of the nurses who had been in the delivery room with my mother. The woman told me everything she could. How my grandmother had taken the child from my mother's arms and handed it off to another woman. One with a cane with a silver cross on it."

"You're telling me Leigh knew someone with that cane?" Liam growled.

"Everyone except my father," Katherine confirmed. "The nurse told me that after everyone left, the woman with the cane returned. The only reason she noticed was because the argument they got into was pretty heated, and the woman was escorted out of the facility."

"That makes sense," I told her. "We believe that your mother was a plant inside the McDonough clan. Her job was to seduce your father, marry him, and, at a date of their choosing, assassinate him."

"But then she got pregnant with you and Marianne," Vas interjected. "That wasn't part of the plan. What made it worse was the fact that you weren't Seamus McDonough's blood heirs, either."

"Don't remind me." Katherine narrowed her eyes.

"We believe that someone recognized Remus as Seamus's twin back in Ireland," I informed her. "There isn't much of a paper trail, but we believe that at the same time Sheila was trying to infiltrate, so was he."

"We're not sure when she found out about it," Vas explained. "But at some point, they began working together. I don't even think whoever they were working for knew that Seamus had been switched with Remus. Not until we started digging ourselves."

"We have one fucked up family." Ava chuckled darkly.

"Indeed," Katherine gave a small laugh.

"Tell us what happened the night you were taken."

"Marianne caught me rifling through everything." She sniffed, wiping her eyes on her sleeve. "I confronted her about it. I still didn't know she was my sister. Not until she came to Portland. She spewed some lie about finding it in her parents' attic before we left for college. That she hadn't confronted them about it. I believed her lies. Casting aside any doubts I had and the fact that she had looked exactly like my mother melted away as she cried in my arms about how they had hidden her entire childhood from her.

"That night, they came for me. I was getting ready for bed, and the next thing I knew, I was waking up in one of Elias's bedrooms." She paused to take a calming breath. There was a slight sheen of sweat collecting along her brow, and her eyes were constricted. She was getting ready to run.

"I think that is good for now," I told her gently. Relief washed over her face, and Ava smiled at me gratefully. "What we need to figure out is where the McDonoughs disappeared to and who the hell sent those men to my club."

"Timbres are known for guarding the Dollhouse." Kenzi spoke up from the corner. "So we know that those impetus fucks must have sent them."

"That can't be their actual name." Vas shook his head.

"That's more like a subtitle and not a moniker for a secret society."

"If that's the case, then we're fucked," Seamus grunted. "Do you know how many secret societies there are?" Kiernan shot him a look.

"They aren't so secret if you know about them, are they?"

"Fuck you, Kiernan," Seamus sneered at his brother. "I'm just saying that if all we have is their tag line, it's going to make it a lot harder."

"Not necessarily," Bridget cut in. "We know that most upper echelon members of the society carry a cane with a silver cross, which means all we have to do is create a program that monitors CCTV footage to look for that specific variable."

"That could take forever," Mark complained. "Not to mention that they picked a cane that is highly popular. There could be hundreds, if not thousands, of people walking around the world with that same exact cane."

The kid had a point.

"Except," Bridget narrowed her eyes at him, "if we have the program dig into each individual's background looking for more specific variables, we can weed out anyone who doesn't fit a specific criterion."

"And how are you going to do that?" Andrei asked. "How would you know what variables to look for in their background?"

"Because everyone with a society cane is a fake," Ava murmured. We all turned to look at her. "Matthias told me what he and Bridget discovered. The society is made up of men and women with fabricated backgrounds. Missing children of high society members. Women abducted for sex auction. Babies born the wrong gender or in the wrong order. These are all known variables that would make it easier to find them. Sheila had a squeaky-clean background tailored to fit exactly what my great-grandparents were looking for when it came to a bride for their son."

"The Dollhouse trains women and men to blend in." Kenzi spoke up. "You're trained to seduce by being the exact fantasy of the target. A chameleon. Once an operation is complete, that identity disappears."

"Except," Mark snapped his fingers, "you can't make an identity disappear. Not like how you make one appear. Once a social security number hits the system, it can't be removed. Some of the best hackers have tried."

"But it can be reassigned." Bridget let out a breathy laugh. "They would be able to reuse a social security number multiple times by reframing everything attached to it."

"It's genius and nearly foolproof."

"Get started on that, then." I looked to Liam, who nodded. "Take Bridget with you." Mark made a face but didn't argue. Smart kid.

"We'll keep looking for the McDonoughs in the meantime," Vas said. "I have everyone on high alert. They aren't getting out of the state without us knowing." I nodded.

"Kenzi was right about the men at the club," Dante confirmed, proudly looking at his daughter, who was all but ignoring him. "They didn't have any tongues, but they did have this." He pulled out his phone, sharing it to the projector screen. "My men sent this to me about an hour ago. Wouldn't have known it was there if your black light behind the bar hadn't been shattered."

It was the same symbol carved into the canes. What had Ivan called them? The Seal of Solomon and the Eye of Providence.

"Those are two very powerful symbols," my father pointed out. "From two very different cultures, but both are considered religious symbols."

"I thought the hexagram was pagan," Seamus said.

Andrei shook his head. "The hexagram was actually said to have first appeared in a synagogue in Israel in the third to fourth century. It was purely a motif. It wasn't until the eighteenth century that it began to take on a more mystical undertone."

"Well, the tagline makes more sense now," Kiernan muttered. "Power over all. God's all-seeing power. All knowing. Always watching. That is what many people believe the Eye of Providence means."

"Just what we need." Liam sighed.

"Let's stick with what we have," I sighed. "We know the men link back to the society. Now what we need to figure out is why they suddenly attacked."

"They were testing you." Kenzi shrugged. "If they wanted to get rid of you, why not just send an assassin?"

Andrei snorted. "Maybe because the last one didn't go according to plan?"

Kenzi rolled her eyes. "I've been thinking about that too, actually." She licked her bottom lip nervously. "You said that the woman on the phone sounded exasperated with Kirill. What was her name?"

"Caesar," I recalled. Kenzi's eyebrows shot up at the name. "You know that name."

The brunette nodded. "Anonymity is key with the society. No one knows who anyone is except one person."

"I'll give you one guess as to who," Andrei deadpanned. Kenzi smirked.

"Everyone knows what she sounds like, but no one knows who she is," Kenzi explained. "I remember rumors flying around the Dollhouse about the great and mighty Caesar. In training, they teach you to worship her. That everything is because of her. That our lives were in her hands. But no one, including Madam Therese, had ever seen her."

"Your lives have become a soap opera." Andrei chuckled. "Complete with people coming back from the dead. At this point, I might never return to Russia. This is much more fun."

"Speak for yourself," Liam muttered. "I'm getting too old for this shit."

"Speaking of too old." Dante yawned. "Let's take what we have for now and reconvene when we have more information. I'll have my guys keep a lookout, but right now, I've got my sights set on Augustu. He's up to something, and I don't think we're going to like what's coming down the pipeline."

I inclined my head at him and shook his hand when he stood to leave. He glanced back at Kenzi with a look of fatherly longing in his eyes, but she was steadfastly ignoring it. It would take time for that bond to heal, if it ever did. Kendra was a large obstacle in their way of truly mending, but there was nothing either of them could do about that.

"Come on, baby." Taking Ava's hand, I helped her up from her chair, smirking when she winced slightly at the movement. I had fucked her hard enough that she would feel me for days.

"Do you think this will ever be over?" Ava yawned as we entered our room. Sighing, I closed the door gently behind me.

"I don't know, baby," I answered her honestly as I

followed her into the bedroom. We both went through our nightly routine in a comfortable silence. Ava snuggled down into the light feathered comforter with her back to my front. Snaking an arm around her waist, I pulled her until she was flush against me. "But know I will never leave your side again."

"Good," she grumbled. "Because you still have so many more orgasms to give me before you're forgiven."

I couldn't help the laugh that escaped me. How had I ever thought that loving Ava was a weakness when all I felt every day was lighter and stronger?

What a damn fool I had been.

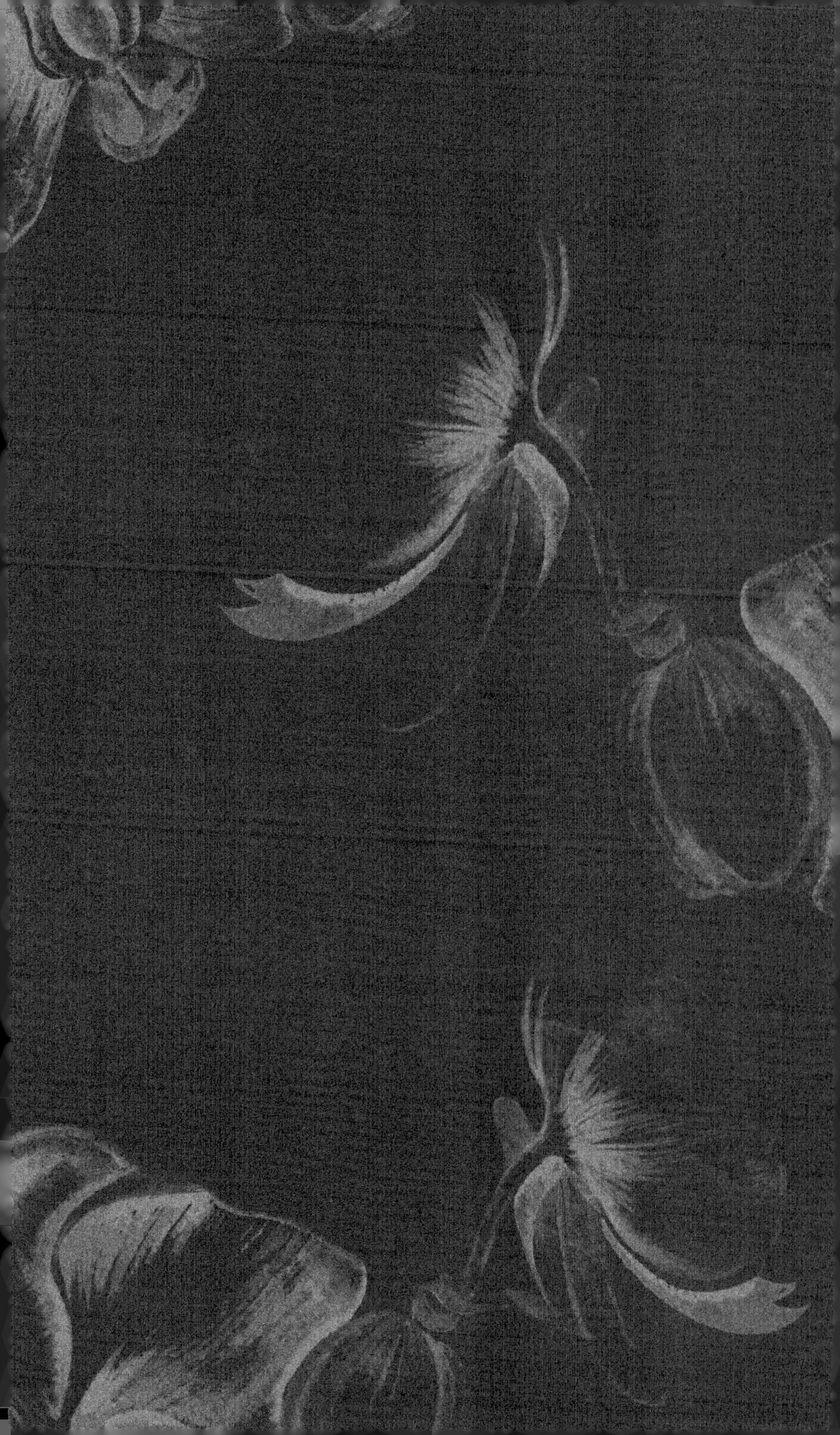

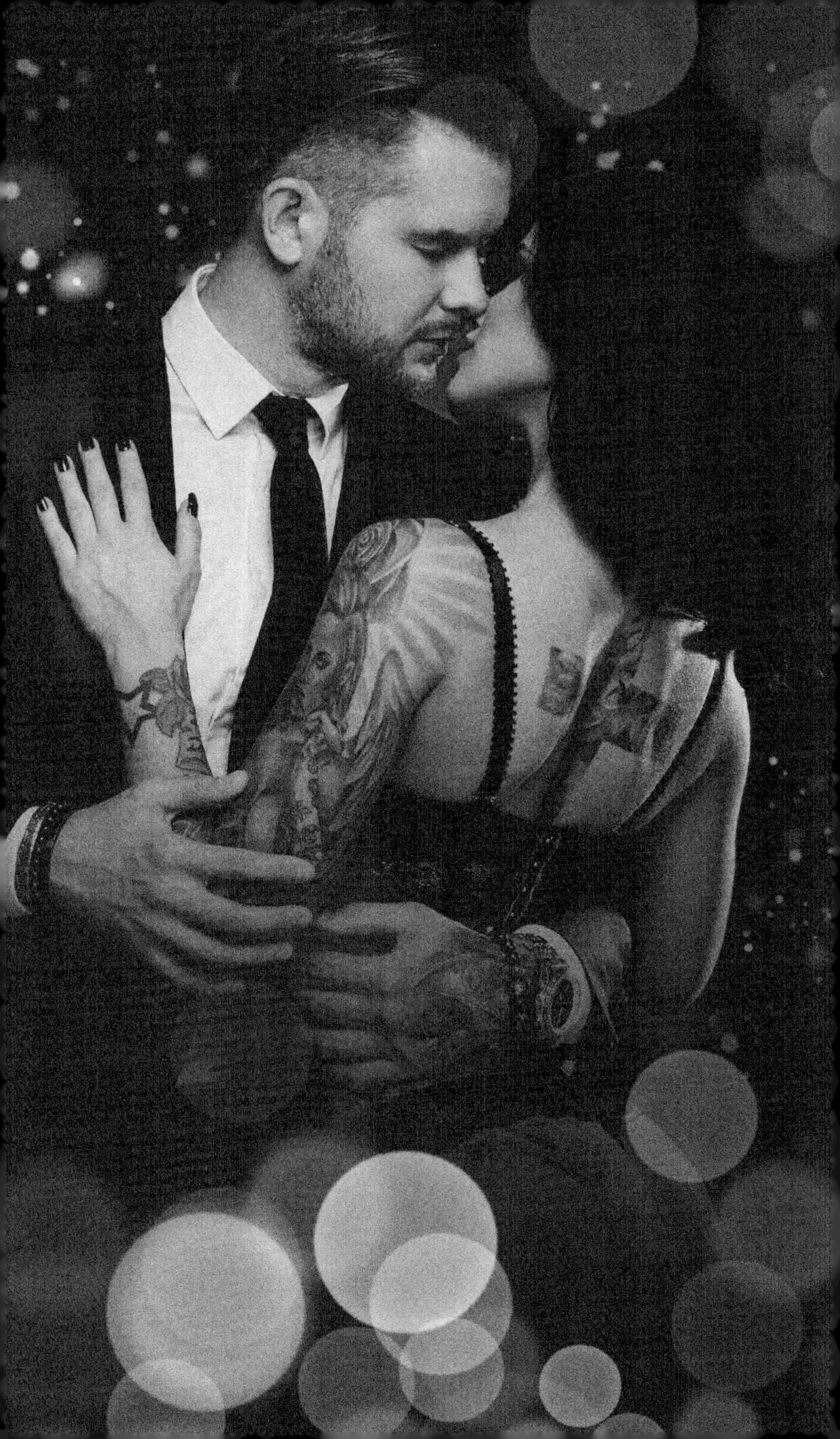

TWENTY-EIGHT

Ava

Something was buzzing.

A phone maybe? Groaning, I opened my eyes to see my cell phone screen lit up and bouncing against the nightstand. Yep, definitely my phone. Picking it up, I frowned when I didn't recognize the number. I pressed the answer key and brought the phone to my ear.

"Hello?" I asked, my voice thick with sleep.

"It's about time you answer your phone, Ava Dashkov," a voice on the other end chirped brightly. It was a female, one with a lilting accent I couldn't place. "This was my third attempt to get a hold of you, and I was afraid my present would go to waste. It would have been a pity if it had."

Sitting up, I nudged at Matthias, who groaned and stirred next to me. When he saw me sitting up in bed, he bolted upright, a frown on his face. Placing a finger to my lips, I brought the phone down and hit the speakerphone button.

"Who is this?" I asked. The woman laughed, a bell chime on the wind.

"Oh, please," she tutted. "Like you don't know."

"I don't." I ground my teeth to keep from snapping at her. "That's why I'm asking."

Another laugh.

"I'm known by many names, dear," she admitted loftily. "But you can call me Caesar. All hail her reign."

That's some narcissism right there.

"What can I do for you, Caesar?" I questioned, eyeing Matthias, who was tapping away silently on his cell phone. No doubt trying to see if Mark or Bridget could trace the call.

"Oh, dear," she chimed. "It's not what you can do for me, not yet anyway. And all about what I have done for you."

My brow creased in confusion. "And what have you done for me?"

"Why don't you go look out your bedroom window, poppet," she urged me. "I'm sure you'll be so grateful for my grand gesture."

I swung my feet over the side of the bed and walked to the window on shaky legs.

"Don't be afraid," she assured me. "I won't hurt you. You have nothing to be afraid of."

Swallowing past the lump in my throat, I reached a hand out to the curtain and ripped it aside.

Then I promptly screamed.

Matthias was at my side in less than a second, his body covering mine as if we were under attack.

"Shit," he cursed under his breath, less affected by the gruesome scene just outside our window than me. In fact, the moment he let me go, I sank to my knees and hurled all over the carpet. When Nan got back from Ireland, she was going to kill me.

"Did you like my surprise, poppet?" The woman laughed. It was almost dainty, childlike.

"No," I croaked, trying to get the image out of my head. They hung outside our window on the opposite wall, which was barely four feet away, their bodies split from their chests to their navels, insides strewn out. Their faces hadn't been touched except the tongue that was nailed to their foreheads.

They were meant for me to be able to identify.

No wonder we hadn't found them. Sheila and Remus McDonough were dead, hanging for me to see. The room had begun to fill with the rest of our dysfunctional family, but I barely paid them any attention. Kenzi knelt by my side, rubbing her hand soothingly along my back. She didn't recognize this woman's voice, and whispered as much to my father, but when Matthias had mentioned her name, she stiffened.

"Oh, come on now." The bitch was smirking. "I saved you all that time and effort of looking for them."

"And sent an army after my husband," I hissed at her. She just laughed.

"Oh please." She brushed it off. "That was just my way of introducing myself."

Unbelievable.

"Well, it was not nice to meet you," I snarled. "Now, leave us the fuck alone."

Another laugh, but this one sent a cold chill up my spine.

Shit, my goose bumps had goose bumps.

"Trust me, poppet. This is far from over."

"Why?"

"Because you have something of mine, and I want it back."

Cold dread filled my heart at her words as my gaze caught my sister's.

I asked the question I already knew the answer to. There was only one thing she could want, but there was no way in hell I was giving it to her. Not in a million years.

"Kenzi."

"Go to hell," I snarled. "She isn't yours."

Another icy laugh that left my skin chilled.

"Oh, but she is, and I'll be coming to collect her very soon." The words were nearly cooed. A stark contrast to the malicious laugh that had nearly frozen my heart. "Be a good girl, Kenzi."

Then the line went dead, and chaos erupted.

Kenzi's body stiffened at the woman's words, and I realized too late exactly what had happened. Rolling out of the way, I missed the punch she threw at me by centimeters.

Fuck.

Her body had gone into fight mode, and all she saw was the enemy. That was what they had molded her to be, and the woman had just flipped on the switch. Or at least I thought she had, but none of the moves she used to take anyone down did anything more than incapacitate them.

"Kenzi, wait," I pleaded, clutching my stomach where she had managed to land a solid kick when I had tried to take her down. Dead eyes stared back at me. Her crystalline gaze muted and cold. I didn't have a chance to say another word before she was gone, taking a piece of my heart with her.

What I did know, though, was that I wasn't going to give up on her.

I had let my sister down once already, and I would be damned if I did it again.

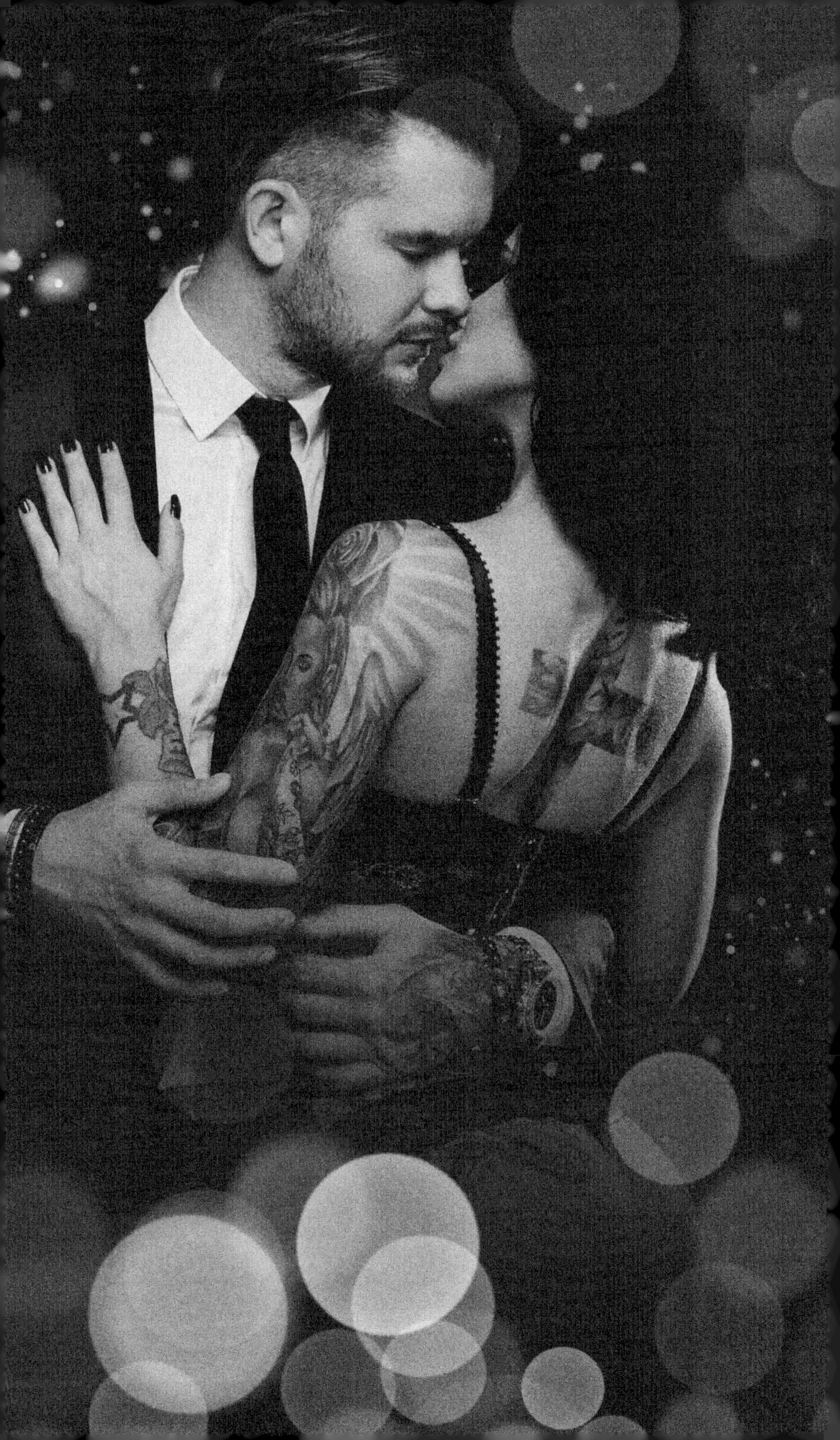

TWENTY-NINE
1 MONTH LATER

Matthias

I stood over the freshly dug grave site, my hand clenching Ava's tightly, but she hadn't once complained. Tears streaked down her porcelain face for a woman she had never met. My Little Red might have turned into a little psychopath, but she never lost her ability to empathize.

My father stood to my right, his face hard and impassive, unwilling to break down in front of his men as he watched them lower his long-lost wife into the crypt. It wasn't until this moment that I realized how truly lucky I was. Compared to him and Ivan, I had gotten so much more time with her. Time none of them would ever get.

Ivan stood on the other side of my father. If it wasn't such a somber event, I might have laughed earlier when he tried to approach Ava. The only reason she hadn't decked him was out of respect for my father.

It was nearly summer in Russia, but the wind was still

biting cold. The graveyard was nearly filled to the brim with the men and woman who had come to support their *Pakhans*. Even Tomas, who had once sworn to me he would never step foot in his home country again, was here, standing just behind me with Vas and my brothers in arms.

What I wouldn't do to turn back time to save her, but then I wouldn't have all of this. I wouldn't have Ava, the goddess beside me, and that was unacceptable. Seamus and Kiernan had joined us as an extension of our alliance with the Kavanaughs, but Liam had stayed behind to keep an eye on Katherine, who, despite the progress she had been making, wasn't clear to fly long distances.

"You know," my father mused once the pomp and circumstance was finished. "Your mother used to sing to you in the womb."

Ivan groaned, but I just smiled.

"*Bayu Bayushki*." My father beamed at me. "She sang it to me every night."

"I tried to keep that tradition going when she—" He swallowed hard. "But Ivan and Antony told me I sounded like a tone-deaf opera singer that had a cat's yowl for a voice."

Ava snorted.

"And that was being generous," Ivan muttered. My father winked at Ava and me.

"It wasn't so bad."

"The entire lullaby was bad," Ivan argued.

Andrei shrugged. "She liked it, and that's all that mattered."

"Gave Antony nightmares."

The three of us stood over her grave, swapping stories about the woman none of us ever truly got to know. Even after eleven years with her, my mother was still as much a mystery to me as she was to the man she had been married to and the other child she birthed. Because the woman I grew up with had been changed by the cruel world that had taken her.

Ava stood by my side quietly, her eyes drifting closed as she leaned into me. My Little Red had been fighting jetlag for half the day. I picked her up in my arms, and she gave a small groan of protest before I narrowed my eyes at her in warning. That shut her up fast, and instead, she leaned her head against my shoulder as I walked through the cemetery toward the line of SUVs waiting for us. By the time I reached the car, she was fast asleep in my arms.

Vas opened the back door, and I gently slid inside, careful not to wake her. Once Vas was behind the wheel, I nodded at him that we were good to go. He pulled out from the curb, following the route to take us to the hotel.

My phone dinged in my pocket, and I dug it out.

Tell her to stop looking.

It came from an unknown number, but it could only be one person.

You know I can't do that, Kenzi.

Day after day, my wife had been leaving messages for her sister to come home. She had Mark scouring every inch of CCTV footage she could get her hands on, hoping to catch a glimpse of her sister.

It's too dangerous. I could have seriously hurt her.

That was an excuse.

But you didn't.

I'd bet money that Kenzi hadn't known about the hidden phrase she'd been trained to obey. It wasn't uncommon practice when brainwashing someone to hide a subliminal message deep in their consciousness. We had been lucky that Kenzi seemed to be relatively immune to it.

And you won't.

She didn't answer, but I sent her another text anyway.

June 24th. I'll send you a pin for the address. Don't miss your sister's big day because you are too scared to face it and too prideful to ask for help.

I threw my phone on the seat of the car and wrapped my arms tighter around the woman snuggled up to my chest.
My life.
My love.
The woman who had stolen my heart and would never give it back.
I watched the wreckage of my childhood fly by out the windows as we drove through St. Petersburg. My mother's family had been buried here for generations, and it was where she had always wanted to be buried as well.
I thought it would be painful to come back here, even after all the time that had passed, but I realized that the

memories were only painful if I let them be. My childhood had been paved with blood and pain, my life often hanging on by the tip of a knife, but none of that mattered anymore. Because each and every decision had led me to this exact moment and to the woman I loved.

Sometimes the most beautiful things were forged from the pain of the past.

And I wouldn't change any of it for the world.

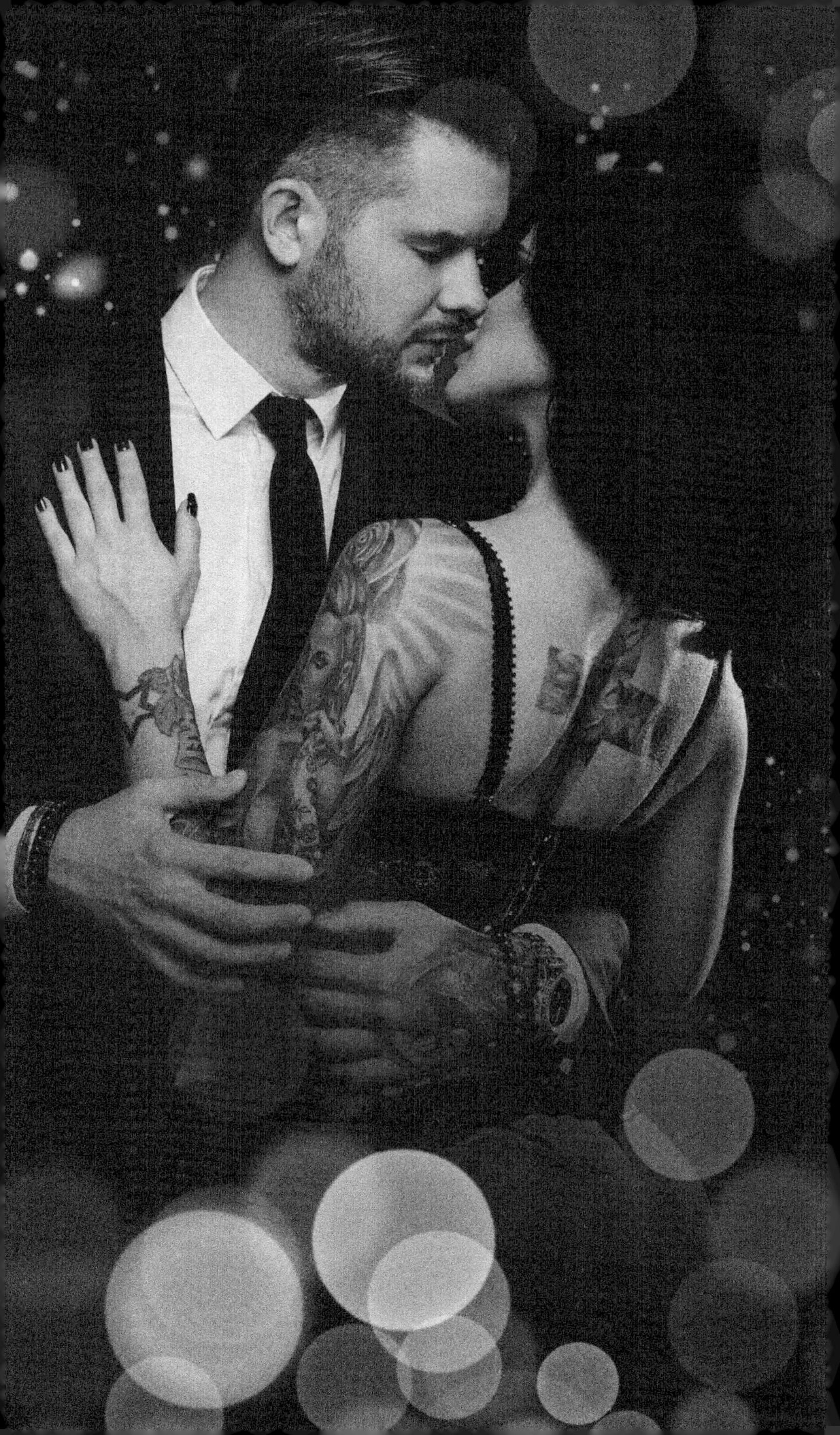

THIRTY

THREE MONTHS LATER

Ava

I wanted her to be here, but there hadn't been any sign of her since that fateful night four months ago. Kenzi had all but dropped off the map. Matthias said that there was hope for her since she hadn't seemed to respond fully to the built-in command she had been given over the phone.

A phrase.

A trigger.

Fuck.

I still called her phone every day and left messages. She had to be listening to them, otherwise her voice mail would be full, so at least I knew she was listening. Which was why I was currently waiting for the nondescript beep to sound.

Beep.

"I know you're listening to these messages, Kenzi." I sighed into the phone. "Please come home. You're my sister. You were my sister the moment I stepped into that horrible house after my mother died and you snuck cookies into my room and held me as I cried. You will always be my sister, no matter what they did to you. Growing up, I tried to save you from everything Elias had done to me, but I didn't save you at all. You saved me. Every single day. And it breaks my heart that you aren't here right now. We talked about this day, remember? Made vision boards and laughed about who would be the lucky one. I miss you. Pleas..."

Beep.

Fucking machine cut me off.

With a huff, I threw the phone down. This was the happiest day of my life, and yet the three people I had always imagined sharing it with weren't here. Libby was dead. I still hadn't managed to find Maleah, and now Kenzi was in the wind as well.

So much for that.

Still, even with them not being here, I couldn't help but love that he had done this for me. Given me exactly what I dreamed of and hadn't told me until precisely six this morning when he dragged me out of bed after eating me out to within an inch of my life. Who needed an alarm clock when you had a husband who couldn't get enough of you?

At least this one wasn't a fraud wedding.

Apparently, he even got a real minister.

One who wasn't bribed this time.

"You look beautiful," my mother whispered, tears shining in her eyes as she took me in. A vision in ivory. Matthias, the possessive, controlling asshat that he was, had even picked out the dress. It was, begrudgingly, exactly what I had always dreamed of wearing. It was a delicate vintage lace ivory sheath with small, capped sleeves. My red curls hung loosely around my face, which had only the slightest hint of makeup on it. Exactly how I had always planned it.

"So do you," I whispered softly, my voice hitching slightly. She wore a sage green maxi halter dress that clung to her developing curves. She'd taken on a good amount of weight now that she wasn't living off bottled nutrition. Her red hair, which had been shorn while she had been in a coma, now came down to just above her shoulders in gentle ginger waves.

A sob threatened to crawl its way up my throat at the sight of her.

I never thought in my wildest dreams that my mother would ever get the chance to walk me down the aisle, and now I not only had her, but my birth father as well.

A loving family.

A dysfunctional, loving family, but a family, nonetheless.

"No crying, now," she chastised playfully. "You'll ruin your makeup."

"Totally worth it." I sniffed.

She smiled softly at me and held out her hand.

"Come on," she whispered. "He's waiting for you."

"Maybe we should make a run for it?" I smirked. My mother laughed.

"I looked into that option for you," she admitted. "He has guards on every entrance and exit. Good luck."

We laughed as she led me from the room and into the large foyer of our new home. That was the other surprise he had laid out for me. The man had gone and purchased a Queen Ann Victorian, that was, admittedly, built in 2008, but it held a perfect old-world charm that blended perfectly with his need for modern structure.

"We'll move in right after our honeymoon," he had

whispered in my ear. "Our house. Our home." I had smirked when I took in the three other smaller buildings spread across the vast property he had managed to secure in the middle of Seattle.

Matthias had shrugged and said, "Well, this specific house is ours. The other ones are for the guys. And your mom if she wants it."

It was perfect.

With a small smile, my mother handed me off to my father, who waited by a set of double doors that led into the large solarium. He was wearing a sharp black suit, his graying hair styled neatly.

"Well, lass," he winked at me. "You sure clean up well."

"So do you." I laughed and took the arm he offered me.

He leaned down until he could whisper in my ear. "Now," he whispered seriously. "There are four exit possibilities by door. Seven by window. We could easily take out a few of the guards before he notices. The twins offered to provide a distraction if needed, but time's a ticking sweet girl."

Throwing my head back, I laughed, long and hard, squeezing my father's arm tightly in a hug. The doors had swung open, and everyone had turned to look at me while I laughed like a maniac.

Whoops.

Matthias narrowed his eyes at my father, no doubt guessing exactly what he had said, but when his gaze shifted to me, he froze. The man had seen me in a wedding dress before, but something about this was different. We weren't playacting or on guard, waiting for an attack.

It was just us.

Me and him and all the orgasms he still owed me for breaking my heart.

This was definitely a step in the right direction.

The music began to play a soft instrumental rendition of "Without You" by Ursine Vulpine. This was our song. Our promise twisted into the words of the song like a creeping vine.

We were in this together.

Forever by each other's side.

And that was all that either of us needed.

It was well past ten by the time everyone had said their goodbyes and we were on our way to the airport. Matthias was finishing up some work on his laptop before we arrived at the airfield so that he wouldn't be required to work on our honeymoon.

Le sigh.

A honeymoon. Although the fucker still hadn't told me where we were going. He even packed my suitcase so I couldn't guess. I was hoping for somewhere warm and tropical, where I could drink margaritas all day by the pool and get a tan.

A real tan.

Not a Washington tan.

My phone beeped in my hand, and I turned it over to see who had texted me. I thought it might be my mother, who I was still nervous about leaving on her own, but Matthias had assured me everything was taken care of, and that Liam was going to watch out for her while we were gone.

That did nothing to assuage my anxiety.

She'd moved out of my father's apartments over a month ago and into an apartment downtown. Matthias had gotten her a job as the assistant to one of his attorneys. I had told him she could be my assistant, but my husband had to go and be all logical about my mother needing her own space.

Whatever.

Guilt gnawed at me when I brushed that statement off, because he was right. She was my mother, but she needed to have her own identity and be her own person. I wasn't a kid anymore, and I knew that was hard for her. Sometimes I caught her looking at me with a sad sort of nostalgic aura bleeding heavily around her.

She missed out on so much of my life.

Not that it was spectacular or anything.

Still, all of those firsts were gone.

Sighing, I looked down at the text on my screen. It was from an unknown number.

A picture of me in my wedding dress walking down the aisle popped up, and under it was a message.

I'm so proud of you, big sister. You will always be my hero, but it isn't safe for me to be around anyone right now. Stop calling. I love you. -K

I snorted. Like that was going to happen.

Looking back at the photo, I realized that Kenzi would have had to be right out the front window of the solarium to get this shot. Had she been close by or was this using a telephoto lens? Either way, she had been there for me. Again. Watching from the shadows.

Typing a message, I pressed send and tossed the phone into my bag as our car came to a stop outside of the small, private airport. I wasn't giving up on her, and I wouldn't stop looking.

Fola roimh gach ní eile.

Blood before all else.

This war was far from over, but right now, I would take the win and be happy for what it had given me.

A loving family and a man I couldn't live without.

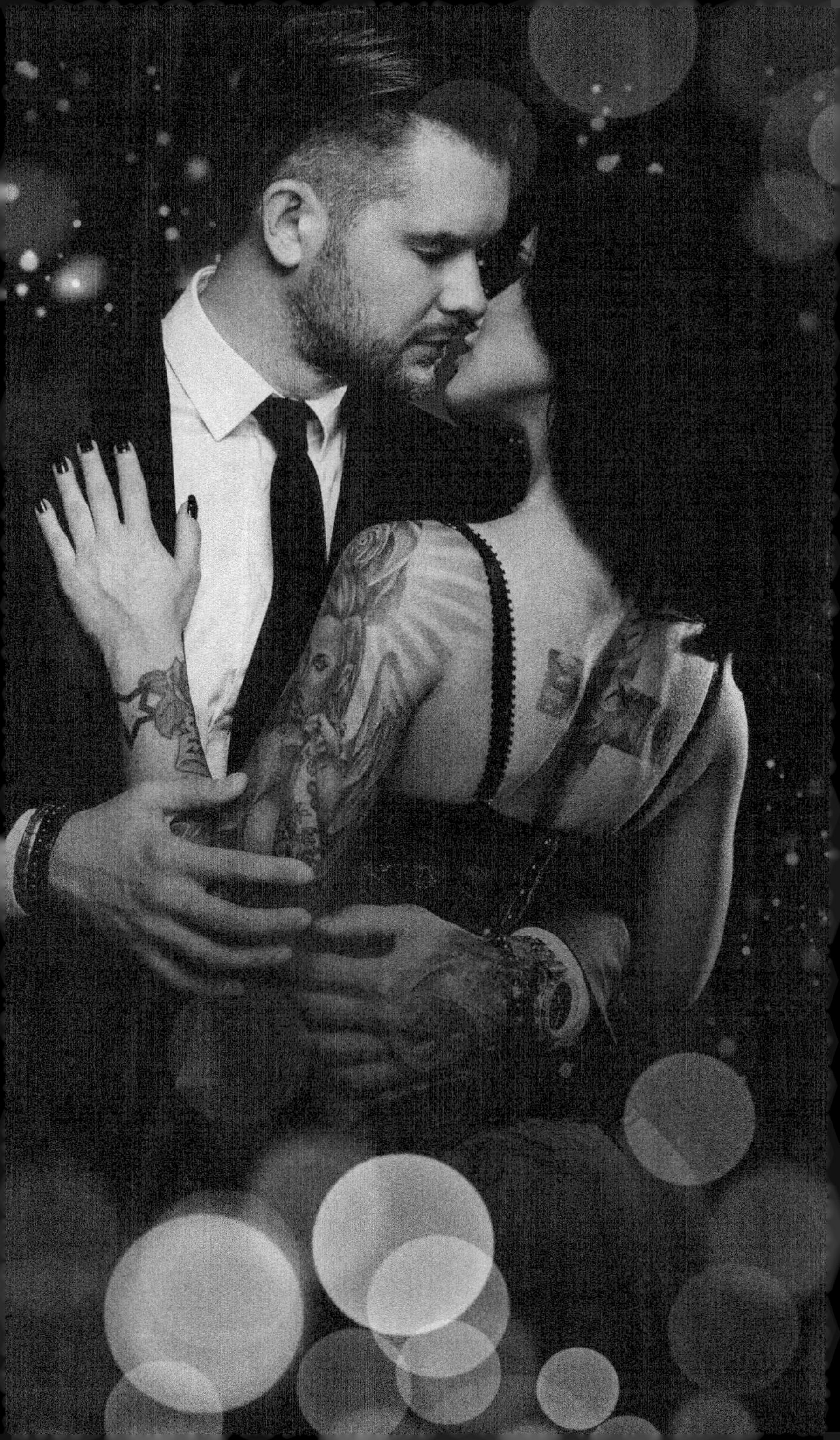

EPILOGUE 1

Kenzi

Ducking through the alley, I pulled my hoodie high over my head to obscure my face from the cameras. Ava would have Mark scouring CCTV footage for my face. The bag in my hand was heavy, filled to the brim with the supplies I would need to make this work.

I couldn't risk putting them in harm's way again.

It had been a fluke that Caesar's trigger phrase hadn't worked properly. Something I still didn't understand. The sudden urge to slaughter had slid into my mind like a shadow, twisting until all I saw was the walls coated in red. Then I'd taken a swing at my sister, intending to crush her skull with my hands, but the moment she cried out in pain, the urge to kill had dissipated.

Be a good girl, Kenzi.

Fucking bitch. I was going to wrap my fucking hands around her throat and strangle her until her eyes popped out of her fucking head. I was no one's fucking puppet, and I would make sure it stayed that way.

The lock of the hotel room door clicked when I pressed my key against the sensor. I pushed my way inside, bypassing the main room in favor of the bathroom.

Shutting the door, I got to work, and by the time I was done, I barely recognized myself.

My long brunette hair was cut short, ending just below my chin in a layered bob, and now a dark emerald green. I slid a pair of colored lenses into my eyes, turning my blue ones a soft brown. Mark's program identified variables such as hair color and eye color. It wouldn't completely fool his system, but it was a start and would give me the time I needed to find the woman who called herself Caesar and hang her by her intestines.

My phone beeped.

Fuck. Ava was a persistent bitch, and normally I loved her for it. Not right now, though. Not when those texts and calls could be traced.

Damn, I missed her so much. I felt like I had finally had my life back. Until that one moment that ruined everything. Things were supposed to get better. I was supposed to be free. Now, I was just a ticking time bomb.

A deadly explosion waiting to happen.

The timer on my watch beeped.

Shit, I was going to be late.

I hurried out the door, still being sure to keep my head down and away from the cameras, but I didn't want to appear too suspicious. I'd spent years learning how to be a chameleon, but this was different. Those targets never knew who I was. How I thought and moved. Mark and Ava did. Caesar too. She was the one who had created the program, after all.

Taking the bus out to where Matthias had dropped the pin was easier said than done. I ended up Ubering it the last few miles. Tipping the driver, I stepped out of the car, stopping to admire the view. Fuck, that man had gone all out.

The outside looked Victorian, but the construction looked too new to be truly vintage. Not that it would matter to Ava. She had always wanted the aesthetic without all the issues that went into owning an actual Victorian. Not to mention that I doubted Matthias would move into a house that couldn't accommodate his state-of-the-art security system or his fancy coffee machine that no honest Victorian would be able to handle without burning down.

Tucking my chin, I followed the flow of guests toward the front door, slipping around to the back before anyone could notice. The lawn was fucking immaculate. Lucky too, because Ava did not have a green thumb to try and make these garden beds herself.

I found the perfect spot to watch the ceremony, perched on a small bench just far enough away that no one could see me, but not too far that my camera wouldn't be able to catch the action.

Hopefully, this wedding went down better than the last.

Sorrow weighed down my heart when I thought about Libby. I tried not to think about her too often because the pain in my chest always seemed to grow immeasurably when I did. My sweet Libby. She would be so happy to see Ava getting married in the way she had always dreamed of. An Ivory dress, flowers, and a groom who looked at her as if she was the world.

We had our weddings planned out by the time we were thirteen years old. Our plan was to be each other's maids of honor. Dad would walk us down the aisle with a smile on his face and give us away to the men of our dreams.

Ugh, if that wasn't the fakest bullshit on the planet, fuck it all.

Those dreams were squashed like pumpkins the day after Halloween.

Elias wasn't really my father. My mother was a lying, whoring bitch. Libby was six feet under and not coming back any time soon, and well—who would want to marry someone who was damaged goods and could accidentally kill you at the drop of a wrong word?

Sighing, I set aside the depressive pity party thoughts in favor of watching my big sister have the moment she deserved. Life had never been fair to her, growing up in Elias's home. I only wished I had known it sooner. Maybe some of the bloodshed and pain could have been stopped.

I sat on the bench for hours, watching the guests mill around. None of them came back here, though. It was late by the time everyone left and I packed up my camera. Ava had left me another message earlier before the ceremony. I'd listened to it like I had all the other ones.

But it was time to stop.

Taking out my new burner phone, I shot her a quick text, telling her how proud I was of her and that she needed to stop searching. Stop looking. It wasn't worth the risk.

Two seconds later, I got a response, and for the second time in over two and a half years, I cried.

Never. Sisters always stick together. I love you.

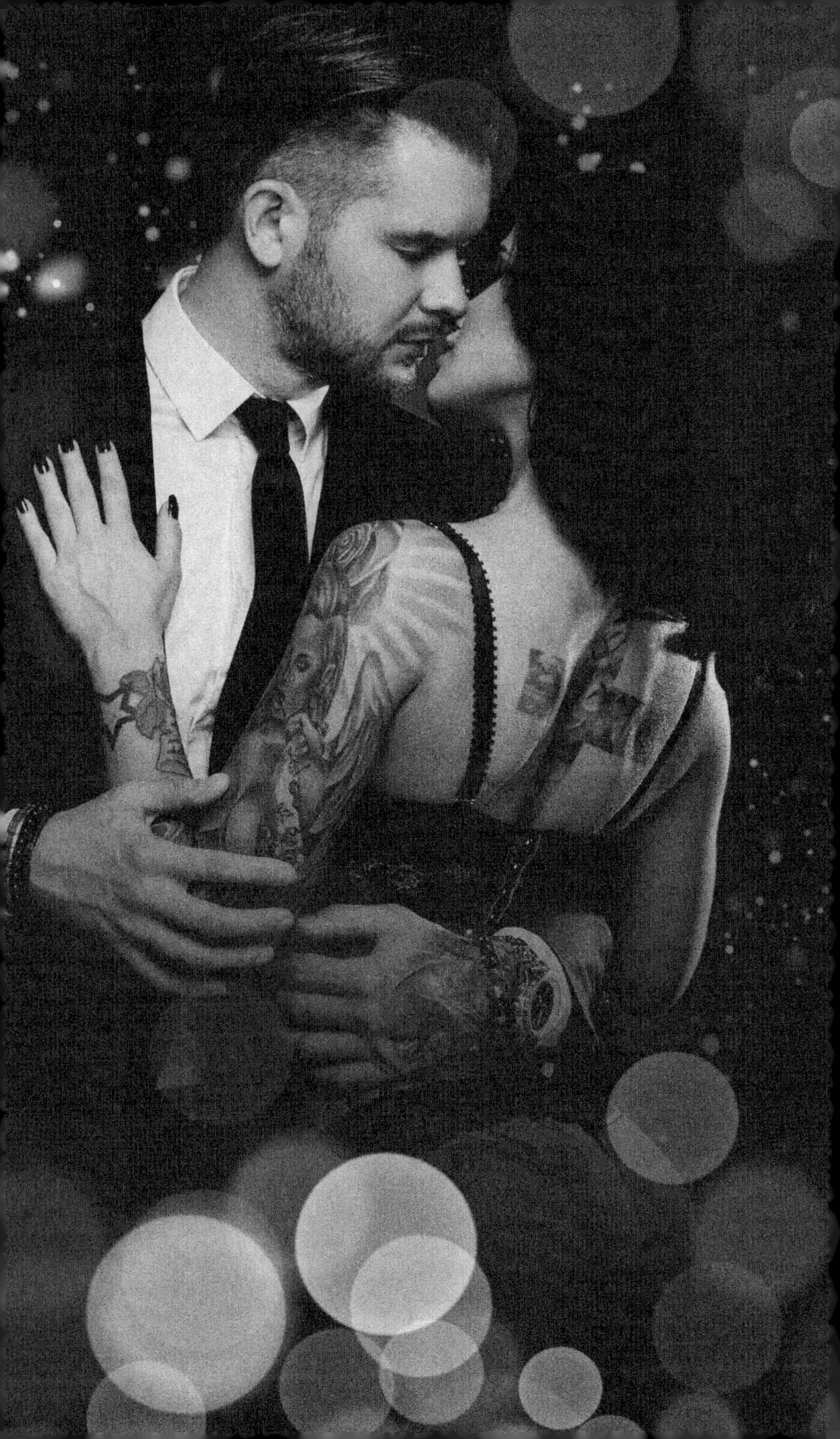

EPILOGUE 2

Katherine

My keys jangled as I shoved them in the lock. Turning the key, I gripped the handle and nudged the door open. Balancing groceries was not something I had ever been good at. Ava kept telling me about how I could order groceries to be delivered now, but the thought of some random stranger knowing where I lived didn't sit well with me.

My daughter had also told me that I didn't need an apartment of my own. There was plenty of room in the new home Matthias had bought for them. The man had not only purchased their home, but every home for several city blocks. He'd torn most of them down to build god knows what.

I respectfully declined the invitation. Living that close to my daughter and her new husband was not my idea of a good time. Not that I didn't want to be near her, and her offer came from a good place, but I had spent the last thirteen plus years under constant watch, able to hear and feel everything without the ability to do shit about it.

Sighing, I set the groceries on the marble island. The apartment was small, but cozy, with floor-to-ceiling windows and a large balcony. It was enough to keep me from feeling stifled and closed in. Matthias had offered me a job at the attorney's office, which I gratefully accepted. The money from the McDonough estate would be enough to tide me over for a decent amount of time. The bulk of my father's fortune had been squandered by Sheila and Remus over the years and it looked as if whoever was behind their extracurricular activities of selling women had taken that money and run with it.

Not that I wanted it.

The McDonough mafia was done for. I'd flown back to Boston to hand over the seat of power to one of my father's men who had been exiled for questioning Remus. He had been my father's second for nearly thirty years and deserved to take it over. There wasn't much left, but he had been confident that he could build it back up to what it once was.

I knew my family's legacy was in good hands.

Pain pierced my heart when I thought about the darkness that had woven its way through my family for generations. I couldn't fault Remus and Marianne for the pain they felt at being cast aside, or even my mother for harboring such hate toward my father and grandmother. It was how it all came about that disgusted me. That, and the fact that my mother so easily cast me aside for being the chosen twin. It was in no way my fault for being born a minute earlier than my sister.

"Hello, Kat."

A cry of surprise erupted from my throat, and I turned

to face who had spoken. He was sitting in one of the overly plush chairs I had stuffed into a corner, half covered in shadow. Hazel eyes shot icy daggers at me. His body was relaxed, one ankle thrown carelessly over the opposite knee, a gun in his hand, the barrel pointed straight at my chest.

His voice was all smoke and gravel, almost hoarse.

Why did it sound so familiar yet also so foreign?

I hadn't turned any of the lights on, so the only source of light came from the windows, which made it hard to see his full form. As if sensing this, he reached a gloved hand out toward the standing lamp next to him, and with a soft click, a warm glow filled the darkened space.

My lips parted slightly, eyes widening in recognition and horror when his face was revealed. He looked different from when I had last seen him, then again, he had been burned to death after being shot.

At least he was supposed to have been.

Noah Kelly.

Fear surged through me unbidden, and goosebumps broke out over my skin, causing me to shiver slightly. The left side of his face was a scarred mess of skin. His lips on that side were missing, causing a permanent sneer, and his left eye was glassy and unmoving.

Clenching my jaw, I swallowed back the bile that threatened to rise in my throat. "Noah."

The right side of his face lifted into what was no doubt supposed to be a smile but resembled more of a grimace.

"What a surprise to find you alive after all these years." He waved his gun at me. "You're as beautiful as I remember."

"Can't say the same for you."

I wasn't going to be pulling any punches. Not with this monster.

Sparks of anger flickered in his steely eyes, but they quickly diminished as if they hadn't existed in the first place. He'd always been quick to anger when we were younger. Constantly getting in fist fights and striking out. We'd been engaged once, but I had been in love with Liam.

That was when everything changed.

"How cruel the years have been to both of us." He inclined his head.

"If you're trying to bond with me over shared trauma," I sniffed haughtily, "it isn't going to work."

He chuckled.

"Oh, little Kat." His words slithered around me like a snake, and I could feel my skin crawling. "We have so much to bond over. But first." He stood from the chair and sauntered toward me. I shuffled back, trying to keep distance between us, but was stopped when I hit the immovable force of the island. Noah smirked, his large body crowding mine against the cold marble. He leaned down until his lips were at my ear. "You are going to do something for me."

I shook my head, unable to speak with how close he was. Lightning fast, his gloved hand gripped my chin in a bruising hold, his fingers digging into my cheeks as he forced me to look at him.

"This isn't a negotiation, Kitty-kat," he snarled menacingly, venom dripping from his words. I flinched at the use of my old nickname. "You are going to do exactly as I say, or I'll put a bullet through your ex-lover's head." He tilted his head to the side, eyes lighting with fire. "Or maybe I will put one through your daughter's and watch her burn."

"Go to hell," I hissed through clenched teeth.

Noah simply laughed and released his grip on my chin, but he didn't step back. He continued to crowd me, his dark essence washing over me like a wave crashing upon a sandcastle on the beach. With one pull of the trigger, he could wash me away.

"I've been there, Kat," he shrugged. "They didn't have what I wanted."

"And what is that?" I asked, afraid of the answer.

"You."

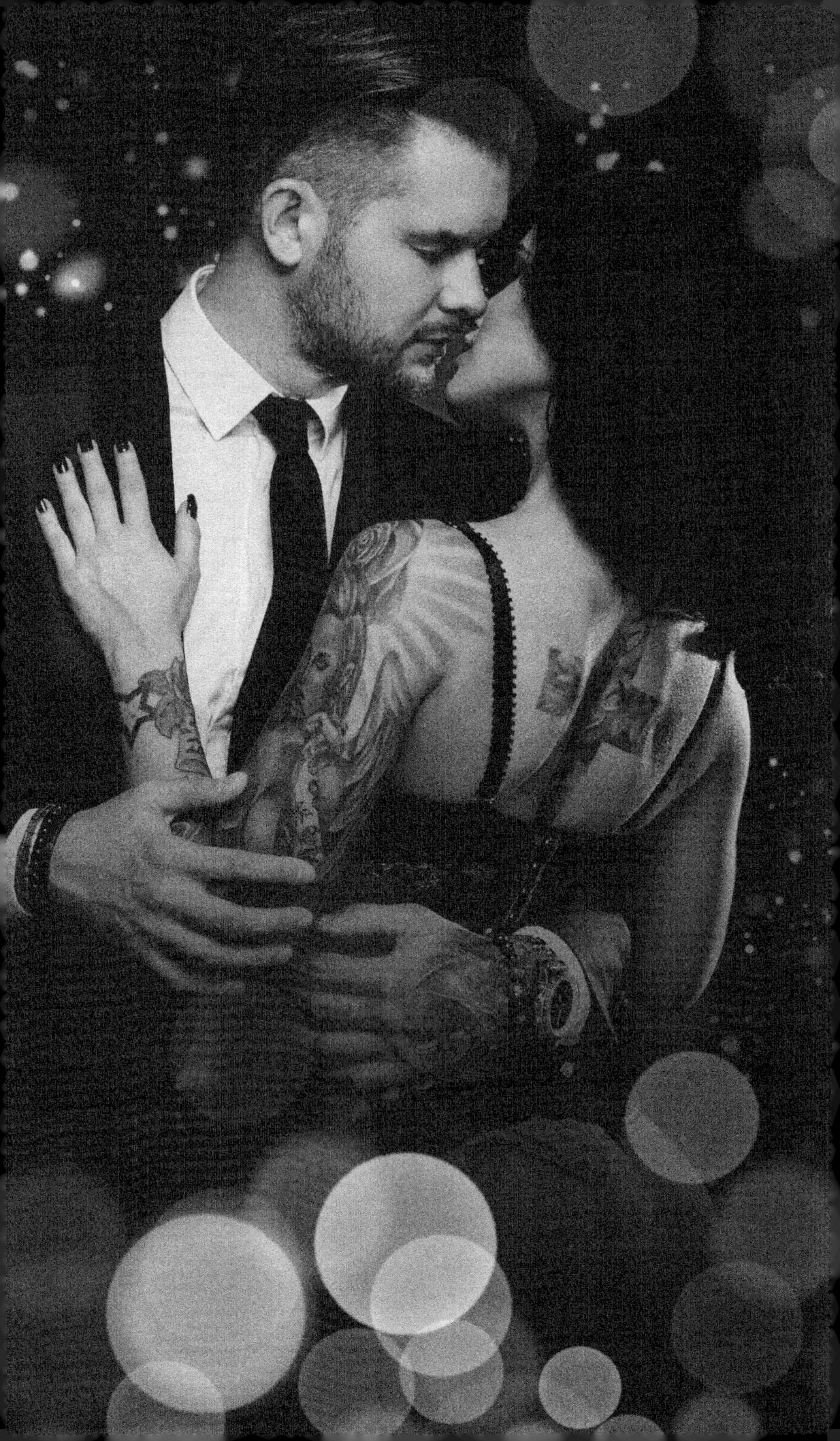

EPILOGUE 3
SEVERAL MONTHS LATER

Dante

The smell of hospitals made me sick to my stomach. Poorly concealed death. That was what it smelled like. I paced the length of the empty birthing room after they had taken Kendra into the OR. Her placenta had ruptured, and now they were going to have to do an emergency C-section.

Fear gripped my heart as they wheeled her away. All that mattered was that the baby was safe. Kendra could rot in hell for all I cared, but I still couldn't follow them. Not after what had happened to my first wife, Lia. I had watched her die giving birth to my daughter, Sestra. It was why I never came to the hospital. Why I had my own private team of doctors, but even they didn't have the skills needed to perform this procedure.

Cazzo.

Nine months.

Nine fucking months was how long I had kept Kendra safe from those who sought vengeance against her. That list wasn't short, either. Much like Elias, Kendra had lied and manipulated her way through society, and now her bridges were burned, and all she had was me.

Lucky fucking me.

Jesus. Being with her had been a mistake. Even if that mistake had given me two beautiful daughters, I should have ended the affair long before they were born. But old habits are hard to turn away from.

I had been drowning in grief at the loss of my wife, Lia, when it started, and Kendra capitalized on that. *Lia*. I still missed her, even after all these years. I could say that Kendra seduced me, using her wiles against me, but I knew I could have ended it an any time, and I should have.

Hindsight was a bitch.

The scent of the hospital was getting to me, my vision blurring slightly as panic settled into my bones. I could handle losing Kendra but losing the baby might just kill me. It was a loss I didn't think I could deal with. Armando and Sestra, my children with Lia, were waiting for me downstairs in the lobby. The hospital had a policy about visitors during emergency surgeries.

They had both suspected the affair growing up, but neither one had mentioned it. When I told them she was pregnant, they hadn't been the least bit surprised or angry. I had been afraid they would see it as a betrayal to their mother's memory.

My phone rang, the shrill sound causing me to start slightly in my agitated state. Fucking hospitals.

Pressing the green button, I brought the phone up to my ear. "Yeah?"

"It's me," the voice on the other line sighed. He sounded

exhausted and worn, like he had been up all night. "I've got her."

"Maleah?" I questioned just to be sure he wasn't talking about Kenzi, who had disappeared without a trace several months ago after she had nearly attacked her sister. If I ever got my hands on the arrogant asshat who called herself Caesar—

"Yeah," he responded tightly. "She's in bad shape. Sick fucker had her strung from the ceiling. She's got a dislocated shoulder, broken leg, several cracked ribs. Her body is wrecked with scar tissue. I don't know what to do."

Running a hand down my face, I groaned in frustration. This was not what I needed right now. "Take care of her," I told him.

I was met with silence. There was a time when Neil had been head over heels for the Ford girl, but rough times had changed him as much as they have undoubtedly changed her. It didn't matter though.

The moment I laid eyes on Maleah Ford, she became mine. My obsession. And I wasn't going to stop until she was begging to be mine and only mine.

"I don't know..." He trailed off, no doubt hesitant about the job I was giving him.

There was a reason I had tasked Neil with finding her. He needed redemption and this was how I was going to give it to him. "You owe her this much, *nipote*."

"Mr. Romano?" The doctor strode through the double doors, holding a small bundle in his arms. I hung up on Neil without saying goodbye and shoved the phone into my pocket as I approached the doctor.

"Congratulations, Mr. Romano." The doctor handed me the infant, swaddled in a pink hospital blanket. There was a smile on his face, but it didn't reach his eyes, which were drawn with sadness and regret. "It's a girl."

I stared down at the bundle in my arms, and my heart filled with a warmth that it hadn't felt since the birth of my daughter. That day, as happy as it had been, was tinged with sadness. Sestra still refused to celebrate her birthday on that day, opting instead for a Halloween celebration each year. The doctor's next words barely filtered through my ears as I continued to gaze at the baby girl I held tightly to my chest.

Kendra was dead. There had been no saving her.

It didn't matter.

No one would miss her.

"Congratulations, Dad." Armando walked into the room with a smile on his face and the car seat in his hand with his sister trailing behind him holding the hospital bag I had packed.

"*Papá.*" Sestra placed the bag on a chair and strode over to give me a kiss on the cheek. She looked down at her new sister and cooed. "She's so beautiful. *Bella.*" The infant in my arms yawned and opened her dazzling blue eyes, peering up at us curiously.

"*Bella,*" I repeated thoughtfully, and the baby cooed. Kendra hadn't bothered to think up a name for her own child. Over the past few months, she had become withdrawn and frustrated at once again being pregnant. She had never wanted the child, and had originally planned on doing away with the pregnancy until it became the only thing keeping her alive. I chuckled at the girl's reaction. "Do you like that *piccolo*?"

The bundle smiled.

"I think she does." Armando chuckled as he leaned in to catch a glimpse of her.

"Then little Isabella it is," I whispered lovingly. "My beautiful girl. You will always be loved and cherished and protected."

Her siblings looked up and smiled at me.

"Forever."

The End....For Now

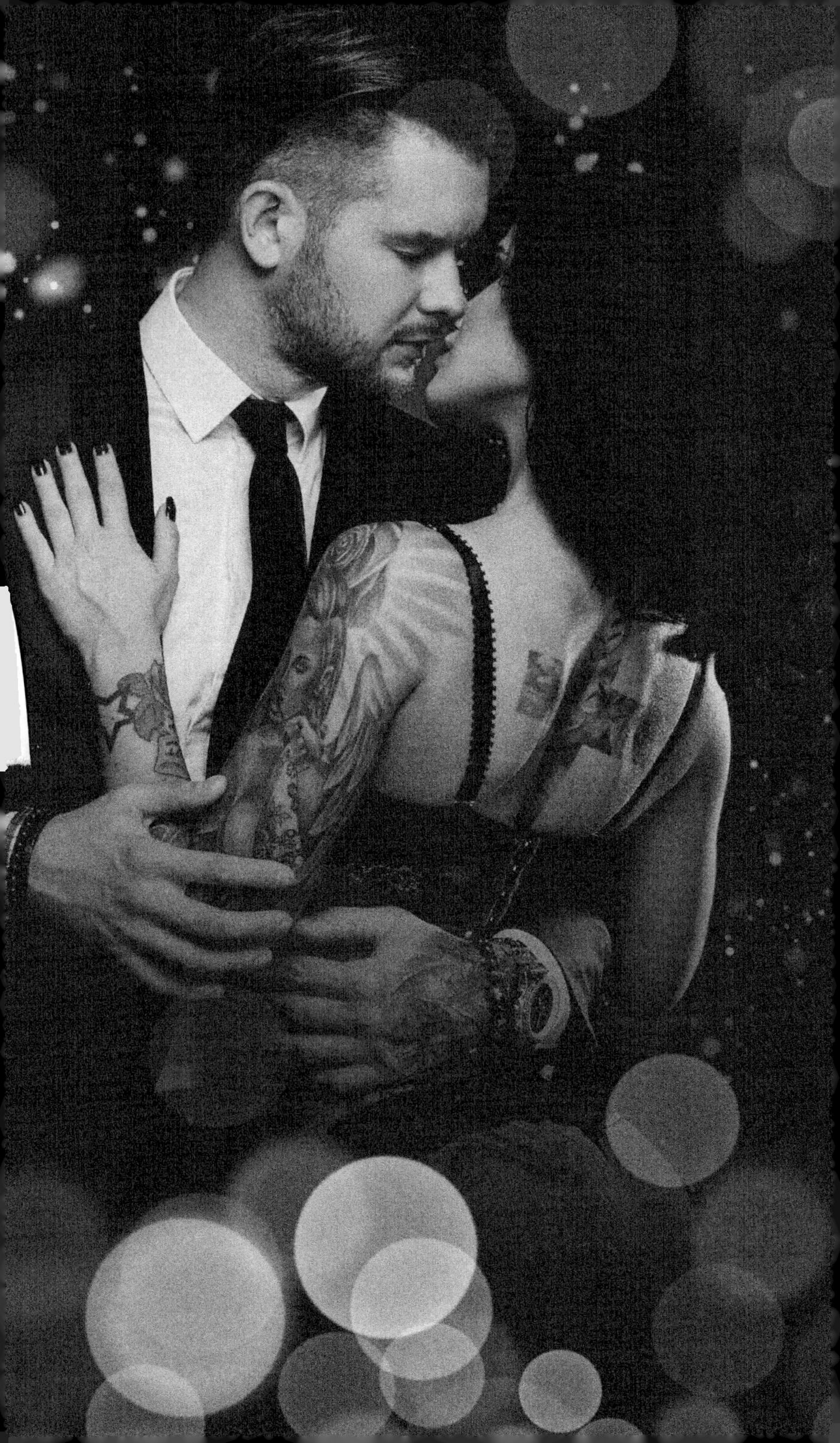

SNEAK PEEK OF SAVAGE
BOOK 1 IN THE SAVAGE KINGS DUET

R iver

The satin red dress clung to my every curve like a second skin. Its ruched sides left my upper thighs nearly bare, showcasing the vivid colored artwork needled into them. I was every man's wet dream tonight. My raven hair was tucked beneath a long blonde wig, my face painted with the utmost care in varying shades of neutrals that didn't detract from the red matte lipstick that graced my plumps lips.

I pulled anxiously at the decorative mask that hid my identity. Not that anyone would recognize me in this place. It wasn't my usual kind of job. The people in this room were dangerous and powerful, far more than the rich, opulent politicians and socialites I tended to target.

But this was a hired job and despite the constant red flags that were booming fireworks in my mind, it was a job that paid well. Really well and I needed the extra cash, despite the possible danger.

Naturally I wasn't going to say no to a payday that big.

A low whistle escaped through my lips as I took in the grandeur surrounding me. Shit, maybe I had been targeting the wrong people all along. These men lived like kings. Not that it surprised me. The men who owned this mansion were all members of the King Syndicate, an organization made of the most powerful mafia houses in Seattle history. They ruled the Seattle underground with an iron first. Drugs, prostitution, weapons. You name it and they had a hand in it.

Not that anyone could prove that.

Even if they could, there was no one to take them down.

Not anymore.

Not since the Blackout.

It happened when I was still a wide-eyed child believing the world to be made of unicorn farts and fairy sprinkles.

That died quickly.

No one knew how it started. Only that the world was plunged into darkness, and everything was gone.

Running water? None.

Electricity? Zilch.

Money nearly became extinct. It was a hard time to learn that the dollar signs in the bank were just a bunch of ones and zeros. The world sunk into a new era of depression that made the 1930's seem like a cake walk. Stock market crash? Hell, there was no fucking stock market anymore.

And humanity? Sometimes I wondered if that existed in the first place.

The new world was dangerous and deadly. The wild west where outlaws came out to play, and politicians turned sour. In the twenty years since the Blackout things had begun to move, but the world would never be the same.

I'd been trained from an early age how to evade attention and go unnoticed. Even dressed as provocatively as I was now. It wasn't all that hard in this crowd to blend in and go unseen. Everyone around me was dressed to the nines in fancy evening wear and a wide assortment of masks. Women hung off the arms of prominent businessmen, lavishing the attention they were given, each one hoping to score longer than one night in their bed.

There wasn't much out there anymore for anyone, let alone women.

Poverty was at an all-time high. Most working people lived in abandoned buildings, snatching electricity from the powerlines under the radar. The men who lived here didn't seem to have an issue with power or money. A grand chandelier was lit up brightly above me, dripping crystals that cast rainbows around the large room painted in delicate neutral tones with large, garish blood red velvet curtains.

People on the streets were starving, barely able to afford food to feed their children and yet there was a gluttony of it littering the tables around me. A buffet for the pawns of the Kings. How very passe. I milled around the room, making idle conversation with random groups of people here and there. To anyone who looked my way it would seem as if I belonged. My bright exuberant smile and enthusiastic conversation made it easy to fool whoever was watching. If I didn't interact with people, it would be suspicious. Most people in this circle knew one another, even with the masks firmly in place.

In circles like these ones there was never any anonymity. Not truly.

I let my gaze wander, making precise notes of exits. My mind conjured up a mental map of barricades, the number of guards and where they were stationed, and *them*.

The kings of the city.

The men who called themselves the King Syndicate.

But there were only two of them sitting up on the dais, their eyes lazily roaming the room as they silently conversed between themselves. Garren and Ivan King, the leaders of two of the most powerful mafia families on the West Coast. None of the Kings were related by blood, but rather, bonded by loyalty.

I was too far away to read their lips, but they were on edge, bodies tense, muscles coiled and ready to lunge at any given moment. Was there something specific that had them riled or was that a constant state they kept themselves in?

Then again, if you were two of the most powerful in the city, it paid to be on guard.

Shifting my gaze, I searched for the third member of their triad. A man whose reputation was written in blood all over the city. He was nowhere to be found and that could prove to be a problem for me. I couldn't afford to be seen taking the diamond. Even if my identity was concealed behind a mask.

They were ruthless in their pursuits of their enemies, and I didn't want to become one.

Even if I was here to steal from them.

I found it rather odd what the anonymous client had asked me to steal. Without electronic banking, the world was back to using the old nickel and dime system. Cash and trade only. Banks no longer existed other than for cash exchange and even then, you never knew what you were getting. Banks contained more counterfeit bills than a monopoly game.

Millionaires weren't really a thing either. The entire world was bankrupt after all. Sure, people were still rich, but the one percent had become more like the quarter percent. They were rich because the economy was in the toilet, and they had hoarded money in their homes. A tad bit wiser than having a safety deposit box.

It was later learned through backwater channels such as morse code, that a single-minded group of
terrorists had simultaneously set off large groups of electromagnetic bombs all around the world. This essentially pulled the world back into the dark ages.

There was utter chaos in the weeks and months following the Blackout. Cities burned. People were dragged from their homes and shot. Even now, twenty years later, we were barely getting back on our feet again.

The item my client had paid me to procure was something that could in no way be sold or bargained for the price it was worth.

A 15.6 carat, princess cut diamond set in a custom gold lead necklace worth more than $4.5 million dollars on pre-Blackout market. No one had that kind of money anymore. Not even overseas buyers would be able to sling up that much cash. Unless the client planned to bargain it for something bigger. Maybe rights to the Panama Canal? That was the only thing I could think of that would be worth that much money. It took approximately ten years for international trade to start up again.

Only problem?

The electromagnetic bombs had pretty much fried anything electrical and there was no one to fix them. Not to say that we were back to using horses and buggies. Cars, motorcycles, mopeds, and other forms of ground transportation were easily fixed. They didn't require sat navs or towers of any kind to track progress. Planes on the other hand—

those were still a work in progress. The one thing every country had at their disposal were ships. Most ships could use sonar and radar to track their trips. Easy enough, I supposed.

On light feet, I made my way toward the large terrace just off the elegant ballroom. Intel told me that the diamond was on display in the garden at parties like this one where guests could fawn over the extravagant jewel like gaping fish.

The cold chill of the last vestiges of winter kept most of the partygoers indoors, relishing in the heat. I could see why the Kings chose this house. It was old. One of the oldest homes in Seattle, which meant it ran on a boiler system for heat, distributing steam through the pipes to radiators and convectors instead of using precious electricity. Not that it probably mattered to these people how they were kept warm. Just as long as they were. They would all soon return to their homes that were run off electric heat, eating up the meters while those who barely made ends meet suffered through the cold.

Twenty years was a drop in the ocean of time when it came to getting the city back on its feet. If we'd had well-meaning politicians and appointees that focused on the needs of the people, we might not have had people dying in their sleep from pneumonia and hypothermia. The system was too corrupt. There were no votes or ballots. People took what they wanted. Killed for what they deemed was theirs.

Washington was under militant rule now.

Militia forces patrolled the streets, there were checkpoints everywhere requiring passes to enter certain sectors. You couldn't freely travel the city any longer. Police drones roamed the skied and criminals roamed the streets. But none of that mattered because the rich pigs sat loftily on their thrones not giving a fuck about anyone below. My heels clacked quietly on the cement steps as I descended into the lower gardens. It was the tail end of winter so there was very little to see outside of the snow dusted evergreen bushes and flowering Camellias. In the center of the garden, surrounded by ornately carved stone benches, sat the very thing I had come for.

The jewel was nestled on a black velvet cushion that sat upon a large stone pedestal for all to see its grandeur. It was surrounded by an octangular glass dome that shone iridescently in the moonlight. It was an odd place to have such a unique item. Most people didn't know what I knew, however. That I know of.

The dome was pressure sensitive and if I was to look closely enough, I would be able to see the faint rippling of the red security sensor that would alert them if the dome was shifted or moved. My plan had been to cut through the glass and use a small hook and line to remove the necklace. The dome might have been pressure sensitive but the pillow it rested on wasn't.

Lucky for me because I had nowhere to hide a bag of precisely measured marbles to compensate for the missing weight. I could see why no one had the balls to steal it, but here I was.

Being ballsy and all that.

"It's beautiful, isn't it?"

Startled at having been snuck up on, my lips parted, and I let out a small puff of air. I'd been so caught up in analyzing the case that I hadn't bothered to check my surroundings. Not wanting to look suspicious at being the only one willingly out in the freezing garden ogling the stone, I schooled my features. I was prepared to put on the ditzy blonde act. The one where I was too drunk to know any better. I turned my head and readied my Oscar worthy performance.

Only to come face to face with the final member of The King Syndicate.

Killian King.

ACKNOWLEDGMENTS

OMG!

It's the end!

The finale!

The big cheese!

This journey has been the best of my life. Every late night, every tear I shed in utter frustration was well worth the love and reception you have all given Ava and Matthias's story.

Their story leads into a much larger world that I can't wait to share with all of you.

THANK YOU ALL FOR YOUR AMAZING SUPPORT THROUGH ALL OF THIS!

Beth at VB Edits, thank you so much for always being there for my endless questions. You are an amazing editor and I couldn't have done this without you.

Kay, you absolutely amaze me and I am so glad we became such amazing friends! I look forward to sharing so much more with you as both of our careers progress.

ROBIN! My gal Friday! Thank you for listening to my endless plot changes and sudden spider takeovers. You get the worst part of everything because you hear all of my wild theories and watch me change them a million times. You are amazing and I am so thankful for your friendship.

Rebecca, your endless emojis and constant attention to detail made this process so much easier. So do all those hilarious tiktoks you seem to send me at just the right time! Thank you so much for being my Alpha Reader.

To all my amazing BETA Readers! Your support and willingness to give me the honest truth is what made this all possible! You are all amazing and I love the support.

And to all my ARC readers and those who have kept reading throughout this journey! You all kept me writing. Your love for Matthias and Ava kept me going when all I wanted to do was give up.

Thank you all from the bottom of my heart!

> "You never know what's around the corner. It could be everything. Or it could be nothing. You keep putting one foot in front of the other, and then one day you look back and you've climbed a mountain."
> -Tom Hiddleston

ALSO BY JO MCCALL

SHATTERED WORLD

Shattered Pieces

Shattered Remnants

Shattered Empire

Shattered Revelations

SHATTERED WORLD STANDALONES

Shattered Revenge

KAVANAUGH CRIME FAMILY

Stolen Obsession

Twisted Crown

Crooked Fate

SAVAGE KINGS DUET

Savage

Kings

STANDALONES

Hunted By Them

STALK ME

@jomccallauthor

BookBub
Amazon Profile
Goodreads
Wicked Romance Book Box

Printed in Great Britain
by Amazon